About the Author

Rachael Johns, an English teacher by trade and a mum 24/7, is the bestselling ABIA-winning author of *The Patterson Girls* and a number of other romance and women's fiction books including *The Art of Keeping Secrets*. She is currently Australia's leading writer of contemporary relationship stories around women's issues, a genre she has coined 'life-lit'. Rachael lives in the Perth hills with her hyperactive husband, three mostly gorgeous heroes-in-training and a very badly behaved dog. She rarely sleeps and never irons.

Also by Rachael Johns:

Man Drought
Talk of the Town

The Hope Junction novels
Jilted
The Road to Hope

The Bunyip Bay novels
Outback Dreams
Outback Blaze
Outback Ghost
Outback Sisters

The Kissing Season (e-novella)
The Next Season (e-novella)

Secret Confessions Down and Dusty:
Casey (e-novella)

The Patterson Girls

The Art of Keeping Secrets

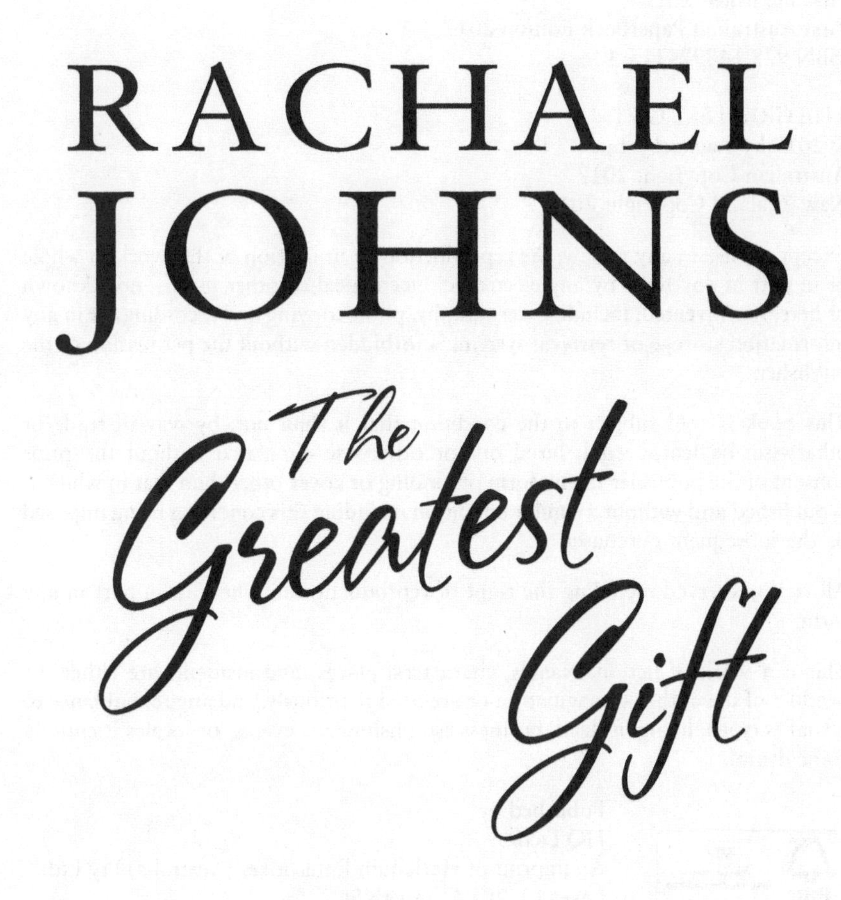
RACHAEL
JOHNS
The
Greatest
Gift

FICTION
HQ

Author note:

I've tried to be as accurate as possible when depicting medical procedures in this book and have consulted with a number of professionals involved in neonatal intensive care, but some small hospital procedures I may have ignored for the plot—please forgive me this creative licence.

First Published 2017
First Australian Paperback Edition 2017
ISBN 978 148924115 3

Published by
HQ Fiction
An imprint of Harlequin Enterprises (Australia) Pty Ltd.
Level 13, 201 Elizabeth St
SYDNEY NSW 2000
AUSTRALIA

Cataloguing-in-Publication details are available from the National Library of Australia www.librariesaustralia.nla.gov.au

Printed and bound in Australia by McPherson's Printing Group

To all the wonderful women who have donated their eggs so that other families could be created. You are true heroines!

mother /'mʌðə/ *n.*
Female parent of a child

mum /mʌm/ *n. Colloq.*
The woman who nurtures, raises and loves a child

Prologue

2001

Please God, let this not be happening to me.

Although she was not usually a person who prayed, these words had been on repeat in her head since she'd opened her student diary last night and almost had a heart attack. She was late. Not late on her next essay—she'd never been late for school work in her life. But nor had she ever skipped a period since that first one when she was eleven years old.

Thankful the university bathroom appeared empty, she screwed up her nose at the pungent smell that hit her as she entered and took the package she'd bought that morning into a cubicle. With trembling hands she locked the door, then sat on the closed toilet seat and removed the test kit from the brown paper bag. It had been easy to find in the pharmacy—right next to the condoms for some bizarre reason—but taking it up to the counter and handing over her money had been mortifying. Her cheeks had burnt so badly she felt as if they were actually on fire. She'd imagined what the middle-aged woman who served her was thinking.

Another silly girl who's been careless with contraception.

But that's just it, she hadn't been—she took the pill religiously—so there had to be some other explanation. With this thought calming her a little, she opened the box and read the instructions. They seemed relatively straightforward, so after a deep breath, she followed them.

The kit said it could be three minutes before a result appeared, and she just knew they'd be the most agonising minutes of her life.

But in the end she didn't have to wait a fraction of that time.

Two little blue lines appeared right beneath her eyes as she held the stick tightly in her hand.

'No!' She let out a gut-wrenching sob as she stared down at the result. This could *not* be happening.

But perhaps it was wrong. That happened, right? Maybe she'd bought a faulty kit. She ripped the plastic off the second stick and did it all over again. This result took a fraction longer to appear and for a few wonderful seconds, she thought she was off the hook, but then reality came crashing down in the form of two more lines.

She spun around and dropped to the floor just in time. Clutching the toilet bowl, tears streamed down her face as she heaved up her breakfast. Was this morning sickness already? Or just a violent reaction to the devastating news?

At nineteen years old, two years into her degree, she wasn't ready to be a mother. She was pretty damn certain she'd never be. If she did this, she'd need support and that was sorely lacking in her life right now. Her older sister had flown off only a week ago to take up a PhD position in Antarctica and her mum was even less reliable than her boyfriend.

This was her worst nightmare come true.

Chapter One

AUGUST 2016

Harper Drummond, unarguably one of the best interviewers in the country, pulled off her headphones and stood. Although only thirty-four herself, her radio show—*Afternoons with Harper*—appealed to young and old alike. When people tuned in they never knew exactly what they were going to get but they were guaranteed entertainment and enrichment. Harper had a knack of getting to the nitty-gritty of people's lives, an ability that many journalists with years more experience than her just didn't possess. Leading up to election time, she interviewed potential PMs and politicians. When international celebrities came down under she put them in her hot seat, grilling them about everything from their career highlights to their deepest fears and a whole host of other juicy topics. It was a rare afternoon where Harper didn't uncover some snippet of information that had never been spilled before.

But political wannabes, film stars and musical hotshots weren't the only people she invited on air. She also chatted with the less obvious heroes of society. A young obstetrician who cared for abandoned mothers and delivered babies in Niger. Ex-homicide detectives. Bestselling authors. Stand-up comics. Prisoners. Recovering drug users. Teenage inventors. A man who'd grown up in a cult. Famous feminists. Sex workers. The list was endless, and yet everyone who came on *Afternoons with Harper* was made to feel as if they were the most interesting person she'd ever interviewed. She was meticulous about research, so that by the time she was sitting opposite someone she could hold an hour-long conversation without ever once looking down at her notes. People were her obsession—the intricacies of their lives fascinated her—and that came across to the listeners who, day after day, kept coming back for more.

Guests were selected in a variety of ways. Publicists across the country sent interview requests by the dozen, but Harper and her hotshot producer Lilia only granted a small fraction of these. Mostly they preferred to select potential interviewees themselves—people they'd read or heard about from one source or another. And, until today, Harper had never had an ulterior motive for inviting a specific person—or in this case people—onto the show.

She smiled through the glass at the trio who had just arrived and were speaking with Lilia, then she opened the studio door and went out to greet them.

'Hi,' she said brightly. 'I'm Harper Drummond, lovely to meet you all.'

Lilia glanced at her watch and then went through the introductions. She gestured first to the tall, thin woman by her side that reminded Harper a little of Mary Poppins, all perfect dark hair, glowing cheeks and a smile that looked like it had a life of its own. 'This is Mel Sharman.'

'Hello. Nice to meet you.' Mel's smile grew even more as she and Harper exchanged handshakes.

Next was the couple. 'And this is Amy and Shep Bird.'

Joined at the hands and pressed so close together Harper couldn't see light between them, they had to let go of each other to accept her hand. She shook the man's first—he had a firm grip, but slightly sweaty palms, which made her want to wipe her hand against her black tailored pants. She resisted and slipped it into his wife's hand, which shook a little, instead.

'Thanks so much for coming in to talk to us,' Harper said, wanting to put them all at ease.

'Oh, it's our pleasure,' gushed Amy. 'I adore your show. I can't listen live normally 'cos I'm at work, so I listen to the podcast in the evenings when I walk the dog.' She rubbed her hand over her bulging bump, drawing Harper's eyes to it. Did pregnant women realise they did that? Was it a considered action—*hey everyone, look I'm pregnant!*—or was it a subconscious thing?

She shook the thought from her head. 'Thank you. I'm glad you like it. Now, shall we head on into the studio?'

Her three guests nodded enthusiastically and as Harper ushered them into the room, Lilia said, 'I'll get you each a glass of water.'

'Thanks,' Harper called and then shut the door behind them. Mel, Amy and Shep stood like dummies just inside the door, gazing at the multiple computer screens on the studio desk and the microphones lined up on the guests' side. She could tell immediately that none of them had been on air before, but she preferred it that way. People who'd been on radio, even only once, often thought themselves experts and sometimes tried to take over, as if they knew how to do her job better than she did.

Smiling encouragingly at her guests, Harper walked around behind the desk and nodded towards the mics. 'They don't bite, I promise. Take a seat on one of the stools and get comfortable.' She glanced at the time on the bottom of one of her computer screens as she put her headphones on again. 'We're on air in sixty seconds.'

At this news, the trio scooted forward and took their positions at the desk.

'Do we need to wear headphones as well?' Shep asked.

'No. I wear these so Lilia can speak to me. You don't need to lean forward or shout into the microphones either. Just talk as if we're all having a normal conversation.'

They nodded as the door opened and Lilia entered carrying three glasses of water. She placed one in front of each of the guests, said 'Good luck, have fun,' and then left the studio just as Lucy wrapped up the weather report.

'Enjoy today's lovely spring weather because tomorrow you'll all want your winter coats and scarves again. Now, back to *Afternoons with Harper*. I'll be back in an hour with another news update.'

Harper launched straight into the next segment of her show. 'Today we have three guests on *Afternoons*. Three guests, but one story. One in six Australian couples struggles with infertility and although the reason varies from case to case, the struggle is real and it's not something that we as a society spend much time talking about. But perhaps it's time this changed as the emotional fallout can have a devastating impact on women, men, families and relationships. With me today are Amy and Shep Bird.'

She smiled at them. 'Thirty-three year old Amy is a primary school teacher and thirty-six year old Shep is a pilot. Shep, can you tell me a little about the day you met your wife?'

A grin sprouted on his face as he reached over and took hold of Amy's hand. 'I was working up in the Northern Territory taking tourists on scenic flights over Kakadu—'

'And I was backpacking around Australia,' Amy interjected.

'With her best friend.' Shep smiled at her. 'We met at a bar one night and she started flirting with me, hoping I might give her—'

'A free flight.' Amy shrugged. 'I was a student, I needed to watch my pennies.'

'I told her I would,' Shep said, '*if* she agreed to go on a date with me.'

'It was hardly a hardship,' Amy mused. 'He was gorgeous and I'd have gone out with him even without the freebie.'

'So I'm guessing that first date went well,' Harper said. 'Was it a whirlwind romance?'

Amy nodded. 'I didn't believe in love at first sight until I met Shep, but by the end of our first date I knew he was the one. We were married six weeks later in—'

'Bali in front of a whole host of our family and friends,' Shep concluded.

'Sounds magical,' Harper said. It was easy to visualise golden-headed Amy as a blushing bride. 'And what was the plan after that? How did you navigate the long-distance relationship?'

Shep winked. 'Amy couldn't bear to be away from me so she moved up to the Territory with me.'

His wife rolled her eyes. 'The way I recall it you begged me to move, but I guess my arm didn't take much twisting. I worked in a pub up there and we stayed while Shep got the experience he needed to apply for a job with a bigger airline. Then we came to Sydney, which was where we were both from anyway.'

Harper nodded. The way these two interacted—finishing each other's sentences and barely able to take their eyes off each other—it was clear they were still as smitten as they day they met, but her research told her they'd had their fair share of disappointments. 'And did you decide to have a family immediately?'

'No.' Amy again caressed her bump, as if to remind herself this story had a happy ending. 'Although we both wanted kids, we thought it would be sensible to establish ourselves—buy a house, that sort of thing—before we brought a new life into the world. We were married five years before we started trying.'

'And did you expect to conceive easily? Was there any family history of infertility?'

'I'm one of five kids,' Shep told her, 'and Amy is one of three. It never crossed our minds that it wouldn't be smooth sailing.'

'I'd done enough reading to know it might take a few months to get the timing right, but after six months with no success, taking my temperature daily, using ovulation kits, keeping my legs up in the air after ... you know—' Amy blushed a little, but continued, '—we went to see our doctor. She told us to come back in six months, but that we'd likely be pregnant by then.'

'But you weren't,' Harper prodded.

'No,' they said in unison, sharing a look between them. Amy explained that after numerous tests they discovered she had premature ovarian failure. 'We immediately started on IVF but after ten failed attempts, we began to lose hope.'

'And why did you feel such a great need to have a baby? To go to such lengths?'

Amy frowned, then shrugged. 'All my life I've imagined being a mother. It just never occurred to us that it might not be possible.'

'So what happened next? What alternatives were presented to you?' Harper asked.

Shep listed the options that they'd contemplated—adoption, surrogacy, fostering, and finally, egg donation—and explained that, in the end, the latter had seemed the best fit for them.

'And that's where today's third guest comes in,' Harper said, giving Mel an encouraging smile. 'Also with us in the studio is Mel Sharman, a thirty-one year old mother of three who did something for Amy and Shep that has changed their lives. Mel gave them the greatest gift anyone could possibly offer another—she donated some of her own eggs so that Amy and Shep could become parents. Until a year ago Mel had never met the Birds, but now Amy is eight months pregnant. She will be the mother in all ways that matter, but the baby is biologically Shep and Mel's. I'm going to dive right in and ask what triggered you to become an egg donor?'

Mel leant forward and spoke into the microphone. 'Late one night while breastfeeding my youngest child I saw a documentary about egg donation, and the pleas of the childless couples touched my heart. Some women had genetic conditions hindering their hopes of getting pregnant and others simply hadn't met the right guy until it was too late. My husband and I got pregnant easily and had been blessed with three gorgeous little girls, but I tried to imagine how I'd feel if I couldn't have them. That was the turning point for me. We felt our family was complete but I knew I had healthy eggs to spare and I wanted to share them.'

'What was your husband's reaction when you told him what you wanted to do?'

'At first he thought lack of sleep had finally got to me—' Mel chuckled, and the others laughed as well, '—but when he realised how serious I was, he actually didn't take long to convince.'

'What did the two of you discuss?'

'He was most worried about the potential effects that donating eggs might have on my body, and he was also concerned about how our daughters might one day feel when they found out that they had technical half-siblings out there. But we spoke to my doctor and we did a lot of research around the issue before we finally made our decision.'

Harper took a breath. 'Let's pause a moment there and discuss the legal aspects of your situation. As I understand it—and please correct me if I'm wrong—egg donation in Australia is an entirely altruistic business. It is illegal to buy or sell human tissue, therefore donors cannot be paid for their eggs, but medical costs may be covered by the recipient couple.'

'That's right,' Mel said, twisting her wedding ring on her finger.

'And once the baby is born, the access the donor has to the baby is not so set in stone. Is that right?'

The three exchanged looks as if deciding who should take the question, and then Mel spoke again. 'Yes, there are two main options available to recipient couples—an anonymous donor or a known donor. Overseas, in countries where you can buy human eggs legally, anonymous donation happens a lot more, but in Australia, it's much more common to use a known donor. And it's up to the donor and the recipients to determine what kind of contact they will have after the embryo transfer.'

'And by "known donor" you don't simply mean a friend or relative of the couple, but sometimes as in your case, a stranger who becomes known during the process. I'm curious. Amy and Shep, how did you find Mel?'

'Mel runs an online group connecting women and couples with potential donors. I signed up to the group and we started chatting.'

The rest of the hour went super fast, talking about the medical process involved in getting pregnant via egg donation, but also emotional ramifications for both parties and their families. Harper found herself surprised at how fascinated she was by their story.

She had many more questions she wanted to ask, but Lilia was on the other side of the glass making wrap-it-up signals with her hands. Her producer ran a tight ship and didn't like their interviews to go overtime any more than she liked mess on her desk.

'We're almost out of time,' Harper said with a reluctant sigh, 'but before we conclude our conversation, tell me, Mel, would you do this again? Either for the Birds or another couple.'

'Actually,' Mel began, 'Amy and Shep's baby will be the second born from my eggs. I also donated to a single mother who delivered a healthy baby boy earlier in the year and I'm currently in discussions with a gorgeous gay couple. But if that match goes ahead, then I think that'll be it for me. Legally my eggs can be given to up to five families, including my own, but my husband and I feel comfortable with four. Though I'd donate again if any of my current families wanted a sibling for their children.'

'Wow, what a generous gift you have given,' Harper concluded, folding her hands together on the desk. 'I want to thank you all for coming into the studio today and sharing your story. And if any listeners are considering donating or receiving eggs and would like more information about any aspect of the process, there'll be a number of useful links in our show notes. I'll be back tomorrow to interview Australia's newest Guinness World Record Holder and you'll be surprised to learn what that record is. But for now, over to Lucy for the four o'clock news.'

As the news jingle sounded around them, Harper once again removed her headset. 'You guys were great. Thanks so much for coming in,' she said, pushing to her feet. She looked to Amy and Shep. 'Best wishes for your new arrival. Be sure to send us a photo when he or she comes.'

'Thank you, we will.' Shep offered his hand in a goodbye shake as Lilia opened the door and hurried into the studio.

'Great job,' she said to the guests, and then ushered them out before they could continue the conversation. Most of the time, Harper appreciated Lilia's efficiency, but today she wouldn't have minded asking Mel a few further questions.

Instead, she left the studio and went into the staff kitchen to grab a coffee. She grabbed a pod for the machine but was staring absently at it, thinking about Amy and Shep's story, when Lilia found her.

The producer paused in the doorway, her eyebrows raised and one hand perched on her hip. 'Do I need to buy you a new watch?'

Harper stifled a smile. So she'd almost gone over time, so what? 'Sorry, but you and I both know the bad news would still have been waiting at five past four.'

Lilia came further into the kitchen and stopped a few inches short of Harper. 'What was all *that* about anyway?'

Harper's insides clenched but she frowned at her colleague and feigned ignorance. 'I don't know what you mean.'

'Do you think I was born yesterday? There was something personal about that interview. You were different—more invested—when asking the questions.'

'I thought I always came across that way,' she exclaimed as she slotted the pod into the machine.

Lilia's expression softened to one of concern. 'Are you and Samuel struggling to get pregnant? Is that it?'

'No! God no.' She almost laughed. 'You know we don't want children.'

'Then what's going on?'

Harper sighed. That was the million-dollar question. 'Do you have time for a drink?' she asked.

Chapter Two

FEBRUARY 2011

As Claire Wallace's best friend and flatmate banged on her bedroom door, she looked longingly at the TV and prayed that her old DVR wouldn't stuff up and fail to record *Packed to the Rafters*.

'Hurry up,' Polly called as she flung open the door. She was wearing the tightest hot pink miniskirt Claire had ever seen, a black tank top that accentuated her very nice cleavage, and knee-high black boots with a sparkly silver trim. Her make-up was impeccable as usual (perks of being a beautician) and she'd spent hours putting her hair into some messy chic up-do.

When Claire didn't make a move to get off her bed, Polly walked over to her and stopped with her hands on her hips. 'Come on. We can't be late or we'll be left with the guys nobody else wants.'

Heaven forbid. Claire wasn't in the market for any man—rejects or otherwise—but she dragged her sorry self off the bed, smoothed down her dress, then grabbed her mobile and handbag. 'It is testament to how much I love you that I'm willing to give up a relaxing night in front of the telly for a stupid Valentine's Day party.'

Polly's mouth exploded into a full-on grin and she jumped up and down on the spot like a two year old needing to pee. 'It's not a *stupid* party, it's a BYO Eligible Friend party. And *we*, my dear, are Eligible with a capital E! Why should all the smug couples be the only ones to have fun on Valentine's?'

'Whatever you want to call it, it still requires me leaving the house when I'd much rather stay at home with my cats, eat crap and watch *Rafters*.'

As Polly grabbed her hand, Claire glanced back at the bed where her two ginger cats Gerry and Sunny lay sprawled across her floral bedspread. 'Those two will still be there when you get back and if your recording stuffs up, I'll buy you the bloody DVD when it comes out. Now, let's get out of here. You look great by the way.'

'Thanks,' Claire said as they hurried down the hallway and out into the balmy late summer night. She had to admit this sunflower-print maxi-dress was one of her favourites.

'Although perhaps it would be better if you were showing a little more skin.' Polly paused momentarily to give Claire a once-over. 'I could lend you something of mine, but—'

Claire opened her mouth to give her friend a polite 'no', but Polly shook her head and added, 'there's no time.'

'What a pity.' Claire didn't bother to hide her sarcasm as they locked up the flat and headed downstairs to her Mini Cooper—the old variety, or vintage as she preferred to call it. She'd volunteered to drive because someone had to stay sober to make sure Polly didn't do anything too outrageous in the name of finding The One.

Polly was obsessed with finding The One, whereas Claire had long ago resigned herself to a life as a singleton. She liked cats so she was halfway there already. And she was fine with this, *really she was*.

The party was only a short drive away at a cream-coloured terrace house in Newtown and, despite them being punctual, the street was already lined with cars when they arrived. In the end they parked so far away that they may as well have walked. Music was blaring from inside the narrow terrace, and crowds of student types were spilling out the door into the tiny front yard. Claire's older brother, Tim, an occupational health and safety officer, would be having conniptions if he were here.

'OMG,' Polly exclaimed, clutching Claire's arm as they went through the open gate and a guy who looked like the Mad Hatter tipped his hat and welcomed them.

'Evening ladies, hope you get lucky tonight.'

Polly batted her eyelashes at him. 'Thanks. You too.'

'Is this a dress-up party as well?' Claire whispered into Polly's ear as they moved inside.

Polly shook her head. 'Nah, don't think so. But if it is, just say you're a summer garden.'

Before Claire could ask who Polly would say she was dressed as—perhaps a streetwalker?—a tall red-headed man stepped in front of them. 'Good evening girls. I'm Scotty and I hope you don't mind me saying how lovely you're both looking this evening.'

'Not at all.' Polly laughed and tilted her head to one side coquettishly. 'I'd think it rude if you didn't. I'm Polly, and this is my friend Claire.'

Redhead grinned back. 'Can I get you girls a drink?'

'Thanks, that'd be great,' Polly replied, before Claire could object. She'd been staring at Scotty's chin, thinking how his ridiculously long goatee was almost the same colour as her cats.

'No, thanks. Not for me,' she said quickly. 'I'm sticking to water, and we'll come with you while you get Polly's drink.' There'd been so many reports of drinks being spiked lately that she wasn't prepared to take any chances.

He nodded, not seeming in the slightest bit offended by her suspicious nature, then turned to Polly. 'Your name is almost as pretty as you are.'

Oh sheesh. We have a smooth-talker. But Polly simpered with glee at Scotty's words. They trekked into the kitchen, which was set up like a makeshift bar. Claire kept one eye on Scotty pouring Polly a wine, while she whispered in her ear. 'Don't you think you should mingle a little before getting cosy with this guy?'

'Nah, I like him. Redheads are always better in bed. But you go mingle. Have fun.' Polly didn't actually shoo Claire away with her hands but her intent was clear. She wanted to get to know Scotty on her lonesome.

'Fine. But *please* be safe,' Claire said, then she nodded towards the back of the house. 'I'm going to get some fresh air. My mobile is on vibrate so I'll feel it if you call. If you're not gonna need a lift home, let me know, because I might just be able to catch the end of *Rafters*.'

'Oh, no, no, no!' Polly shook her finger at Claire. 'You are not leaving this party without getting either a snog or five phone numbers. Deal?'

'Deal,' Claire lied, knowing it was easier to do so than object. Polly was optimistic by nature, but she didn't know the full story behind Claire's stance on men and relationships.

Claire was happy to let her believe she was simply unlucky in the dating department but the truth was much more complicated. She'd give Polly half an hour and if things were still looking good with the redhead, she'd get his details and head home.

The backyard wasn't as populated as inside, but there were people on the verandah smoking. *So much for fresh air.* Claire held her breath and ventured a little further until she came upon an ornate old-fashioned iron table and chair set beneath a massive fig tree.

She'd barely sat down before she heard a deep voice a few feet away. Dammit, this spot wasn't as isolated as she'd hoped.

'That's the best news ever! I'll call Corrine tomorrow but give her my love.'

She looked up and saw that the voice belonged to a man. He had his back to her and was talking on a mobile phone. As she watched, he slipped the phone into his pocket and spun around.

'Hello,' he said, his face filled with the biggest grin she'd ever seen. It was getting dark but there was enough moonlight to see that this guy was gorgeous. *With a capital* G, as Polly would say. Her friend should have looked around a little more before she settled on Scotty.

'Hi,' Claire said back, smiling herself because his was infectious. 'I'm sorry, I didn't know anyone was out here. I didn't mean to eavesdrop.'

'I've just become an uncle,' he said as if he hadn't registered her comment about eavesdropping.

'Really? Congratulations.' She tried not to let her smile falter but she couldn't help the twinge in her heart at the mention of a baby.

'Thanks. Not that I can take the credit. It's my middle sister's first kid.' Clearly oblivious to her discomfort, he sat down on the vacant chair and thrust out his hand. 'Sorry, I'm Jasper Lombard and I'm ...'

When he didn't finish his sentence, she said, 'Lost for words?'

He chuckled. 'Excited. I've never been an uncle before. I can't wait to meet the little sweetheart.'

'I'm Claire. Claire Wallace.'

'Pleased to meet you, Claire.'

'Likewise.' And she meant it. Although babies weren't her favourite topic of conversation, this guy's enthusiasm was refreshing. As much as she didn't want to admit it, a man who liked children appealed to something deep inside her.

After a few moments silence, Jasper said, 'I'm sorry. When you come to a hook-up party, the last thing you probably want to be talking about is babies.'

Ignoring the latter part of this statement, she smiled. 'Actually, this isn't really my scene. I came kicking and screaming with my flatmate. Hey, I don't suppose you could kiss me? I'd be happy with a peck on the cheek, but I promised her I wouldn't leave without getting a snog or at least five phone numbers, and I really wanna bail on this party.'

He leant across the table, and before she could tell him it was a joke, he pressed his mouth against hers in the most gentle but titillating kiss she'd had in her entire life. Her nipples tingled, her toes curled and that tender spot between her legs flooded with warmth. And then he pulled back.

Her cheeks burning, she tried to catch her breath as she met his still-smiling gaze. 'Thank you,' she whispered, resisting the urge to ask him to kiss her again. Suddenly she couldn't even recall the name of the TV show she'd forgone to come here.

'Always happy to help a lady out, but I'll be sorry to see you go. We haven't had a chance to get to know each other yet.'

'Who'd you come with?' she asked. What harm would it be to stay and talk to him a few moments?

'My cousin. I'm visiting him and he said a condition of using his couch was being his eligible friend so he could come. So here I am.'

Her mind latched onto one part of that sentence. 'Oh, are you not from around here?'

Jasper shook his head. 'I live in the Hunter Valley. I came to Sydney to catch up with an old friend who lives overseas now but was back for only a few days.'

'Wow. I haven't been there much, but I love the Hunter Valley,' she said, and then bit her lip to stop herself from grinning like a loony. The Hunter might not be another country but it was far enough away that the chances of developing a relationship were slim. But a quick fling was not out of the question. Claire wasn't normally a one-night-stand kind of girl, but perhaps she could make an exception for this gorgeous guy.

Because he *was* gorgeous. She put Jasper at about a head taller than herself. He had lovely broad shoulders and muscular arms, but he wasn't too big. Still, it was his face she could barely stop from drooling over—his eyes and his smile to be precise. Thanks to the darkness she couldn't quite define his eye colour, but she guessed them a silver blue, and they positively sparkled when the ends of those lovely thick lips twisted upwards. He had lots of dark-blond hair and it was kind of scruffy, but it suited him as much as his close-cut beard of the same colour. Until tonight, she'd have said facial hair turned her off, but right now, she was feeling very turned *on*.

'What about you? Have you always lived in Sydney?' he asked, and she realised she'd been watching his mouth move and that he'd presumably been talking about his home town for a while, but she hadn't registered a word of it.

'Yep,' she said. 'My parents own a bookshop in the inner city. I've spent a few years globetrotting but I came home recently for my older brother's wedding. I wasn't planning on staying, but two kittens were dumped outside my parents' shop and I kinda fell in love.'

A worried look crossed his face. 'You fell in love?'

She was confused for a moment, but then rushed to reassure him that she wasn't bound to anyone. 'With the *kittens*. I was only meant to foster them until they found new homes, but I couldn't bear to part with them, so I moved in with my old friend from school and ... well, almost a year later, here I am.'

'Yes, here you are.' His smile returned. 'And what do you do for a job? Or are you studying?'

'I never was much one for the books. Well, I love reading them, obviously—can't grow up in a bookshop without becoming a bookworm—but I like flowers even more than I like books. So I became a florist.'

'That's cool!'

She raised one eyebrow. 'You like flowers?' In her experience most men just saw them as a means to an end.

'Of course I do. Who doesn't like flowers? What's your favourite?'

'The *Plumeria* "Rosy Posy".' When his expression remained blank, she elaborated. 'It's a rare Australian flower with the most beautiful soft colours—pinks and white and yellows usually—and the petals kind of curl downwards.'

He made a half-laugh impressed noise. 'You learn something new every day.'

Now she decided to test him. 'Do you have a favourite flower?'

He rubbed his lips together and his brow furrowed as if he were in deep contemplation. She'd put her money on the rose, tulip or lily—they were the most commonly requested flowers at the shop. 'I can't choose between the gerbera and the sunflower,' he said, reaching out and gently touching one of the flowers on her dress, right in the middle of her belly. Her stomach quivered beneath his touch.

'What about you? What do you do for work?' She held up her hand. 'No wait, let me guess.'

He tilted his head to one side making his smile appear lopsided. 'Go on then.'

'Teacher?' She could imagine him with a classroom of kids sitting at his feet while he read a picture book.

'Nope.'

'Accountant.'

'Do I look *that* boring?'

She laughed. 'Dentist.'

'Not even close.' He grimaced and then ran his tongue over the front row of his teeth. She noticed that they weren't perfectly straight, but they were still nice teeth.

'I give up! What *do* you do for a crust?'

He leant forward ever so slightly across the table and whispered. 'I'm a balloonist.'

'What?' The image of him dressed in a clown suit landed in her head. 'You make little animal models out of those long, skinny balloons.'

'No!' He laughed as if this was the funniest thing he'd ever heard. 'I'm a *hot air* balloonist.'

She let out a long breath. The air was suddenly *hot* out here. 'Seriously? You're not pulling my leg?'

'I wouldn't do that. Honest to God, I'm a hot air balloonist, or as some of us in the industry say, a balloonatic.'

'Wow.' Now, not only was he one of the best-looking guys she'd ever met, he was definitely the most interesting.

She needed all the answers. 'How does one get that job?'

'Well,' he began, leaning back in the seat as if settling in for a long story. 'I come from a long line of hot air balloonists ...'

And for the next hour or so, Jasper told her the fascinating history of his family. They were French—she should have guessed from the way he pronounced his surname—and apparently his ancestors were some of the earliest hot air balloonists, descended from the Montgolfier brothers. 'Or so my dad reckons—he's obsessed with tracing our family tree.'

'Did the Montgolfier brothers invent the hot air balloon?' she asked.

He shook his head. 'No. The first known balloon flight, carrying test animals—a sheep, a duck and a rooster—was in a balloon invented by Pilatre de Roziar, a scientist, in 1783.'

Claire laughed, half amused, half horrified. 'Those poor animals!'

'Hey,' he shrugged. 'They went down in history—they're probably the most famous sheep, duck and rooster of all time.'

She shook her head, chuckling. 'I think Dolly was the most famous sheep.'

'Perhaps,' he conceded. 'Anyhow, not long after Pilatre came Joseph and Etienne Montgolfier. They flew from Paris and are considered the forefathers of hot air ballooning. Apparently Joseph first got the idea of building a flying machine when he noticed laundry drying over a fire form pockets that billowed upwards. He was the inventor in the family, but his brother Etienne had a brain for business.'

He paused a moment. 'Am I boring you yet?'

'Not at all.' His voice relaxed her and the story was fascinating. 'Tell me more.'

And so he did—giving her a crash course in hot air ballooning and his family's passion for the pastime. Although Jasper still had relatives in France, his great-grandfather had married an English girl and set up a ballooning business with her in Cornwall.

'That company grew and is now run by my great uncle and his family. They've got outlets in Devon, London, Hampshire, Oxford, York, the list goes on.'

'I never knew ballooning was such a big business.'

He grinned. 'Probably because big business isn't usually synonymous with fun, and ballooning is quite possibly the most fun you can have with your clothes on.'

'Is that a fact?' she asked, her mouth going a little dry at the thought of Jasper naked.

He nodded.

'So how did your family end up in Australia?'

'Love,' he said. And then elaborated. 'My dad came down under to compete in a ballooning competition at Canowindra and met my mum.'

'Was she a balloonist too?'

'No, she worked at the hotel he stayed in. And by the time he was due to fly home, he was smitten. They were married six months later and my sister arrived five months after the wedding.'

Claire laughed. 'Did he win the competition?'

'No, but whenever he tells the story and anyone asks that question, he looks at Mum and says he still got the prize.'

'That's sweet,' she said. If Jasper's dad was half as good-looking and charismatic as him it was easy to see why his mum fell hard and fast.

'There you are, I've been looking everywhere for you,' came Polly's slurred voice from the direction of the verandah. Claire's heart sank a little that this magical time with Jasper was likely over.

She turned to see her friend and the redhead stumbling over to them. If the hot pink lipstick all over his face was anything to go by, they'd gotten up close and personal already. Claire and Jasper stood as the drunken duo arrived in front of them.

'Jasper, I'd like you to meet my friend, Polly, and her ... *friend*, Scotty.'

Jasper tipped his head. 'Nice to meet you Polly, and as it happens, Scotty and I are already acquainted. His is the couch I was telling you about.'

'He's your cousin?' She couldn't hide her surprise. Obviously Jasper had gotten the lion's share of the handsome genes.

'Don't hold it against me,' he said with a chuckle.

'Can ya giz Pol and I a liftbacktomyplace,' Scotty asked, his head lolling a little from side to side. 'I'm gonna show her my bedroom.'

He and Polly laughed as if this was the most hilarious thing in the world. Claire and Jasper exchanged the knowing look of two people who were the only sober ones in a sea of drunks.

'Yeah, mate,' Jasper said, clamping his hand down on his cousin's shoulder. 'Do you think you can make it to the car?'

Polly spun around quickly and threw up into a nearby bush.

Claire sighed. 'I think maybe it would be better if I took Polly home to her own bed and they reconnect another day.'

'Good idea.' Jasper nodded.

'How did they get drunk so fast? What have they been drinking?'

Jasper glanced at his watch. 'Wow. We've actually been sitting out here for almost four hours.'

'What?!' Time had never gone so fast in the company of another person before.

'I know,' he said, his eyes meeting hers as if he were thinking exactly the same thing.

Polly chucked again and Claire, remembering her duty as the doting friend, rushed forward to hold her hair back from her face.

'I'll go see if I can find some water,' Jasper said.

When he returned, they helped Polly clean up and then supported their friend and cousin as they negotiated their way through the crowd inside, down the hallway and out the front door. It turned out Jasper had parked a lot closer, so they put Polly and

Scotty into the back seat and then Claire climbed in the front next to him.

'I hope she doesn't throw up again,' she said.

Jasper chuckled. 'This is Scotty's car.'

'Oh! Hah! Good.'

After the short drive down the road, Jasper helped her transfer Polly from Scotty's car to hers. When he shut the back door, the two of them stood on the side of the road looking at each other. It almost felt like the end of a first date—if she could forget about her drunk friend only centimetres away. She wanted to kiss Jasper again, but more than that she wanted him to ask for her number.

You could ask him, said a pesky little voice inside her head. She wasn't sure whether it was her good or bad conscience because another voice also sounded—*This will only end in tears*.

He shoved his hands in his pockets and cleared his throat. 'I've really enjoyed talking to you this evening, Claire.'

'Me too,' she rushed. 'I've never met a hot air balloonist before.'

'About that,' he began. 'I was wondering ... would you like to go up in a hot air balloon?'

'With you?'

He nodded. 'That was my idea, but if you'd rather someone else, I can get Mum or Dad to take you.'

Alarm bells rang inside her head—not because she thought Jasper dangerous in a serial killer type of way but because she knew if she saw him again, she was likely to start falling in love. Hell, it might already be too late.

And she didn't *do* relationships.

When she was still deliberating after a few moments, he shook his head and his cheeks turned beetroot under the street lights. 'Sorry, stupid idea. Forget I asked.'

'No.' She shook *her* head. She would never be able to forget, and she knew if she didn't say yes, she'd never forgive herself either. So what if she was playing with fire? She'd always wanted to go up in a hot air balloon and here was a gorgeous, lovely man offering to take her up for free. He wasn't asking her to marry him, just taking her for a joyride. 'I'd love to. Yes, please. When? Where?'

Now she was babbling. She sounded like an idiot but he didn't seem to care.

The colour softened in his cheeks and his mouth twisted into that beautiful smile again. 'When's your next day off?'

Chapter Three

JULY 2016

Thank God it's Friday, Harper thought as she turned her key in the front door of her Paddington town house and dumped the pile of reading she'd brought home on the hall table. Usually she spent her weekends enthusiastically devouring background research on upcoming guests, but right now all she wanted to do was curl up on the couch with a big bowl of Coco Pops and watch old episodes of *Friends* until she fell asleep or Samuel came home. Whichever came first.

She dropped her keys and handbag, toed off her high heels and shrugged out of her winter coat. As she walked towards the kitchen, she reached around under her shirt and unclasped her bra. She manoeuvred her arms out and slipped the undergarment through her sleeve and then draped it over the back of a stool alongside the breakfast bench.

'That's better,' she said aloud as she opened the cupboard and retrieved a carton of Coco Pops from its hiding space behind rows of tinned tuna. She was in dire need of her go-to comfort food. After some nasty dental work yesterday, Lilia hadn't been able to eat anything but mush today, so Harper had done her best not to eat too much in front of her at work. Now she was hungry enough that she could eat the box as well as its contents.

She grabbed a bowl, a spoon, milk from the fridge and took these items and the cereal to the coffee table in the lounge room. After setting up *Friends* series five on the DVD player—thank God for the box set—she curled up on the couch and proceeded to devour her first bowl of Coco Pops.

'Man you taste good,' she said, gazing lovingly at the little brown bubbles as she lifted the spoon to her mouth.

How sad to be having a one-sided conversation with my cereal. Maybe I should get a pet.

It would give her someone to talk to during the evenings Samuel worked late, which was most evenings. Surely talking to an animal was better than talking to cereal. You'd think because she spoke to people for a living, she'd enjoy a little solitude at night, but lately she'd been feeling a little off-kilter.

Harper sighed and tried to focus on the screen where Chandler and Monica were sneaking behind their friends' backs trying to keep their relationship a secret and Phoebe was giving birth to triplets. Even Phoebe—one of the least together characters in the history of TV—was doing something amazing with her life. What was Harper doing?

Today she'd interviewed Sophie-Anne Romero, a woman she'd gone to school with and who now volunteered in Niger as an obstetrician. During the interview, Sophie-Anne had spoken about her passion for improving conditions for pregnant women and new mothers in third world countries. Afterwards, when she'd said farewell and wished her a safe return trip, Harper had felt an aching hole inside her.

The hole had been growing for months—every time she met another selfless person doing something wonderful to make the world a better place, she couldn't help wondering what the hell her role was? When the people she interviewed died they'd have remarkable epitaphs on their gravestones, and what would she have? Sure, people enjoyed listening to her show, and yes, she had a great reputation as a journalist and an interviewer, but all she did was report on *other people's* lives.

If Lilia presented *her* as an interview candidate, Harper would knock herself back for being boring.

When her spoon scraped the bottom of the empty bowl, she refilled and then leant back against the couch, trying to focus on the screen and not on the nagging feeling within her that something wasn't quite right. If only her friends were available for a night out, but Lilia was out of town for a weekend on one of her frequent recharge trips and Harper's other close friends—Juliet and Renee—had both recently become mothers within a matter of months. Even if they could come out, all they'd talk about was how little sleep they were getting and their fears they'd never fit into their jeans again. Lord, the way new mothers spoke about babies, it was a wonder anyone willingly got pregnant.

She could call her sister, except Willow was in the throes of a brand new relationship and thus spent every evening, especially Fridays, with her girlfriend.

She could call her mum. *Now you really are scraping the bottom of the barrel, Harper.*

Instead she went out into the hallway, retrieved her mobile from her bag and took it back to the couch where she texted Samuel:

Hey honey, hope your day was good. What time do you think you'll get home? Want me to order takeaway? xo

Neither of them ever felt like cooking on work days so he wouldn't read anything worrying into her message. What she really wanted to write was: *Please come home. I think I'm having a midlife crisis and I need distraction.*

Samuel was *very good* at distracting her but she didn't want to sound needy. Part of their attraction to each other was that both were diehard workaholics and neither minded the other one putting work first.

The episode of *Friends* had ended, the next one started and she'd eaten another bowl of cereal before he replied.

Sorry babe, think it'll be a late one tonight. But how's breakfast in bed sound?

As she read his message, tears prickled at the corners of her eyes. She wiped them away angrily and then punched out a reply.

Fresh croissants from the bakery?

Is there any other breakfast?

She forced a laugh, telling herself to stop being such a wet blanket.

That sounds wonderful. Love you.

Love you too.

With another long sigh, she tossed her phone aside and turned back to the TV screen. Sometime before midnight, she woke up on the couch, her neck hurting from lying at an awkward angle and a little puddle of drool on the white cushion beside her. *Friends* series five had ended and the house was dark, except for the TV screen frozen on the episode list.

Harper stood, stretched and then picked up the empty box of Coco Pops, the milk carton, and the other damning evidence from the coffee table. The lounge room perfect again, she got rid of the box, put her bowl and spoon in the dishwasher and then went upstairs to bed.

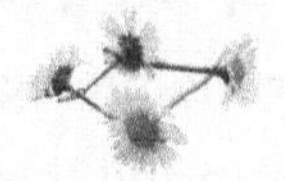

'Rise and shine, sleeping beauty.'

Harper woke to Samuel's ridiculously chirpy voice as he peeled back their bedroom curtains. Lying at the bottom of his side of the bed was a tray laden with croissants, butter, jam and two champagne flutes. She sat up as her husband came to join her. In his hand was the bottle of the champagne they had been keeping in the back of their fridge in anticipation of a very special occasion.

'Oh my God,' she exclaimed. 'You've made partner?'

Samuel was employed by a prestigious law firm and had been working his arse off for the last decade in the hope of one day buying into the company. Their marriage had actually been part of this plan. Apparently the partners still thought a married man a better bet than a single one. As long as she could keep her own name, Harper didn't see how a wedding ring could make much of a difference to their lives and so she'd agreed. Samuel had joked that to avoid all the family hoo-ha they should elope to Vegas and get married by an Elvis impersonator. She'd surprised him by agreeing and in the end it had actually been very romantic.

'No.' Although he shook his head, his smile didn't fade. 'Not yet, but I'm sure it won't be long. One of the partners gave me the heads-up that they'll be promoting someone next year. I'm pretty sure I've got it in the bag.'

'That's wonderful,' she said as he popped the cork. 'And you totally deserve it. All that hard work has finally paid off.'

'I know.' He started pouring the fizz into their best crystal flutes and then offered her one. 'I'd better not have too much of this as

I've got lots of work to do today. Can't afford to slack off at the last hurdle.'

'Of course not.' She held up her glass and forced a smile as she made a toast. 'To my wonderful, intelligent, sexy husband.'

'Thanks, babe.' He took a sip and then leant back into the pillows beside her. She was happy for him, truly she was, but that niggling feeling that had eluded her during sleep returned. Samuel's epitaph would also be impressive—he helped people get a fair trial in court and she knew, after listening to him for years, that there were a number of innocent people in this country (and others) wrongly imprisoned because they didn't have good defence. So his job was an important one.

As they sipped bubbles and devoured the deliciously light croissants from the fab French bakery just down the road, Samuel chattered on about current cases he was doing and Harper tried to make the right noises in all the right places, but she just couldn't garner her usual enthusiasm.

After about ten minutes, he put his now-empty flute down on his bedside table and turned to face her better. 'Babe, is something wrong? I noticed an empty box of Coco Pops in the bin when I came in last night and I saw the *Friends* box set on the coffee table.'

Sprung. She obviously hadn't covered her tracks as well as she'd thought. There hadn't been many times during their ten years together where Harper had needed a double dose of comfort in the form of *Friends* and bad-for-you cereal, but whenever she had a particularly draining interview at work or her mother was being more demanding than normal, she often turned to one or the other to make her feel better.

She shrugged and took another sip of champagne. 'I can't really explain it but I guess I've been feeling a little flat lately.'

He frowned as he reached for the bottle and refilled her glass. 'Flat? What do you mean? Is it your mother? Your job? Us?' There was a hitch in his voice on this last word.

'That's just it, it's none of those things. I can't even really pinpoint the problem but I just feel there's something missing from my life. That I should be doing something more meaningful.'

Samuel raised an eyebrow. 'You're one of the most successful radio interviewers in the country, and you're a woman and half the age of most of the others.' She knew he didn't mean offence by the 'woman' comment—he believed in equal rights for all, but he knew that not everyone felt that way and that women often had to work harder than men to prove themselves.

'I know.' She sighed. 'I told you. I just can't explain it. I was thinking maybe we should get a pet.'

He startled as if she'd suggested they get an alien. 'Look, in theory a dog or a cat would be nice, but you know we'd both end up feeling guilty about neglecting it because we're out of the house so much. And animals tie you down—it'd be like having children. We couldn't just take off for the weekend on a whim.'

Before she could ask him when exactly they'd last had a weekend away together, he reached out, took her drink and put it on the bedside table next to his. 'I'm sorry I've been so occupied lately ...'

She refrained from mentioning that he'd been occupied from the moment they'd met—he hadn't changed, but something inside *her* had.

'But I promise I'll make it up to you when I make partner. We'll go on holiday to Europe to celebrate. In the meantime, how about I give you a little taster of some of the things we might get up to when visiting Rome, Paris—all those wonderful places we've dreamed of going together?'

'Won't you be even busier when you make partner?' she asked. 'And anyway, I don't think that's the issue, I ...'

Her voice drifted off again, but Samuel didn't appear to be listening anymore anyway. He carefully removed the tray from the bed, placed it on the floor and then dived under the covers.

While he did his best to distract her, she stared at the ceiling and thought of England. He was a talented lover and could usually turn her into a panting mess very quickly. Today however, her body refused to get with the program and she had to do something she'd never needed to do with him before. She did a Meg Ryan, and it must have been an impressive performance because seconds after she'd finished moaning, groaning, writhing and shuddering, his face reappeared from under the covers wearing an expression that said he was pleased with his efforts. Seconds later he was inside her.

Afterwards he held her for the obligatory few moments, before planting a quick kiss on her forehead and then rolling over to climb out of bed.

'I'm going for a ride and then I have to work for a bit, but how about we go out for dinner tonight?'

He was making an effort to cheer her up, saying all the things he was supposed to be saying, but the thought of having to dress up and leave the house made her even more depressed. 'That would be lovely.'

'You know,' Samuel said, his back to her as he rifled through his drawers for his cycling gear, 'you could always come out with me.'

'What? Now? Go riding with you?' She laughed at the notion. 'I'd never be able to keep up.' A graceful swim through the pool three mornings a week gave her all the exercise she needed.

He chuckled. 'It was just a thought.'

'And it was a lovely one, but I think I'll have a shower and then spend a lazy morning reading the Saturday papers. Have fun, and don't pull any muscles.' She tried to sound chirpy, giving Samuel a free pass to go off and enjoy his morning without worrying about her. Like most men, whenever she admitted she had a problem, he wanted to fix it, but she wasn't sure he could fix this one.

This niggling feeling of disenchantment was something she needed to sort out for herself, and she doubted a day in bed flicking through the papers and watching more episodes of *Friends* would give her the answer, but she didn't have the motivation for anything else.

'Bye, babe.' Samuel came across to the bed again a few moments later when he was all suited up in his expensive lycra. 'I look forward to our dinner date tonight.'

Then he kissed her again and swaggered out of the bedroom.

Chapter Four

FEBRUARY 2011

'I can't believe you're driving all the way to the Hunter Valley to spend the night with a guy you've only met once,' Polly said, standing next to Claire's car as she threw her overnight bag onto the passenger seat.

'Says she who didn't come home at all yesterday because she was spending the night with a guy *she'd* met only once before.'

Polly opened her mouth, no doubt to explain how that was different, but Claire got in first.

'Anyway, I'm not spending the night with him in the way your dirty mind would like to think. He lives with his parents and I'll be staying with them, in the *spare* room.'

Polly sniggered. 'If he's got to—what is he? Twenty-six? Twenty-seven?—and he's still living at home, then I'm sure he has tricks for sneaking you into his boudoir.'

'Oh stop!' Claire waved a hand at her friend and then turned to walk around to the driver's side, which meant Polly couldn't see the blush on her cheeks. The truth was if Jasper should decide to make a midnight visit, she probably wouldn't turn him away.

'Don't forget to feed the cats and bring them in from outside tonight,' Claire called as she climbed into the car.

'You can count on me,' Polly said, already waving. As Claire reversed out of her car spot, Polly called out loud enough for half of the suburb to hear, 'Don't do anything I wouldn't do!'

'That leaves the options wide open,' Claire muttered to herself as she started down the road, ready to navigate the afternoon rush hour traffic out of the city. She turned her radio up and tried to ignore the little voice in her head that kept asking her what game she was playing. She'd been arguing with it ever since she'd agreed to make this trip.

Although she'd only met Jasper once, this pesky voice kept insisting that he was family man material, and thus wouldn't want to be with someone like her. She argued back that it was possible for a man and a woman to be good friends and that they lived so far from each other that that's all she and he could ever be anyway. Despite this reasoning, on the two-and-a-half hour drive up the freeway she almost turned back more than once. Her head swam with potential excuses. Yet, once she passed Newcastle, she decided she was going to do this whether it was a bad idea or not. If her heart got hurt, at least she'd be able to say she'd been up in a hot air balloon. And, if you were going to do it, the Hunter Valley had to be one of the most gorgeous places in Australia to do so.

Following the directions Jasper had given her when they'd spoken on the phone, Claire drove through seemingly endless paddocks of vineyards in full leaf until she finally reached Lovedale and slowed her car in front of a handsome wooden gate. Her stomach tightening, she followed the tree-lined gravel drive until she came upon a traditional whitewashed Australian homestead. The gardens surrounding it were perfectly manicured but they didn't feel showy or pompous at all. Of course she noticed the flowers—among a number of native shrubs were beds of stunning roses—and it pleased her to think that someone in Jasper's family had a green thumb. If she lived here she'd spend all day every day out in the garden and she would *never* want to leave.

In the middle of the garden a hot air balloon sculpture had pride of place—she'd obviously come to the right address.

As she parked her car out the front, she saw Jasper stepping off the verandah, waving as he came towards her. Her breath left her lungs and all her nerves and second thoughts fled with it.

Too late to back out now. And anyway, she didn't want to. She couldn't get out of the car fast enough and almost tripped in her haste.

'You okay?' Jasper asked, rushing over and reaching out to steady her. Claire's mouth went dry—he was even more gorgeous than she remembered.

She managed a quick nod. 'Guess my feet are a little unsteady after the drive.'

'It's good to see you. To be honest, I wasn't sure whether you'd come or not.'

She smiled up at him. 'If you think I'd pass up a free ride in a hot air balloon, you don't know me at all. This is bucket list stuff. I have to confess I did look your family up online and check out your story to make sure this wasn't some elaborate scheme to lure me to a cabin in the woods and have your wicked way.'

'Thank God for Google, hey?' He laughed, then nodded towards her bag on the front seat. 'Can I get that for you?'

'Oh, I can carry it,' she said, rushing around to the passenger side.

Jasper was right behind her. 'I'm sure you *can*, but my mother is very old fashioned and if she sees you carrying your own luggage inside, she'll box my ears.'

Claire couldn't imagine anyone daring to box any part of Jasper's muscular physique but she liked the sound of his mother. 'We can't have that,' she said, conceding.

His parents must have been lingering just inside, for the moment she and Jasper stepped onto the verandah the fly screen door flew open. A tall, wiry man with salt-and-pepper hair, matching beard and silver-rimmed spectacles held it open as a woman who couldn't have been much taller than five foot stepped out. Two words came to mind when Claire looked at her—cuddly and chirpy. She wore an apron with a hot air balloon print around her waist and had smile lines round eyes that were the same unusual colour as Jasper's.

'Good evening,' Jasper's dad said at the same time his mother grabbed Claire in a hug. 'Welcome, my dear. You must be tired after such a long drive from Sydney.'

'It's not that long, Mum,' said Jasper.

His mother ignored him. 'I'm Wendy and this is my husband Jean-Paul, but we all call him Paul and you must too. Now, can I get you a cup of cocoa or would you prefer a nice glass of wine before bed?'

It was barely eight o'clock but Jasper had warned her that in the world of hot air balloons people went to bed early and rose before the sun. 'Cocoa sounds lovely,' she said.

'That's settled then. You come into the kitchen and we'll have a good natter while the milk heats.' Wendy linked her arm through Claire's and ushered her down a hallway lined with photographs and paintings of hot air balloons, calling back over her shoulder. 'Jasper, put Claire's bag in the guest room.'

'*Yes, Mum.*'

Claire smiled at his bemused tone and hoped he'd join them in the kitchen soon. This situation was weird enough without being grilled by the mother of a guy she'd only just met. Wendy, with Paul following closely behind, led her into a large, country style kitchen with a table in the middle of the room. Yellow roses sat in a vase shaped like a hot air balloon and as she looked around, she couldn't help but notice all the other hot air balloon–themed stuff: balloon placemats on the table, multi-coloured balloon ornaments hanging from the ceiling, balloon magnets on the fridge, balloon print tea towels hung over the big Aga oven.

'You'd be forgiven for thinking we like balloons,' Paul said.

'I love them. They're amazing,' she gushed, one hundred percent genuine in her praise. The room was almost like a hot air balloon museum—or perhaps the gift shop. 'I always wanted to collect something but I never found anything that kept my interest long enough.'

Wendy crossed over to the fridge and retrieved a carton of milk, speaking as she proceeded to pour some into a saucepan over a stove. 'Take a seat, love. And fetch my biscuit tin, will you, Paul.'

Both Claire and Paul did as they were told and Wendy kept talking as she worked. 'Jasper tells me you're a florist.'

'Yes, that's right.'

'And that your parents own a bookshop?'

Paul returned to the table with a balloon-shaped biscuit tin. He removed the lid and offered it to Claire. 'Wendy's a big reader,' he said as she took what looked to be a homemade melting moment cookie.

'Thank you. What kind of books do you like?'

'I'm a sucker for a good romance,' Wendy admitted, whisking the milk. 'Speaking of which, Jasper tells me you two were reluctant attendees at a BYO Eligible Friend party.'

'A what?' Paul asked, his chair scraping on the floor tiles as he pulled it back to sit.

'Scotty dragged me along,' Jasper said as he entered the kitchen.

Claire's belly did a somersault as she laid eyes on him again and she almost choked on a mouthful of the most delicious melting moment she'd ever tasted.

Paul gave a brief nod. 'Scotty, huh? Ah, that explains it.'

'You okay?' Jasper crossed to Claire and put his hand on her back, gently patting it as she coughed. 'Can I get you some water?'

She nodded, unable to speak.

Moments later he handed her a glass of ice-cold water and she downed it, hoping to clear her throat and to lower her temperature—which had skyrocketed when his hand landed on her back.

Get a grip, Claire.

'I was just admiring your parents' hot air balloons,' she said when she'd recovered.

'You should see their bedroom,' he muttered as he sat down on the seat next to hers.

I'm more interested in yours, she thought.

Wendy arrived at the table with the hot mugs of cocoa and immediately started her motherly interrogation. First thing she wanted to know was why Claire had become a florist.

'Actually,' she said, lowering her glass back to the table, 'I developed a thing for flowers when I was in hospital as a child.'

'Did you have your tonsils out?' Paul asked. 'I remember when Jasper got his tonsils out when he was five. He refused to wear the operating gown because he said dresses were for girls.'

Claire looked up to see Jasper blushing and forced a laugh. 'It was a little more serious than tonsillitis. I had a form of leukaemia.'

'Oh Mary, Joseph and Jesus,' Wendy gasped. 'How terrible.'

'It's okay,' Claire reassured her. 'I survived. Obviously. But there were a few awful years there and flowers became the thing to take my mind off the pain and my hair falling out. Whenever I saw a flower, I couldn't be sad or even scared that I might die. I became obsessed—friends and family bought me flowers, even the nurses—and when I went into remission, Mum and Dad celebrated by giving me a patch of the garden for my own. I grew every flower I could possibly get my hands on. Then I'd pick them and arrange them and give them to my friends. In fact, I love flowers so much I even named my cats after them.'

'Oh really?' Wendy's face lit up at this news. 'What are their names?'

'Gerry and Sunny, short for Geranium and Sunflower.'

'Aw, that's just lovely.' Wendy sniffed and reached across to grab a tissue from the box on the table. It might have been the only thing in the room (maybe even the house) without a balloon on it.

Claire felt Jasper's knee press against hers under the table and she could tell from the way it lingered there that it wasn't an accident. Warmth spread from that spot right through her body.

'I really like your garden,' she said, looking from Wendy to Paul as she tried to take her mind off their son's knee and also ward off any further questions about her childhood illness. She didn't often talk about it and couldn't quite understand why she'd opened up to these virtual strangers. Perhaps because they didn't *feel* like strangers.

'Paul's actually the green thumb around here,' Wendy said, 'but I do love to spend a Sunday afternoon sitting among the blooms reading a good book. Speaking of books, I'm trying to recall if I've ever visited your parents' bookshop in Sydney. How long have they owned it?'

'For as long as I can remember,' Claire replied. 'They were both teachers before then, but it was always Dad's dream to either write a book or own a bookshop, and the latter seemed the easier option.'

Everyone laughed. Wendy seemed to want to know as much as Claire was willing to share about her family, so as they sat drinking cocoa and eating biscuits, she told them more about her parents—both only children—and her grandparents—both sets alive and kicking. 'They're actually very good friends and at the moment they're grey-nomading around Australia together.'

'Sounds like fun,' Paul said, dusting biscuit crumbs from his beard.

'And do you have any siblings?' Wendy asked.

'I have one brother. Tim. He got married a year ago and doesn't live far from me, so I see him and his wife quite a lot.'

'Do they have children?'

'Give them time, Mum. They've only been married a year.'

Wendy and Paul laughed and Claire forced herself to chuckle alongside them, even though the mention of children always set the hairs on the back of her neck on edge. 'No children yet,' she said.

'I became a grandmother on Monday—a Valentine's baby—can you believe it?' Wendy asked.

'Congratulations. Jasper told me at the party. It must be very exciting for you.'

The older woman beamed. 'It is. Would you like to see a photo?'

'I'd love to,' Claire lied, the cocoa and biscuit suddenly sitting heavily in her gut.

Wendy bustled out of the room, quickly returned with an iPad and then sat again, dragging her chair closer to Claire. She swiped her finger across the screen and seconds later the first baby photo appeared. Claire tried to smile as a chubby, red, squished up face stared back at her.

'Isn't she simply divine? I could just eat her up. Her name is Cadence Rose. Isn't that beautiful?' Wendy kept swiping, sentencing Claire to photo after photo of newborn baby in different positions and various states of undress. Then she came to a photo of a woman—gorgeous despite her messy golden-blonde hair, sweat-glistened face and tired eyes—lying on a hospital bed snuggling the baby. Her love for the child shone from the screen and Claire felt her throat closing over.

Oblivious, Wendy continued. 'This is my middle daughter, Corrine. Sadly she and her hubby live in WA. The baby was early so I wasn't there, but I'm leaving tomorrow night to go stay with them for a month.'

Claire somehow managed to speak. 'What do they do over there?'

'Two of my sisters married balloonists in other parts of the world,' Jasper said. 'Celine and her husband live in Denmark. Corrine, as Mum said, is in the Wheatbelt of Western Australia, and my youngest sister and her partner haven't settled anywhere yet. Caroline is into competition ballooning and when she's not doing that, they travel around the world working for friends and family.'

'So you are *all* balloonists?' Claire asked. This topic was much more comfortable than the baby one.

Wendy shook her head. 'Caroline's partner, Noah, is crew, like me, but the rest of the tribe all have pilot's licences and Noah is working towards his.'

'What does it take to become a hot air balloon pilot?'

Paul and Jasper both went to answer at once—it was clear they were passionate about their vocation. Taking turns, they explained that most people started out as ground crew for private balloon teams or commercial companies. Crew members who wanted to become pilots could learn a lot on the ground, studying weather patterns and picking up the tricks of the trade.

'Then you get a student ballooning licence and you have to do a certain number of hours instruction with a qualified pilot before you get a private certificate. When other dads were teaching their kids to drive, mine was teaching me to fly,' Jasper said, before downing the last of his cocoa.

'To get a commercial licence the hours are even more on top of that,' continued Paul. 'In Australia, it's—'

'Now, now, you'll bore Claire with all this industry speak,' Wendy said, clutching her iPad to her chest as if she'd much rather still be showing and telling baby photos.

'I'm not bored at all.' But Claire *was* terrified that the conversation might return to children.

'Anyway,' Paul yawned and pushed back his seat to stand. 'We should probably be getting to bed. As lovely as it's been chatting to you, Claire, we all have early mornings.'

'Dad's taking up a group tomorrow morning. Two of our employees will be crewing for him and—'

'I'll be crewing for Jasper,' Wendy finished, smiling again at the prospect. 'He'll have to leave earlier than us to go and check the weather reports and air currents at the launch site, so set your alarm for four o'clock, and I'll meet you in the kitchen with a cuppa.'

'Can't wait,' Claire said, offering her host a smile.

Jasper stood. 'Come on, I'll show you to your room.'

'Thanks for supper,' she said to his parents as she pushed her seat back and stood. 'It was lovely to meet you both, and thank you so much for letting me stay here tonight.'

'It's our pleasure,' they replied in unison.

Once they were out of the kitchen, Jasper took her hand and her heart hitched a beat as he led her down the corridor. He paused in front of an open door. 'This is the bathroom. There are fresh towels on your bed.'

'Thank you.' She was so full of conflict—half of her wanting to hold his hand forever and the other half telling her to run. Not to her bedroom, but right out of the house and back to Sydney. They may only have known each other a couple of days, but already Jasper made her feel things she'd managed to repress for years.

They continued down the hallway. 'That's my bedroom in there,' he said, indicating a closed door, 'and this one is yours.' He stopped, and still holding her hand, opened the door with his other one to reveal a fairytale bedroom. Like the rest of the house, the décor was balloon themed. Light spilled gently across the room from a hot air balloon lamp beside the bed. The bed itself looked as puffy as a cloud and she couldn't wait to climb into it.

'This is gorgeous,' she said.

'Not sick of hot air balloons yet?' he asked.

'Strangely, no.' She turned to face him. He was looking down at her and she struggled to breathe under his intent gaze. For a second, she thought he might kiss her goodnight—her lips craved this—but instead he gently let go of her hand.

'Hope you have a good night's sleep. I'll see you bright and early.' And then he turned and headed back down the corridor.

Claire went into the bedroom and closed the door behind her. She unzipped her bag on the bed, took out her toiletries and the various outfits she'd brought for tomorrow. She knew she shouldn't be putting this much thought into what to wear to go hot air ballooning—Jasper had told her comfortable, casual clothes were the go with walking shoes and a cap to stop her hair from flying away in the wind—but she wanted to look her best.

Finally deciding on her favourite pair of jeans, which just happened to accentuate her good butt (or so Polly told her), a long sleeved floral-print t-shirt and a bright yellow jacket, she laid them on the chair and headed for the bathroom. After admiring the balloon-shaped soap dispenser, she had a quick shower, put on her PJs and brushed her teeth. As she tiptoed back towards the guest bedroom, the low murmur of voices drifted up the hallway from the kitchen—Jasper and his mum. Although slightly ashamed, she couldn't help cocking an ear to eavesdrop.

'I really like her.'

'I can see that, son, and I have to say I approve with all my heart. She's lovely. And she has a C name, so she'll be like the fourth daughter I never had.'

Claire didn't hear any more. Her heart pounding and tears welling in her eyes, she fled back to the bedroom and closed the door firmly but quietly behind her. Dropping her toiletries bag and towel to the floor, she leant back against the door. Hearing that Jasper liked her should have been the most wonderful thing in the world, because she couldn't remember ever liking anyone as much as she liked him, but this realisation meant two things. One, they could never be just good friends, and two, going up in the hot air balloon and spending the day getting to know him even better would be unfair to them both.

There was only one thing for it.

Chapter Five

AUGUST 2016

'So, how's your parents' mission to find you a husband?' Harper asked as she looked across the table. She and Lilia were sitting outside a wine bar not too far from the radio station and Lilia looked all business.

'Oh, no you don't!' Lilia put down the glass she was about to sip from and waved her finger at Harper as if she were a naughty child. 'We're not here to talk about my depressing, non-existent, love life. We're here to talk about you. Why the Spanish Inquisition with Mel, Amy and Shep this afternoon?'

Harper cringed. 'Did it really come across like that?'

'Only to me because I know you so well. I'm sure Mel, Amy and Shep had no idea, but something's been off with you for a while. What's going on?'

Harper swallowed. How could she explain this to her friend when she didn't even know how to explain it to herself?

'I want to donate my eggs to help a couple that can't have children on their own.'

'You *what*?' Lilia's eyes widened and she coughed as if she'd choked on air. In their five years of working together, Harper had never seen her visibly surprised by anything. Perhaps she should have worked her way up to the subject, rather than just blurting it out like that.

'I've decided I want to give my eggs to a couple like Amy and Shep. A deserving, lovely couple who want a baby more than anything in the world.' Her voice shook a little as she spoke. It was the first time Harper had told anyone what she'd been contemplating, and although she'd felt for some time that this was something she wanted to do, she wasn't sure how people would react.

'Holy shit.' Lilia rarely swore—she had far too good a vocabulary to need to. 'Why? When? When did this possibility even enter your head? Does Samuel know?'

One question at a time. And 'when' was the easiest to answer.

'It started a couple of months ago. There was only this niggling feeling at first but then every interview I did, it got worse. At one stage I even considered taking some leave because it was doing my head in, but then I thought, what would I do if I didn't work?'

'*What* was doing your head in?' Lilia asked.

'Sorry.' Harper shook her head and took a quick breath. 'We're always interviewing these amazing people doing all these selfless and world-bettering things and I just started thinking about my contribution. What am I giving? What's the purpose of my life on this planet?'

'Whoa,' Lilia said, eyeing her drink. 'Maybe I need something stronger than wine.'

Harper let out a half laugh.

Lilia held up a finger. 'One, I never realised you felt this way and that makes me a pretty crap friend. I'm sorry. I should have asked when I sensed something was off in your world.'

'Don't be silly, you couldn't have—'

'Two,' Lilia interrupted, holding up a second finger. 'Your contribution is spreading the word, garnering support for all those wonderful causes and all those people we interview, and that's important too. And quite aside from that, you're entertaining. How many emails and tweets do we get from folks who say your show is the highlight of their day? Don't underestimate that. People need shows like ours for entertainment, education and relaxation.'

'I know,' Harper said on a sigh. In theory she agreed but her head and her heart were divided over this one. Her heart needed something more, something bigger—she needed to do something that made an obvious difference, even if just to one person. 'That's exactly what Samuel said. I can't explain it properly because I don't completely understand it myself, but I just feel this is something I need to do.' Maybe she hadn't allowed herself to truly analyse exactly why *this* made sense. A tiny voice inside her asked if it had something to do with her past, but she nudged it aside. Did it really matter what her motivation was?

Lilia's eyebrows rose slowly until they almost touched her hairline. 'So you've told him about your plans?'

'Not yet. He knows I've been feeling unsettled, but I haven't mentioned anything specific. You're the first person I've spoken to about what I've decided to do.'

'And how exactly did you come to the decision that donating your eggs was the thing you needed to do?'

'Remember we interviewed my friend who works in Niger?'

Lilia nodded. 'The obstetrician. Wow—some of her stories brought tears to my eyes, and you know how hard that is to do.'

'Mine too.' Harper admitted. 'I went home feeling worse than I had in months. I spent all night on the couch eating Coco Pops and watching *Friends* and when I woke up in the morning I was still feeling off. I told Samuel. He couldn't understand either and he tried to distract me, but when he went off for his morning ride, I lay in bed reading the papers. And that's when I saw it—an ad from a gay couple looking for an egg donor. They had a surrogate, they just needed the donor. And I thought ... I could do that. I could help them.'

'You're going to donate to a gay couple?' There was no judgement in Lilia's tone.

'No.' Harper shrugged. 'I don't know. Maybe. I haven't chosen a couple yet. I hope the couple I saw in the advert have a donor by now, but there are plenty of others like them, and like Amy and Shep. However, the first step is talking to a doctor, checking I'm physically able to do this.'

'Right.' Lilia nodded slowly as if digesting this news.

'And then I'll start looking for a suitable recipient couple. I might even donate to a single woman, a career woman who hasn't found Mr Right but wants to be a mother.'

'Are you sure *you* don't want to be a mother?' Lilia asked, her tone sceptical.

'Have I ever given you any indication that's what I want?' It was a rhetorical question. 'I'm quite happy focusing on my marriage and my career.'

Lilia raised only one eyebrow this time. 'But you just said you're *not* happy, that something about your life is disillusioning you.'

Harper's grip tightened around her wine glass. 'It's not that I don't like my job or my life, I just want to do something worthwhile, something meaningful, and this is something I can do. Look, you asked what was going on and I've told you, but if you're going to be all negative about it then we may as well—'

Again Lilia interrupted her, holding up one hand. 'Sorry. I'm not meaning to be negative. This came as a surprise, that's all. But if this is what you want to do, then as your friend, you have my support one hundred percent. And as your producer, just give me as much advance notice as you can when you have medical appointments and we'll work around it.'

'Thank you.' Harper let out a big breath, feeling some of the pressure inside her ease out. 'But this won't affect my work. I promise.'

'Just one thing,' Lilia continued, as Harper took another sip of wine. 'I mightn't know much about marriage, but this seems a pretty big step to take without even talking to Samuel about it. You heard what Mel said—she couldn't have done what she did without the support of her partner, her family and friends. I think he needs to be next in line to hear this news, *before* you see the doctor.'

Harper swallowed her mouthful and nodded. 'Oh, I am going to tell him. I promise. He's been so busy at work lately that he probably wouldn't even notice anything going on. But as my husband I actually need his consent to do this.'

'Seriously?' Lilia's eyes boggled.

'It's because of any current or future children we might have,' Harper explained. 'He needs to be involved in discussions about how a baby born to a recipient couple might be part of our lives, or the lives of any of our future children. But that won't be a problem because he's never wanted kids of his own.'

'And what does his mum think about that?' Lilia asked, smirking a little.

Harper smiled back. 'Of course she'd prefer us to procreate, but considering she has five other children and three of them have already started breeding, she's begrudgingly accepting of our decision.'

'Good.' Lilia nodded and glanced at her watch. 'Look, I hate to run but Mum has a friend of an old friend bringing her son round for dinner tonight, and she'll skin me alive if I'm late.'

'Go,' Harper said. 'And good luck.'

Lilia rolled her eyes. 'Not holding my breath. I might have to resort to the internet yet.'

Harper laughed. Her friend was such a contradiction—a staunch career woman but also a devout daughter who wanted to please her parents by being happy in love, like they were. 'I'll just finish this,' she gestured at her glass, 'and then I'll head home too. Hopefully Samuel won't be too late and we'll be able to have the discussion tonight.'

Lilia leant over and hugged Harper briefly. 'I look forward to hearing how it goes.'

When Harper finished her glass of wine, she considered another one, but the bar was filling up with professionals coming in from work and she didn't want to look like the sad sack drinking alone.

Pushing back the stool, she hitched her handbag over her shoulder and walked out into the street to flag a taxi. Usually she took the bus to and from work, but this afternoon she couldn't be bothered dealing with other commuters. She wanted to get home and work out a script for telling Samuel her decision. He was a logical, intelligent man and the best way to handle this situation was to present him with the facts, leave emotion out of it, demonstrate that she'd done her research and have ready answers for any questions or opposition he might throw at her.

As she paid and thanked the taxi driver, she glanced at the clock on the dashboard. It was only six o'clock, so she figured she had at least another couple of hours before Samuel graced her with his presence. By that time she'd be fully prepared.

Yet when she pushed open the front door, she was met by the sound of gentle classical music and the aroma of her favourite candles. Instinctively, she breathed in the salted caramel scent. She dropped her bag on the hall table and was halfway to the kitchen when Samuel stepped through the doorway with a glass of wine in his hand.

'Good evening gorgeous,' he said, wrapping an arm around her waist and drawing her up against his hard body. He pressed his lips down on hers and pushed his tongue into her mouth in a way that made the blood heat in her veins. A desire she hadn't felt in months kicked up inside her and she kissed him back.

'Well, hello there,' she said when they finally came up for air. 'This is a lovely surprise. What are you doing home so early?'

He handed her the wine, then grinned. 'I kicked arse in court today so I thought I'd come home and celebrate with the love of my life.'

She laughed as she lifted the glass to her lips. 'How much of this have you had already? And didn't you want to celebrate with your colleagues?' That was usually the way when one of them won a big case.

'I can celebrate with them anytime, but I've been thinking about you a lot lately, and worrying, if I'm honest.'

'Really?'

'Yes. Ever since you told me you weren't happy, I've been wracking my mind for how to help. I know I've not been the best husband of late and I want to make it up to you. We need to spend more time together. Starting tonight. I've made dinner but I can run you a bath first if you'd prefer.'

'Who *are* you and what have you done with my husband?' Harper asked and then took a sip of her very favourite wine. He really *had* gone all out.

'Hey, I'm not that bad, am I?' Although Samuel laughed, there was a hint of neediness in his question.

'No. You're not bad at all,' she rushed to assure him, reaching out to link her hand through his.

'Dinner or bath first, then?' he asked as he led her into the dining room.

She blinked at the sight of their table laid out with all their good stuff and the room lit with candles on every available surface. 'This is beautiful.'

'Thanks.' He sounded proud as punch. 'But I think you should see the bathroom before you make your decision.'

'Intriguing,' she said with a smile.

He led her up the stairs to the master bedroom, which looked like the set for a seduction scene in a rom-com. The bed was covered in rose petals and he'd obviously bought more candles, because she was sure she didn't own this many.

'Oh Samuel.' She turned and kissed him again. 'Thank you. This is magical.'

He grinned. 'You haven't seen the bath yet.'

He pushed open the door to the ensuite to reveal the full spa scattered with more rose petals.

'I don't think I've ever had a bath with flowers in it.'

'Then let's fix that.' He took her wine glass and placed it down on the vanity. Then he stepped close and started to undress her. 'We might have to top it up with hot water.'

As Harper let Samuel take off all her clothes, her body tingled with awareness. Neither of them had made this much effort in a long while. Was this all she'd needed to feel special about herself—a little extra TLC from her man? Or was it the fact that she'd made the decision about donating her eggs that meant she was finally able to relax now?

She wrapped her arms around his still-clothed body and lowered them to his butt, feeling his hardness press against her core. 'You coming in with me?'

'The dinner might burn if I do.'

'I don't care. Come on.' She yanked open the top buttons of his shirt, then slid her hands onto his hot, bare skin.

Five seconds later they were both naked and sitting spooned against each other in the bath. Samuel's hands roved teasingly over her body and Harper let her head fall back against his chest as he took her over the edge. Afterwards, when they were both entirely aroused, she turned around, straddled his lap and a few moments later they came gloriously together in the water.

'The benefits of having a big bath,' Harper said when she could finally speak again.

'The benefits of having a hot, sexy wife,' Samuel replied. 'Now, let's get out and dry off so I can impress you some more with my culinary skills.'

He climbed out and held a towel for her as she stepped over the edge of the bath. They dressed in the fluffy white robes they'd bought from an expensive hotel on a weekend away in Melbourne, then went downstairs to eat. Samuel insisted she sit in the dining room with another glass of wine while he plated up in the kitchen. And as she sat there, swishing wine around her glass, she contemplated the conversation she'd planned on having.

Was now really the right time to tell him? They were having such a lovely evening, celebrating the two of them as a couple, and she didn't want to ruin that. But then again, maybe this moment, when he was so focused on her, was the perfect opportunity.

Harper took a large sip of wine, hoping the alcohol would help ease the nerves that were brewing inside her. Why should this be such a big deal anyway? It wasn't like donating her eggs would affect Samuel's life at all.

By the time he returned with two plates of roast beef and vegetables, she'd made the decision.

'This smells delicious. Thank you,' she said as he went back out into the kitchen to get the gravy.

'Let's hope it tastes as good as it smells.' He smiled as he put the fancy gravy boat they'd got as a wedding present on the table.

'I'm sure it will.' Harper poured gravy over her vegetables—she didn't like it on meat—and then picked up her knife and fork.

'How was work today?' Samuel asked as he refilled both their glasses.

She stared at him as if he'd asked the question in a foreign language. Then she put down her fork, knowing she wouldn't be able to swallow one bite until she'd done what she'd told Lilia she was going to do. 'Samuel, there's something I want to talk to you about.'

He put down his cutlery and she saw worry enter his eyes. 'O-kay. I'm all ears.'

'I actually interviewed three people today.' She paused, letting him digest this difference. 'Two were a couple; the woman is infertile and they desperately want to have a family. And the third person was a lady who donated her eggs so they could achieve this dream.'

'Nice thing of her to do,' Samuel said, picking up his glass and taking a sip. He obviously didn't see what it had to do with them.

She nodded. 'Yes, it is. But the reason I asked them on the show was a personal one.'

His brow furrowed. 'What do you mean?'

'You know how I told you I wanted to do something more meaningful with my life.'

'Yes.' He sounded wary now.

'Well, a little while ago I stumbled across this advertisement for a couple looking for an egg donor and something clicked inside me. This was something altruistic I could do. I've decided I want to donate my eggs to someone, to a couple who can't have children themselves.'

'Are you insane?' Samuel didn't sound angry, just completely blindsided. 'Why would you want to do something like that?'

She clenched her jaw, trying not to get annoyed at his derisive tone. 'I just want to do something good for someone.'

'Do you know anything about what's involved? You'll need to give up alcohol. You'll have to go on drugs.'

'Drugs!' She felt her patience slipping. 'You make it sound like I'll need to develop a crystal meth addiction. I've done my research Samuel and yes, there'll be blood tests and examinations and I'll need to take medication to stimulate my ovaries, but thousands of women go through this kind of treatment for IVF every year. If it was that dangerous, don't you think we'd hear more warnings? And pregnant women stop drinking every day.'

'I guess so. But all those tests sound expensive.'

Money wasn't a problem—they both had good incomes, paid their mortgage easily and had no other debts. 'IVF isn't cheap,' she admitted, 'but all my medical expenses will be taken care of by the recipients.'

'Will they pay you for the eggs?' he asked.

'No. In Australia it's against the law to be paid for donating eggs, but I'm not doing this for the money. I'm doing it because I want to help someone,' she added quickly before he could ask her a question she couldn't quite explain.

'Very noble of you.' Samuel shook his head slightly as if he couldn't believe they were having this conversation. 'Have you thought about the legalities? What happens once the baby is born? Will you be part of its life? What if the child asks where they come from and wants to meet its *real* mother?'

His questions surprised her, but no doubt in law school they'd discussed these kinds of issues.

'How will you feel knowing you have a biological child walking around?' he continued.

Harper took a deep breath; luckily she'd prepared an answer for everything. 'There'll be a contract between myself and the recipient couple. In Australia the majority of egg donation is not anonymous, which means I'll likely meet the couple I decide to go with and together we'll discuss what any child born from our arrangement will be told.'

Both she and her recipients would be required to undertake counselling and she guessed these were some of the things they would work through.

'As for the future, you probably know—' better to flatter him, '—that in New South Wales anyone who donates an egg must go on a register so that any children conceived from the donation can contact them when they are eighteen.'

'And you don't mind that?' he asked. 'A child coming into our lives eighteen years from now? Last I heard, we didn't want children.'

'And that hasn't changed, but they won't be a child by then, will they?' she retorted. She knew she'd have to be prepared for a child conceived with her eggs to come looking for her one day. But by then, their birth parents would have done the hard work of raising them and she wouldn't be able to mess them up. Instead she'd be able to sit down and have a grown-up conversation explaining why she'd done what she'd done. In fact, she quite liked the idea of developing a friendship with the child down the track.

Ignoring this logic, he hit her with another question. 'You don't even know if you *can* have babies. How do you know you aren't infertile like the couples you want to help?'

Oh, I know. She'd gotten pregnant easily once before and there was no reason to think she couldn't again. But she kept that thought to herself—because what would be the point in coming out with that secret after all these years? That episode in her life had nothing to do with this.

Harper took a quick breath. 'That's what the initial testing will be for. Obviously if I'm not a suitable candidate to donate, then I won't, but I *need* to do this. I need to find out if I can.'

He sighed and ran a hand through his hair, suddenly looking a lot older than his thirty-seven years. 'Maybe you just need a hobby? Another interest outside of work. Why don't you train for a marathon or something?'

When she made a face at that, he said, 'Okay then, what about CrossFit? A couple of receptionists at work have just taken it up. It sounds a lot of fun, why don't you give that a try?'

She scoffed. 'I'm not paying to join a fitness cult. And I don't need a hobby.'

'How about a pet? You mentioned a while back that you might like to get one.'

'But as *you* reminded me, a pet won't fit in with our busy lifestyle. And can you imagine what a dog or cat would do to our lovely white couches?' She shook her head. 'I don't need a hobby, I don't want to do a marathon or join CrossFit or get a pet. I want to help someone have a baby. What's really your opposition here?'

Samuel took a sip of wine, obviously thinking carefully about his answer. 'I just can't fathom why you would want to. There's no financial gain. I might be able to understand if you were doing it for your sister or even a friend, but strangers? What's the point? Why would you *want* to put yourself through this? Why would you want to put *us* through it?'

Harper took a moment to try and find the words that would make him see sense. She loved her husband and she didn't want this to come between them.

'This isn't about *us*, Samuel. It's about me. This is something I just really need to do. I can't explain it any more than that, but I'd really like your blessing. In fact I need it.'

'What do you mean "need it"?' he asked.

'When I find the right couple, both myself and that couple will have to do counselling before we are able to go ahead. And both the counsellor *and* the clinic will want to know that you, as my husband, are okay with me doing this.'

'Why does my opinion matter?' He sounded like a petulant child.

She clenched her jaw, trying not to lose her cool. 'Because,' she began, 'although we don't have children now, they want to know how you feel about the possibility of any future children being related to the donor child or children.'

He scowled. 'There won't be any children.'

'I know.' Harper nodded.

She and Samuel had met outside a courtroom in their mid-twenties—she'd been reporting on a case his firm were defending. Harper had dropped her notebook when she got accidentally caught up with the accused, his family and his lawyers trying to escape the courthouse and avoid the media frenzy. Samuel had been the only one of the group who'd bothered to stop. He'd plucked her notebook from the ground and handed it back to her.

Their eyes had met, a zing had passed between them and she remembered thinking how she'd never met anyone with such perfect teeth. He was so gorgeous that she'd been tongue-tied, barely able to utter a coherent thanks. But Samuel wasn't flummoxed at all. After checking she was okay, he said he had to run but did she have a card as he'd love to call her later. Somehow, despite her heart fluttering madly away in her chest in the manner of guileless romance heroines she'd always despised, she retrieved her business card from her purse and gave it to him.

For two days, she'd barely let go of her mobile long enough to go to the bathroom. She didn't even know his name, but try as she might she couldn't get the mystery man out of her head. And then just when she'd given up on ever seeing him again, he'd called. They met for a drink and the chemistry that had flickered between them at the courthouse near on exploded. Neither he nor she were beat-around-the-bush types, so within a few hours of that first drink, they were in bed together. In both their minds it was only ever going to be a one-night stand—a few weeks fling at the absolute most. Harper, far too focused on climbing the career ladder, never meant to fall into a relationship and she certainly never meant to fall in love.

But they couldn't keep their hands off each other. One night turned into a week, a week turned into a month and before long they were headed down a track neither of them had planned for.

'I'm going to be blatantly honest with you,' Samuel had told her late one night when they were lingering in his bed in a post-sex haze. 'I don't want to have children.'

He mistook her shocked silence for distress and went on to explain. 'I really like you, Harper, but I grew up having to share every damn thing from my clothes to school books to my bedroom, and now I value my freedom, my things and my space.'

By this time, they'd exchanged their stories of childhood woe—he knew things about her mother she'd never told anyone and she knew he'd grown up with Catholic parents who didn't believe in contraception even when they couldn't afford another baby. He hadn't specifically said it, but she'd have been a fool not to see that his drive to succeed and his desire to buy his own house, wear nice clothes, have quality things, came from a childhood of doing without. As someone who had also missed out on many of these things, she understood.

'I've fallen in love with you,' he added, 'but that hasn't changed my position on children. Besides, hasn't the world got enough babies? And who would want to bring one into today's climate anyway? Babies might be cute at first but I think far too many people have children because that's just what society expects of them and ...'

A tear slipped down her cheek and he stopped midsentence.

'Oh Harper, I'm sorry.' His face fell and he drew her into his arms. 'I shouldn't have let things go on this long. It wasn't fair to you but it's just I couldn't help myself.'

'You love me?' she asked, sniffing as she looked into his serious brown eyes.

He nodded, his expression grave as if he were admitting a terrible sin.

'And you don't want children?'

He shook his head. 'Not at all. I came from a big family but I have no desire to emulate that.'

In response, Harper all but threw herself at him again. She pulled him tight against her body and pressed her lips against his. She couldn't believe her luck. Here was an unbelievably good-looking man who turned her inside out just by looking at her, a man who was driven, intelligent and kind, but suddenly the most attractive thing about him was the fact that he didn't want to go forth and multiply.

'I love you too,' she admitted, tearing her lips from his once again. 'And I don't want children either.'

'What? Are you serious?' Samuel frowned. 'You're not just saying that to placate me, because you think that in time you'll be able to change my mind?'

'Give me a little credit. If there's one thing I've learnt about you in the past few months it's that you are a man of your word. But so am I. And I'm too much of a career woman to ever want children. Besides, I couldn't think of anything worse than going through nine months of pregnancy, never mind the eighteen or so years afterwards.'

He laughed and shook his head. 'So we're not breaking up?'

'No way. In fact, we're moving in together. I don't want to spend another night not in your arms.'

'Did you hear what I said?' Samuel asked, bringing her back to the present.

Harper blinked. 'Sorry, I got lost there for a minute. I was thinking about the day we met.'

His lips quirked at the edges. 'That was a good day.'

'It was,' she agreed.

'Anyway,' he said. 'What I was *trying* to say was that if this is something you really want to do, then I'm not going to try to stop you. Lord knows I may not understand, but if you think you need to do this, then I wish you the best.'

'Really?' The word came out on a whisper.

He nodded, a bemused expression on his face.

'Thank you,' she said. 'I promise, aside from one brief session of counselling and your consent, this won't affect your life at all.'

'Counselling?' he groaned. 'You're damn lucky I love you.'

Harper laughed and went around the table to give him a hug.

Chapter Six

APRIL 2011

Claire was sitting on the bed stroking her cats, stuffing her face with corn chips and watching a mind-numbing reality TV show when the door to her bedroom burst open and Polly appeared, the most gigantic grin on her face. A smile wasn't unusual on Polly, but there was something different about this one that made Claire sit up and take notice.

'Have you won the lottery?' Perhaps she'd ask for a loan so she could get away for a while.

'Better than that.' Polly bounced over to the bed and thrust her hand out.

'Oh my God!' Claire shrieked, almost blinded by the sparkly square diamond on her friend's ring finger and momentarily forgetting her own disillusion. 'Is that what I think it is?'

'Do you think it's an engagement ring?' Polly didn't give Claire a chance to reply. 'Because then you'd be right.' She squealed. 'Scotty and I are getting married.'

'Wow, that was fast.' Claire didn't mean to sound bitter but the mention of Jasper's cousin sent a cold jab to her heart. She hadn't spoken to Jasper since she'd fled from his house in the middle of the night, and although she cringed every time she thought about it, he'd refused to get out of her head. She thought about him constantly—always wondering if she'd been too hasty in her decision.

Polly, too consumed with her own happiness, didn't appear to notice. 'I know, but when you know, you know, right? Apparently everyone in Scotty's family gets married quick when they find The One. It's a tradition. Besides, we might have a teensy tiny reason to hurry things up.'

Before Claire could ask her what she meant, Polly's hand dropped to her stomach and her grin grew even wider. 'I'm going to be a mother!'

Claire's mouth fell open as bitter cold flowed from her heart to the rest of her body. She tried to recover quickly and not show anything but excitement for her closest friend.

'Oh my God!' She blinked back stupid tears, praying Polly would assume they were tears of joy. 'Congratulations.'

'Thank you.' Polly flopped onto the bed beside Claire, causing Gerry and Sunny to leap off in disgust. As they stalked out of the room, she said, 'I don't think I've ever been this happy in my entire life. A baby might not have been planned, but who doesn't want kids, right?'

It was obviously a rhetorical question but Claire's heart squeezed in reply. What you wanted and what you got weren't always compatible.

'And,' Polly continued, 'I can't imagine anyone I'd rather have a family with than Scotty. Honestly, he's just the best guy ever.'

As her friend prattled on about the virtues of her new fiancé, Claire prayed that he and Jasper weren't particularly close and didn't see each other that often. In the couple of months that they'd been dating, Polly had never once mentioned Scotty talking about his cousin.

'Do you want to hear how he proposed?' Polly asked, jolting Claire's thoughts.

'Sure.' She forced a smile and settled herself back on the pillows.

'Well, remember his cousin Jasper? The one who *almost* took you up in a hot air balloon?'

Claire nodded—her stomach turning to cement. She'd told Polly she'd chickened out, but she hadn't mentioned her midnight dash, or the fact that she'd avoided Jasper's calls afterwards until he'd eventually given up.

'He and this other guy that works for him came down from the Hunter Valley and met Scotty and me on the foreshore, then Jasper took us up in a balloon over Sydney Harbour. It was the most magical thing I've ever experienced and honestly it wasn't scary in the slightest. I'm such a dimwit but I was so overwhelmed by the whole thing that I didn't even suspect Scotty was going to propose up there. When he did, I burst into tears and then kissed him so hard I almost knocked him out of the balloon. Jasper popped champagne—non-alcoholic stuff because, well, don't want to hurt the baby—and we all toasted our happily ever after.'

Claire kept smiling, even though her heart ached—at the talk of Jasper, at the fact that Polly had experienced the hot air balloon ride that Claire had forfeited, but mostly because Polly had so easily achieved something that she never would. 'That's some story to tell the grandkids,' she managed.

'I know. Now, the important business. You'll be my maid of honour, won't you?'

'Well, I ...' Claire searched her mind for an excuse—right now the prospect of standing alongside a pregnant Polly didn't fill her with joy, but she swallowed her sour grapes. She wouldn't abandon her best friend on the most important day of her life. 'Of course I will. When's the wedding?'

'As soon as we can book a venue and find a dress. You can choose your own bridesmaid outfit—I don't care what colour you wear either. Ooh, I'm so excited. And did I tell you who the best man's gonna be?'

Claire's already heavy heart filled with dread.

She knew the answer even before Polly said it. 'Jasper! That won't be awkward, will it? You never did properly tell me what happened between you two.'

'*Nothing* happened,' Claire said, perhaps a tad too forcefully. Thankfully when Claire had returned from the Hunter Valley, Polly had been so consumed with Scotty that she hadn't pressed her for more information when she'd cited a fear of heights. 'Of course it'll be fine.'

So fine that the thought of it made her want to run out into the bathroom and throw up all the chips she'd just eaten.

'Great! Because Scotty and Jasper are out in the lounge room now ready to talk details. Come on.' The baby not yet hindering her movement, Polly leapt off the bed, grabbed Claire's hand and started tugging.

Claire didn't budge an inch. 'He's out there *now*?' Although she had whispered, she sounded hysterical even to herself.

'That's what I said.' Polly frowned. 'I thought you said seeing him wouldn't be a problem?'

She'd lied about that but she'd also thought she'd have time to prepare herself for such an occurrence. 'It's not, I'm just surprised at the speed all this is happening. Give me a couple of moments to throw on some company-worthy clothes—' she gestured to her stained *Cats* the musical t-shirt and her decade-old tracksuit pants, '—and I'll be with you.'

'Okay, but don't take too long,' Polly said, before floating out of the room.

Claire scrambled off the bed and shut the door. She turned around and stared at her window, contemplating climbing out of it—who cared that they were three storeys off the ground?—and running the hell away. Again. But that solution would only be a temporary one. She couldn't leave the cats for long, and when she returned Polly would still be pregnant and engaged to Jasper's cousin.

The thought of going out there and acting all polite and friendly to Jasper, acting as if he hadn't been pretty much the only thing she'd thought about in months, filled her with dread. Would he even speak to her? He had every right to be angry at her for leaving without so much as a note and then ignoring his attempts to make contact.

Telling herself that if she didn't make an appearance soon Polly would come looking for her, Claire tugged off her round-the-house clothes and replaced them with a pair of jeans and a jumper from her favourite market stall. She did the necessary fingers through the hair and then applied foundation, lip gloss and mascara. Although she didn't want to make it look like she'd gone to too much trouble, she couldn't confront Jasper again looking less than her best.

Finally, after inhaling a massive gulp of air, she summoned a carefree smile, pushed her shoulders back and opened the bedroom door to the sound of happy voices in their living room. Due to the tiny size of their apartment, she only had to take a few steps before she entered said room and her heart, predictably, leapt up into her throat. Jasper was sitting on their couch, leaning back against her favourite throw cushions as if being here was the most natural thing in the world. If possible he was even more gorgeous than the last time she'd seen him. Added to that, her damn traitorous cats—felines who usually didn't give the time of day to anyone but Claire—were rubbing themselves affectionately around his legs.

He glanced up and caught her looking. She hadn't known what to expect but he hit her with a melt-your-insides smile. 'Lovely to see you again, Claire. I can see why you fell in love with these guys.' Then, while she failed to remember how to speak, he scooped up Gerry and dumped him in his lap. Gerry never even sat in *her* lap!

'Oh look, the evil cats like him,' Polly said, laughing as she got comfortable on Scotty's lap.

'Evil?' Jasper said. 'They're literally pussycats.'

'They're not usually,' Claire said, finding her voice and her feet as she ventured further into the room and perched herself on the other end of the couch. Seating options were limited in their apartment and Polly and Scotty had claimed the armchair, leaving Claire no option but to sit next to Jasper, stand or take the floor. The latter two, she decided, would make it appear as if she were uncomfortable with this whole situation. *Hardi-hah!*

'Now that we're all here, I think we should have a toast,' Scotty exclaimed, raising a glass of what looked suspiciously like orange juice.

Until that moment, Claire hadn't noticed the bottle and the three other glasses on the table.

'Pretend it's champers,' Polly said, picking up one of the glasses and indicating that Jasper and Claire should do the same. 'Scotty didn't think it was fair that you guys drink when I couldn't, so he bought the most expensive orange juice he could find instead.'

'Very thoughtful of him,' Claire said, although right now she would really appreciate a nice alcoholic beverage. Preferably a very, very strong one.

Jasper picked up two glasses and then handed one to her—their fingers brushed in the exchange but she couldn't work out whether it was on purpose or accidental. Either way, her pulse skittered.

'Thank you,' she said, quickly looking away and raising the glass for the toast. Polly and Scotty looked at them expectantly. Was she supposed to make a speech? She wasn't sure she could say anything without falling apart.

Luckily, Jasper did the honours. 'Congratulations Scotty. I think it's definitely a good idea to put a ring on it before this lovely lass realises what a buffoon you are.'

Scotty showed Jasper his middle finger but laughed good-naturedly.

'Nah, seriously. I'm stoked for you guys. Scott's a good bloke Polly and I hope you'll both be very happy together.' He lifted his glass. 'To Scott and Pollyanna and their already growing family.'

'Thanks, mate!' Scotty clinked glasses with his cousin.

Polly sniffed. 'That was beautiful.'

'To Polly and Scott,' Claire added, hoping her smile looked more real than it felt.

The four of them clinked and sipped. Talk immediately turned to the upcoming nuptials. Claire tried to make the right noises in the right places—occasionally she registered words such as 'cake', 'invitations', 'honeymoon'—but mostly she was thinking about how close Jasper was and how much she wished things could be different. Why couldn't *she* be the one accidentally pregnant and flashing around an engagement ring?

'Do you mind if Claire and I step outside for a moment?' Jasper said.

She looked at him blankly, thinking that she must have imagined his words, but then he added, 'Secret bridesmaid and best man business,' and winked at her.

Claire's insides twisted as Scotty said, 'Sure mate. Polly and I will be able to keep ourselves occupied, won't we, my little minx?'

In reply, Polly wrapped her arms around her fiancé's neck. 'I'm sure we'll think of something.'

Jasper put Gerry on the couch beside him, then stood and looked down at Claire expectantly. 'I promise this won't take long.'

'Okay.' She nodded and pushed herself to her feet, swallowing as she anticipated a confrontation. She'd had almost two months to think of an excuse for why she'd fled, so why the hell hadn't she come up with one?

Probably because she hadn't allowed herself to even dream of the possibility of seeing him again.

They walked in silence out of the apartment and down the three flights of stairs. Jasper led her across the road to a park where people were walking their dogs and children were playing on the play equipment, their parents watching from not too far away. He sat down on a wooden bench and patted the space beside him. 'I won't bite, Claire, I'd just like a few answers.'

She gulped, nodded and lowered herself to the seat, trying not to look like a wooden soldier.

'It's good to see you again,' he began.

'It's good to see you again too,' she said, without even thinking about how that sounded. But no matter how torturous it was to have him so close again, it was also unbelievably wonderful. She'd never felt so conflicted in her life.

He quirked an eyebrow. 'Then why did you leave my house without even so much as a note? And why didn't you answer any of my calls?'

She cringed at his hurt tone. 'Would you believe me if I said I was afraid of heights?'

'Nope.' He shook his head. 'But I think you're afraid of something.'

When she didn't say anything, he added, 'Was it my mother? She can be a little overwhelming when you first meet her but she means well. Or is it that I live with my parents? Too weird? I promise you it's only while I'm saving to buy a house of my own. Property isn't cheap in the Hunter Valley.'

'Your mother's lovely.'

'So it's me.' He sighed. 'Did I come on too strong? I didn't mean to but I gotta be honest, I really liked you, Claire. Hell, against my better judgement, I *still* like you, so I have to know. Are you just not into me or is there something more going on? Because I can't get you out of my head and not knowing if I could have done something different is driving me crazy. And now that Polly and Scotty are getting married, we'll have to see each other again.'

'Oh God.' She brought her hands up to cover her face as tears spurted from her eyes. This was pure hell. 'It's *so* not you,' she managed between sobs. 'You are wonderful and fascinating and your family is lovely, but I'm broken. And it would be wrong of me to lead you on, to let you fall in love with me, when I can't ever give you what you deserve.'

'Claire!' Jasper grabbed her hands from her face and drew them up against his chest, forcing her to look at him. 'What are you talking about?'

'I'm infertile,' she all but spat. 'I can't have babies.'

'Oh, Claire.' Pity squeezed his facial features together as he drew her close and wrapped her in his arms. Her head told her to pull away—that her heart couldn't handle what being loved by him might feel like—but she couldn't bring herself to do so.

Claire cried like she hadn't cried in years, ever since that devastating conversation with her parents in her teens. For so long, she'd managed to trick herself into believing that the life of a cat-loving spinster would be enough, but meeting Jasper had made her realise otherwise. She wanted love. She wanted *him*. He was the first person outside her family she'd ever told.

'How do you know?' he asked when her tears finally started to subside.

'I found out when I was fourteen,' she said, swallowing hard in an effort to stop the flow of tears. 'Friends of our family had a baby and we went to visit them in hospital. She was the most beautiful, magical little thing and I fell utterly in love. Like some girls get obsessed with horses, I got obsessed with babies. I told my parents I couldn't wait to have a family of my own, and one day when I was listing off the names of my future children, Mum burst into tears. I demanded to know what was the matter and they decided that it was time to tell me.'

She took a deep breath—even over a decade later it was painful to recall.

'They told me that because my leukaemia was pre-puberty the chemotherapy had caused ovarian failure and the doctors couldn't do anything to save my fertility. I had to have hormone therapy to kickstart puberty but I hadn't even realised that's what I was taking. I thought the pills were just something to keep me healthy, like multivitamins. My parents didn't want to upset me unnecessarily, but ...' The tears she'd been trying to fight came rushing back, the memory of that awful night still as strong as if it were yesterday.

After beating cancer she'd thought herself invincible—she'd *thought* she could achieve anything—but this news had been a blow like nothing else before or since.

'I'm sorry you had to go through all that, Claire,' Jasper said, still rubbing his hand up and down her back. 'But you're absolutely wrong if you think what you've just told me makes me want you any less.'

She chanced a look up into his beautiful face and seeing that his eyes also glistened, she pushed away the tiny hope that had flared in her heart and pulled herself out of his embrace. 'You can't tell me you don't want children.'

He nodded. 'You're right. I can't tell you that, because I would love to be a father one day, but only with the right woman, and—'

'And I'm not *that* woman, because I *can't* give you babies. *Ever*. So what's the point in starting something that is only going to end in tears?'

Jasper sighed deeply and ran a hand through his hair. 'What I was going to say is that none of us know what the future holds. You know you can't have children, but I have no idea whether I can or not. For all we know I could be just as infertile as you are. I don't have a crystal ball. Anything could happen—aliens might invade and take over Earth, Donald Trump might become President of the United States.'

Claire felt a small smile tug at her lips. 'As if *that* would ever happen!'

He smiled and took her hand again. 'Okay, perhaps not, but what I do know is that I like you more than I've ever liked any woman before, and I want to get to know you better. I also know that this is the twenty-first century—if things go well between us and we decide we want to have a family, then there are many different ways to go about it. There's adoption, there's fostering, there's surrogacy, and probably a hundred more ways I don't even know about.'

Claire blinked, unable to believe his response. She'd expected him to run a mile. What kind of man was willing to consider these things when he'd only just met a woman?

'But I don't want to worry about any of that right now,' Jasper continued. 'I just want to get to know you, focus on this feeling inside my chest that I get whenever you're near. And if the fact that you can't have children the usual way is the only reason for rejecting me, then I hope you'll reconsider. I'd still really love to take you up in my hot air balloon, but if that's too full-on, then perhaps we could start with a coffee date? What do you say, lovely Claire?'

As magical as his words were, as much as she wanted to believe him, she couldn't quite let it go. 'Are you absolutely sure? There may be alternatives for having children, but they're not fail-safe. If we got together and really couldn't have children, would you regret being with me?'

'Life isn't fail-safe,' Jasper said, his expression solemn. 'There are never any guarantees, but I can tell you that I'd rather spend my life childless with someone I really loved and respected, than have ten kids in an unhappy marriage. Besides, how many couples get together and only later find out that they can't have babies? At least we know from the get-go. Please, give us a chance, Claire. I promise you I already feel more for you than I have about anyone I've ever dated and you'll break my heart if you say no.'

So, unable to believe her luck and against her better judgement, she answered him with a kiss, hoping against hope that he truly meant what he said, because she was already falling for him and his heart wasn't the only one on the line.

Chapter Seven

AUGUST 2016

On Saturday afternoon, Harper met her sister Willow outside the front of their mum's rundown rental in Waterloo. She hadn't seen either of them in a couple of months and while that was normal with her mother, it wasn't with her sister.

'Hi there, long time no see,' she joked as Willow kissed her on the cheek. She was dressed in her usual uniform of jeans, a casual shirt and Doc Marten boots, but it looked as if she'd put on a little weight since the last time Harper had seen her. For someone who'd struggled with an eating disorder since her teens, this wasn't a bad thing. Love obviously agreed with her. 'How's Miriam?' Her partner was the senior executive to the deputy police commissioner.

Willow let out a long, dreamy sigh. 'Wonderful. In fact, so wonderful that not even a summons from Mum can put me in a bad mood.'

'That's a big call,' Harper said, glancing ominously towards the front door. 'I wonder what she wants this time.'

'Money. It's always money. She's probably got herself into some kind of debt again or has another crazy idea for a business and needs some start-up funds. Welcome to *Shark Tank*—where you and I are the sharks.'

Harper laughed, knowing Willow was probably right. Laura Drummond wasn't the mothering type—at least she hadn't been for as long as Harper could remember—and most of the time her daughters were an afterthought. So many times as children they'd been left home alone, sometimes for days on end, while Laura spent time with her latest lover, hoping that this one would finally fill the void left in her heart by the death of her late husband. More often than not, she'd left them with hardly any food; either because she didn't have the funds or because she'd simply forgotten to buy it altogether. Needless to say, Laura Drummond had never held down a job longer than a few days in her life.

It was amazing that Harper and Willow had turned out so normal. But if their mother had done one thing for them it was teach them that they didn't want to be like her. They didn't want to spend their lives trying (and failing) to please man after man. They wanted to be self-sufficient and independent. As a result she and Willow had worked their butts off at school, studying hard and working secret jobs to save money they made sure Laura never knew about. All this had paid off and now they both had good careers, homes of their own and money for luxuries as well as the food and essentials they'd often gone without as children.

Thus, finally they were useful to their mother who had conveniently rewritten history to make herself out as a hero who had sacrificed everything to raise them. Now, she believed, it was their turn to pay her back.

Samuel often asked Harper and Willow why they didn't just cut the apron strings once and for all. Sometimes Harper wondered this herself, but when push came to shove she simply couldn't bring herself to do it. Laura wasn't a bad person, she just wasn't a great mother, and Harper honestly believed she didn't even realise this. Either way, there were plenty of worse mums in the world. Mothers who physically abused their children or worse. She shuddered as she remembered an interview she'd done a couple of years ago with a father who had lost both his sons when his ex-wife committed murder/suicide.

'Well,' she said, pushing that dark memory aside and linking her arm through Willow's. 'Let's face the music.'

Together they approached their mother's front door. Five seconds after Willow knocked, Laura answered.

'My girls,' she said, hugging them both at the same time. 'It's so good to see you. Come on inside. I've made scones for morning tea.'

'You baked?' Willow asked. The one time Laura had tried to make a cake (a packet mix) during their childhood she'd almost burnt the house down.

'I've been doing a lot of baking lately,' Laura said, closing the door behind them. 'There's lots of good instructional videos on YouTube.'

Harper gave Willow a look behind their mother's back. Since when had Laura known how to use a computer? Willow had given her a laptop for Christmas a few years ago and even tried giving her a few lessons in the hope that maybe she could pick up some typing work, but that had ended in tears on both their parts. As far as the girls thought, the laptop had been gathering dust ever since, alongside everything else in the house.

They emerged into the kitchen to see the laptop set up on one end of the table and the other end laden with a basket of fresh scones, jam, cream and clean plates. Even more surprising was that they could actually see the bench surfaces, and that the sink wasn't full of dirty dishes. Again Harper and Willow exchanged looks of surprise. Something weird was going on.

'Wow, these smell good,' Harper said, nodding towards the basket of scones.

Laura beamed. 'Wait till you taste them. Now you girls take a seat and help yourself while I put the kettle on. I have some very exciting news.'

'Can't wait.'

Harper detected the sarcasm in her sister's voice as they both pulled out chairs and sat, but she didn't think their mother did. She plucked a scone from the top of the basket.

'You're actually going to eat one,' whispered Willow, her eyes wide.

Harper shrugged. 'What's the worst that can happen?'

'You die of food poisoning.'

Harper chuckled as she cut the scone in half and proceeded to apply jam and cream. Willow wasn't exactly joking—Laura might never have intentionally poisoned her children, but there were a few times in their childhood when she'd accidentally come close. She never quite understood why you should keep cleaning, gardening and cooking supplies separate.

'So, how's the lovely Samuel?' Laura asked as she carried tea supplies over to the table. 'Still busy, busy, busy?'

'He's great. Hopefully he'll be making partner at the firm soon.' Harper took a surreptitious sniff of her scone before taking a bite. It wasn't actually that bad.

'Lovely, lovely.' Laura sat opposite the girls and poured tea into fine china cups from a teapot Harper had never seen in her life. She smiled across at Willow. 'And what about Mary? How's she these days?'

'*Miriam* is great, thanks for asking. Now, what's this news you have?' Willow had never possessed a lot of patience, but right now

Harper didn't mind her hurrying things up because she had a doctor's appointment to go to soon.

'Well.' Laura clasped her hands in front of her on the table as if she were about to launch into prayer.

Was that it? Had she found Jesus? Maybe this was where Laura sat them down and finally apologised for being such a shitty mother.

'I've met someone!' The grin Laura had been wearing from the moment they arrived somehow managed to grow even wider.

Here we go again.

'Is that it?' Willow didn't even try to hide her annoyance. 'You dragged us all the way over here on a Saturday to tell us about another dropkick guy you've met at some seedy bar? Don't you know we don't care anymore?'

'No!' Laura shook her head, her smile only slightly dimming. 'He's not a dropkick and I didn't meet him in some seedy bar. This time it's different. I feel it in my bones—and it's actually thanks to you I've found him, Willow.'

'How the hell do you figure that?'

Harper reached under the table and put her hand on Willow's knee. They were grown-ups now. No stupid boyfriend of their mother's could hurt either of them ever again.

'After you girls nagging at me that I needed to get a job, I decided to learn myself some computer skills. I signed up to a course at the local library and they got me online.'

'Wow, that's great,' Harper said, seriously impressed that her mum even knew where the library was.

Laura beamed at her. 'Thanks, honey. And that's how I met Mack.'

'At the library?' Willow sounded sceptical.

'No, *online*. There's a whole world of cyber dating out there. You don't even need to leave the house. I had to sort through a lot of losers to get to Mack, but we've fallen in love and we're going to get married.'

'Well, congratulations,' Willow said, not sounding congratulatory in the slightest. 'When do we get to meet the lucky man? Is this where he steps out of the pantry?'

'Actually, he's from Montana.'

'Montana as in America?' Harper exclaimed, pushing the plate with her unfinished scone on it away from her.

'Yes. He's a cowboy. Has a ranch and everything and he wants me to move over there! Isn't it exciting? Willow, you and what's-her-name could come visit me and get married. It's legal for lesbians to tie the knot in Montana you know.'

'Oh my Lord.' Willow clicked her tongue and shook her head, ignoring the reference to her own possible nuptials. 'So you haven't actually met him yet? He could be a serial killer.'

'He's definitely not. We've talked online *and* on the phone. Here's proof.' Laura grabbed a piece of paper from near her laptop and thrust it at Willow.

Harper looked over her sister's shoulder and saw that it was a phone bill.

'How the hell are you going to pay this?' Willow asked as Harper's gaze landed on an amount owing well into the thousands. 'Doesn't your boyfriend ever call *you*?'

Their mother had the good sense to look a little contrite. 'He does, but I don't want to send him broke. I was hoping you two could give me a loan.' Before they could reply, *hell no*, she added, 'And while you're at it, could you lend me the money for a plane ticket as well? *Pretty please*.'

Hearing *pretty please* from a child infuriated Harper, but hearing it coming from her mother made her homicidal. She dug her fingernails into her palms and silently counted to ten. In that time, she considered the possibility that perhaps sending their mother off to the other side of the world to be some stranger's responsibility was not such a bad idea. So what if she didn't have the best track record with relationships?

It appeared that Willow was on the same page, for before Harper had got to eight, she said, 'Okay.' Then she folded the phone bill until it was small enough to shove into her shirt pocket and added, 'But this is the last time, Mother. We'll pay the bill and buy you your flight to Montana, but it'll be a one-way ticket. We're not bailing you out again if this doesn't work out, understood?'

'*What?*' Harper exclaimed.

At the same time, Laura sprang from her seat, rushed around the table and threw her arms around Willow. 'I knew I raised you right. Thank you. Once I'm settled, maybe you can all come for Christmas.'

'And maybe the Pope will convert to Scientology,' Willow replied, extracting herself from their mother's embrace.

'Do you want to see a photo of Mack?' Laura asked, clapping her hands together in excitement. 'Or better still, maybe we could Skype him.'

'A photo will be fine,' Harper said. 'I've got some place to be shortly.'

'Okay then.' Laura grabbed the laptop from the other end of the table and set it in front of Harper and Willow. She knelt on the floor between them and brought up a folder of photos dedicated totally to him.

As their mother clicked it open, Harper looked at her sister and mouthed, 'Montana?'

Willow shrugged and then gave her two thumbs up.

'There he is! Isn't he gorgeous?'

Harper turned back to the screen not sure what she was expecting to see, but she had to concede that for a man in his late fifties he was quite good-looking. For a bald guy. He smiled back at them from the photo and he seemed genuinely warm and friendly. 'So what's he like?' she asked.

Laura opened a browser and logged into the dating website. 'Here's his profile. It tells you the basics, but as I said, he's a cowboy. Years ago he used to be a bull rider, but he's retired from that and these days his ranch keeps him pretty busy.'

Harper read how Mack was a lonely widower looking for another lost heart to help him find his way again. He wanted someone who wasn't afraid of hard work and who'd enjoy working on the ranch with him. Laura was pretty much the exact opposite of what he was looking for.

'I want to see your profile,' Willow said, taking over the laptop and finding their mother's details. 'Holy hell. How old is that photo? Did you say you've Skyped? Mack knows you no longer look like this right?'

Laura frowned and then patted her stomach. 'I've taken up jogging and I'm almost back to the weight I was before you two ruined my body, but Mack cares more about what's inside. We have so much in common. He brings out the best in me. He makes me want to be a better person.'

'Well, congratulations then,' Willow said, pushing to her feet. 'I hope you'll both be very happy. You sort yourself a passport and then we'll organise your ticket, but we better be off now. Harper has somewhere to be.'

'Okay, my darlings, I'll be in touch.'

Not really knowing what had just happened, Harper gave her mum a quick hug and then followed Willow outside. Laura shut the door behind them and as they started off down the cracked path towards the road, Harper said, 'I thought you weren't lending Laura any more money? And I do believe you just said that we'd *both* pay her bills and buy her an airline ticket.'

Willow waved her hand in dismissal. 'Didn't you hear what she said? She's moving to *America*. I'd remortgage my house for that. She won't be able to call us to get her out of sticky situations so easily from the other side of the planet. Now, where shall we go for a celebratory lunch?'

Harper smiled at her sister's enthusiasm. 'She's not on the plane yet. Maybe when she tells Mack he'll get cold feet and ask her not to come.'

Willow stopped dead in her tracks and horror crossed her face as she looked up to the sky. 'You wouldn't be that cruel! Would you, God?'

Harper laughed—last she heard Willow was an atheist.

'Hey, we should call Miriam and Samuel and see if they can come to lunch too.'

'Maybe another time,' Harper said. 'Samuel's at the office and I wasn't lying about having somewhere else to be. I've got a doctor's appointment.'

'Oh. Is something wrong? Not a pap test, is it?' Willow screwed up her nose. 'I had mine the other week. Ugh.'

'Actually, nothing's wrong and I'm not getting a pap test.' Harper had been waiting to see her sister face-to-face before sharing her news, but after Samuel and Lilia's initial reactions, she felt a little hesitant. 'I've been doing a lot of thinking lately and have come to a decision. Have you heard of egg donation?'

'You mean when a woman donates her eggs to another woman to have a baby? Of course I have. Oh my God!' Willow put out her hand and touched Harper's arm. 'Is there something wrong with your eggs? Are you going to see a fertility doctor? Do you need *my* eggs?'

'No.' She half-laughed, swallowing her slight irritation. 'You know I don't want children—I've never had that maternal urge—and anyway, your eggs would be considered too old for donation.'

'Oh.' Willow shrugged, her face relaxing again. 'I thought maybe you'd changed your mind. Plenty of women do when they hit thirty-five.'

Harper shook her head. Why did everyone assume that just because she was almost thirty-five she must want to have babies? Even her own sister didn't believe her when she said she didn't want to be a mum. Harper would be a billionaire if she had a dollar for every time someone asked her or Samuel when they were going to have kids. She always felt a little guilty answering this question—as if not wanting to have children made her weird—but Samuel had perfected his response. He always went on about it being an ethical response to climate change, sometimes even quoting statistics about how the planet was already overpopulated, and thus not having children was the morally right thing to do. If the interrogator persisted, he'd add something about the world being a nasty place these days and him not wanting to bring a child into it.

It was all bullshit—he just didn't want to sacrifice his comfortable life—but he was smart enough to know if he simply *said* he didn't want children, folks would try to convince him otherwise. As it was, people generally accepted his reasoning much quicker than they did hers. For all the western world was supposed to be a progressive place these days, many people still felt uncomfortable with the idea of a woman who didn't have a maternal bone in her body.

But Harper had known from about seven or eight that she didn't want to have children—she'd never liked playing with dolls and she hadn't gone through the craze that many of her friends had, wanting to start their own babysitter's club after reading the popular book series. She must have been the only girl in her class who never even read one of them. Like her sister, she was far more interested in getting a good job and being able to look after herself in the way her mother never had.

Why did she and Samuel even need a reason anyway? Why was it anyone else's business if they didn't want to procreate?

Feeling suddenly defensive, she blurted, 'I want to donate my eggs to someone else!'

Willow took a moment to digest the news. 'Oh wow—that's fantastic! What a great thing to do.'

Harper blinked. 'Seriously? You don't think it's totally insane?'

'No, I think it's a wonderful idea. You're giving away something that has the power to change someone else's life. There are so many people who are desperate to have children. If you can give them that, well, I think that would pretty much make you a hero.'

Harper didn't want to be a hero, she just wanted to feel she'd done something good with her life, but Willow's enthusiasm cemented her decision.

'Thank you,' she whispered, tearing up a little as she dragged her sister into a hug.

'Do you want me to come to the doctor with you?' Willow asked as they pulled apart. 'Then we can get a bite to eat.'

'That would be great.' It wasn't that Harper needed anyone to hold her hand, but they hadn't spent much time together since her sister had started dating Miriam and she missed her.

'Excellent. I'll drive and we can pick your car up afterwards,' Willow said, linking her arm through Harper's.

Half an hour later when she was sitting in the office of the GP she'd been seeing for almost a decade, Harper was glad of Willow's company.

'This is a big decision,' Dr Rimmer told her, tapping her long gel fingernails on her desk. 'Are you sure you've thought this through?'

Why did everyone keep saying that? Harper gritted her teeth. It wasn't like she was donating a kidney and people gave *them* away all the time. Did men get grilled like this when they wanted to donate sperm?

'She's not asking your permission,' Willow said, taking hold of Harper's hand and giving it a squeeze. 'She's simply asking you if there's anything she needs to do to prepare her body. Is it the same as if she were wanting to get pregnant? Should she be taking folate supplements or something?'

Ignoring Willow, Dr Rimmer spoke again. 'Donating your eggs isn't entirely risk free. There's a possibility, a small one I admit, that your own fertility might be sacrificed.'

'That wouldn't be a problem. I'm certain about doing this, Doctor,' Harper said, tossing her sister a grateful smile. 'I just wanted a general check-up before I proceed with looking for a recipient couple. I don't want to get anyone's hopes up if I'm not a good candidate.'

'Well.' Dr Rimmer let out a long, clearly disapproving sigh. '*If* you've done your research, you'll know that the IVF clinic will undertake thorough testing when you've found your couple, but I suppose I could send you for an AMH blood test.'

When both Willow and Harper looked at her blankly, she explained. 'This will give us an idea of whether you have good quality eggs left in your ovarian reserve. At thirty-four, you're nearing the age where your fertility is dropping off. But if that's positive and you're still sure of your decision, then yes, it will pay to start getting your body in optimal condition. I recommend a healthy balanced diet, regular exercise and, as Willow suggested, a good folate supplement, which will improve egg quality.'

Harper nodded, making mental notes of all of this—*buy folate tablets.*

'So, when can I have the blood test?' she asked. Despite her doctor's less than enthusiastic response, she couldn't wait to get started.

Chapter Eight

SEPTEMBER 2016

As Jasper raised his champagne flute and entertained the crowd in the local café with the story of why balloonists traditionally drank champagne after a successful flight, Claire surreptitiously slipped her iPhone out of her pocket.

'Legend has it that early French balloonists carried champagne to appease the angry farmers whose fields they landed in ...' he began. Claire had heard the spiel a million times since their first flight together five years ago, so she took the chance to check her email while the eager eyes of the tourists were glued on her animated husband.

She held her breath, her stomach tightening in hopeful anticipation as she waited for the mail app to open. In the last few days she'd become obsessed, checking her email ten times an hour like a woman who was trying to get pregnant might check her body temperature to see if she was ovulating. *Come on*, she silently pleaded, cursing her slow internet connection and willing Jasper to keep talking. Once he'd finished, they'd share a toast and then breakfast would be served, during which she'd have to be social, chatting with and answering questions from this morning's passengers. That wasn't a bad thing—she loved her job and liked nothing better than sharing her and Jasper's passion—but first she wanted to see if they'd had any replies to their ad.

Last week, after months of research and many late night conversations with Jasper about what they wanted in a donor, they'd finally taken the plunge and posted their request in an online forum that matched people like them with women wanting to donate their eggs. It wasn't the way you were supposed to get pregnant but hey, a lot of things in the world happened in non-traditional ways these days. They may as well make the most of the medical advances available to them. Without such things she'd likely have died as a child anyway. The fact she hadn't made her a big believer in medical intervention.

Clicking publish on their post had been the most exciting and terrifying thing she'd ever done. The only other time she'd ever felt such butterflies was during her very first hot air balloon flight. Back then she'd been nervous—not so much about possibly crashing or falling from the sky—but about taking this plunge with Jasper.

But that had been the best risk she'd ever taken.

If she hadn't already been in love with him before the balloon had left the ground, she was well and truly head over heels by the time it landed again. Up in the air, she'd felt on top of the world, as if anything was possible, and it was Jasper's enthusiasm for life that made her feel this way. During that one hour flight they talked about everything under the sun. She told him more about her childhood cancer, how spending so much time in hospital had got her behind in her schooling and also made friendships difficult. People felt sorry for her but they didn't want to get too close—as if cancer was something they might catch. So even before she'd found out about her infertility, she'd felt different and somehow less than everyone else.

Jasper explained how school hadn't been a walk in the park for him either. Kids had teased him about his family's weird passion. Claire had found this hard to believe. Up in the sky, looking over the endless rows of vines, she couldn't understand how anyone wouldn't find this thrilling. She decided during that very first flight that she wanted to learn everything there was to know about hot air ballooning. And she didn't simply want to *learn* it, she wanted to *experience* it. She wanted to fly a balloon herself! To personally feel the thrill she'd seen on Jasper's face when they were cruising at 2000 feet over the Hunter Valley.

After that, Claire spent every second weekend with Jasper and his family, learning the ropes of the business and working towards attaining her private ballooning licence. On the weekends she had to work at the florist, Jasper came down to Sydney and they played house, eating together, watching TV together and lazing in bed on Sunday mornings. When Polly officially moved in with Scotty, she and Claire gave up the flat, and Claire and the cats moved to the Hunter Valley. Although she was offered a job at the local florist, she took one in the hot air balloon office instead, which only ensconced her in Jasper's family more.

And it was true what Scotty had said about people in he and Jasper's family moving fast. Like Polly and Scotty, Claire and Jasper's was a whirlwind romance. They were married five months after her first balloon ride in a beautiful ceremony on the Lombards' smallholding, only *theirs* wasn't a shotgun wedding. Claire didn't let that bother her—finding Jasper had restored her faith in the goodness of life and she believed her dream of having a baby would one day come true as well. But for a while, she was simply happy to spend time with her love and pursue their other passions together.

They honeymooned in New Mexico and Jasper took part in the Albuquerque International Balloon Fiesta, something that had been on his bucket list since he'd first heard his parents talking about it many years ago. As they'd sailed alongside hundreds of other balloons in all different shapes, colours and sizes, with the desert beneath them and the Rocky Mountains as their backdrop, he'd told Claire how glad he was that they could experience this magic together.

The five years that followed had truly been a fairytale, filled with more fun and happiness than she'd ever imagined possible. As a wedding gift Wendy and Paul had given them the deposit on a house. Now Claire had a new career flying balloons in the family business, but in her free time she nurtured her other love—flowers. Her garden already rivalled her father-in-law's. Everything she planted grew and thrived, and people often marvelled at her green thumb.

And until recently, all these wonderful things had been enough.

Jasper had been enough.

But when Claire turned thirty, a switch flicked inside her and a longing she'd buried years ago sprouted and blossomed like one of her flowers. Everywhere she turned she suddenly started seeing pregnant bellies or women about her age gazing adoringly into prams as they strolled along the street. She'd been caught staring in the local café at a chubby baby sitting in a high chair—his gorgeous rolls of blubber had made her happy and despondent all at once. When Polly brought her tribe to visit, Claire practically inhaled her youngest; she wished she could smell that sweet baby aroma every single day. As if Big Brother truly was watching, ads for maternity clothes and baby massage classes started appearing in her Facebook feed. She took this as a sign from above and secretly started researching the options available to a woman like her.

When she had all the facts, she took them to her husband. Jasper had at first seemed surprised when she'd confessed her desire to look for an egg donor.

'I didn't know you were this desperate to have a baby.'

She opposed the word *desperate*. 'You know I've always wanted to have kids. I told you how much the day we decided to start dating.'

'Yeah, I know.' He twitched his nose in the way he did whenever he was confused. 'I guess we just haven't really talked about it since then. I thought we were happy as we are.'

Claire couldn't believe it when he admitted he'd just assumed they wouldn't be parents, but would embrace a different, equally as satisfying life together. He talked of plans to travel the world—tick all the exotic balloon festivals off their list, maybe even participate in a few challenges. And while part of her agreed that this life sounded amazing, it wouldn't fill the baby-shaped hole inside her.

'I need to try,' she'd told him. 'If it doesn't work, then I'll accept that. But if we don't try, I'll always wonder.'

And it wasn't just her own feelings that worried her. Jasper would make a wonderful dad—he loved it when his nieces and nephews or Polly and Scotty's kids came to visit and would play silly games with them for hours without complaint. They adored him too. Who wouldn't? Not only was Jasper very pleasing to look at, he was also one of the really good guys. It would be a sin to let his good genes go to waste simply because she couldn't breed, and she couldn't bear the thought that down the track he might look at her and feel resentment because he'd never been a dad.

She remembered the night they met. His excitement about becoming an uncle was still as fresh in her mind as if it were yesterday. How much more elated would he be if it were his baby?

'How about adoption then?' he'd asked.

And she *had* given that option a lot of thought.

'One, it's not as easy as the celebrities make out. In Australia there are far more couples looking to adopt than babies available. It was different years ago when being a young single mother was frowned upon, but these days most people either get rid of unwanted pregnancies or they go through with them. The shame isn't there, so there aren't as many babies to adopt. And international adoptions are hard because many countries are putting in place laws about babies being raised in foreign places.'

'You have done your research, haven't you?'

She nodded, pleased by his impressed tone.

'Then I guess you've ruled out fostering as well?'

Claire loved that Jasper would consider such a thing, but she was selfish. She wanted to feel a baby grow inside her and then nuzzle against her breasts. She craved the full-on mum experience and because Jasper never judged, she admitted this.

'I'm just not as good a person as you,' she added once she'd explained.

He'd pulled her into his arms and told her what utter bollocks that was. 'You are the best person I know, and if you're sure you're okay with going through IVF and all the gruelling stuff that involves, then let's do it!'

A chair scraped alongside her and Claire realised that Jasper had finished his post-flight speech and the passengers were getting up to help themselves to the hot buffet breakfast. As usual there was a buzz in the room—everyone still on a high from their experience up in the sky. She smiled at the lady who'd been sitting beside her and then slipped her phone back into her jacket pocket with a long, internal sigh.

She needed coffee. From the moment they'd decided to go ahead with the egg donation, Claire had been preparing her body—taking folic acid tablets, eating better and exercising more often. She'd even given up caffeine, which Jasper had said was a testament to how much she wanted this. But with no egg donor possibilities yet in sight, she decided one cup wouldn't hurt, and it might give her the lift necessary to mingle with the enthusiastic crowd.

As she stood in line at the tea and coffee station, Jasper came up behind her. He slipped his arms around her waist and then leant in to whisper in her ear. 'Well? Any responses?'

She shook her head, blinking back tears and feeling a little silly about being caught checking. So much for being surreptitious, but then again, she'd never been able to get anything past him. Jasper knew her better than anyone.

'Give it time, gorgeous.' He pressed a quick kiss against the top of her head. 'It's only been a few days.'

And while logically she knew he was right, she couldn't help wondering if they could do something more to enhance their chances. She'd posted their ad on two Facebook forums and an online site specifically for egg donation, but maybe they needed to try a newspaper advertisement as well. There were so many other people looking for egg donors and their pleas all seemed equally as heartfelt and deserving. Women who were carriers of genetic diseases, others who had already been on IVF for years and experienced miscarriage after miscarriage. But no matter how much she felt for these women, it didn't make her own yearning to have a child any less.

'Maybe we need to reassess our advert,' she said, keeping her voice low.

Jasper shook his head. 'Our advert is fine. We've been open and honest about who we are and what we're looking for. The right donor will come along if we're patient.'

Claire couldn't hide what she thought of that. She shrugged off his arm, not in the mood to be placated.

'You know,' he whispered, 'if you really don't want to wait, Polly's offer is still open. She and Scotty have made that clear.'

'No!' she said, a tad louder and firmer than she'd meant to. When Polly had been pregnant with Loretta (their first), she'd been so gung-ho in her efforts for Claire to join the motherhood brigade that Claire had finally confessed her inability to have children—and the feelings of guilt and inadequacy that came with it. Of course her friend had been suitably devastated for her; and recently when Claire had told her about the egg donation idea, Polly had immediately offered her services.

But as much as she adored Polly, Scotty and their brood—which they'd added to at a rate of one a year since the first had arrived—she couldn't deny the feelings of jealousy she harboured towards her friend for being so damn fertile. Besides, it just felt a little incestuous. Jasper and Polly might only be related (loosely) through marriage but then their kids would be cousins *and* half-siblings. Claire couldn't get her head around that and although she'd only admit it to herself, she didn't like the idea of Jasper making babies with her best friend.

Jasper sighed, clearly losing his patience. 'Look, I love you, but now isn't the time to discuss this. We need to focus on our clients.'

She nodded, knowing he was right, but at the moment it was hard to concentrate on anything but her desire to get pregnant. Maybe Jasper was right. Maybe she was desperate, but she was also determined, and just like she'd fought childhood cancer and won, she would fight her infertility and win.

Chapter Nine

EGG DONOR WANTED: Loving couple (Ellen, 43 and Owen, 45) desperate to complete our family. We conceived our first daughter (Gemma) on Clomid when I was 40 and have been trying to give her a sibling ever since. After five failed IVF attempts and two miscarriages, our doctor has suggested donor eggs ...

IN NEED OF A GIFT OF LIFE: We are a heterosexual couple who have been TTC for many years with no success ...

PLEASE HELP: I am the carrier of a genetic condition called Fragile X, which means that if I have a baby with my own eggs it will be born handicapped. Due to my condition, I also have a low egg reserve. My boyfriend and I have been together for five years, we are financially established ...

LOOKING FOR AN EGG DONOR: I'm Joel and my partner is Jonathon. We married in Canada last year and are now desperate to take the next step to consolidate our love. One of our friends has generously offered to be our surrogate, but we're looking for an egg donor to help make our dreams come true ...

Oh sheesh. Harper stared at her computer screen, utterly bewildered. She'd thought that the moment she'd made her decision and told all the people that mattered—Samuel, Lilia, her sister and her two closest friends—she'd just go online to one of the many forums she'd discovered when researching egg donation and pick a recipient couple, but it had turned out to be far more complicated than that.

She was usually a very decisive person—someone you could rely on not to dilly-dally but to get a job done—but she hadn't expected to feel such emotion when reading these people's stories. There were literally *hundreds* of people online crying out for the assistance of someone like her. And they all seemed equally deserving. How on earth could she pick? Even when she narrowed her search to potential recipients in NSW it didn't help at all.

Some of the ads were short and concise. Generally she'd approve of such succinctness, but in this situation she wondered if it meant they weren't as invested as those who'd obviously gone to a lot of time and effort to craft theirs. The majority of ads were from middle-aged couples who'd either met each other later in life or had left the decision to have a family too late. Were they more deserving than the younger ones because their time was running out? Were older parents with more life experience a better choice than younger parents with energy and enthusiasm?

Argh—this was doing her head in. The least she could do was to make sure her eggs went to people who would do their best by them, but how on earth could she know that?

Harper pushed back her seat from where she was sitting at the dining room table and went into the kitchen to check out the contents of the fridge. Nothing appealed—it was all healthy stuff. Since deciding to donate, she'd joined Samuel on his permanent health kick. She'd even disposed of the last secret box of Coco Pops, but there were a couple of bottles of wine lingering in the fridge door. Samuel's obsession with health and fitness seemed to overlook a little alcohol, or maybe he reasoned that as wine was made from grapes, it was healthy.

She hadn't yet chosen a recipient, so surely one glass wouldn't hurt.

As she went to unscrew the lid, a thought struck her. Although this wasn't a job interview as such, when employers were looking for the best candidate for a position, they usually had a number of people on the panel. Perhaps she too should enlist some help.

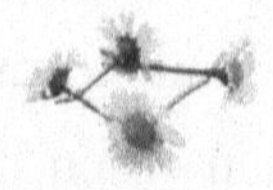

A few hours later, Harper sat down at the dining room table again, but this time she wasn't alone. Beside her was Samuel, who'd begrudgingly agreed to being involved—she wanted him because he saw everything from a practical, logical angle. And he was male, therefore brought a different viewpoint to the table. Lilia sat on her other side—she'd chosen her for her skills at getting people talking and because Harper respected and trusted her implicitly. Opposite the three of them, Willow and Miriam were snuggled close and at either end of the table were Juliet and Renee, who'd miraculously managed to escape without their babies. Like a jury, she'd called upon all her friends to help her with the decision. Individually they might have personal biases, but together they could have a logical, well-thought-out discussion. At least that's what she hoped.

Many women might have called upon their parents at a time like this, but her mother hadn't been there for any other important occasions or decisions in her life, so Harper wasn't about to invite her opinion on this one—she'd not told her anything about her plans. Besides, Laura was busy packing up her house for her upcoming move to Montana.

'Thank you all for coming at such short notice,' she said, once she'd made sure everyone had a full glass of wine.

'Thanks for inviting us,' Juliet said, her wire-rimmed glasses reflecting as she raised her glass. 'Do you know how long it's been since I had a night out?'

'Or been able to eat in peace,' Renee added, her dark hair falling over her face as she leant forward and snaffled a cracker with cheese from the platter on the table.

She smiled from one friend to the other—Juliet and Renee certainly didn't make the whole motherhood thing sound appealing, yet she'd invited them because they understood what it was like to *want* a baby. She hoped they might be able to read between the lines of the ads and pick out those women and couples who wanted this the most, because when she handed over her eggs she wanted to be damn certain she was giving them to people who'd love them with everything they had.

Willow, Miriam and Lilia smiled in encouragement; Samuel simply lifted his glass and took a sip.

'So, as you know, I'm looking for a woman, or a couple, to give my eggs. There are a number of avenues I can take to look for a recipient—newspaper ads, online forums, websites, Facebook groups, or I could even choose someone we already know. Don't suppose any of you have a friend in need?'

They all shook their heads.

Harper nodded. That idea had just come into her head anyway, but was discarded as quickly as it had arrived. 'Right, then I've decided to start with one Australian donor website because it's far too overwhelming looking across the board.'

'If people are really serious about this,' Miriam said, 'then they've probably got ads across multiple platforms, so I think that's a good idea.'

Willow beamed at her girlfriend and Harper smiled inwardly at how cute they were together. She hadn't seen her sister this smitten in years, perhaps ever, and she liked Miriam's logic.

'Thank you,' Harper said. 'To make this easier, I've narrowed it down to my top ten couples this afternoon.' Even that had been difficult. 'And I've printed off the ads for you to read through.'

She picked up a pile of papers from next to her laptop and passed them round the table like a teacher handing out tests. She'd also made sure everyone had a pen so they could make notes.

'Do you want to read through them separately or shall we discuss each one as they come up?' she asked.

'Let's read through separately and then discuss,' Samuel said, peering down at the paper with the most interest he'd shown since she announced her decision. He'd always liked studying and this probably felt a little like preparing for a test.

Everyone agreed and the room fell silent. All that could be heard was the rustling of papers as her husband, sister and friends starting flicking through the ads. Harper glanced down at the papers in front of her, but she'd already practically memorised them so instead she looked from face to face, trying to read their expressions. She appreciated that they all seemed to be taking this task seriously, but she wished they'd hurry up. Butterflies were churning through her stomach, making the cheese she'd scoffed while preparing turn in her gut.

'I'm just going to the bathroom,' Harper said after what felt like an hour but was probably more like five minutes. She pushed back her seat and fled from the room, needing to busy herself while the others did their reading. It would be stupid to rush them as she wanted their considered opinions. After walking upstairs and straightening the expensive prints that Samuel had bought from some gallery in The Rocks, she went back down again.

As she descended the stairs, she could hear that an animated discussion had begun.

'What do you all think?' she blurted as she hurried back into the dining room. 'Shall we take a vote? Are there any stand-outs?'

'Before we talk, I'd like to know whether you've thought about the ethics of doing this?' Renee asked, frowning up at her. 'How will the child feel years down the track when they find out how they were conceived? And what will happen to any leftover embryos afterwards? Will they be destroyed or will they offer them to another couple?'

Irritation flared within Harper. She knew that if anyone, Renee, with her religious background, would be the one to find objection to what she was proposing to do, but why hadn't she mentioned it on the phone?

'Of course I've thought about the ethics. As I've already told you, this isn't a decision I've made lightly, and as for the child that might be born, they'll know the truth as early as they are able to understand it so it *won't* come as a shock. All the research I've read shows that kids who know where they come from—wherever that is—are less likely to suffer psychologically. But when I've found a couple to go ahead with, we'll be required to have counselling and *all* these issues will be discussed.'

Renee twirled her wine glass between her fingers. 'Sorry. I didn't mean to sound negative. I'm just curious about how it's all going to work.'

'It's okay. I appreciate that you've taken the time to help me choose.' Harper pulled out her chair and sat. 'Speaking of which, are there any favourites?'

They shook their heads and Lilia spoke. 'Sorry Harps, we're completely divided.'

'I reckon this woman,' Samuel said, tapping his pen on the page in front of him. 'She's fifty years old, has paid off her mortgage and is desperate for a baby before she's too old and the IVF age limit kicks in.'

Juliet frowned. 'I think fifty is already too old.'

'I agree,' Renee said, reaching for another cracker with cheese. 'Being a mum is exhausting. You can't comprehend the energy it requires until you're living it. And it also means a lot of self-sacrifice. This woman has already been on the planet for half a century—she'd be too stuck in her ways for a child.'

'That's a bit unfair,' Lilia piped up. 'You don't know her. She could be the fittest fifty year old around. She might have more energy than you and Juliet put together.'

'And you haven't got a child, so what would you know?' Juliet retorted, narrowing her eyes at Lilia. 'What happens if she dies? Fifty might not be old but it's not young either. Who would look after the kid then?'

'I'm sure she's thought about what would happen in such a scenario,' Lilia snapped.

Harper's three closest friends had never gotten along very well—they endured each other when necessary but somehow her old school friends Juliet and Renee believed Lilia was the one discouraging her from having a baby. She didn't know how on earth they had got this impression, because she'd always made her position on motherhood perfectly clear.

'Let's not get carried away—we're not here to insult each other, but to help Harper make a good decision,' Miriam said, obviously sensing the discord in the room. Harper hadn't spent much time with Willow's girlfriend but she liked her immensely—she was exactly the kind of no-nonsense person she needed.

She threw her a grateful look as Miriam added, 'Let's look at this logically. Perhaps you should choose the recipient couple who have been waiting the longest.'

Harper picked up her papers but before she'd worked out who this was, Lilia countered with, 'But what if there's a reason they're still waiting? Like, what if they've already been rejected by a number of donors because they're weird or something?'

Samuel sighed and ran a hand through his hair. 'Does it matter if they're weird? This isn't a dating site—it's not as if we have to *like* these people.'

As Harper reached out to refill his wine glass—she sensed him losing patience—Willow said, 'We don't have to like them, but we're giving them an egg, and any baby created from that egg will be biologically related to Harper and me, so I think it's our duty to make sure it goes to good people. Like this couple.' She held up a page with the smiling faces of two gorgeous men at the top.

'Are they gay?' Renee asked, then shook her head. 'Such a waste.'

Juliet giggled.

'It doesn't say anything about women in their life,' Lilia said, frowning as she scrutinised the page in front of her. 'And while I'm all for the right of gay couples to have children, I do believe any kids—boys or girls—need male and female influences in their lives. So while these guys seem great, I'd want to know what the child will have available in terms of aunties and grandmas around them.'

'Fair point,' Juliet said, offering Lilia a rare smile.

'Thank you,' Lilia replied.

'I'm sure that information would be easy to find,' Willow said, sounding a little defensive.

Harper began to wonder if inviting them all here together had been a terrible idea.

'Perhaps we should make a list of what you want in a recipient and then work out who of these people fit?' Miriam suggested.

'Well, I've kind of already done that,' Harper said. 'I wanted people with tertiary educations, no religious affiliations and who were financially able to provide for a baby.'

'What about race?' Willow asked. 'Does that matter to you?'

Harper pondered that a moment. 'No. I don't think so. Plenty of adoptions are interracial.'

Samuel glanced at his watch. 'All right then, how about we all give you our definite noes, which will narrow down the possible yeses.'

'Good idea,' Miriam agreed with a nod.

'Okay,' Harper said. 'That's a good idea. Who wants to start?'

'The fifty year old woman is out for me,' Juliet began.

'Me too,' added Renee. 'And I agree with Lilia so I think for now we rule out the gay couple as well.'

'I didn't say we rule out the gay couple,' Lilia said. 'Just that you should make some more enquiries before agreeing to anything, which I'm assuming you'll do whoever you contact first. They're a yes for me.'

'The single women are noes in my opinion,' Willow said. 'You know how much Laura struggled with being a single mother. And remember how we hated Father's Day?'

Harper grimaced. She'd loved school—generally it was a happier place to be than at home—except at that time of the year when all the other kids were making cards and presents and their dads came in for special assemblies. When she was little Harper had sat in the corner of the classroom and cried; as she got older, she'd often feigned illnesses to avoid such events.

'I wouldn't wish that on anyone,' Willow concluded as they shared a look.

'I agree to an extent,' Miriam said. 'Two parents might be better than one in theory, but there's no such thing as a normal family these days, so I'm thinking schools will be more sensitive to these kinds of things.'

The discussion went on around the table for another twenty minutes. No one seemed to agree on anything and Harper's head started to throb. Maybe asking for help wasn't such a good idea after all. Perhaps this was a decision she needed to make on her own, or maybe it was a stupid idea altogether. If she didn't think *she'd* make a suitable mum, how the heck was she supposed to know if someone else would?

She pushed back her chair and picked up the near-empty platter from the table. 'Look everyone, thank you for your help. I appreciate all your thoughts. You've given me lots to think about but I realise that ultimately I'm the one who needs to make this decision.'

Although she didn't exactly tell them she wanted them to go, they all knew her well enough to hear it in her voice. She wanted to be alone with her thoughts.

Samuel was the first to stand, looking like a little kid who'd just been let out of detention early. 'Night all,' he said, then he turned to Harper, kissed her on the cheek and added, 'leave the mess, I'll help clear it up in the morning.'

Juliet and Renee stood next—both of them yawned as if suddenly realising how tired they were. 'Thanks for including us, Harps,' Renee said. 'We three need to get together more often.'

'Yes,' Juliet agreed. 'Call us.' They collected their bags and then headed down the hallway.

Lilia started collecting the empty wine glasses from the table.

'Leave them,' Harper said.

'You sure?' asked Lilia and Willow in unison. They both looked at her with concerned expressions.

'I'm sure,' Harper promised. 'I'll see you all out.'

As she walked them to the door, Miriam said, 'I suggest an Excel spreadsheet. Put all the possible recipients down one side and list your requirements along the top. And maybe make them more specific—then you'll be able to tick off who has what and you'll get a visual idea of the best choice. If you email me your requirements, I can do up a spreadsheet for you.' Her eyes gleamed at this suggestion.

'Thanks, that would be great,' she said, feeling it would be easier to agree than turn her down. And perhaps it would help, but right now all she wanted to do was crawl into a hole. She'd been *so* excited about doing this, but now she wasn't sure. Maybe Samuel was right, maybe she should take up CrossFit. Pity she despised organised exercise.

One by one, Lilia, Willow and Miriam hugged her goodbye, with Willow promising to call to check in tomorrow and Lilia saying, 'See you Monday.'

When Harper closed the front door behind them, she let out a long, deep sigh. How had what she'd thought would be an easy task become such an emotional headache?

Feeling disillusioned, she headed back into the dining room to clear up. Although Samuel would keep his promise about helping in the morning, she didn't like going to bed with a mess downstairs.

As she picked up her empty wine glass, Harper glanced down at her laptop still open on the table and her eyes were drawn to a brand new ad at the very top of the page, which must have popped up while they'd been talking. It was the accompanying photo that initially caught her attention—a smiley young couple, him with golden scruffy hair and her with beautiful long honey locks, standing in the basket of a bright multi-coloured hot air balloon.

Dragging her chair out and sitting down again, she clicked on the link to read the rest of their advertisement.

> *ARE YOU OUR EGG DONOR ANGEL? Hi there, I'm Claire and my gorgeous husband of five years is Jasper. We live in the Hunter Valley with our two ginger cats and a garden just waiting for a child to play in it. I was a florist before I met Jasper, but now I work alongside him in his family business helping people tick hot air balloon ride off their bucket lists.*
>
> *We consider ourselves extremely blessed to have found love, to be living in such a magical part of the country and to be doing a job we love. Hot air ballooning is so fun that it almost feels wrong to call it work. I believe each day is a gift as when I was seven years old I was diagnosed with leukaemia. Although I was one of the lucky ones who conquered this disease, the price I paid was my fertility.*
>
> *There are so many wonderful people in need of an egg donor and we can't tell you that we are more deserving than any of them, but if you're reading this, we can give you this promise: We want this child with all our hearts and we will love it with everything we've got.*

Although they hadn't specifically said they were financially secure like many of the other potential recipients and they hadn't even mentioned religion or education, something about Claire's plea tugged at Harper's heartstrings. And they were hot air balloonists! Had she ever heard anything so delightful? *And* they had cats. Although she'd never had a pet herself, she liked the idea of children growing up with animals. Hadn't she read somewhere that pets were good for them? Or maybe that child psychology expert she'd interviewed had mentioned it. Either way, the cats felt like a good sign—if they could look after animals, then they were obviously nurturing and responsible people. Then there was the fact they lived in the Hunter Valley. She liked the idea of the baby enjoying an outdoor lifestyle and smiled at the empty wine bottles on the table. They just happened to be from her favourite winery in that region.

If that wasn't a sign, she didn't know what was.

Chapter Ten

Dear Claire and Jasper,

My name is Harper Drummond and I'm reaching out to you after reading your advertisement for an egg donor.

A little bit of background about me: I'm 34 years old, married (with no children) and I work in the media. I grew up in Sydney (where I now live) but have worked in various parts of the world on location as a journalist. I love travelling, watching Friends *on TV, reading crime novels and biographies, hanging out with my sister and swimming, which I do three mornings a week.*

I've attached a recent photo, but here are my physical details as well: dark brown, straight hair; pale green eyes; 170cm; 76kg; fair skin (parents both Caucasian, fourth generation Aussies with English heritage). As far as I know there are no genetic illnesses in my family and I have had no health issues in my life thus far.

For personal and professional reasons, my husband, Samuel, and I have decided not to have children of our own. However, I recently interviewed an egg donor and her recipient couple for my work and their story really touched my heart. I thought, if I don't want to use my eggs, why not give them to someone who does? I have been to see my GP and have had an AMH test, which showed that I am a good candidate to donate eggs. I feel like this is something I would love to do and my husband is supportive of my decision.

If you feel I may be your donor, I look forward to hearing from you and would be happy to answer any further questions you may have, and/or arrange a face-to-face meeting to chat.

Kind regards,

Harper

'Oh my God!' Claire hissed the words under her breath as she leant towards her computer screen and re-read the email that had landed in her inbox only seconds ago. She wanted to be sure she hadn't imagined it before she dragged Jasper in here to take a look.

They'd finally had their first reply and this woman sounded absolutely perfect. As she jolted to her feet, her office swivel chair skidded across the floor. She sprinted into the shed where Jasper and his dad were busy doing their post-flight check and maintenance.

'Jasper,' she shrieked, loud enough to be heard over the Cold Chisel song blaring from the stereo. 'Quick. Come. I need to show you something.'

His lips twisted at the edges as he looked up from the floor where he'd been replacing a skid on the bottom of a basket. The basket lay on its side and Jasper had a sheen of sweat across his brow. 'What's going on?'

'Is it arvo tea time, love?' Paul asked, wiping his hands on his old work shorts.

Claire shook her head at her father-in-law and grabbed her husband by his hands, hauling him up off the ground with a strength she didn't know she had. 'We've had a reply to our ad.'

'What? Seriously? Just now?'

'Yes, just now,' she said as they hurried back towards the office.

'Sit,' she ordered, rescuing the chair from the other side of the room and rolling it back in front of the computer. 'Email's on the screen.'

Jasper did as he was told, his hand caressing the mouse as he scrolled down Harper's letter.

'Doesn't she sound wonderful?' Claire couldn't stop bouncing up and down. With the adrenalin racing through her body right now she felt like she could touch the shed's high ceiling.

'Give me a chance to finish reading,' he said, not sounding at all as excited as she was.

'Sorry.' She stopped moving, clasped her hands together and read over his shoulder, although by now she could almost recite the stranger's words by heart.

Finally Jasper looked up from the screen, his brow creasing as he spoke. 'Harper Drummond? That name sounds vaguely familiar.'

Quite frankly, Claire didn't care if she was Prince Harry's latest squeeze—she just wanted to send a reply. Right this second. *Instantly.* But she knew Jasper liked to think important things through.

'Shall we Google her?' she suggested.

'Good idea.' He opened another window and typed her name in the search engine. Moments later numerous entries flooded the screen. 'She even has a Wikipedia entry.'

Claire reached over and took control of the mouse, clicking on the first link. There was a headshot of her—more professional looking than the one she'd sent them—and a lot more detail than she'd provided in her letter. Her husband was a defence lawyer, her sister an environmental activist and she herself a successful journalist. She'd won numerous awards in her early career and now she had her own radio show.

'*Afternoons with Harper*,' Jasper exclaimed, spinning round on the chair to look properly at Claire. 'That's why I've heard of her. Dad and I listen to that show in the shed sometimes. He was only joking last week that we should try and get on there to talk about ballooning.'

Claire tried not to show her irritation, but at this moment she didn't give two hoots about ballooning or the fact that Harper was some kind of radio celebrity. All she cared about was that this woman had eggs to spare and had all but offered them to her and Jasper. 'So you like her? Shall we reply? Let me sit down. I can type faster than you can.'

'Hang on a moment.' Jasper held up his hand. 'This isn't something we should rush into. She sounds pretty smart.'

'And that's a bad thing?'

'No. It's just that she, her sister, her husband, they're all obviously tertiary educated and we didn't study any further than high school. What if we have a kid that's too bright for us?'

Claire fell into his lap and wrapped her arms around his neck, then looked into the pale blue eyes she'd fallen in love with almost on sight. 'Don't underestimate us. You are one of the most intelligent people I know—no one understands weather patterns better than you—and you can fix things. Lots of things. You read biographies like she does. Just because you don't have a degree, doesn't mean you couldn't get one; you just chose to follow a career path that didn't need one. And if you think I'm a dummy, well ... I resent that.'

He rolled his eyes and chuckled. 'I don't think you're a dummy.' Then he turned back to the screen. 'But the kid would probably have dark hair.'

'And what's wrong with that?' she asked, half-laughing at the ridiculousness of his comment. 'Are you hair-ist or something?'

'No, but we both have lighter hair. It'll be obvious it's not our child.'

'I might not remember much from human bio at school,' she admitted, 'but I recall something about recessive genes. I'm pretty sure you and I could quite possibly breed a dark haired baby too—that's if I could actually breed, which I can't. So this is it. Harper Drummond is our chance to have a family. And I for one don't think we should let hair colour stop us from following our dream.'

Jasper let out a deep sigh as if he wasn't convinced.

'Why are you being so negative?' she asked, tearing her hands from his neck.

'I'm not. It's just—' He looked really, really sad. 'I'm struggling to get my head around having a baby that isn't half you.'

'Oh Jasper.' This time as she leant into him again, she palmed her hand against his stubble-covered cheek. 'Our baby will grow inside of me, we'll feel it kick in my tummy and I'll be the one that screams at you while I'm pushing it out of a ridiculously tiny hole.'

His lips twisted ever so slightly upwards as she continued.

'I love that you want to make a baby with *me* and in an ideal world that's exactly what we'd do, but we *can* make a family together. And family is more than just blood and genetics. Family is what's in here.' She grabbed his hand and brought it up to her chest.

'I know. You're right,' he conceded. 'But what if we do make a family and then down the track the baby wants to follow its biological roots?'

Claire looked deep into his eyes and smiled. 'Didn't you once tell me there were a lot of what ifs in the world? We'll love and nurture our baby, but we won't own it any more than any parent owns a child. And if we're completely open with them from the beginning—if we let them know who their egg donor is and keep in occasional contact—then their beginning won't be a mystery, and they'll never need to go searching for the truth.'

'I guess …' he said, still sounding a tad uncertain.

'If we're honest and open and love our baby unconditionally, they'll feel safe and in the right place with us. That's all any parent can offer.'

His lips cracked into a smile. 'You are an amazing woman, you know that?'

Before she could reply, he grabbed her head in his hands, drew her towards him and planted a kiss on her lips. She smiled even before his mouth left hers.

'So we're gonna do this?' she asked.

'Yep.' He nodded, smiling almost as widely as she was. 'Wow. Parenthood here we come.'

And together they clicked reply.

Chapter Eleven

After a week of exchanging emails with Claire and Jasper Lombard, Harper felt more than ready to meet them. At least she had done when she'd woken up that morning. But now, as she marched towards the café on Oxford Street, her heels click-clacking along the pavement, her stomach tightened in nervous anticipation.

What if this was weird and awkward? She went out for Sunday brunch on a fairly regular basis—sometimes with Samuel, sometimes with her sister and occasionally with a friend, but she'd never had brunch alone with total strangers. Arriving at the café, she peered in through the window, trying to see if she could recognise Claire and Jasper from the photos they'd sent. It almost felt like turning up for a blind date. Before she'd met Samuel, friends had occasionally tried to set her up with 'the perfect man', but Harper had never been interested in such things. Now she kind of wished she had a little experience.

'Excuse me.' A woman emerged from the café juggling four takeaway coffee mugs and an enormous jogging style pram.

'Sorry,' Harper said, stepping aside, and then before she could chicken out, she walked through the open door.

It was then that she finally saw them—sitting right down the back in the corner, huddled together on the booth-style seat on one side of a table. They glanced up, caught her looking and lifted their hands to wave. Their smiles were wide and real, exactly as they had been in their photos, and the knot in her stomach loosened a little. This couple had way more at stake in this meeting than she did. Hitching her bag on her shoulder, she weaved through the tables to get to them.

They stood as she approached and stepped around the table to greet her. The man wore smart-casual black shorts and a red-checked shirt, which did little to hide his broad shoulders and muscly arms. The woman looked a little hippyish in a long floral-print skirt, a black tank top and a chunky beaded necklace with matching earrings. Their eyes sparkled as they looked to her.

'Hi! You must be Harper?' They spoke in unison. Normally that kind of thing would irritate her, but it didn't with these two.

She nodded. 'Claire and Jasper?'

They nodded back and then all three of them burst into smiles. Any nerves that were still fluttering in Harper's belly evaporated as Claire threw her arms around her and drew her into a hug.

'It's so lovely to meet you.'

Not usually one for public displays of affection—especially with strangers—Harper surprised herself when she didn't feel uncomfortable. In fact, hugging Claire felt like coming home; she couldn't remember ever feeling such an instant affinity with anyone.

When they pulled back, Jasper offered his hand and his warm, firm shake was equally as comfortable as his gorgeous wife's hug.

Harper looked from Jasper back to Claire. 'Thank you so much for coming all the way down to Sydney to meet me.'

'Oh, don't be silly,' Claire said, 'if anyone should be thanking anyone, it's us thanking you for agreeing to meet us at all, for even considering doing this.'

Harper smiled.

'Was Samuel not able to make it?' Jasper asked.

'No.' Harper shook her head—embarrassed, annoyed but also slightly relieved that he'd decided to pull out at the last minute. He still believed what she was doing was crazy, and she'd been surprised when he'd offered to come in the first place. 'He said he's really sorry but he's got a big court case kicking off tomorrow and unfortunately couldn't take the time out from preparing.'

'That's okay. We understand. Another time.' Claire gestured to the table. 'Shall we sit?'

'Yes, good idea.' Harper dropped her bag to the floor and sat.

As he and Claire slipped back into the booth seat, Jasper glanced towards the queue at the counter. 'Should we order before we get too deep into conversation?'

Despite the alluring aroma of fresh coffee and the clatter of cutlery scraping plates all around them, Harper had almost forgotten they'd come here to eat as well as talk. Judging by the surprised look on Claire's face she had too, but tall and strapping Jasper looked like a guy who needed his food, so Harper picked up the menu on the table and took a look. She decided on poached eggs and smashed avocado on sourdough and waited until it looked like the others had made their selections, before grabbing her purse from her bag and pushing back her seat.

'What can I get for you guys?' she asked.

Claire also stood. 'Oh no you don't. Jasper and I are shouting you.'

They argued in a friendly manner for a few moments and then finally agreed to go Dutch.

Jasper chuckled. 'This is a little too much like a first date.' The women laughed along with him.

Once the orders were placed, they returned to their table.

'So, did you drive down from the Hunter Valley this morning?' Harper asked, not sure how they were meant to start this conversation. This was really just protocol—unless they'd turned out to be fruitcakes in person, she'd already decided that Claire and Jasper were the people she wanted to help.

Claire shook her head. 'No, we came down yesterday afternoon and spent the night with Jasper's cousin. He's married to my best friend, and they have five children.'

'Five?' Harper hoped they didn't notice her shudder.

Jasper laughed. 'Some people just don't know when to stop.'

'Either that or they haven't discovered contraception,' Claire said and Harper wondered if there was a hint of bitterness in her voice.

'I imagine it must be difficult being around others, especially friends, who can so easily have children.'

Claire looked to Jasper and reached out to take his hand. 'We try to remain grateful for what we do have,' she began, 'but I must admit, it's been getting more and more difficult the last year or so. It's hard to see everyone around us—or at least it sometimes feels that way—getting pregnant so easily, when I know that for us to have a baby it will be a lot more complicated. I've actually had murderous thoughts about people who declare they accidentally conceived.'

Harper cringed inwardly, hoping her guilt didn't show on her face.

'It got to the point where I decided it was time to do something about it, or risk becoming the kind of person I don't like. That's when I told Jasper I wanted to look into egg donation.'

Interesting. It sounded very much like this had been Claire's decision. Was Jasper perhaps not quite so keen to do this?

'What about you?' Harper asked, looking to him. 'Did you have the same deep yearning to have a baby?'

'I come from a big family,' Jasper began, leaning forward slightly. 'I've got three sisters and they all have kids of their own now. My parents have been happily married for almost forty years, and growing up I always assumed that would be me one day. Until I met Claire, I'd not really considered the possibility that maybe I wouldn't be able to have kids. Infertility was an alien concept until Claire hit me hard with it even before we'd had our first real date.'

When Harper raised an eyebrow, the couple looked at each other and smiled.

'Until *I* met Jasper, I'd resigned myself to a single life with no kids, so I rarely even went on dates. But with Jasper, I wanted the date he offered. I wanted a lot more, but I didn't want to hurt either of us. I tried to protect us both—tried to make him think I wasn't interested—but then my best friend got engaged to his cousin and suddenly avoiding him was near-on impossible. He confronted me, asked me outright why I'd ghosted him and that's when I told him I was infertile.'

Harper had read all about Claire's childhood cancer in her emails—she'd described in detail how the chemotherapy she'd had for acute lymphoblastic leukaemia pre-puberty had caused ovarian failure—but hearing this lovely young woman announce her infertility made her feel more emotional than she knew herself capable of. Claire looked so healthy, it seemed inconceivable that she'd ever been so sick, and even more unlikely that she was barren.

'And how did you feel about that?' she asked, looking to Jasper.

'I was shocked. Having kids isn't usually something you speak about so early in a relationship—at least in my experience—but although I knew I wanted a family, I couldn't walk away from Claire.' He looked to her then and his eyes swam with adoration as he smiled, sniffed and then continued. 'She's the best damn thing that ever happened to me and since that day she's always been enough. Saying that, there's nothing in the world I'd like more than to have a family with her, as long as there's no physical risk to Claire in the process.'

Harper thought of her GP's warnings. 'There's a physical risk to every pregnancy.'

'I know that,' Jasper said with a nod as he drew his wife into his side. 'I just can't help being a little protective.'

Harper smiled, experiencing a smidgen of jealousy at the beautiful relationship these two obviously shared. They were so full of love, she had no doubt they had plenty to give to a child. She tried to imagine what a baby combining her genetics with Jasper's would look like. He was a very good-looking man—chiselled facial features, thick golden hair and the palest blue eyes she'd ever seen. Although he was a similar height and build to Samuel, she got the impression his muscles weren't earned at the gym.

'That's fair enough,' she said, thinking that if Jasper was half as protective of their baby, he'd make an awesome dad.

'Skinny latte, hot chocolate and strong black?' Announced a young waiter arriving at their table.

'So tell me all about hot air ballooning?' Harper asked when their waiter retreated. She didn't want to sound like she was interviewing them but was truly fascinated by their unusual career.

'What do you want to know?' they asked, again speaking at the same time.

She smiled. 'Absolutely everything. How long have you been ballooning? Was it something you always wanted to do?'

'I'd never been in a hot air balloon until I met Jasper,' Claire admitted, 'but I think I fell in love with him and ballooning at the same time. His family however, have a very long history in the industry.'

Harper nodded encouragingly. 'Do tell.'

Jasper's eyes lit up when he spoke about his family's heritage and their passion for hot air ballooning and she could tell he loved it almost as much as he loved his wife. Harper barely noticed the arrival of the food, so transfixed was she by his story. She couldn't help thinking he'd make the perfect guest for her show. Perhaps once this was all over, she'd invite him on.

'So you both fly now?' she asked once he'd finished.

'Yep. Claire decided on her first flight that she wanted her own licence and I taught her myself.'

'Can kids go up in hot air balloons?'

'In Australia it's up to the discretion of the pilot,' Claire said, 'but there's really not a lot of point in bringing a child until they can see over the sides of the basket properly, so we've set a minimum age of five years.'

'And will you both still work once the baby's born?' Harper asked, speaking as if Claire were already pregnant.

'We plan to share the parenting responsibilities as evenly as possible. Jasper wants to be a hands-on dad as much as I want to be a full-time mum, but I guess we're pretty lucky in that working for the family business, we can be flexible. Currently we work together—when Jasper flies, I'm chasing on the ground, and vice versa, but once the baby is born we'll rework the rosters. In addition to Jasper's parents, we have a number of other employees to fly and crew.'

Harper nodded, but then it suddenly struck her that if both of them were killed in a balloon accident, the baby would be left an orphan. 'Isn't hot air ballooning dangerous?'

Jasper laughed as he placed his knife and fork down on his now-empty plate. 'Ballooning statistics are incredibly boring to read because there are so few crashes. Occasionally a balloon clips a tree during landing, but usually the only thing damaged is the pilot's ego.'

'Most people don't think twice about climbing into a car,' Claire said, 'but you're way more likely to die on the roads than in the air.'

Then, as if she could read Harper's mind, she added, 'However, we won't be taking any unnecessary risks so I won't be flying once I get pregnant—the landings can sometimes be a little bumpy—and once the baby is born, then Jasper and I have decided never to go up in a balloon together. It's probably a ridiculous precaution, but at least then if something happens to one of us, the other one will still be around.'

'That sounds sensible.'

'We've rambled on about our career. What about you?' Claire asked. 'Did you always want to be an interviewer?'

'For as long as I can really remember. From an early age, I was fascinated by people and also by current affairs, but I did best in English and drama at school so after lots of discussions with my older sister, I decided journalism might be a good fit.'

'And you love it?' Jasper smiled, his cheeks reddening slightly. 'I promised Claire I wouldn't be all embarrassing but I have to tell you, my dad and I are huge fans of your show. We often listen while we're doing maintenance. Even Dad's old dog listens. Usually he sleeps in the doorway of the shed so he can keep an eye on anything happening outside, but when your show comes on, he gets as close to our old radio as he can.'

Harper chuckled, chuffed by Jasper's confession. 'That's really cute. I'm glad you enjoy the show.'

'Do you have any pets?' Claire asked.

She shook her head. 'Samuel and I are both such workaholics that we don't feel it would be fair to bring an animal into our lives, but I do love them. I always wanted a pet as a child but my mother could barely remember to feed her own children, so thankfully we never got one.'

'Are you not close to your mum then?' Jasper asked.

Harper sighed. 'No. Not really. My mother is a ... My dad died when I was a baby and she never quite got over the loss.'

'Oh, I'm so sorry,' said Claire. 'That must have been hard.'

'Well, I can't really remember that time. I was really young, but let's just say Laura's a complex person. In fact, she's just moved overseas to become a cowgirl in Montana or something ridiculous like that.'

Jasper laughed. 'Sounds exciting.'

'We'll see how long she lasts,' Harper said, then quickly changed the direction of the conversation. 'What about your families? Are they supportive of your decision to try egg donation?'

Claire and Jasper exchanged a look and then looked back to Harper. 'We've decided not to tell them yet,' Claire said. 'It's not that we don't think they'll be supportive, but ...'

Jasper picked up where she left off. 'But we're well aware this whole thing might not be smooth sailing and we don't want to have them constantly asking us how we're doing. This is something we want to do by ourselves.'

'But I'm sure our families would be encouraging,' Claire said. 'Both our parents already have grandchildren and would be overjoyed for more. My brother and his wife had a baby not long ago and his wife is an only child. They both know I'm infertile so I don't think they're holding out for a cousin for their little boy—if this works out, it'll hopefully be a lovely surprise for everyone in our family.'

Harper smiled. She felt warm and fuzzy all over knowing that not only would this baby be embraced and loved by its parents, but it would have a big extended family of aunts, uncles, cousins and grandparents to love it as well.

Claire drained the last of her hot chocolate and then placed the mug down on the table with a thunk. 'Harper, *if* you decide to donate an egg to us and *if* we are successful in getting pregnant, we want to be as open as possible with our child and that means we'd like our donor to be involved in their life. How do you feel about that?'

She hesitated a moment. 'What kind of involvement are you thinking about?'

Jasper took hold of Claire's hand over the table again and his eyes turned serious as he looked to Harper. 'We don't want to live in each other's pockets, but we thought it would be nice meeting up maybe once or twice a year. As soon as the child is old enough we'd like to tell him or her about her beginnings. All the reading we've done suggests that's the best way for the child.'

She hadn't planned on being involved at all once a fertilised embryo was transferred, but once or twice a year wasn't much of an ask. 'So I'd be like an aunty of sorts?' she asked, thinking of Samuel's nieces and nephews who she didn't see very often but enjoyed when she did.

Claire smiled. 'Yes, exactly.'

'I think that would be good,' Harper said. Now that she thought about it, it might be quite nice to follow the progress of a child grown from her egg. And these were the people—she felt it in her bones.

The three of them grinned at each other like they were in on some big wonderful secret, which she supposed in a way they were. Silence rang between them but it wasn't awkward at all. A lump had formed in Harper's throat at the thought of these lovely people becoming a family because of something *she'd* given them.

She waited until the lump had lessened a little, then she reached across the table and placed her hand on top of Claire and Jasper's joined ones. 'I've loved talking to both of you today,' she said, 'and if you want to do this, then there's no one else I'd rather give my eggs to.'

Chapter Twelve

The door of the fertility clinic slid open and Claire looked up from the magazine she'd been attempting to read, but it was only a couple of strangers. Her heart sank.

'She'll be here,' Jasper whispered, patting her knee. 'Don't stress.'

She hoped he was right, but until they'd begun the actual process of egg donation, until a fertilised embryo had been implanted into her uterus, Claire wasn't sure she would be able to relax. She and Jasper had survived the two private counselling sessions required by the clinic, and Harper and her mysterious husband, Samuel, had also done theirs. Now they only had one mandatory group session to go before they could begin.

Whenever she thought about what this process might result in, she felt like a kid at Christmas. This time next year they might be very close to becoming parents and that would be the greatest Christmas gift ever.

The door whined as it opened and this time when she looked up she was rewarded with the sight of Harper stepping inside.

She waved as Harper scanned the waiting room, her eyes lighting up when she saw them. In the few weeks since they'd met in person, they hadn't seen each other again but they'd spoken on the phone a number of times, and weirdly, Harper now felt like an old friend.

As Harper—looking all professional in a black pencil skirt, lilac business shirt and her shoulder-length brown hair immaculately straight—strode towards them, Claire and Jasper stood to greet her. They exchanged hugs and then Harper took the plastic seat next to Claire's.

'Sorry I'm late,' she said. 'I got held up at the station.'

Claire and Jasper spoke as one. 'Not a problem. We haven't been called up yet.'

'Oh good.' Harper leant back in her seat as if to catch her breath.

They'd decided on a fertility clinic in Sydney. Newcastle would have been closer for Jasper and Claire but their schedules were more flexible than Harper's and they wanted to make things as easy as possible for her.

'Could Samuel not make it?' Jasper asked, leaning forward slightly to look past Claire.

Harper shook her head. 'Until this morning he was planning to, but some guy and his girlfriend had a fight last night and she ended up falling from their balcony. It looks like she might not make it and he's been called in to represent the guy.'

Jasper made a face. 'Must take a special kind of person to stand up in court for criminals.'

'Innocent until proven guilty,' Claire said, giving him a pointed look. She didn't want to offend Harper.

Harper shrugged. 'It doesn't matter, he's given his consent, so we don't need him here anyway.'

Before either of them could reply, their names were called and they looked up to see their counsellor, Jessica Warren, waiting by the reception desk.

'Good afternoon.' Jessica greeted them and then indicated an open door halfway down a long corridor. She wasn't one for small talk and although she smiled, no warmth emanated from her. Weren't counsellors supposed to be warm and fuzzy people? This one was the opposite of everything Claire imagined she should be. But the bottom line was that this last session was just a formality—Jessica's personality was neither here nor there.

Once they were all in the office, Jessica shut the door and indicated they should take one of the two white leather couches. She lowered herself into an armchair and crossed her legs.

'From our previous conversations, it's clear that you all have a strong grasp of what is involved in donating and receiving eggs, so today we're going to go over some of the legal and psychological issues relating to the process. Your situation is less common than most in that generally egg donors have already finished having their own family when they decide to donate. However,' she paused for emphasis, 'there are never any certainties in life, so we need to consider the possible relationship between any children conceived by the donor agreement and any children Harper and Samuel may subsequently have. I see he couldn't join us today.'

'I've already told you,' Harper interrupted, her tone stern, 'we don't want to have children. Both of us are far too busy with work and we wouldn't want to bring a child into the world when we wouldn't have time to give them the attention they deserve. I promise you that is not going to change, so such a discussion is unnecessary.'

Jessica pursed her lips together, then sighed. 'Okay, then.' She glanced down at her notes. 'I see you've decided that the three of you and the child will keep in contact after he or she is born. Have you discussed how this contact will work?'

They all nodded.

'I'll probably visit Claire and Jasper in the Hunter Valley once a year,' Harper said.

'And we come to Sydney at least every couple of months to see my parents and our friends, so we'll try to catch up with Harper some of those times as well,' Claire added.

Jessica nodded and made a note on her clipboard. 'And, Jasper and Claire, have you decided what you will tell the child about their origins?'

'We want to be honest from the start,' Jasper said. 'We've read all the material you've given us and agree that the earlier our child knows where they came from, the easier it will be for them to come to terms with it. So we'll be starting discussions when the child is about three or four.'

'That's good. And just remember that the most important thing for any child is a secure and loving relationship with their parents. If a child feels loved, they can handle almost anything.'

Again they nodded. Claire just wanted to hurry this up.

'There are a few final things that need to be considered before taking the next step,' Jessica said. 'I want to be sure you all understand your legal rights. Under Australian law, egg donors can withdraw or change their consent at any time prior to insemination or fertilisation of the eggs. After that, all financial and legal responsibilities are transferred to the recipient couple and the donor has no rights over the pregnancy or the child.'

'We understand that,' Harper said tersely, and Claire bit her lip to stifle a smile.

'Good. And I want to make sure you also understand that Claire and Jasper will become guardians to any leftover embryos. They will be free to use them themselves for subsequent pregnancies, to donate them to another recipient or to destroy them.'

Claire clenched her jaw. Did this woman think they were idiots? They knew all this. They'd done their research, sat through the obligatory counselling sessions and now they wanted to get on with it.

As if sensing her frustration, Jasper put his hand on her knee again.

Harper nodded. 'I understand all of that and I trust Claire and Jasper will do whatever they feel is right. Whatever decision they make will be fine by me.'

Claire smiled her thanks at Harper—she sometimes had to pinch herself when she thought about how lucky they were to have found her.

A few more questions about their values and anticipated parenting styles—which Harper said were no concern of hers—and Jessica finally put her notes down. This time when she smiled it actually looked like she meant it. 'Well then,' she said, 'I'm confident you are all on the same page, so I wish you the absolute best as you go forward. Harper, this is a good thing you are doing, and Claire and Jasper, I can't wait to hear news of your bundle of joy. Good luck.'

That was it? Claire felt like leaping across the coffee table and throwing her arms around Jessica, but she turned to Jasper and hugged him instead. Then they both stood and hugged Harper. This might only be the beginning, but it felt like a moment to celebrate.

After the counsellor dismissed them, they had a short wait before the fertility doctor called them into his office. Dr Ballantine—a white-haired, smiley man with a rounded tummy pressing against his grey shirt—welcomed them as if they were long-lost friends. He wore a tie covered in storks carrying babies and the walls of his office were plastered with baby photos, birth announcements and thank you cards. Claire couldn't take her eyes off them.

As they sat down, the doctor caught her looking and chuckled in a very Santa-like manner. 'Aren't they all gorgeous? Not long and your little boy or girl will be up there.'

Claire sniffed and smiled back at him, unable to speak past the emotion that climbed into her throat at that thought. Would they have a boy or a girl? She didn't care. As long as it was healthy, and theirs.

Jasper squeezed her hand. 'We're really looking forward to that, doctor.'

'Good good.' Dr Ballantine leant back in his leather chair and folded his hands across his belly. 'I want to start by congratulating all three of you for taking this big leap. I won't pretend it's going to be a walk in the park. Egg donation requires a huge commitment from both the donor and the recipient uterus, and you won't get off scot-free either.' He winked at Jasper. 'Some of our dads get stage fright when it gets to the making love into a cup stage.'

'I'll think I'll manage.'

Claire glanced at her husband to see he'd turned a bright shade of red. Not much embarrassed Jasper, so she couldn't help but laugh.

'I'm sure you will,' the doctor replied and then started to explain the physical process they were about to begin, the genetic screening and tests Harper would have to undergo.

'Once we've deemed Harper a suitable candidate for donor, the next step is synchronising your menstrual cycles. This involves some hormone treatment for you and nasal sprays and injections of follicle stimulant hormone for Harper.'

Claire glanced over at Harper and saw that her normally radiant skin had turned slightly green at the mention of needles. She wished she could take the pain for this generous woman or at least pay her for her efforts. It felt wrong to be taking something so big and not giving *anything* back.

Yet at the same time, what price could you put on a child?

'Now.' Dr Ballantine straightened in his chair and planted his hands on his desk to help him stand. 'Let's get this party started. Harper, if you could jump up on my examination table over there so we can take a little squiz at your ovaries.'

'Sure.' Harper followed him to the other side of his office.

She climbed up onto the table and Claire and Jasper looked at each other with relief when the doctor pulled a curtain to block their view. He might only be examining Harper's abdomen, but an ultrasound felt like an intimate thing and it was a little weird being in the room while a woman who'd been a complete stranger to them until a few weeks ago had one.

They sat silently, holding hands and staring at the surrounding baby photos as they listened for news from behind the curtain.

Harper squealed. 'Ouch, that's cold.'

'Sorry.' The doctor chuckled. 'Even after all these years I forget to warn my patients about that.'

There were a few long moments of silence and Claire held her breath waiting for something else. This was more nerve-wracking than anything she'd ever experienced—what if he found something wrong with Harper? What if, like Claire, she had no eggs?

'Won't be long and you'll be on that table having an ultrasound,' Jasper whispered, leaning close.

Wow. She allowed herself a tiny smile at that thought. For so long she'd resigned herself to the fact that she'd never have a pregnant belly to be examined. Could she dare to hope their dreams of a family might actually come true?

Then Dr Ballantine's voice broke into her fantasy. 'What a star! Nice healthy egg follicles. From the looks of things, she's the perfect candidate, folks.'

Claire let out the breath she'd been holding and wrapped her arms around her husband. This wasn't the way she'd like to have a baby with him—but it *was* the only way and she couldn't be happier right now.

The doctor reappeared a few moments later, his grin broader than ever.

'Now, we've got some paperwork to fill out—your medical histories, etcetera—and then I'll be sending you off to pathology.'

Harper appeared again, looking pretty damn pleased with herself, and Jasper gave her a thumbs up. Claire felt a pinch of jealousy at the knowledge that this woman could do something for her husband which she could not, but she quickly forced that feeling aside. She needed to stay positive. And focused.

If everything went according to plan, then in the not-too-distant future she and Jasper would have the baby they craved. And, when that little bundle was placed into her arms, Claire knew it wouldn't matter where he or she had got their start.

Chapter Thirteen

NOVEMBER 2016

Harper lifted her pyjama top, positioned the needle, closed her eyes and held her breath as she plunged it into her flesh. Today was the seventh day she'd done this and she still broke out in a sweat every single time.

As she was putting away the injection kit, Samuel appeared from their ensuite, a fluffy white towel wrapped around his torso. 'Been shooting up again?' he asked, with a chuckle.

'It's not funny. It hurts,' she said, although truthfully the anticipation was worse than the actual act.

'If it's that bad, don't do it.' He dropped his towel to the floor and began to get dressed for work.

Harper let out a frustrated sigh. After a week of this, she should have known better than to say anything. The first time she'd brought out the kit, Samuel had watched as she'd tried to garner the courage to perform the injection. Dr Ballantine had suggested that if she was squeamish, she could get her husband to do the honours but Samuel scoffed at that.

'Do I look like a doctor? I can barely watch, never mind inflict it on you. I think you're insane to be putting yourself through all this.'

But he hadn't met Claire and Jasper—he didn't know what wonderful people they were and how grateful they felt towards her—so she'd swallowed her fear and done the deed herself. All her life she'd been driven to succeed and this was no different. She wanted to see this process through to the end and for Claire and Jasper to have a healthy baby to show for all her efforts. Then she could get on with her life with the knowledge she'd done something that made a difference, even if only on a small scale.

'Do you think you might finish in court today?' she asked, deliberately changing the subject. All week Samuel had been defending a high school teacher accused of having a relationship with a student.

'Hope so,' he said, pulling on his expensive navy trousers. 'We've got the firm's Christmas party tonight and it would be good to walk into that with a win on my hands to impress the partners.'

She had to bite her tongue to stop herself groaning out loud. With everything else going on, she'd totally forgotten that this event had crept up on them. She'd been planning on spending the whole weekend on the couch watching Netflix. It wasn't that she minded Samuel's work parties—they weren't frequent and were usually held at swanky restaurants. Expensive champagne would flow and she usually enjoyed listening to his colleagues, but tonight she wouldn't be able to drink a drop.

Dr Ballantine had been right—the process of preparing her body for egg retrieval had been harder than she'd anticipated. It wasn't just the daily injections. From the moment she woke up in the morning to when her head hit the pillow again at night, the responsibility of what she was doing weighed heavy on her mind. She thought more carefully than ever about what she put into her body and suddenly started seeing dangers she'd never noticed before as she walked down the street.

'Fingers crossed,' Harper said, injecting enthusiasm she didn't feel into her voice. 'What time does it start again?'

'Eight o'clock.' He sat on the edge of the bed to pull on his socks. 'Who are you interviewing today?'

'Um ...' For a moment, she couldn't find the name of her guest anywhere in her head. All she could think about was the ultrasound she had coming up this morning to see how her egg follicles were going.

Samuel glanced up and she noticed his socks didn't match. She quirked a smile as the answer to his question came to her. 'A doctor who specialises in obsessive-compulsive disorder. Lilia found her. Apparently she's trialling a new type of therapy.'

'Fascinating. Is she going to use Lil as a guinea pig?'

Harper laughed. 'I think she plans on listening very carefully and self-medicating.' Everyone at the station teased Lilia about having OCD and although Harper didn't believe she did—she just liked her clothes to match and everything around her to be neat and tidy—her friend herself was starting to get a little paranoid that maybe she did have a problem. 'Are you all finished with the bathroom now?'

'Yep.' Samuel nodded as he went over to select a tie, leaving his wet towel on the tiles. Sometimes she wished the two of them had OCD. 'It's all yours.'

'Thanks.' Harper stood. 'Do you want me to meet you at the restaurant tonight or will you be home in time for us to go together?'

'Not sure yet. I'll text you. Have a great day.' And then, knotting his silver tie as he walked, he headed out of the bedroom.

Harper took her time in the shower, letting the hot water gush over her belly in an effort to try to ease the slight bloating feeling. She ran her hand over the tiny mound that had grown over the last few days. If she didn't know any better, she'd think *she* was pregnant. Screwing up her nose at that thought, she wrenched off the taps and then went back into the bedroom to get ready.

Her usual morning routine consisted of coffee and a pastry at her local café while she read the papers and caught up with the news and current affairs. But since the go ahead she'd been abstaining from caffeine, so today she bypassed the café and headed straight to the fertility clinic for her scan.

'Good morning.' Dr Ballantine greeted her with his usual cheerful grin. 'I listened to your show for the first time last night. My wife's got me onto podcasts and I've subscribed to yours.'

'I hope you enjoyed it,' Harper said, feeling weirdly nervous.

'Immensely.' He indicated she hop up onto the table. 'I had to drive around the block a couple of times when I got home so I could hear the end of it before heading inside.'

'I'd love to interview you one day about all the different things you do here,' she said, leaning back and lifting up her work blouse. 'Would you be interested in that?'

The doctor turned a bright shade of red. 'I would love that.'

'Great. I'll get my producer to call and set up a time.'

'Splendid. Now, let's take a look at those lovely ovaries of yours.' He lifted the tube of lubricant and squeezed a dollop over her stomach.

Again, she flinched at the coolness. Or, at least that's what she put it down to, but the truth was every time a doctor touched her stomach, it reminded her of another time. A time she'd spent over a decade trying to forget.

'Any problems with the medication?' he asked.

She swallowed. 'No. But I'll be glad when the injections are over.'

Dr Ballantine chuckled, then his expression turned serious as he touched the wand against her lower abdomen. He turned his head to look at the screen beside them and Harper held her breath as she followed his gaze, not sure what to expect.

'Excellent, excellent,' he said after a few moments. 'I think you were born to do this.'

'Really?' She couldn't hide her surprise—although quickly told herself that the doctor meant she was physically suitable for the job. Actually *being* a mum was a whole other thing.

'Yes.' He nodded. 'There's a good number of follicles here and if things keep developing at this rate, I'd say we might be able to schedule the retrieval for next Tuesday.'

'That's great,' she said, pushing her other thoughts aside and trying to recall who they were scheduled to interview on Tuesday. Hopefully their guest would be open to doing a pre-record because she had to go under general anaesthetic for the procedure and wouldn't be able to work that day.

'Right then.' Dr Ballantine handed her a paper towel to wipe her stomach. 'We'll do another scan on Monday to be sure, but we'll plan for Tuesday.'

Harper could barely contain her excitement as she climbed off the table and said goodbye to the doctor. Although she knew the clinic would be calling Claire and Jasper to book them in for Tuesday as well, she wanted to deliver the good news, so the moment she stepped out of the building she brought up Claire on her phone.

'Hi Harper,' Claire answered after a few rings. 'How are you?'

'I'm full of egg follicles!'

Claire laughed. 'Did you just have your scan?'

'Yep—and Dr Ballantine reckons we'll be ready for the procedure on Tuesday.'

'Oh my God! This is really gonna happen?' She could hear the mixture of excitement, fear and shock in Claire's voice.

'It looks like it. The clinic will be calling you soon to make the appointment, but I wanted you guys to know right away.'

'Thank you. Thank you so much.' There was a moment of silence on the line. 'For everything.'

Harper grinned. 'Don't thank me yet, but you're absolutely welcome. I'll see you next week.'

They disconnected so that Claire could go tell Jasper, and Harper tried to switch focus from the follicle excitement to her day job, but when she got to the office, she still couldn't wipe the smile from her face.

'You look like the cat that got the canary,' Lilia said, pushing her glasses up onto her head. 'Did the scan go well then?'

Harper nodded as she dumped her handbag onto the floor and flopped into her swivel chair, resisting the urge to spin around like an excited child. 'Really well. Which means I need next Tuesday off. Is that going to be a problem?'

Lilia turned to her screen and flicked to next week's schedule. 'Oh dear, you're interviewing that debut thriller author from Perth who hit the *New York Times* bestseller lists. Apparently she's a total diva.'

'Well, tell the diva's publicist that if she wants an interview, she can do a pre-record on Monday.' An appearance on *Afternoons with Harper* was sought after enough that the publicist would likely advise the author to accept this offer, and if she didn't, well, they had plenty of other hopeful guests to call on. Harper could ask Dr Ballantine or even Jasper to fill the spot.

'I'll see what I can do. But don't you worry about it. I'll mark you as sick for Tuesday. Will you need Wednesday as well?'

Harper shook her head. The doctor had advised her that she might be a little tender after the egg retrieval but that's what painkillers were for.

'Did you get to see the spunky husband today?' Lilia asked, her eyes gleaming.

Harper laughed. When she'd first shown her friend the photo of Claire and Jasper, Lil had been unable to take her eyes off him. She was gutted to hear he didn't have a brother and Harper couldn't blame her. Jasper looked like he'd stepped right off the page of a fireman charity calendar.

'No. Today was just me, but I'll see him *and* his lovely wife again next week.'

Lilia blew out a deep sigh, her thick, dark fringe flicking up off her face in the process.

'How was your date last night anyway?' Harper asked. 'Any luck with the pilot?'

They'd both had high hopes for this guy—Lilia loved travel, so whenever a pilot appeared on one of her dating sites she contacted him immediately.

'I don't want to talk about it.'

But Harper took a sip from her water bottle and waited.

Two seconds later her friend elaborated. 'He flies international for Qantas and he had the audacity to ask me to go halves on dinner. What the *hell*?'

'Maybe he didn't want to offend you by assuming traditional gender roles.'

'Ugh. Just because I'm a feminist doesn't mean I don't appreciate chivalry and romance. Makes me think he's a tight-arse with his money and I can't stand people like that. If that wasn't bad enough, he assumed I'd want a second date and suggested bowling for Saturday night.'

Harper snorted and almost spat out the water she'd just sipped. Anyone could see Lilia wasn't a bowling kind of girl.

'Think I'll give up on the man scene and accept my destiny,' Lilia said. 'Dating requires way too much effort.'

'Good idea.' Although Harper didn't believe for a second Lilia would actually follow through on it.

After that, they got down to business, going through the schedule for the following week. They had some interesting guests coming up—a beekeeper, a woman who wrote the captions in greeting cards, a photographer who worked in war-torn regions and a ghost hunter—and Harper looked forward to researching and speaking to all of them. After a few hours making notes, Harper and Lilia scoffed salad sandwiches and then migrated to the studio for their afternoon on air.

The OCD expert was truly fascinating—she'd discovered a chemical receptor in the brains of mice that might hold the key to helping humans with obsessive-compulsive disorder—but Harper's mind was only half on the job. Her hand kept drifting to her stomach as she contemplated the eggs forming there. More than once Lilia caught her staring off into space and smiling.

Finally the day was over.

'Any big plans for the weekend?' Lilia asked as they hitched their handbags to their shoulders and swiped their security cards to let them out of the building.

'Dammit. Until you mentioned it, I'd completely forgotten. I have Samuel's work Christmas party tonight.'

Lilia smirked. 'Have fun.'

Harper poked out her tongue at her friend. 'I'll see you Monday.'

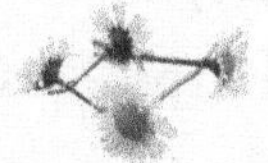

'There's my sexy wife!' Samuel announced as Harper entered the small function room his firm had hired at a harbourside restaurant.

Pasting a smile on her face, she started towards him, not feeling particularly sexy with her bloated belly. She'd spent almost an hour trying to find a dress that would hide it and hoped the red one she'd eventually chosen did the trick.

'Hello darling,' he said, planting a kiss on her cheek and drawing her into his side. She could tell he'd already had a fair bit to drink, which made her think he'd won his court case today. Samuel wasn't one for drowning his sorrows.

'Hiya.' She greeted the crowd of his colleagues gathered around him.

Niceties were exchanged—she kissed the men, hugged the women and complimented the partners' wives on their outfits. Samuel smiled pleasingly at her as she did this. The firm was a medium sized general law company with employees that practised in a number of areas. As well as Samuel, there was one other criminal solicitor, with whom he shared a personal assistant. There were two partners and seven other ambitious solicitors all, like Samuel, hoping to achieve partner status ASAP. So while all these people were friendly to each other, she knew, beneath the façade, they would stop at nothing to get ahead. There were also two paralegals and three receptionists.

Harper had met almost everyone (and their significant others), except the newest receptionist.

'This is Annika,' Samuel told her.

One look at this woman told Harper she was the one responsible for the CrossFit obsession sweeping through the firm.

'Can we get you a drink, Harper?' asked Elizabeth Carter, one of the partners' wives as she looked around for a waitperson.

Within seconds a boy who looked barely legal appeared wearing the standard black and white uniform of restaurant wait staff.

'I'll have a soda water, thanks,' Harper said.

'Can I grab another soda and lime?' Annika lifted her empty glass, confirming Harper's CrossFit suspicion. You didn't get a body like that without treating it like a temple.

'Don't tell me you've joined this ridiculous cult as well.' Tracey Slater, the other partner's wife, tutted. She took a large gulp of her red wine.

Harper opened her mouth to say 'yes' as that would be the easiest explanation, but Elizabeth got in first.

'Oh my goodness! Are you pregnant?'

The chatter in the room died instantly as all eyes snapped to her and Samuel. Her stomach tightened.

Samuel snorted loudly. 'You know our stance on babies.'

Harper cringed. Of course they did. Everyone who knew them knew 'their' stance on babies—how due to climate change, world poverty, war, famine, blah, blah, blah, it wasn't smart to bring *more* babies into the world—but it embarrassed her when he went on about it in front of people who already had children, like many of the people at this party. She'd called him out on this once and he'd retorted with, 'Well, why shouldn't we make them question their decision? They sure as hell try to make us question ours.'

And although he might have a point, it still made for awkward social situations, but tonight he surprised her.

'Harper's abstaining from alcohol because she's in the process of donating her eggs to a childless couple. You should see how brave she is, injecting herself every morning.'

The pride that shone from his voice was new—so far he'd given no indication that he admired her for what she was doing. Aside from a few condescending remarks, he'd shown so little interest that she'd hardly told him anything about Jasper and Claire.

Was he simply using her situation to make himself look good in front of the partners?

Whatever Samuel's reason, she couldn't help feeling a little pissed off that he'd made this public announcement. She hadn't wanted anyone except her close friends knowing. Although she wasn't exactly Kardashian famous, as a public figure she preferred to keep her private life just that. And there was also Claire and Jasper's privacy to consider.

'Wow, Harper, do you know the couple you're doing this for?' asked one of the paralegals.

'Um … no.' She bit down on her annoyance. 'Well, I didn't when I first set out but we've kind of become friends now.'

Everyone had something to say about this. The overall consensus was that donating her eggs made her some kind of angel and although this sentiment made Harper uncomfortable, it was preferable to the alternative.

'I could *never* do something like that,' Annika exclaimed, swishing her soda and lime around in her glass.

Nobody asked you to. Harper gritted her teeth and forced a smile.

But the worst came from one of the female solicitors, who'd recently returned from maternity leave. Isobel had twins and her husband was a stay-at-home dad. 'How can you give away your babies like that?' she spat, the expression on her face saying she could barely even stand to look at Harper.

'They're not *babies*. They're not even embryos. They're just eggs,' Elizabeth said in her defence. 'I think it's a very noble thing to do. Infertility can be heartbreaking and I think what you're doing is a priceless gift. Well done.'

Elizabeth raised her glass in a toast and no more was said in opposition; no one dared voice a contrary opinion to one of the partners' wives.

Uncomfortable with all the eyes on her, Harper whispered her thanks, then took a sip of her soda, wishing it was alcoholic.

Thankfully, two wait staff entered the room with trays of bite-sized nibbles, the circles broke into smaller clusters and the focus of conversation changed from Samuel's announcement. Harper stood on the edge of her group, smiling and making occasional comments as she listened to Annika harp on about the virtues of CrossFit. A couple of the younger male lawyers seemed very eager—and on more than one occasion Harper caught their eyes drifting down to the high split in the young woman's skirt.

Nearby, Isobel and some of the other women were loudly lamenting the difficulties of getting their children into the best kindergartens.

When everyone had eaten their fill of hors d'oeuvres, they migrated to the two long tables dressed in stylish gold and silver cloths. Stanley Carter sat in top spot at the end of one table and the other partner, Rodger Slater, sat on the other. As the meals—salmon or rare beef depending on where you were sitting—were distributed, the two men stood and tapped their spoons against their wine glasses in unison. Everyone looked up as they began an obviously prepared speech, alternating sentences between them. Although they praised all their employees, there was no mention of a possible new partner and Harper had to wonder if they were simply stringing their juniors along.

Once the speech was over, Christmas cards were passed around and Harper knew from experience they'd contain a rather nice bonus cheque. As everyone got progressively more drunk, their voices rose as the lawyers tried to out-perform each other in front of the bosses. Once again Harper found herself glancing longingly at her glass. Samuel's colleagues were bearable with the assistance of alcohol but stone-cold sober she found them utter self-obsessed bores.

Dessert was the only highlight of the evening. And although she'd been so good this past month, steering clear of high-sugar items, she scoffed the decadent chocolate lava cake as if it were the last meal she'd ever have. And when Samuel finally said they should make a move, she couldn't get out of there fast enough.

They flagged a taxi and as the driver weaved through the city streets on the way to their place, Samuel snuggled against Harper in the back seat.

'You're the best wife ever,' he all but purred. 'You don't need CrossFit. Coco Pops are obviously working for you.'

She forced a laugh as he put his hand suggestively on her thigh, but inside she was still seething and confused over the way he'd spoken about her egg donation. If it weren't for the taxi driver, she would say something.

Samuel, seemingly oblivious to her irritation, leant in for a kiss and moved his hand a little higher. Despite her mood and the fact she hadn't had a drop to drink all night, her traitorous body reacted predictably at his touch. It had never been able to resist him.

By the time they arrived at the house, they were ready to rip off each other's clothes. Harper thrust a fifty dollar note at their driver and told him to keep the change. Samuel fumbled with his key to open their door. And before he'd kicked it shut behind them, he had her slammed up against it and his hands under her dress.

She moaned as their mouths found each other again and his fingers slipped inside her knickers. After years together, he knew exactly what to do to bring her to the edge. She palmed her hands against the door, crying out as her first orgasm rolled over her. Meanwhile Samuel shoved down his trousers and freed himself.

He was about to enter her when alarm bells blared inside her head and she all but shoved him off her.

'What the hell?' Samuel stumbled back and caught his naked butt on the edge of the hall table.

'Condom!' she spluttered.

'What? You are kidding, right?' He straightened and rubbed his butt.

'I'm so damn fertile that if we had unprotected sex right now we'd probably have triplets.'

A look of horror flashed across Samuel's face and his erection wilted right before her eyes.

'I'm sorry.' She smiled apologetically. 'But it won't be for long.'

'Oh for fuck's sake.' He ran a hand through his hair in frustration.

'Excuse me?' Harper blinked at his harsh tone and coarse words, her arousal diminishing by the second. 'You sounded proud of what I was doing tonight when you told *everyone* at the party. Or was that all just for show?'

For a moment he looked slightly chastised. 'I *am* proud of you, it's just ...' He sighed. 'Do we even *have* any condoms?'

As it happened, she had bought a packet of protection, but ... 'We don't have to have sex, you know,' she snapped as she tugged her dress down and straightened the skirt.

'See?' He threw his hands up in the air. 'This is exactly what I was worried about when you decided to do this *thing*. I knew it would come between us.'

'It doesn't have to come between us,' she scoffed. 'You just need to stop acting like a spoilt brat and think about someone besides yourself for once.'

He recoiled as if she'd shoved him again and she felt a flicker of guilt at the hurt in his eyes, but she'd lost all desire for intimacy with him right now. 'Fine,' he said, yanking up his trousers. 'If that's the way you feel, I guess I'll see you in the morning.'

And with that, he stormed into the lounge room and slammed the door behind him.

Harper resisted the impulse to go after him. She wasn't the one who'd ruined their 'moment'. Was it too much to ask for a bit of support from her husband?

Yet, as she climbed the stairs and crawled into their king-size bed, which felt ridiculously huge without him, that gnawing feeling of guilt ate at her insides and she began to wonder if she'd done the right thing making the decision to donate her eggs. Perhaps it was an extreme thing to do in the name of trying to make her life more meaningful? But she hadn't felt so good about herself in months. And besides, it was too late to back out now.

Chapter Fourteen

It was the morning of egg retrieval and all through Polly and Scotty's house not a creature was stirring, except Claire who, unable to sleep, had decided to cook pancakes for everyone. She tried to keep the noise down as she searched in the cupboards for the ingredients and cooking utensils, but before long Polly appeared carrying their youngest on her hip.

'Do you always rise and shine this early?' her friend asked as she dumped the baby in the high chair.

'Only on very, very special days.'

Beaming, Polly threw her arms around Claire and they jumped up and down together like two schoolgirls. 'I'm so excited for you. I can't believe this is actually happening.'

'I know. Neither can I.' Claire clung to her friend as tears sprouted in her eyes. She'd promised Jasper she wouldn't get too emotional today, and here she was falling at the first hurdle. But she didn't care—nothing could dampen her mood.

The baby started grizzling and Polly pulled back. 'You'd better get used to early mornings anyway. Once you have a kid, you no longer have any control over your own sleep.'

As if to prove her point, Scotty entered at that moment—his bright red hair stuck up messily on his head and a toddler clinging to each leg. 'I can't believe it's morning already,' he grumbled.

'You making cakes, Aunty C?' asked three year old Daisy. She looked a hundred times more awake than her father. 'I love cakes.'

'I'm making pancakes, yes. Do you want to help?'

Claire realised the stupidity of her question when Daisy *and* her two year old brother, Jake, both wanted to assist. She had a lot to learn about parenting, but then motherhood had been thrust upon Polly and she'd taken to it like a duck to water. Claire couldn't wait for all the lessons their baby would teach them.

The pancakes took a little longer than they usually would due to her enthusiastic assistants, but by the time the table was set and the pancakes piled high on a plate in the middle, Polly's other son, Bobby, and daughter, Loretta, had also appeared.

'I'd better go wake Jasper,' Claire said as the ravenous kids all but dived upon the pancakes.

'I don't know how he's managed to sleep through all this noise,' Scotty said, nursing his second coffee in less than half an hour.

Claire didn't know how Jasper had managed to sleep full stop, but as he was usually an early riser for work, he took the chance to laze in bed whenever he could. When she opened the door to their room and flicked on the light, Jasper groaned and pulled the sheets up over his head.

She crossed the room and plopped down on the bed, laughing. 'Wake up, sleepyhead. Today is the first day of the rest of our lives.'

In a few hours Harper's eggs would be inseminated with Jasper's sperm and within days they'd hopefully have embryos ready for implantation. The thought made her giddy.

'How long have you been awake?' Jasper asked.

'Long enough to make pancakes.'

'Did someone say pancakes?' He grabbed her into a hug and she laughed as he pulled her down beside him. 'That must be why you smell so delicious.'

As he kissed the side of her neck, something fizzed inside of her and her body melted against his. Oh how she'd love to throw her leg over him and have her wicked way, but that was against the rules. In order to ensure Jasper had the highest possible sperm count for the procedure, they'd abstained from sex for the past week. They hadn't been celibate for this long since they'd met and Jasper had complained about having blue balls more than once, but it was for a good cause. The very *best* cause.

With this thought, she pressed a quick kiss against his lips and then escaped his embrace.

He groaned again, but then threw the covers off and climbed out of bed. He pulled jeans on over the top of his boxers and she tossed him a t-shirt, which he yanked on before following her out of the room.

As noise from the kitchen wafted down the hallway, Jasper grabbed Claire's hand and swung her round to look at him. 'Hear that?' he said, his eyes wide in faux-horror. 'Are you sure you want that kind of chaos in our lives? It's not too late to back out.'

She whacked him playfully and dragged him after her. 'That is *exactly* the kind of chaos I want for us. Now let's get this show on the road.'

Although she'd made breakfast for everyone else, Claire couldn't eat a bite, so she snuck off to shower while the others were still busy in the kitchen. Then she and Jasper helped Polly and Scotty ready their tribe for delivery to their various day care centres and schools, which helped kill the time until they could head off to their early appointment.

'Thank God they booked us in first thing,' she said to Jasper as they arrived at the fertility clinic. 'Having to wait till the afternoon would have been unbearable.'

As they climbed out of their car, a sleek black Audi turned into the car park and moments later Harper emerged carrying a small overnight bag. They waved and Claire tried to get a look at the driver—was it Samuel, her elusive husband?—but whoever it was left in a hurry.

'Hi guys. Excited?' Harper asked as she approached.

'That is an understatement,' Jasper said, leaning forward to kiss her on the cheek. 'Claire was worse than a kid at Christmas this morning.'

Harper laughed as she and Claire exchanged hugs. 'I was the same. I hope we get a good egg haul.'

She sounded nervous and Claire tried to put her at ease as they walked towards the building. 'Dr Ballantine's nurse told me he felt very positive after your scan yesterday. It'll be fine.'

She silently prayed this was the truth, although realistically she knew that the majority of couples didn't hit the jackpot first time.

They registered their arrival at the reception desk and then sat down to wait until Harper's name was called. Dr Ballantine had explained to them that Harper would be taken into surgery for the retrieval and while she was under general anaesthetic, Jasper would be given a private room to do his thing.

After what felt like days rather than minutes, a woman wearing green scrubs appeared. 'Harper Drummond?' she called into the waiting room.

'Oh my God, that's you.' Claire felt as if she could burst into tears.

'It is.' Harper smiled, leant down to collect her bag off the floor and then stood gracefully.

Claire and Jasper stood as well and each gave her a quick hug. 'Good luck,' they said in unison, holding hands as the woman who had the power to change their world walked off to be readied for surgery.

Time dragged. People came and left the waiting room. Claire and Jasper tried to pass the time by road-testing baby names.

After making a mental list of possible boys' names—James, Cameron and William were the highest contenders—Jasper said, 'If it's a girl, it has to begin with a C. We can't break my family tradition.'

'Yes, we can—all the good ones are taken now anyway. If it's a girl, I like Anaya.' She'd read it in a baby name book she'd found in Polly's bookshelf early that morning.

'Anaya? Is that even a name?'

She laughed. 'Yes. It means "God answered". Isn't that perfect for us?'

He raised an eyebrow. 'I didn't think you were religious. And anyway, I thought you'd want a flower name like Clover or Camellia.'

Before she could reply, another nurse appeared and called Jasper's name.

Claire sprang off her seat and grabbed his hand. 'Come on, you're up.'

After introducing herself and giving them a few instructions, the woman led them into a small, sparsely furnished room. The floor was vinyl and the air smelt of disinfectant. There was one plastic chair in the room and a pile of dirty magazines on a small table beside it. Claire didn't know what she'd been expecting exactly but she'd hoped for somewhere a little more atmospheric. They'd had a choice between 'producing the specimen' here or at home, and she and Jasper had thought this would be preferable to doing it at Polly and Scotty's place with a house full of kids.

The nurse indicated the stack of specimen cups on a shelf in one corner. 'Good luck. I'll be in the office next door, so let me know when you're done.'

Then she left the room and closed the door behind her.

Claire locked the door, trying not to think about how many other men had wanked in here before them, and when she turned around to face Jasper the look on his face told her he was having similar thoughts.

'This is gonna be fun,' he said, picking a magazine off the top of the pile. He flicked through a couple of pages and then held a photo up to her. 'But I'm not sure I want to think about this woman when I'm trying to create our baby.'

She stepped forward, snatched the magazine from his grasp and dropped it. 'That is why I'm here,' she said, slowly undoing the top few buttons of her shirt and looking at him with the come-to-bed expression that never failed to get his attention. Although they'd been told Jasper could do this alone, she'd wanted to help him so that she at least had some involvement in the conception of their child, and now she tried to keep that thought first and foremost in her mind.

Jasper walked to the side of the room and rapped on one of the walls. 'I wonder how thin these are? Do you think she can hear us?'

Claire shuddered, but tried not to let it show on her face. 'Forget about her. This is about us.' Slightly panicked that he might not follow through with this, she grabbed his hand and turned him back to face her. Then she slid her hands beneath his t-shirt and smoothed them over his warm, hard torso. His body never failed to turn her on and even in this cold, clinical space, she found her desire gathering strength. But it wasn't herself she needed to work into a state.

'Remember how much you've wanted to touch me this last week?' she whispered seductively into his ear. 'Well, touch away, baby. I'm all yours.'

She saw Jasper's Adam's apple move up and down as he swallowed, his arousal clearly starting to fight the discomfort of their situation. 'Or would you rather *I* touch *you*?'

Without waiting for a reply, she dropped to her knees, yanked open the button of his jeans and then pulled them down his legs. Claire wasn't sure this was what the nurses meant when they'd told her she could help, but she'd always loved giving Jasper head and he'd never failed to respond to the touch of her tongue. She wanted this moment to be special and memorable for both of them.

Seconds after she took him into her mouth, his hands found the back of her head and his fingers twisted through her hair as she felt his body begin to respond. She licked up his length, cupping his balls as she swirled her tongue around his delicious cock. It wasn't long before his breathing grew faster, deeper, and he reached his hand down to halt her efforts.

'Jar!' He uttered. 'Now.'

While he held still, Claire grabbed said jar, unscrewed the lid and handed it to him. As she watched his semen spurt into the little container, she beamed. This was it. They were really doing this and she couldn't be happier.

When they had a full jar of sperm, he claimed her mouth in a victorious kiss.

'Careful,' she said, pulling back and glancing down at their little pot of gold. 'Don't spill it.'

He laughed as she retrieved the lid and screwed it on tight. Neither of them could stop smiling down at it.

'Our baby could be in there,' she whispered, feeling as if she could burst with love for her husband and the child that was still barely more than a twinkle in his eye.

They left the room like a couple of teenagers who were sneaking out of the school store cupboard after getting up to no good. Except that everyone in this building knew exactly what they'd been getting up to. But they were too euphoric to be embarrassed.

'How long will Harper be?' Claire asked their nurse.

She glanced down at her purple fob watch. 'She must almost be in recovery. You can take a seat in the waiting room again and you'll be called up when she's okay for a visitor.'

'Thank you.' Jasper smiled, much more relaxed now, as he and Claire went off to wait.

It wasn't long before her phone beeped in her bag. She snatched it up and shrieked loudly when she saw it was from Harper. Jasper read over her shoulder:

We got 15 eggs. Apparently that's good and it sounds like a lucky number to me!

'Oh my God!' they exclaimed together like two kids in a candy store.

'What shall I say back?'

'Thank her and ask her how she's feeling,' he said.

That's wonderful. Thank you. How are you feeling? x

Aside from a little tenderness I feel fine. They've just given me some lovely sandwiches and a nice cup of tea.

Claire's own stomach rumbled at the message—until now, she'd been too strung up with nerves to eat anything.

Enjoy.

About fifteen minutes later, the nurse who'd taken Harper away came to collect them. 'Want to come keep Ms Drummond company in recovery?' she asked. 'It won't be long and she'll be able to go home.'

They found Harper sitting in a chair, still wearing a surgery gown, and sipping a cup of tea alongside a few other women. She looked up and grinned when Claire and Jasper approached.

Claire rushed to her side. 'Are you sure you're okay? Is there anything I can do or get for you?'

'Honestly I'm fine.'

Jasper shook his head good-naturedly at Claire. 'Don't mind her, she's a bit of a fusspot.'

'Hey!'

Harper laughed. 'I think being a fusspot is requirement number one for being a good mum. And I'm so excited for you. I know you'll both make fantastic parents.'

Claire's eyes prickled with tears at their donor's words and she tried but failed to swallow the lump that had formed in her throat. Unable to speak, she reached out and squeezed her new friend's hand.

At that moment, somewhere else in this building, Harper's fifteen ova were being placed into a petri dish with Jasper's sperm. In as little as twenty-four hours they would know whether fertilisation had been a success.

Chapter Fifteen

DECEMBER 2016

The doorbell rang. Harper wiped her hands on the apron she wore once in a blue moon and ran down the hallway to answer it.

'Merry Christmas Eve,' said Willow as Harper opened the door to find her sister and Miriam standing there in the most ridiculous Christmas t-shirts she'd ever laid eyes on.

'You're early,' she blurted.

'And you're covered in flour,' Willow said, throwing an arm around her sister in a hug. In the other hand she held a bottle of Baileys Irish Cream.

'Hi Harper. Merry Christmas.' Miriam smiled from over Willow's shoulder. She was holding a couple of large bags with presents poking out the top. 'Sorry we're so early, but this one said we might as well come over and start drinking the Christmas cheer.'

Harper laughed as she pulled back from her sister's embrace and then kissed Miriam on the cheek. 'That is the best idea I've heard all week. Come on. Get yourselves inside.'

Their early arrival was most welcome—perhaps they'd help take her mind off Claire and Jasper for a while. She'd thought she'd be able to move on after the egg retrieval, but while she didn't miss the daily injections, she still found herself thinking about her recipient couple frequently. Luckily *Afternoons with Harper* wrapped up for two weeks over the Christmas and New Year period, so her distracted state didn't affect her work.

She'd been trying to keep busy but no matter what she was doing, she found herself wondering about the embryo that had been transferred into Claire's uterus. Had it taken hold? The clinic had declared her PUPO—pregnant until proven otherwise—but Harper knew the odds were against them. The chances were that this first time wouldn't work and they'd need to use one of the other embryos that had been frozen. Although she wouldn't have to go through the process again unless all these embryos failed, she still felt anxious for Claire and Jasper who had buried their way into her heart.

She'd never imagined feeling this invested, but now wherever she went she saw pregnant women and hot air balloons. The oldest of their nieces and nephews were getting remote controlled hot air balloons for Christmas; she'd bought her mother-in-law some hot air balloon print tea towels for her collection; and she'd even bought Samuel a pair of gold hot air balloon cufflinks. Harper didn't know whether hot air balloons were in fashion this year or she'd simply never noticed how popular they were before now.

'Since when did you bake?' Willow asked as they entered the kitchen. The bench was covered in shortbread dough which Harper had cut into various shapes.

'Since I finished buying all the presents for Samuel's nieces and nephews and exhausted all my kind of shows on Netflix. I decided I could start watching them all over again or I could try and garner some festive cheer.'

Willow snorted. 'You're full of surprises lately, sister dear.' Then she glanced at Miriam. 'Harper doesn't like holidays from work. And she married The Grinch.'

'I did not,' Harper objected, trying not to smile at her sister's description of Samuel. But it was actually pretty close to the truth. She had her reasons for hating Christmas—as a child it had never been the exciting time it should be. Laura had never forked out for photos on Santa's lap and the only trees they ever had were the branches Harper and Willow dragged in from outside and decorated with the things they'd made at school. Christmas lunch was the same as any other lunch—generally it consisted of toasted cheese sandwiches that they had to make themselves.

On the other hand, Samuel's childhood Christmases were everything Harper imagined a family Christmas should be. Lots of delicious home-cooked food, a tree so big it took up most of the lounge room with presents spilling out from underneath it, carols playing on the stereo in the background and everyone mucking in and helping cook up a storm in the kitchen. Still, they only made the trek to his parents' place in Parramatta for Christmas every few years. Most Decembers they flew away to somewhere exotic to escape the festivities—somewhere with cocktails on tap—but this year Samuel hadn't wanted to take too much time off work and as they were in the country, they felt obliged to spend the day with his family.

'Speaking of surprises,' Willow said, retrieving three glasses from one of the kitchen cupboards, 'any news from Claire and Jasper yet?'

Harper glared at her sister as she started to put the trays of biscuits into the oven.

'What?' Willow exclaimed.

She sighed. 'No news. Claire's got a test scheduled for next week and to be honest, I'm struggling to think about anything else.'

'Think about how much worse it must be for them,' Miriam said, pulling out a stool at the breakfast bar and sitting herself down.

Harper nodded—she felt like she was in some kind of weird limbo place and could only imagine how anxious Claire and Jasper must be feeling. 'I know. We've exchanged a couple of text messages over the last week and she's sounding positive, but I hope she's not getting her hopes up.'

'I reckon it would be hard not to,' Miriam said. 'When my younger sister and her husband were trying to conceive a couple of years ago, she couldn't talk about anything else.'

'And she didn't have any fertility issues, did she?' Willow asked as she found ice in the freezer and proceeded to pour three glasses of Baileys.

'Nope. None. She got pregnant after two months of trying, but for those two months she was unbearable. I'm surprised my brother-in-law didn't divorce her.' Miriam chuckled. 'I must admit my resulting nephew is pretty damn cute though.'

'I'll toast to that.' Willow handed Harper and Miriam a glass. 'Shall we go out onto the deck to drink these?'

Harper glanced at the oven. 'Okay. But don't let me forget to come back in and get these out. I don't want my only contribution to Samuel's family Christmas lunch to be burnt biscuits.'

The others laughed.

'When will he be home?' Miriam asked as she slid off the stool and followed the sisters to the back door.

Harper glanced at her watch. 'I'm guessing anytime. They usually take an early mark and have a few post-work drinks on Christmas Eve, but everyone else will be eager to get home to their families.'

'Won't Samuel be eager to get home too?' Miriam asked.

'The Grinch, remember,' Willow said as they stepped out onto the deck. 'And he's a workaholic—he and Harper are perfectly matched. As are you and I.'

Miriam smiled at Willow with gooey eyes that made Harper smile as well. She was glad her sister finally seemed to have found the perfect woman.

'Oh, I should get some nibblies,' she exclaimed just as she was about to sit down on the wicker outdoor lounge. 'I really am a terrible host.'

Willow waved her hand. 'Don't worry about it. We can get some when we refill the drinks.'

'Or when we get your shortbread out of the oven,' Miriam suggested.

'Good plan.' Harper leant back in the seat and tried to relax. She looked to Miriam. 'So what do your family do for Christmas?'

'My folks are sort of beach bums, so our Christmases are usually spent eating seafood, swimming and playing cricket on the sand.'

'Beach bums!' Willow snorted. 'They have a mansion practically on Palm Beach.'

'Sounds like bliss,' Harper said.

Miriam's expression turned serious. 'Willow's told me a bit about your Christmases growing up, and having met your mum it's not hard to imagine. I'm sorry your childhood wasn't ideal. I guess I was lucky—but I just took it all for granted. Can't wait to take Willow to meet everyone tomorrow. She's already met Mum and Dad and my sisters of course, but all our extended family will be there for me to show her off. You know, you and Samuel are welcome to come up too if you like.'

'Thanks. We'll be at his parents' place for lunch but we'll think about driving up afterwards.'

'Driving up where?'

They all turned to see the man in question standing in the doorway, tugging off his tie as he surveyed the scene in front of him.

'Hey honey.' Harper smiled up at him. 'Miriam was just telling us about her parents' place in Palm Beach; she's invited us to visit tomorrow if we want.'

'Sounds good, but right now I'm going upstairs to get changed and then I'm coming down to join you in a drink. Back in a moment.'

While Samuel headed upstairs, Harper went inside to check on the biscuits. She saw her laptop closed on the bench and remembered they'd arranged to talk to their mother on Skype. Forgetting the shortbread, she went back outside.

'What time are we supposed to be Skyping Mum?'

Willow picked up her phone and glanced at the screen. 'If she got her time differences right, in fifteen minutes.' She sighed. 'You know, I'm not really in the mood to talk to her. We're having fun. Maybe we should be the ones to forget about her for a change?'

Remembering the number of times Laura had promised to come watch her at school assemblies and hadn't shown up, Harper was sorely tempted, but she knew she'd spend the rest of the night feeling guilty. 'I'll bring the laptop out here,' she said, heading back inside.

Five minutes later, Samuel had joined them and they'd refilled their glasses. The laptop was on the outdoor coffee table and Harper and Willow were sitting opposite it on one of the wicker couches.

'Remember, please don't say anything about what I'm doing for Claire and Jasper,' Harper said. 'She'll somehow find a way to make it about herself and I don't want to deal with her opinions.'

'Our lips are sealed,' Miriam said.

Emphasising the point, Willow pinched her thumb and index finger together and lifted them to her mouth and mimed doing exactly this.

Samuel didn't say anything but Harper knew he wouldn't mention it anyway. The tension that had come between them while she'd been preparing for the egg retrieval was gone now, but as far as he was concerned, the less said on that subject, the better.

'Thanks,' she said. 'Now, who's supposed to be calling who?'

'Let's call her and get it out of the way. If she doesn't answer, too bad; at least then we can say we tried.'

'You guys really don't like your mother, do you?' Miriam asked.

Samuel glanced down at his glass and swished the liquid around.

'It's not that we don't like her,' Willow said.

'Not exactly,' Harper added, just as Skype started buzzing on the screen.

'Oh my God, it's her. And on time. What is the world coming to?' Willow's finger shot forward to accept the call.

Seconds later their mother appeared on the screen wearing a knitted Christmas jumper that was ten times as ridiculous as the t-shirts Willow and Miriam had on.

'It's worked.' She clapped her hands and grinned at the screen. 'Mack, come and say Merry Christmas to my daughters.'

'Hi Laura,' Harper and Willow said at the same time as a tall, bald man in his early sixties appeared on the screen.

He grinned at them from the other side of the world and Harper noticed the smile lines around his eyes. 'Well, hello beautiful girls—so great to finally chat with you both. It's clear that you have your mother's good looks. Merry Christmas. I'm so sorry I'm keeping her from you this year.'

'We're just about managing without her,' Willow said sarcastically.

Harper elbowed her sister and stifled a smile. 'It's great to finally talk to you, Mack. Gorgeous house you have there.'

It looked like some kind of log cabin, with so much more warmth in the décor than any of the rental houses they'd grown up in. Then again, they'd moved so many times that Harper had lost count, and they'd certainly never stayed anywhere long enough for it to feel like home.

'You girls and your partners are welcome here anytime,' Mack said, wrapping an arm around their mother and dropping a kiss on the top of her head. 'Any friends or family of Laura's are friends and family of mine. Nothing more important than family in my opinion.'

Laura beamed up at him. 'I couldn't agree more. I miss you girls so much, but I've found my happy place here with Mack.'

Harper and Willow exchanged a look, their eyes boggling.

'Are Samuel and Martha there?' Laura asked. 'Let me and Mack say Hi.'

'It's *Miriam*, Mum,' Willow snapped.

'Hi, Laura,' Samuel and Miriam said together as they leant in from where they were both perched on opposite ends of the outdoor couch.

'Oh look at you all sitting there. What are you drinking?'

'Baileys,' Harper replied and took a much-needed sip. This was proving to be a very weird conversation.

'Mack's going to teach me how to make egg nog tomorrow night,' Laura said. 'What are you all doing for Christmas?'

They told them their plans and enquired after Laura and Mack's. It sounded like they had a whole host of people coming round to the ranch on Christmas Day. Harper just hoped Mack wasn't relying on their mother to cook the festive feast.

'So have you anything exciting to tell me?' Laura asked. 'What's happening in your worlds?'

'Samuel and I are just busy with work as usual,' Harper said.

'Ah yes.' Mack nodded. 'Your mother told me how famous you are in Australia and we worked out how to listen to your show online. I really enjoyed your interview with the ghost hunter.'

Harper chuckled, surprised and bemused by his comment. 'I wouldn't say I'm famous, but I'm glad you like the show.'

They talked for another half an hour, Mack asking questions of all of them, seemingly genuinely interested in their lives. Finally Samuel sniffed and said, 'Is something burning?'

'Shit!' Harper shot to a stand.

'We'd better be going anyway,' Laura said, 'but it's been lovely chatting. We must do it again soon. Have a lovely Christmas.'

As Willow shut the laptop, Harper raced into the kitchen and yanked open the oven, only to be greeted by belching smoke and a tray of blackened shapes.

Samuel came up beside her. 'Since when do you bake?' he asked, repeating Willow's earlier sentiment.

She glared at him, unsure whether to laugh or cry. 'I wanted to take something to your parents' tomorrow.'

His lips twisted into the smile that had given her butterflies that first day outside the courthouse. 'It's okay,' he said, pulling her close. 'I didn't marry you for your cooking skills and you know there'll be way too much food anyway. Now come on outside again and have a drink.'

She nodded and together they opened packets of crackers and cut up gourmet cheeses to take out onto the deck.

'Do we dare ask about the biscuits?' Miriam asked with a playful smile when they emerged.

Samuel made a face and shook his head dramatically.

Harper poked her tongue out at him and then plonked herself back down on the couch. 'So, Laura,' she said looking to Willow. 'What the heck is going on with her? I don't think I've ever seen her smile as much as she did tonight.'

'I know. Wonders never cease. I was certain she wouldn't last two weeks on some ranch. I felt sure that once Mack saw her true colours he'd send her back to Australia, but I have to admit she almost seems like a different person. I almost like her when she's over there.'

Harper laughed.

'From what you've told me,' Miriam said, leaning forward and popping some brie onto a cracker, 'your mother is the type of woman who needs a man to make her happy. I know that's no excuse for the way she neglected you two, but maybe she's finally found another person to bring out the best in her.'

'But what happens when he dumps her? Or worse, dies?' Willow asked.

Harper shuddered and shook her head. 'Let's not go there tonight. Let's just enjoy our own night together.'

And for the next few hours she managed to take her own advice, not once thinking about Jasper and Claire and whether or not they'd get their Christmas wish.

Chapter Sixteen

While Jasper slept soundly in the bed beside her, Claire crept across the room and into the ensuite. She closed the door behind her without making a noise and then clicked it locked, something she never ever did. But she was about to do something she'd promised her husband she wouldn't, hence her stealth-like behaviour. She opened the bathroom cupboard and retrieved the paper bag she'd hidden there yesterday. It crackled slightly when she removed the little box within and she froze, listening for sounds from the bedroom.

All she heard was the comforting noise of Jasper snoring.

Having read and memorised the instructions for the pregnancy test kit before hiding it, she didn't waste time going over them again. Her hand trembling a little, she took the stick out of the box and then lifted the lid off to reveal the strip of testing paper. Then she lowered her knickers, lifted her summer nightie, sat down on the toilet and peed as directed.

Once done, she recapped the stick and held her breath.

One blue line appeared immediately, telling her the test was functional, but she needed two.

The eleven days since the implantation of one of their fertilised embryos had been the longest eleven days of her life; she felt every little twinge in her breasts and her belly, praying they were pregnancy symptoms. She'd been a pain to live with—unable to focus or even talk about anything else except their possibility of parenthood—but she couldn't help it. It was hard to get into the Christmas spirit when all she could think about was whether or not she was pregnant.

Testing at home was against the clinic recommendations—they preferred to do a blood test to find out whether pregnancy had been achieved—but as the clinic was closed today *and* tomorrow on the days she'd be ready to test, she'd decided to take things into her own hands. Jasper had warned her strongly against doing so—worried about how she'd feel if they got a negative result on Christmas Day. Logically she agreed with him, but the thought of not knowing till after Boxing Day ...

Nope, that was way too long.

Yet, sitting on the edge of the toilet seat now, listening to the sounds of a crow welcoming the morning outside, time dragged. The days leading up to this moment felt like nothing compared to the two minutes of waiting she'd just done, and the hope she'd felt when she woke up began to fade. What had made her think that her stupid barren body would be able to handle an egg from someone else?

She blinked back tears as they formed in the corners of her eyes and was lifting her arm to hurl the blasted stick into the bin when she noticed that another line had appeared alongside the first thin blue one. Terrified she was hallucinating, she brought it closer to her face and her heart stopped beating as she registered what it meant.

There were definitely two lines. She was pregnant.

Oh my God!

Now the tears she'd been fighting seconds earlier broke free, pouring happiness down her cheeks. Clutching her good news in one hand, she yanked up her knickers with the other and slammed the lid down on the toilet seat, no longer caring about keeping quiet. If she were a more patient person, she might have taken a few moments to think of a wonderful and unique way to tell Jasper. But as patience had never been her virtue, Claire wiped her eyes on a towel then flung open the bathroom door and took a running leap onto the bed.

'What the hell!' Her husband woke with a start and looked up at her like she'd lost the plot.

'Santa came,' she exclaimed, holding up the positive pregnancy test right before his eyes. 'Merry Christmas, Daddy.'

'What?' He blinked, rubbed the sleep from his eyes and stared at the stick as if it were a UFO. 'Is that what I think it is?'

She nodded. 'Look! Two beautiful blue lines. We're pregnant!'

Jasper opened his mouth as if to say something, then closed it again. This happened a few more times, making her giggle, before he finally said, 'I thought you promised you wouldn't take a home test?'

She rolled her eyes. 'Forget that. We're pregnant!'

He took the little stick from her and held it up between them. 'Are you sure it's not too early?'

'These tests are as accurate as the doctor's ones these days. And today is the day Dr Ballantine would have done the blood test, so if this says I'm pregnant, then I am!' She couldn't keep the excitement from her voice.

'Well, then.' Slowly, his lips twisted up into a grin and he pulled her into a hug. 'I think this is the best Christmas present ever.'

'I agree.' She'd known he wouldn't be able to hold onto his irritation that she'd snuck behind his back. It had definitely been worth the risk.

'Oh, my God, Claire,' Jasper exclaimed as if it was only just dawning on him. 'I thought for sure it'd take a few times before we made a baby.'

They'd been told by the clinic that it could be a long road ahead, that it might take numerous attempts before they were successful. 'Me too,' she said, 'but this was obviously meant to be.' Rolling out of his embrace, she stretched over to the bedside table to collect her mobile.

'What are you doing?'

'We need to phone Harper. Let her know.'

'At this time of the morning?' Jasper exclaimed.

She gave him a look that told him it would be better to just go along with her craziness—she was pregnant and hormonal after all. 'It's after six. Besides, everyone gets up early on Christmas morning.'

Jasper chuckled. 'I suppose she did tell us to call her the moment we found out.'

Claire put the phone on speaker and held it between them as it dialled.

It rang four times before Harper picked up. 'Hello?'

'Hi Harper, it's Claire and Jasper.' Caller ID would have told her this but she sounded sleepy so Claire announced it just to be sure.

'Who is it?' came a strange deep voice.

'Go back to sleep,' Harper said. 'Hi guys. Merry Christmas.'

'It is indeed a Merry Christmas,' Jasper said, grinning at Claire.

'Isn't it just?' Claire replied.

They waited a moment for Harper to catch on.

'Oh my God,' she said, sounding suddenly much more awake. 'Are you trying to tell me something? Isn't it too early to know?'

'Claire has the patience of a small child. She took a home test just now.'

'And I'm pregnant!'

'Oh wow,' Harper said. She sounded a little choked up and took a moment to add, 'That's wonderful. I'm so happy I don't know what to say.'

They all half-laughed, half-cried for a few moments, then Claire said, 'I wish you lived closer so I could come around and give you a great big hug.'

'Me too,' Jasper added. 'We can't thank you enough.'

'It was my absolute pleasure. Maybe we could get together in the new year to celebrate.'

'That's a great idea,' Claire said. 'In fact, why don't you and Samuel come up to the Hunter Valley one weekend and we can give you a romantic hot air balloon ride? Well, Jasper can. I'm grounded for the time being.'

They all laughed.

'That would be wonderful,' Harper said.

Jasper leant closer to the phone. 'We'll let you go now, but thanks again and have a wonderful Christmas.'

'Yes, thank you,' Claire added. She could say those words a million times and it would still never be enough.

'Merry Christmas to you guys too,' Harper said, then disconnected.

Jasper and Claire snuggled back into the cushions for another hour—talking, fantasising about the future with their baby and marvelling at the miracle that Harper had given them. By next Christmas their lives would have changed irrevocably and they couldn't be more excited about the prospect. Although Claire wanted to fly up in a balloon and shout their news from the skies, Jasper convinced her otherwise.

'I'm as excited as you are,' he said, 'but you know I've always been a little superstitious. I don't want to take any risks by telling anyone until we're past the three month mark.'

'Not even Polly and Scotty?' Although she understood his reasoning, Claire didn't know if keeping this big a secret from her best friends was possible, especially when they knew about the egg donation.

Polly and Scotty were their only family that did. Everyone else knew about Claire's infertility, so they never asked when they were going to have children like strangers did.

'Can you at least wait until we've had the blood test confirmation?'

She sighed and smiled at him. 'I suppose I can try and learn a little patience.'

Chapter Seventeen

FEBRUARY 2017

'Rise and shine.' Harper chuckled at the role reversal as she silenced the alarm on her mobile phone. Apart from during a brief dalliance with breakfast radio years ago, Samuel had always got up earlier than she did. But not today.

When there wasn't so much as a blip in his deep sleep breathing, she switched on the bedside lamp and tried to shake him awake. 'Come on, get up! We have places to go, people to see.'

He groaned predictably. 'You're fucking kidding me. It must still be the middle of the night.'

Last night over dinner at a gorgeous little Italian restaurant, she'd told him she had a surprise for him in the morning and that he'd have to get up early, but they'd indulged in a few drinks and retreated to their little boutique hotel room and he'd obviously forgotten her warning.

'Not kidding at all.' She climbed out of bed, tugging the covers right off along with her, revealing Samuel's gorgeous naked body. Thanks to his daily early morning trips to the gym and his weekend bike rides, he was as toned and terrific as the day they'd met and he still sent her heart racing when she looked at him. But today there was no time for distractions. 'I'll have the first shower. Don't go back to sleep.'

Two minutes later he joined her in the ensuite. As she scrubbed her body, she heard him brushing his teeth and a few seconds later he pulled back the glass shower door and stepped in beside her. She glanced down and saw that he'd well and truly woken up. He hit her with a look she knew all too well and then dipped his head and claimed her mouth with his. Her breasts pressed against his hard chest and when something else firm of his pressed against her belly, she had to summon all her self-control not to give in.

'We don't have time for that,' she said, palming her hands against his chest before stepping past him and out of the shower.

'What's the point of getting up at this time of the day if I can't get my rocks off?'

She laughed. 'I promise you it'll be worth it. Now hurry up. We have to be there by five.'

'Where are we going? Can't you give me a clue?' he asked when they were in the car.

A few weeks ago she'd booked them a romantic getaway to the Hunter Valley and so last night when she'd mentioned the need to get up early, she'd felt certain he'd put two and two together. He knew her recipient couple lived in the Valley and that they were balloonists, so the fact he hadn't guessed they were going ballooning irked her a little, but she swallowed her irritation and shook her head. This weekend was about having fun and spending rare time together and she didn't want to spoil it with resentful thoughts. To be fair, she hadn't spoken about Claire and Jasper since telling Samuel the procedure had been a success—it had been easier not to—and he did have a lot of other things occupying his brain space.

Things at the firm seemed busier than ever and still no promotion to partner had been forthcoming.

'Try to relax and enjoy not being in control for once in your life,' she said, reaching out and squeezing his knee before putting her hand back on the steering wheel.

'It's hard to relax when you've banned me from checking my email,' he grumbled. He couldn't believe it when they'd arrived at their hotel last night and she told him she'd specifically chosen a place that didn't have wi-fi.

She laughed. 'It's not even daylight yet. I doubt you'll have anything too urgent, but if it makes you feel better we can schedule some screen time after breakfast.'

He sighed and then chuckled. 'When you put it that way ... Ah, maybe it is a good idea to totally detach from our work lives for a few days.' Then, as if to prove he meant it, he dug his mobile out of his pocket and switched it off.

'Wow, I'm impressed. Grab mine out of my bag and do the same.'

He did as she asked and they both laughed as if they'd done something terribly naughty. It was a rare and freeing feeling to know they couldn't be interrupted by anyone.

The GPS spoke, informing them they were almost at their destination, and a few moments later a balloon-shaped sign loomed up on one side of the road just before a gravel drive.

'We're here!' she announced, excited at the prospect of doing something unusual and adventurous but also at seeing Claire and Jasper again.

Samuel glanced out the window and pointed to the sign. 'Seriously? We're going up in a balloon?'

He sounded sceptical, but Harper couldn't quite tell whether it was the hot air ballooning or if he'd finally put two and two together and come up with Jasper and Claire.

She decided to plough on regardless. 'Surprise! I packed caps and jackets for us; they're in the back seat. Apparently it can get pretty cool up there,' she said as she turned off the road and followed another car towards some lights and a corrugated iron building up ahead.

'Are we meeting the couple you gave your eggs to?' he asked.

So he did remember. 'Yes, Claire and Jasper. They've offered to take us up in one of their balloons to say thanks. Haven't you always wanted to go hot air ballooning?'

'Can't say I've ever given it much thought.'

'You're not scared, are you?' she asked as she parked in front of a large shed with Big Basket Ballooning painted across it in bold, bright letters. Spotlights shone from either side onto the name so you could read it in the dark.

'Don't be ridiculous,' he said. 'I just think it's a bit weird hanging out with the people you donated your eggs to.'

'I don't see why. They're nice people. And haven't we been meaning to get away for a weekend forever?'

The expression on Samuel's face suggested he wasn't sure a ride in a hot air balloon counted.

'We'll only be with them for a couple of hours this morning,' she said. 'After breakfast we'll hit the wineries and tonight we can enjoy a quiet dinner back at the hotel.' She thought the lure of good wine would put a smile on his face and it did.

'All right then. Let's do this.' And with that, Samuel leant into the back seat and retrieved the caps and jackets she'd packed.

Letting out a puff of breath that he hadn't kicked up a fuss, Harper climbed out of the car.

'How many other people are doing this?' Samuel said, glancing at the cars pulling up alongside theirs.

She shrugged. 'No idea, but Jasper told me they're pretty much fully booked all year round.'

He shook his head slightly as if he couldn't quite comprehend the popularity and together they headed towards the building.

There was already a crowd of excited people inside, but Claire and Jasper sought them out almost immediately.

'Harper!' Claire let go of Jasper's hand and threw her arms around her.

In contrast to the intense period of frequent contact leading up to the procedure, over the last couple of months they'd merely exchanged a couple of text messages. As she returned Claire's hug, Harper realised she'd actually missed her. She pulled back and took a good look.

'You look fabulous,' she exclaimed. Although Claire wasn't showing yet, she definitely looked pregnant. Her skin positively glowed and her smile was—if possible—even wider than Harper remembered.

'Thank you. I feel fabulous,' Claire said as Jasper jokingly nudged her out of the way.

'My turn. It's great to see you, Harps.' He kissed her on the cheek and then turned to Samuel standing beside her. 'And you must be Samuel. I'm Jasper and this is Claire. Great to finally meet you.'

He held out his hand and Samuel shook it, glancing around at the photos and memorabilia as he replied. '*Interesting* business you've got here.'

Jasper laughed, thankfully not sounding at all offended by Samuel's condescending tone. 'It keeps us busy. Did you guys have a good drive up last night?'

Samuel nodded and the boys embarked on a little small talk about city driving versus country and the boutique hotel they were staying at.

Meanwhile, Claire spoke to Harper. 'We've just started telling our friends and family, so Jasper's parents want to come over and meet you. Do you mind?' Claire's hand drifted protectively to her stomach, but the gesture didn't annoy Harper in the way it sometimes did on other women. Instead she felt a lovely warmth inside at the knowledge she'd helped this woman achieve a dream.

'Of course not,' she replied. 'I can't wait to meet them.'

'You're lucky my parents aren't here as well, or you'd be at risk of being hugged to death,' Claire added. 'My parents are ecstatic about the prospect of another grandchild—especially my mum. We only just told them about the baby and she's already maxed out their credit cards buying stuff.'

Harper laughed as Jasper clapped his hands together.

'Right,' he said. 'Let's go say a quick hi before we head off to the launch site. It'll be good to get out of here before Dad goes through the safety spiel with these guys, but I'll fill you two in on our way.'

'We're not going with them?' Samuel asked, nodding towards the gathered crowd.

Claire shook her head. 'Jasper and I are treating you two to a private romantic flight—well, as romantic as it can be with Jasper chaperoning.'

They laughed and then Jasper grabbed hold of Claire's hand again. Harper and Samuel followed them over to a middle-aged woman holding a clipboard and ticking off names. She paused in the task and stepped away from their paying passengers, her eyes lighting up as she laid them on Harper.

'Harper and Samuel, I'd like you to meet my mum, Wendy.' Jasper didn't say anything more than this, but the smile on the older woman's face said she knew exactly who they were.

'Oh, it's so lovely to meet you both. I hope you'll enjoy your hot air balloon ride.'

'We're very much looking forward to it,' Harper said, as a tall man stepped up beside Wendy and put an arm around her shoulder.

Jasper introduced his father Paul, but there wasn't time for small talk as Paul and Wendy had to get back to their passengers. Then, still holding Claire's hand, he led Harper and Samuel outside and into the adjoining shed. Harper tried to remember the last time they'd held hands in public. Had they ever? But the way Jasper and Claire frequently touched each other warmed her heart and reinforced her feelings that she'd chosen the right couple to give her gift to.

After a quick visit to the rest rooms, they piled into a four-wheel drive with a trailer that carried the balloon and the wicker basket. As they drove out of the balloon base and down dirt roads to their launch site, Samuel asked Claire and Jasper about the mechanisms of ballooning. Harper smiled as she listened to the answers, happy that he seemed to be enjoying himself.

'How do you choose where to take off and when to land?'

'It's all down to the weather,' Claire explained. 'We watch the weather and monitor the winds before a flight. Jasper went out earlier this morning and let out a few testing balloons. It's perfect ballooning weather today.'

'We can never guarantee exactly where we'll land,' Jasper added, glancing into the rear-view mirror, 'but we *can* guesstimate and Claire will chase us on the ground anyway.'

'So you land pretty much anywhere?' Samuel asked. Harper could practically see his brain contemplating the legal ramifications.

Claire and Jasper laughed.

'Yes and no,' she said.

'Most of the landowners around here know us and we have their permission to land as long as we respect their crops, stock and vines. Balloonists occasionally have an unscheduled landing, but most folks don't have a problem with it,' Jasper elaborated.

'Especially if we offer them a free ride from time to time,' added Claire with a smile.

After a discussion of ballooning safety—which seemed mostly common sense—and more questions from Samuel about the exotic places their hosts had flown, they arrived at their destination.

Claire got out of the four-wheel drive and opened the gate to what looked like a paddock in someone's farm. It was still dark, so Jasper kept the headlights on while he got out and unhooked the trailer, then he turned the vehicle around so they illuminated the trailer.

'Give us a hand unloading the basket, will you mate?' Jasper asked, looking to Samuel.

For a moment Samuel looked a little flummoxed—Harper had forgotten to mention that part of the ballooning experience was helping set up and pack up at the other end.

After the men had finished unloading the trailer, Harper decided she couldn't just stand around like a spare part. She wanted to experience the whole shebang, so she and Samuel followed Jasper's instructions, helping him get the basket on its side and rolling the balloon envelope out in front of it.

'It's a lot bigger than I imagined,' Samuel noted, his tone full of wonder.

She smiled and nodded her agreement, happy that her husband seemed to be getting caught up in the excitement. Hopefully meeting Jasper and Claire and seeing what wonderful people they were would make Samuel think more favourably about what she'd done for them.

Once the balloon was laid out on the ground, they set up two big fans in front of the basket and Jasper instructed her and Samuel to hold one side of the balloon up a little as he began to propel air into it. Even though this wasn't physically hard work, he refused to let Claire in on the action, so she stood on the side commenting.

'We fill the balloon mostly with cool air to start with and then once it's about three-quarters blown up, we start with the hot air.'

By the time they got to that part, the sun was slowly rising over the horizon and the local wildlife were waking up, with bird calls just audible over the noise of the generator.

Claire took out her phone and snapped a few shots of Harper and Samuel in action.

'Thanks,' Harper said. She didn't want to get her phone out and interrupt the magic of this experience, but it would be nice to have the memories later.

Finally, after about half an hour of cold and occasionally hot air being pumped into the balloon, Jasper announced it was time to get it off the ground. Harper and Samuel helped him turn the basket off its side. Although it was now upright, ropes pegged to the dirt kept it grounded.

Harper gazed up at the massive balloon, transfixed.

'Now comes the fun part,' Claire said as Jasper climbed into the basket and then delivered another burst of hot air skyward. 'Harper, you climb in first. Samuel, wait till she's in position and then you go.'

They did as instructed, and Claire began unhooking the ropes. Harper's pulse began to race. Usually she just listened to other people describe their adventures, so getting to experience one first-hand was magic. She could only imagine the excitement of the very first balloonists.

'Careful, Claire,' Jasper instructed, his tone anxious.

'Stop being a stress head,' she replied.

He shrugged. 'Sorry, can't help it.'

Claire had confided to Harper earlier that ever since the positive pregnancy test, Jasper had been treating her as if she were made of china. Apparently he felt a little anxious that they'd had such a smooth run, but Claire believed it only proved this baby was meant to be, and Harper agreed.

'I'm pregnant, not an invalid,' Claire said. 'I've done this a million times before. Just focus on our guests, please.'

Jasper laughed and looked to Samuel. 'Do you get bossed around like this too?'

Although Samuel chuckled and nodded in agreement, Harper knew he only did so to be polite. They never bossed each other around—not even in jest. Samuel didn't have much of a sense of humour but she'd fallen in love with his other attributes. After the sexual attraction that had sparked their relationship—and still blazed between them—she'd fallen in love with his intelligence, his ambition and of course the fact that he was on the same page as her regarding having a family.

'All done. Have fun. I'll see you soon.' Claire stepped back and waved as Jasper directed another shot of hot air up into the balloon and it lifted a few feet off the ground.

Harper waved down at Claire as they slowly floated upwards. For a little while, none of them said anything—Jasper did his thing, letting them watch in awe as the beautiful Hunter Valley passed beneath them, the rising of the sun painting a spectacular backdrop.

As she gazed down, Harper tried to recall ever doing anything quite so relaxing before. She hadn't known what it would be like and had even wondered if she'd be scared being so high up in the sky, but it was impossible to be scared when she felt so full of wonder and awe. Something flipped inside her when she glanced across to Samuel and he grinned back at her. A happy contentment that she hadn't felt in a while bubbled within her. Part of it was to do with what she'd done for Jasper and Claire, but now she realised that another part was down to being up here, experiencing something so special with her husband. They smiled at each other for a few long moments and she made a silent vow to try and spend more time together.

In the busyness of their lives she'd forgotten how much they enjoyed each other's company. Sure they loved their jobs—their careers were important—but what was the point of being married if they didn't love each other more?

The sound of dogs beneath them jolted Harper's eyes from Samuel. Once again she looked down to the land below. She laughed as they crossed over a town and dogs ran crazily around backyards barking up at the sky.

'Bet the people in those houses get annoyed by you flying overhead,' she commented. 'You'd think the dogs would be used to balloons flying overhead by now.'

Jasper chuckled. 'I think dogs have short memories, but we also don't travel the same flight path every day, so we annoy *different* dogs.'

'How high up are we?' Samuel asked, still peering down over the edge of the basket.

'Right now? About two-and-a-half thousand feet, but it varies—we go anywhere from fourteen hundred to five thousand feet depending on the weather.'

'And do you always fly at sunrise?'

'Pretty much. Although we do the occasional sunset flight. The winds are calmer at these times. As the sun warms the earth, thermals occur and the winds increase, which can make landing more difficult.'

While Jasper and Samuel chatted about the instruments used to monitor ascending and descending, Harper simply enjoyed the feeling of doing something so outside their normal lives. She still wanted to get Jasper and/or his dad on her show, but she couldn't imagine how he could possibly convey to her listeners the actual experience of flying a hot air balloon. Until she was up in the air, she'd had no idea it would be like this. Although she knew they were moving, it actually felt like the earth was scrolling by beneath them and they were motionless. It was magic and she could stay up here forever.

Unfortunately, not long after thinking this, Jasper pointed out Claire and the four-wheel drive waiting in a paddock a little way off. She glanced at her watch and couldn't believe they'd been up in the air almost an hour.

They descended quickly and Jasper reminded them to bend their knees and hold onto the handles inside the basket as he brought the balloon back down to earth. It hit the ground and then bounced up and along again three more times before they finally came to rest.

'That was amazing,' Harper said, straightening again.

Jasper grinned. 'That was a pretty smooth landing. Glad you guys liked it.'

'Loved it, mate, thanks.' Samuel clapped their host on the shoulder and grinned in a way he hadn't in a long while. In fact, Harper couldn't remember her husband ever wearing such a full and natural smile.

Claire pulled up in the four-wheel drive and leapt out. 'How was it?' she asked, excitedly.

Samuel and Harper replied in unison: 'Bloody marvellous,' and 'I want to do it again. Right now.'

Claire laughed as she began to grab the ropes to secure them to the ground. 'That's exactly how I felt after my first flight.' She looked to Jasper, who was anxiously watching her work. 'We might have a couple of new recruits.'

Once the balloon was grounded again, Jasper instructed Samuel and then Harper to disembark and then he finally climbed out. Packing up didn't take quite so long as setting up had, but it was a skilled process. They flattened the deflated balloon envelope out along the ground and then Samuel and Harper helped Jasper roll it in at the edges as he folded it up from the base. She and Samuel marvelled at Jasper's skill in being able to fit the massive balloon back into its plastic covering.

'I can't even put a sleeping bag back into its casing,' Samuel admitted, and Harper knew he was thinking of the one disastrous time they'd agreed to go camping with his massive family.

'It's a skill,' Jasper said, 'but practice definitely makes perfect.'

'Usually after a flight we take our passengers to a gorgeous little café overlooking the river,' said Claire once the balloon and basket were back on the trailer and they were piling into the four-wheel drive, 'but we'd like to invite you back to our place where we won't be distracted by the group that went up with Mum and Dad this morning. Is that okay with you?'

'That sounds lovely,' Harper said.

'Thank you,' Samuel added. 'I'm starving.' Then he shuffled over a little in the back seat, wrapped his arm around Harper's shoulder and kissed her cheek. She snuggled into him, surprised but happy about his rare public display of affection.

Jasper drove them back to the airfield where they collected the Audi and then followed him back to his and Claire's place. Theirs was a relatively new house on about an acre of land and the garden looked like something out of the Chelsea Flower Show.

'Oh my goodness,' Harper exclaimed as they walked towards the house. 'You weren't kidding about Claire being a green thumb.'

Jasper smiled at his wife, pride and adoration shining from his face. 'There's not much Claire isn't good at.'

'Oh, stop.' Claire blushed. 'Come on inside. Samuel is hungry.'

They laughed again—Harper had lost track of the number of times the four of them had done so—and followed Claire into the house, which was as bright and cheerful as the garden outside. The walls were all white but broken up with massive floral paintings in frames and the furniture was colourful and funky. It was easy to imagine kids' toys strewn across these floors and drawings stuck to the fridge.

Jasper and Claire led them into a country style kitchen with a table in the middle of the room and two fat orange cats sitting on top of it.

'Gerry! Sunny!' Claire scolded as she went across to lift them off. 'Sorry about these two. I've told them time and time again that they're not allowed on the table, but they refuse to be trained.'

Harper smiled. 'Don't worry about it.'

As Claire dumped the cats on the floor, Samuel stepped towards them and held out his hand. 'Here kitties,' he said, rubbing his fingers together.

Both animals gave him a look of disgust and then turned and stalked from the room, their tails swishing in the air behind them.

Jasper chuckled. 'Take no offence. Those two rarely like anyone. Now, take a seat and make yourselves at home.' He gestured to the table that was already set for breakfast as Claire turned to switch on the oven.

'I made some blueberry muffins yesterday,' she said, 'but I'll just warm them up a bit. They taste better that way.'

Jasper went across to her, put his hands on her shoulders and steered her towards one of the seats. 'I'll do that. You just sit down a bit and let me look after our guests.'

The way he treated Claire was so cute and made Harper wonder if Samuel would be as over-protective with her if she were carrying their child. Of course that was a moot point, so she put it from her mind.

'How do you guys like your eggs?' he asked as he lifted his hands from his wife's shoulders. 'As well as Claire's delicious muffins, we've got some local bacon and eggs to cook.'

'I like my eggs cooked by someone else,' Samuel said. 'Harper and I aren't all that skilled in the kitchen.'

'Hey,' she exclaimed, pretending to be annoyed. 'I do a mean beans on toast.'

Samuel laughed, then looked to Jasper. 'We eat out a lot.'

'Is there anything I can do to help?' Harper asked, then realised how silly that sounded after Samuel had just declared them incompetent cooks.

'No, you guys just relax. Can I get you some juice or coffee while you wait?'

They decided on coffee since they'd been up since before dawn, and while Jasper worked wonders at the stove, Claire, Samuel and Harper sat at the table talking over the balloon experience. Samuel surprised her by asking further questions and also by the way he truly seemed to be enjoying the time with Claire and Jasper. They didn't associate much with other couples—she had her own friends and Samuel occasionally went out with his pals from law school—so this was a new but fun experience for them. Her husband acted differently around other men than he did when they were alone—a little more blokey—and she quite liked it.

When Jasper had finished cooking up a storm, he laid everything out on the table and then retreated to the fridge and conjured a bottle of champagne.

'It's the tradition of ballooning that we drink champagne after a flight,' he said as he popped it open, 'but today we also have something else very special to celebrate and there's no one we'd rather do so with than you two.'

'Yes.' Claire sniffed and then beamed. 'Thank you both so much for coming up to spend the morning with us. It was a pleasure to share a little bit of our world with you.'

'Thanks for taking us up today,' Samuel said. 'I must admit, I was dubious when Harper told me what we were doing but I enjoyed it way more than I imagined.'

Claire smiled. 'Ballooning is like that. You can't understand the magic until you've actually experienced it.'

'It's a wonderful thing that Harper has done for us,' Jasper said as he began to fill the glasses. 'And we want to thank you as well, for supporting her in her decision.'

He handed each of them a crystal flute filled with golden bubbles.

Samuel shrugged as he took the glass. 'Well, *we* don't want her eggs, so someone else may as well have them.'

Harper cringed a little at his tone. Thankfully it appeared nothing could wipe the joy from their hosts' faces.

Jasper passed a flute of orange juice to Claire and then raised his own glass in a toast. 'To Harper and Claire—the most amazing women I know.'

'To Harper and Claire,' Samuel echoed, a bemused expression on his face as he lifted his glass.

'And to you and our baby,' Claire added.

Following the toast, conversation moved on from ballooning—Jasper enquired about Samuel's job, while Harper asked Claire if she'd experienced any morning sickness.

'Only a little, but it'll all be worth it in the end,' she said, placing a hand against her belly.

Long ago, Harper had experienced a bit of morning sickness herself, but she hadn't been so positive about it—in fact, having to keep rushing off to hurl into the toilet bowl during her lectures had only confirmed that her decision was the right one. She resented the nausea and was scared she'd also resent the child.

'So have you started getting organised for the baby?'

'Jasper wouldn't let me until we got to the three month mark,' Claire replied with a good-natured roll of her eyes, 'but now we have, it's full steam ahead. We're going shopping this week to start looking at the bigger items for the nursery and to choose paint.'

'What colour do you think you'll choose?' Harper asked.

'I'm tossing up between yellow—which is my favourite colour—and this gorgeous mint green I saw in a magazine.'

'And will you find out the baby's gender?'

Although Harper had mostly asked out of politeness, she found she didn't mind talking about their baby plans.

'We've decided on a surprise,' said Jasper, clearly just as excited as his wife.

It wasn't long before Samuel's eyes started to glaze over. Wanting him to remember today as an enjoyable experience, Harper decided it was time to make a move.

She glanced at her watch. 'Thank you so much for the flight and for this wonderful breakfast, but we should probably be heading off. We have a long list of wineries to get through today.'

'You must visit Petal Wines,' Claire said, pushing back her seat to stand. 'They have the most amazing range based on local flora.'

'Wow, sounds great,' Harper said.

Although she and Samuel offered to help with the dishes, Claire and Jasper wouldn't allow it and instead walked them to the front door to see them off.

This time Samuel took the wheel, and as he drove off down the driveway, Harper looked back over her shoulder at Claire and Jasper standing close together on the verandah. She probably wouldn't see them again till after the baby was born and that made her a little sad.

'So, do you think I chose the right people?' she asked, turning to look at Samuel.

He chuckled. 'What kind of question is that? How the hell would I know?'

'You liked them, didn't you?'

'Of course I like them,' he said. 'They're different to the people we usually socialise with and I had thought it might be a little weird, knowing that Claire is pregnant with your egg. But I barely even thought about it. They were fun, the flight was fun, but the best part of it all was hanging out with you. And I must admit, I'm glad to have you all to myself again.'

Chapter Eighteen

JULY 2017

'Hey, honey, I'm heading off now,' Claire called into the shed as she spun her car keys on her finger.

Jasper leapt up from the floor where he'd been working on the burner from one of the balloons and came over to her. He put his hands on her arms and frowned. 'Are you sure you're okay to go on your own?' He glanced back at his dad and the mess of tools and balloon parts strewn across the shed. 'I could probably spare a couple of hours and come with you.'

'No.' She shook her head. 'You're needed here.'

They had their annual visit from the Civil Aviation Safety Authority tomorrow and although they didn't predict any problems, Jasper and Paul were going over everything today, making sure it was all in top-notch condition. Besides, she was looking forward to having a few hours with her mum in Newcastle to browse for baby clothes.

'I don't know.' He sighed and ran a hand through his hair, still looking uncertain.

'Well, I do,' she said firmly. 'This isn't a scan or a blood test; it's just a routine check-up—I'll probably be in and out the doctor's office within five minutes. And Mum's coming up and we're having lunch and going shopping, remember?'

The mention of shopping did the trick. As much as Jasper loved her mum, he couldn't hide his terror. Although excited when they went shopping for big ticket items like their pram and cot, he bored quickly when looking at clothes—even if they were the cute and tiny variety—and he knew that when she was with her mum they were likely to shop for hours. She laughed, stretched up onto her tippy toes and kissed him on the lips.

He grinned goofily at her when they broke apart. 'How come you're so pretty?'

Although inside she glowed at his words, she shook her head and rolled her eyes. 'I'll see you this arvo,' she told him, before waving at her father-in-law and walking out to her car.

As she turned her favourite radio station up to maximum and started towards the main road, Claire felt like a kid playing hooky. Drives completely on her own like this were few and far between and she couldn't wait for some girl-time with her mum. That was the only downside of living in the Hunter—she didn't get to catch up with her parents nearly as much as she would like. As she drove, she fantasised about what they'd do together after the appointment. First on the list was treating themselves to brunch at her favourite café. And then they'd hit the shops until her feet failed her. Maybe they'd even indulge in a little pedicure pampering.

'Be prepared for a work out, Mr Visa,' she said, chuckling to herself as she danced her fingers on the steering wheel in time to the music. On the way home, she'd hopefully be in time to tune into Harper's radio show. Their contact was now sporadic—only the occasional text message to check in—but she'd found she enjoyed listening to *Afternoons with Harper* as much as Jasper and Paul did.

The forty-five minute drive to the city flew by and Claire scored a perfect car spot not far from the offices of her obstetrician. She practically skipped towards the building and was delighted to see her mother waiting for her just outside.

'Mum!' she exclaimed as she rushed over and threw her arms around her. 'Thank you so much for coming up.'

They hugged tightly.

'It's my pleasure, my sweet girl,' Joanne said. When they pulled apart she gazed down at Claire's stomach. 'My! You've doubled in size since the last time I saw you.'

Claire groaned. 'I know. I can't believe I might still have ten weeks until I pop. I'm huge.'

'Huge but gorgeous,' said her mum, linking her arm through Claire's. 'Shall we go in?'

Claire nodded and they entered the reception area filled with other pregnant women sitting flicking through magazines as they waited.

'How's Dad?' Claire asked as she picked up a copy of *My Child* and rested it on her growing bump.

'He's great. Was jealous of me coming up to see you today. He wanted to come but I told him we were going shopping and he changed his mind pretty damn quick. The only thing he's ever been interested in shopping for is books.'

Claire laughed. 'Jasper was the same. This is the first appointment he's missed and he felt bad about me driving *all* the way to Newcastle by myself. Honestly, since I've been pregnant, he wants to wrap me up in cotton wool. The shopping turned him off though.' She leant into her mother. 'As much as I love them, I'm so glad to spend some one-on-one time with you.'

'I know, me too.' Joanne wrapped her arm around Claire and pulled her close. 'I can't believe my baby is actually having a baby.'

'Sometimes I still pinch myself,' Claire said. 'I can't believe what I always thought impossible is actually coming true.'

Before Joanne could reply, the midwife called Claire's name and beckoned her into the consulting room. As she wasn't having an ultrasound, her mum stayed in the waiting room.

'Please don't tell me how much I've put on,' Claire pleaded as she stepped onto the scales and turned her head so she couldn't see the result. Getting fat was the only part she wasn't particularly enjoying about pregnancy, but she'd been ravenous these past few months and didn't want her baby to go hungry because she was a little vain. Anyway, her reading told her that most women lost weight while breastfeeding, and if it didn't work for her, well, she'd worry about that later.

The midwife chuckled. 'You have nothing to worry about, love.'

Five minutes after the midwife announced that Claire was in good health and released her back into the waiting room, it was her turn to see the doctor.

'Claire Lombard,' called her obstetrician from the doorway of her office.

She handed her mum the magazine she'd been flicking through and stood.

'Hi, Dr Manera,' she said with a smile. When they'd first met, the woman's close-cut grey hair and sharp-edged glasses had given the impression she was stern and not very friendly, but the moment the doctor had opened her mouth and introduced herself, Claire had realised otherwise. Her bedside manner was very kind and gentle.

'No Jasper today?' the doctor asked as she closed the door.

'Unfortunately he's busy with work. We have our annual aviation safety check tomorrow, but he'll be here next time.'

'Not a worry. Tell him I said hi. I've decided I'm going to book me and my husband in for a flight for his sixtieth birthday.'

'That's a wonderful idea,' Claire said. 'And of course we'll give you a discount.'

'We'll see about that.' Dr Manera smiled as she sat down at her desk and opened Claire's patient file. 'Now, thirty weeks. That's flown by, hasn't it?'

'Has it?' Claire laughed. 'Sometimes I feel like I'm *never* going to meet my baby.'

'First pregnancies do sometimes tend to drag, but you should enjoy it. Next time round, you'll be run off your feet looking after this one. Now, my midwife's notes say you're very healthy and so unless you have any worries or questions, I'll just do a quick physical examination and then you can go. Have you got anything else on while you're in Newie?'

'My mum's come up from Sydney for the day and we're going to do a bit of shopping together,' Claire said as she climbed onto the examination table and lifted her top.

'Ooh, splendid. I love a little retail therapy.' Dr Manera rubbed her hands together to warm them up as she always did before laying them on Claire's bare skin.

'Are you feeling much movement?' she asked as she pressed firmly around her abdomen.

'Yes.' Claire nodded and smiled affectionately at her bump. 'This one's a night owl. I get the odd kick during the day, but the moment I lay my head on the pillow at night he or she starts going crazy.' Many nights she'd woken Jasper when the baby started kicking and they'd lain there, spooned together in the dark, his hands resting on her stomach as they marvelled at the miracle inside her. The baby might not be biologically hers, but she would be its mother in all the ways that mattered. She already felt an intense love for her little boy or girl.

'I won't tell you the theory that whenever the baby is awake in uterus is also when it'll be awake when it's born then.'

But nothing Dr Manera said could lessen Claire's excitement. She'd eagerly taken the oestrogen tablets to build her lining up for pregnancy and had not even blinked an eye at having to insert progesterone pessaries vaginally in the lead-up to the embryo transfer. *Nothing* could put a dampener on this! She couldn't wait for their baby to be born, just as she couldn't wait to hit the shops and stock up on those ridiculously cute little jumpsuits. As if specifically for her, Bonds had just released a floral range—she'd been eyeing the yellow ones online last night.

Next the doctor checked the baby's heartbeat and Claire grinned from ear to ear as she listened to the thump-thump-thump from the little speakers.

'Nice and strong,' Dr Manera said, putting away her wand and pulling down Claire's top again. 'Your fundal height is measuring well for thirty weeks and the baby is in a good position. I don't need to see you for another four weeks. After that we'll go down to fortnightly appointments. Now, you enjoy your shopping.'

'Thanks. We will.' Claire said goodbye to the obstetrician, made an appointment with the receptionist and then she and her mother went outside.

'Oh no.' Joanne grimaced as she looked up at the sky. 'What happened to this morning's beautiful weather?'

When they'd arrived the weather had perfectly matched Claire's sunny mood, but now grey clouds loomed in the overcast sky. Rain looked imminent but nothing could dampen Claire's joy. She wasn't going to let a little bad weather dampen her special day with her mum.

'Don't worry—we'll be inside eating and then shopping. Come on.' She grabbed her mum's hand and started towards her car. They'd agreed to leave one car in the hospital car park while they shopped.

Fifteen minutes later she was placing their order at a local café while her mum popped into the rest room.

'Thank you.' Claire took her card back from the lady behind the counter and then went to choose a table. It wasn't an accident that the place she chose happened to be next to a couple of women with prams. She gazed into them and they caught her looking.

'Your babies are gorgeous,' she said.

They thanked her then one of them nodded towards her belly. 'When are you due?'

Claire tried to suppress her smile as her hands drifted down to lovingly caress her bump. 'September 11,' she told them, feeling as if she were part of a club she'd never imagined she'd be granted membership to.

'Ooh, a spring baby,' said one of them.

'And you'll never forget that date,' said the other.

This woman wasn't the first person to comment on this. Some people thought having a birthday on the historic date that had changed America—and thus the world—forever was a bad omen, but others believed it would be nice to have something happy to celebrate on such a date. Claire was of the latter thinking, but then again, how often were babies actually born on their due date?

After a few more moments of small talk, her mum arrived and the two women turned back to their babies. They passed a few minutes talking about her brother Tim and his family and then a waitress delivered two massive hamburgers to the table.

Joanne's eyes widened as she gazed at them. 'There goes my diet,' she said with a laugh.

'You don't need to diet, Mum, you're gorgeous just as you are.' Claire devoured her burger and a vanilla milkshake quickly, and then sat back talking while her mum finished hers.

Midway through a conversation about Tim's little boy Theo's upcoming second birthday party, her phone beeped with a message. She slipped it from her handbag and glanced down at the screen, warmth spreading through her body as she read Jasper's message:

Hey gorgeous. How's our little bundle going? x

'Sorry, Mum, just gonna reply to Jasper.' And she smiled.

Dr Manera said we are both healthy and the baby is a good size for thirty weeks. I've just had lunch and am about to hit the shops. XO

So that's why my back pocket is suddenly hurting! Have fun. X

She laughed as she put the phone back on the table.

Joanne wiped her mouth with a paper serviette and then gestured out the window. 'I think we should hit the shops before the storm arrives. I don't want you driving home in that.'

'Nor me you,' Claire said as she saw that the clouds outside had turned even darker.

Soon they were browsing the baby section at David Jones, their arms laden with tiny outfits. Claire was in heaven. Polly had warned her not to go over the top because they'd get more than enough clothes as presents, but Claire couldn't help herself. And nor could her mum.

'You don't know what you're having then?' asked the older woman behind the counter as she rang up all their purchases.

'No, we want a surprise,' Claire replied.

The woman nodded. 'Best way, I reckon. In my day, no one had the option and it was always a lovely surprise at the end of all that pushing.'

Claire laughed—not even scary stories about painful labours could dampen her mood.

They left the department store and continued into other smaller shops, browsing and adding to their purchases until neither of them could carry even one more bag. Due to the weather and Joanne's eagerness for them both to be getting home, they bypassed a pedicure and Claire took her mum back to collect her car instead.

'Thanks for coming up today,' she said as she hugged her goodbye.

'The pleasure was all mine, sweetheart,' Joanne said as she stepped out of Claire's car into the pouring rain. 'Text me when you get home, okay?'

Claire nodded. 'You too.' Sydney drivers always seemed to go a little crazy in a storm.

She waited until her mum was safely in her own car before driving off. As she began to navigate the traffic to the main road, she was almost bouncing in her seat with eagerness to show Jasper everything they'd bought. She was even excited about the prospect of washing all the little outfits and putting them in the nursery in readiness.

'You really are a hopeless case,' she said to herself with a chuckle.

She was on the Expressway heading towards the Hunter Valley, lost in a fantasy about how she was going to fit all the stuff she'd bought into the baby's drawers, when she blinked.

A car was coming towards her from the other direction. And it was travelling *fast*. Way too fast.

Horror drenched her in an icy sweat. Instinctively, she spun the steering wheel to get out of its way.

Am I on the wrong side of the road?

That was Claire's last thought before the other vehicle slammed into her and everything went black.

Chapter Nineteen

'Good morning,' Harper almost sang as she handed Lilia the takeaway coffee. It was her day to bring drinks. 'Did you have a good weekend?'

Lilia raised an eyebrow as she took the cardboard cup and leant back in her swivel seat. 'Sounds like not as good as you. Your smile is blinding me.'

Harper laughed, dropping her bag to the floor as she plonked into her seat. 'It *was* quite a lovely weekend. Samuel finally got promoted to partner on Friday and we've been in celebration mode ever since.'

'Oh wow!' Lilia leant forward, her lips twisting into a smile. 'Weren't you beginning to think it was never going to happen?'

Harper nodded and took a sip of her coffee. 'Yep. But it appears the partners were true to their word, if incredibly slow.'

'Samuel must be beside himself.'

'That is an understatement. We're having dinner at one of the partners' houses tonight so I've booked myself in to get my hair done after work this afternoon.'

'Wow, give him my congratulations.'

'I will. Thanks.' Harper grinned—things had been so great between her and Samuel lately. Since their trip to the Hunter Valley in February, she'd felt closer to him than she had in a long time, and she couldn't be happier that all his hard work had finally paid off. 'I'm going to pick your brain soon about exotic holiday locations, because when things have settled down at work again for Samuel, I want to take him overseas to properly celebrate.'

'Sounds good,' Lilia said with a wistful sigh. 'You know I'm your girl when it comes to all things travel.'

'Anyway, why did you have such a long face when I walked in? I thought you were in new relationship heaven?'

Lilia glowered. 'There's no such thing as heaven. Or the perfect man. Well, mine *might* be perfect if his mother was dead.'

'What?' The cup jolted in Harper's hand—thank God for plastic lids or she could have had a major coffee spillage down her white shirt.

Lilia's lips quirked a little. 'David is divine—I haven't met a guy I've felt this way about before—but his mother hates me.'

'I'm sure she doesn't. How could anyone hate you?'

'She thinks I'm too strong-willed and focused on my career. So much so that she's taken it upon herself to start trying to set David up with other women. Can you believe that?'

Harper couldn't. She was absolutely speechless.

'Maybe we need to interview a hit man,' Lilia said after a few moments. 'Get some tips.'

And Harper laughed, because she knew her producer was only half joking. 'Speaking of work ...'

Dosed up on caffeine, they threw themselves into the day's tasks. That afternoon they had an underwater archaeologist on the show but they also had a pre-record to get done before then and the usual research and preparation.

'And now it's over to Lucy for the news, but I'll be back soon with a very special guest. Here's a clue—there's more to this man's job than *Titanic*.'

Harper removed her headphones, stood and went out to meet the giant of a man waiting beside Lilia. She'd been expecting someone older, a mad professor type, but this guy couldn't be more than thirty and with his mussed-up blond hair and terribly tanned skin, he looked like he'd just stepped off Bondi Beach.

Lilia barely noticed Harper as she stepped out of the studio to join them. In the end she had to clear her throat and then they both spun round to look at her.

'Oh,' Lilia exclaimed as if Harper was the last person she expected to see. 'This is Tr-Troy. Troy Davies ... My ... I mean *our* ... shipwreck guy.'

Harper tried to hide her smirk. Lilia had never before stuttered in her presence. The way Troy and Lilia were making eyes at each other, maybe David with the crazy mum had cause for concern.

'Nice to meet you,' she said as she thrust her hand towards him. 'I'm Harper and I'm really looking forward to talking to you.'

'Likewise,' Troy said. His shake was firm and his palm warm but not sweaty.

'Well, we better get in there. Lucy is almost done with the news.'

Troy nodded, tossed a quick dreamy smile at Lilia and then followed Harper into the studio. She gave him the spiel she gave all her guests about microphone use and then glanced down at her computer screen.

FIND OUT IF HE'S SINGLE.

Harper made a funny noise as she tried to swallow the laugh that erupted in her throat at Lilia's uncharacteristically *un*professional message.

'You all right?' Troy asked, settling into his stool on the other side of the desk.

'Fine.' She smiled widely and gestured to her throat. 'Just swallowed some air the wrong way. You know how it is.'

He nodded slowly, looking at her as if he had no idea.

Harper went to reach for her bottle of water but realised it was empty and *dammit*, Lilia—obviously flustered—had forgotten to bring in the usual glass for their guest either. Oh well, too late now, the news jingle was finishing.

'Welcome back to *Afternoons with Harper*,' she said, not allowing herself to meet Lilia's gaze through the glass. 'Today I have a very interesting man with me in the studio. Troy Davies—can you tell us exactly what an underwater archaeologist does for a living?'

Grinning, Troy leant close to the mic. 'Maritime or underwater archaeology is much the same as regular archaeology. It just happens beneath the ocean rather than on land. There are a number of types of maritime archaeology but my speciality is the study of shipwrecks. Exploring wrecks can give us great insight into the lives of those who lived before us.'

Harper asked what an average day in Troy's world was like, how he had found himself in such a specialised area and if he'd worked on any famous shipwrecks. Troy had fallen into his career after embarking on an arts law degree and choosing archaeology as an elective. He'd always loved the ocean—yes, she was right about her assessment of him as a surfer—and as a child, he remembered reading books about shipwrecks that fascinated him.

'But I never imagined I could explore wrecks for a living. There was only a brief reference to maritime archaeology in the unit I did at uni, but that was enough to pique my interest. Over the next few months, I read everything I could get my hands on about the topic and then when I finished my Bachelor degree I applied for a graduate program in maritime archaeology. I guess the rest, as they say, is history. Since then I've worked on wrecks all over the world.'

'What brought you back to Australia?' Harper asked after he'd talked about some of his favourite shipwrecks.

He blushed a little. 'Love. I got engaged and my fiancée wanted to be back in Sydney close to her family.'

At his words, Harper chanced a glance up at Lilia and saw her scowling. She looked back to Troy. 'Well, congratulations.'

'Not really,' he said with a self-deprecating chuckle. 'She left me at the altar.'

'Oh.' That Harper hadn't been expecting—she looked to Lilia again and saw her hand pressed against her heart. 'I'm sorry.'

Troy shrugged and Harper remembered she was here to talk about his work, not his love life. Damn Lilia.

'Can you tell us a little bit about how shipwrecks are discovered?' she asked, smiling encouragingly.

Indeed he could. Troy talked non-stop about his work and she found herself caught up, almost able to visualise what it would be like exploring history beneath the sea. This is what she loved about her job—the enthusiasm her guests had for their vocations was infectious and she learnt something new and exciting every day. Since donating her eggs to Claire and Jasper, she no longer felt like she was living life on the sidelines. Her contribution might not be as obvious as some of her guests, but she had made a difference to someone, and that was enough.

When Lilia gave her the wrap-up signal, she smiled at Troy again and thanked him for his time.

'It was my pleasure,' he said with a nod.

'And here's Lucy with the four o'clock news.'

As Harper stood and went around the desk to show Troy out, Lucy's voice sounded over the studio speakers.

'In breaking news, a horrific car accident on the Hunter Expressway north-west of Newcastle has claimed the life of a young woman who was thirty weeks pregnant. The male driver of the other vehicle has been taken to hospital with minor injuries.'

Harper halted in her stride, her heart turning to ice at the newsreader's announcement. *No. It can't be.* The rest of her body still frozen, she shook her head vigorously as she repeated this mantra over and over to herself. *It can't be! It can't be!*

She barely registered the door opening and Lilia ushering their guest out. As the news jingle sounded and the drive time announcer's voice came on air from studio two, she rushed out into the corridor and hurried down to the newsroom.

'What do we have on that car accident?' she screamed.

Lucy and the news intern simply stared at her.

'I *said*, what else do you have on that car accident?!' She forced herself past Lucy, shoving her out of the way as she stared at the main news computer screen.

'Excuse me? What are you doing?' Lucy asked, her hands on her hips.

'What's going on?' Lilia's voice came from the doorway and Harper spun around.

'That accident on the Hunter Expressway. Lucy said a pregnant woman has died.' Uncharacteristic tears burst from her eyes and she saw Lucy and the intern look at each other as if she were deranged.

Lilia's eyes widened and her mouth dropped open as understanding dawned. 'Claire,' she whispered.

Harper nodded, barely able to breathe at the possibility.

Lilia marched in and put her hand on Harper's shoulder. 'Let's not jump to conclusions. There must be hundreds of pregnant women in that area.'

'But Claire's thirty weeks.' Harper sniffed.

'What's going on?' Lucy asked, her voice softer now.

Lilia looked to Harper and she nodded, silently giving the producer the okay to explain.

'Harper donated some of her eggs to a childless couple late last year. The woman she gave them to is now thirty weeks pregnant and lives in the Hunter Valley.'

'Wow,' whispered Lucy and the intern at exactly the same time.

Then Lucy added, 'I'm sorry Harper, but no other information has been released yet. You know what it's like. We probably won't get a name until tomorrow at the earliest, but I do know that this accident was closer to Newcastle than the Hunter.'

Harper nodded, her breathing finally starting to slow again. Of course Lilia was right. The likelihood of Claire being the woman who'd died was tiny, but still she had to find out.

'Do you have her number?' the intern asked. 'You could try calling her.'

It was so simple, Harper didn't know why she hadn't thought of it. Without another word to any of them, she raced back into the studio and snatched her mobile up off her desk, found Claire's number and pressed call. It rang a few times, then voicemail clicked in and Claire's effervescent voice told her to leave a message.

But she hung up. What could she say? *Hi Claire, just wondering whether you're still alive?*

'She's not answering,' Harper said, her stomach knotting as Lilia walked into the studio.

'It doesn't mean anything. Try *him*,' Lilia suggested.

Harper nodded, looked down at the phone in her slightly trembling hand and then remembered she didn't have Jasper's number. 'Dammit, I don't have it.'

Lilia frowned. 'I wonder if Samuel has any contacts that might be able to get information for you.'

Harper wasn't sure—the police force didn't tend to look fondly upon defence lawyers—but in the absence of any other ideas it was worth a shot. She pressed his name in her recent calls list and then held the phone up to her ear again. *Come on. Pick up.* But his phone went to voicemail as well, his authoritative voice promising to get back to her when he could.

Her fingers tightened around her mobile as the urge to punch something came over her. 'Why won't anyone pick up?'

She was about to call Samuel's office and tell whichever CrossFit receptionist answered that it was an emergency, when Lilia said, 'Doesn't Willow's girlfriend work for the police?'

'Of course.' Ten seconds later Harper had her big sister on the line. Barely able to string a sentence together, she told her about the accident and her concern that Claire might be involved. 'Would Miriam be able to find out the name of the deceased?'

'I'm not sure, but I'll get back to you as soon as I can,' Willow promised.

Lilia persuaded Harper to go to the bar down the street for a stiff drink while they waited for information and by the time her phone rang fifteen minutes later, she'd almost managed to convince herself that she was being a drama queen and panicking over nothing.

'Willow?' she said, snatching the phone up, her heartbeat halting as she waited for confirmation.

'I'm so sorry, Harper.'

Chapter Twenty

As Jasper popped the lasagna he'd just made into the oven and closed the door, he glanced at the kitchen clock. He was expecting Claire home any moment and although dinner was a few hours away, he wanted it sorted before she came back so they could chill together for a bit. Knowing she'd be exhausted after her busy day shopping, he was contemplating running her a bath when he heard a car turn into the driveway.

Unable to see the front yard from the kitchen window, he jogged through the house to meet Claire but when he opened the door, the smile fell from his face. A police car had pulled up and two of the local officers were climbing out of it. He recognised one of them—Nick Gilbert—as a bloke he'd gone to school with.

Trying to swallow the fear that rose in his throat, he told himself there was a perfectly reasonable explanation for their visit. Maybe they were simply driving by and had decided to pop in and say hi.

Yet, as they got closer, he saw the solemn expressions on their faces. His rib cage tightened around his lungs.

'Hi Jasper,' Nick said, his tone sober, not even a flicker of a smile on his lips. 'This is my colleague, Constable Gail Morrissey. Can we come inside?'

Jasper didn't even glance at the constable. Instead he looked his old friend dead in his eyes. 'Don't bullshit me, Nick. It's Claire, isn't it? Just tell me. What happened? Is she hurt?'

'I'm so sorry, Jasper.' Nick blinked and rubbed beneath his nose as if trying not to cry. 'There's been an accident on the Expressway. She didn't make it.'

'No.' He shook his head as a cold clammy feeling crept over his skin. 'It can't be true. She only messaged me ...'

But he couldn't finish the sentence—she'd messaged him over two hours ago saying she was almost finished shopping. She should have been home an hour ago, but he'd just assumed she'd been distracted and hadn't left when she'd planned to. He'd almost messaged her to check but he hadn't wanted her to look at her phone while driving.

'I'm sorry,' Nick said again.

'What happened?' Jasper heard himself speak, but didn't feel as if he had.

Nick expelled a heavy breath. 'She was heading home from Newcastle I guess, and another vehicle was travelling on the wrong side of the road. It looks like she tried to swerve but the two vehicles collided.'

He went quiet again and the three of them stood there, no one saying a word. Jasper stared at the ground, trying to wrap his head around what the police officers were telling him, but it didn't make any sense. Claire *couldn't* be dead. He remembered her smile and the spring in her step as she'd left the shed that morning—*no*, she was far too full of life to die.

After a while, he realised Nick was speaking again. 'There's a tiny bit of good news though.'

Jasper's head snapped up to look at the sergeant. 'What?'

Nick offered a small smile. 'The paramedics were able to get Claire to hospital quickly and the doctors managed to successfully deliver your baby. You have a little girl. She's in a critical condition, but at thirty weeks, they say she has a fighting chance.'

Chills rolled over Jasper's skin. *My baby?* He didn't give a damn about the baby.

What good was a baby without Claire?

'Is there anyone you want us to call?' Nick said. 'Your parents? We can take you to the hospital now to see your little girl if you like. We'll also need someone to formally identify Claire but if you'd rather not see her like that, then we can ask her parents or use her dental records. Would you like us to have some officers go round and inform her parents or would you prefer to do that yourself?'

Jasper's hands clenched into fists. His head filled with sudden pain. Too many questions. He could only focus on one.

'Identify her?' Hope flickered inside him. Perhaps this was some cruel mistake. 'There's a possibility it's not her?'

Nick and Morrissey exchanged a look and then both turned back to him.

'No, I'm sorry, I don't think there is,' Nick said with a sombre shake of his head. 'Unfortunately this is necessary protocol, but she was driving a car licensed to you and the identification in her purse matched. And then there's the fact that she was pregnant.'

'I need to see her.' He couldn't believe this was true until he'd seen it with his own eyes—and if it was, then he wanted to be the one to identify her. As her husband, it was his duty. He couldn't pass the task to his in-laws like some sort of coward. 'I'll get my car keys.'

'No. We'll take you,' Nick said. 'You shouldn't drive after such a shock.'

If it weren't for the police, he wouldn't have even bothered to lock the door, but Morrissey gently suggested he do so, which reminded him to turn the oven off as well. At least he wouldn't be returning to a burnt down house, although right now his home was the least of his worries.

The drive to the hospital was a blur. Nothing felt real. Nick tried to talk to him for a while but Jasper ignored him and in the end he gave up. Jasper turned his phone over and over in his hand—toying with the idea of calling Claire's parents and his own, but he couldn't bring himself to do so, not yet. He didn't want to worry them until he knew for sure. And he didn't know how he'd be able to make such a call, to actually say the words.

Finally they were there. Jasper followed Nick and Morrissey into the hospital and down a number of corridors before they stopped at a closed door. A moment later it opened and a man dressed in scrubs appeared as if he'd had insider knowledge that they'd arrived.

Nick nodded at the man. 'Hello, I'm Senior Sergeant Nick Gilbert and this is Jasper Lombard. We've come to identify Claire Lombard.'

The man nodded, some words were spoken but they might as well have been gobbledegook for all Jasper understood them. He just wanted to see her, wanted to put this surreal moment behind him.

Constable Morrissey stayed in the corridor but Nick accompanied Jasper and the man into the small cold room. A stark hospital gurney was in the middle, its head against one wall, and lying on the table was his wife.

Jasper's mouth fell open and his hand flew to his chest. The cold he'd felt back at the house had nothing on the ice that filled him now. He felt Nick's hand on his shoulder but he shook him off and took a step towards Claire. Even as he gazed down at her beautiful face all bruised and scratched up, he couldn't believe his eyes. She looked like Claire but the spark had left her. She wore a hospital surgical gown and as his eyes moved lower, he swallowed at the sight of her no longer pregnant body.

He'd gotten so used to that beautiful bump, and the way she caressed it near on constantly, that she didn't look right without it. Instinctively he reached out and touched her hand. It was cool, but then again she'd always had cold hands—they'd often joked about it. She'd spout the old saying, 'cold hands, warm heart,' and he'd retort, 'cold hands, selfish heart.'

He hadn't meant it—Claire didn't have a selfish bone in her body.

Interlocking his fingers with hers, he waited for her to squeeze them as she'd often done when they held hands, but there was no such response. He had to be dreaming, having a nightmare. If she really was dead, he'd be a mess, but although his eyes hurt, he couldn't cry. He felt nothing.

This couldn't be his wife lying before him. It just couldn't be.

Yet even as his heart tried to hold onto her, his head knew the truth. In a matter of moments his whole world had blown apart. And not just his world. He thought of Claire's parents, her brother, Polly. Would it be best they hear this on the phone from him or, as Nick had offered, from a police officer face-to-face? He had no idea.

If only he could ask Claire, he thought, gazing into her beautiful face—she always knew how to handle sticky situations.

'Oh, sweetheart.' Although he still didn't cry, emotion shuddered through his body. He dipped his head and pressed his lips against hers and then wrapped his arms around her lifeless body. Even though logically he knew this wasn't his Claire anymore, he never wanted to let go. He wished he could crawl onto the table beside her, close his eyes and never wake up.

He'd loved her from the moment he'd first laid eyes on her; how was he supposed to go on without her at his side?

Chapter Twenty-one

Harper had never hated rush hour traffic more than she did at that moment. The Pacific Motorway was clogged, cars bumper-to-bumper, torrential rain not doing anything to help the situation. They'd already been in the car for half an hour and had barely made it out of Sydney. Hitching a ride on a snail would be faster.

'Hey,' Willow spoke soothingly from the driver's seat, 'do you want me to put some music on? Maybe it'll help ...'

'What?' Harper snapped at her sister. 'Help me relax?' She shook her head. 'The only thing that will help me relax is if the damn traffic evaporates.'

Willow sighed as a car somewhere beeped its horn.

'I'm sorry,' Harper said. 'I shouldn't be snapping at you. Thank you for driving me. Thank you for being here for me.'

'As if I'd be anywhere else. And there's no way I'd let you drive after the shock you've just had.'

Silence hung in the air a few long moments and then Harper sniffed, digging another tissue out of her handbag. She wasn't usually a crier but since Willow's phone call she hadn't been able to stop the tears.

'I just can't believe it,' she whispered. 'Why Claire? Why now, when she and Jasper were so close to getting the family they craved? Honestly, Willow, you've never met a more loving couple. And Claire would have made the perfect mother—she's kind, caring, good with flowers and animals, she can cook and sew ...' Aware that she sounded like she was describing a nineteen-fifties housewife, she added, 'But she's also really smart. They both are. They might not have degrees—but they're big readers and in the end, none of that matters because they wanted to be parents more than anything and this just absolutely sucks.'

Willow reached across and squeezed her hand. 'There's no logic to life my love, but at least the baby's still got Jasper, and at least he has the baby to live for.'

The surprising news of the baby's survival from Miriam had been bittersweet—and she hadn't really had time to process it. Before she could reply to this, Harper's mobile sounded with the ringtone programmed for Samuel's number. 'Oh God,' she said as she stared at the screen, remembering she was supposed to be getting ready for his first dinner with the partners *as* a partner.

'You going to answer that?' Willow asked.

She was tempted to let it go to voicemail as her call to him had gone that afternoon, but he'd only worry when she didn't turn up at home. He deserved to know what was happening.

'Hi, Samuel,' she said, her voice still sounding choked.

'Where are you? You're supposed to be here getting ready to go out.'

'I tried to call you this afternoon. Something terrible has happened.'

'What's wrong? Is it your sister?' he asked, his tone softer now.

Harper glanced at Willow as she inched the car slowly forward. 'No, Willow's fine. She's sitting right next to me. I'm not sure if you've heard the news, but …' She sniffed, the tears coming all over again. 'A pregnant woman died in a car accident this afternoon. It was Claire.'

He took a moment to respond and she wondered if he even knew who she was talking about. 'Shit. That's terrible. Poor Jasper.'

'I know.' She sniffed again and wiped her eyes. 'But I guess the good news is that the paramedics and doctors miraculously managed to deliver the baby. Claire had a little girl.'

'So Jasper's okay? Was he in the car? Was he driving?'

She shook her head and then realised he couldn't see. 'No, apparently there was a car chase. The police were after some guy on ice who'd stolen a car and he entered the Expressway the wrong way trying to get away from them. They aborted the chase but the guy crashed into Claire.'

'Was he killed as well?' he asked.

'No. Apparently he's suffered serious injuries but they're not life-threatening. Bastard.'

'I wonder if he has representation yet.'

'What?' Harper couldn't believe her ears. Here she'd been thinking Samuel might have half a heart for Jasper and all he'd been thinking about was professional opportunity. 'Who the hell cares? The other guy deserves to *die* for what he's done.'

'You don't know what led him to a drug addiction, Harper.' Samuel spoke to her as if she were a naughty child. 'Anyway, never mind. When will you be home? We have to leave soon.'

Never mind? She felt her blood boiling beneath her skin. 'I'm not going out and what I've told you is confidential. The media doesn't know any of it yet and Miriam could get in big trouble for telling me, so please don't breathe a word of it to anyone.'

'What do you mean you're not going out?'

'I'm on my way to Newcastle to see Jasper and the baby. Willow's driving me.'

'You're *what*?' His voice was so loud she pulled the phone away from her ear. 'I need you beside me tonight. Don't you know how important this evening is? You barely knew those people.'

She took a deep breath, trying to remain calm—or as close to calm as was possible in this hellish situation. What about what *she* needed? 'I'm sorry, Samuel, but I wouldn't be good company tonight anyway. I know you don't understand; I might not have known Claire very long, but we went through something together that formed a bond I can't explain and I need to go and offer Jasper my condolences.' She also needed to see with her own eyes to believe that this nightmare was real.

'You're right,' Samuel said. 'I don't understand.' And then he disconnected the call.

'Sometimes your husband can be a real dick,' Willow said.

Harper didn't have the energy to defend him. 'He's a man. What do you expect?'

She didn't really think that—she knew more lovely men than otherwise and suspected a good husband would be offering to abandon his dinner and come with her at a time like this. Or at least show a little empathy. But emotionally wrung out as she was, she didn't want to analyse her husband or her marriage right now.

'Do you want to stop and get some dinner at a service station?' Willow said, obviously deciding not to enter into such a discussion. 'I need to get some petrol. It won't be fancy but if you're hungry ...'

'I'm not.' Harper shook her head. 'Maybe Samuel's right? Maybe we are crazy driving all the way to Newcastle on a whim. I'm not family. Well, not exactly. Oh God, this is so damn complicated.'

She buried her face in her hands. Their counsellor had never made them contemplate this scenario.

'Forget Samuel,' Willow said firmly. 'Your first instinct was to go to Newcastle and I'm a big believer in following your gut. It's when the head tries to butt in and reason that we start twisting ourselves into ridiculous knots. If the baby hadn't lived, I'd tell you to send a sympathy card and give Jasper space to grieve, but you were planning on going to see the baby when it was born anyway, weren't you? It's up to you,' she added before Harper could answer, 'but if we go home now, will you spend all night wishing you went?'

'I don't know.' Harper's stomach felt like it was twisting into one of those knots Willow had mentioned. She wasn't sure what she could say or do to help Jasper, but something deep inside her told her she needed to go.

'Then let's get petrol and see how you're feeling after a pit stop,' Willow said as she pulled off the road into a service station.

Harper sat numbly in the car while her sister filled it up. She didn't even realise Willow had gone inside to pay until she returned with two cans of Coke and two Violet Crumbles. She handed one of each to Harper, then cracked her own can.

'Might not be the healthiest dinner,' she said, 'but sugar is good for shock.'

And Violet Crumbles were their childhood comfort food—when their mother was busy with her latest boyfriend, they sometimes used to steal money from her purse and buy them from the deli on the corner. Although Harper didn't want to think about Laura right now. This was too stark a reminder of how many people out there didn't deserve to have children, and the cruel contrast with those who did, but couldn't.

As they headed further out of Sydney, both the traffic and the weather eased and Harper found herself sharing her memories of the few times she'd met Claire.

'She really does sound like a special person,' Willow said. 'Will you go to the funeral?'

'Funeral?' She tried the alien word on for size—it seemed wrong to be even talking about the possibility of a funeral for Claire. 'I guess so. Yes, I think I will. I want to show Jasper that I care and I want their baby to one day know that I cared about her mother as well. I think it'll be a big funeral. They have a large extended family and Claire seemed like the type of person to have a lot of friends.'

'I'll come with you as well if you want,' Willow said, glancing across and offering a big-sisterly supportive smile.

'Thank you. I guess we'll both have to get time off work. I wonder when it'll be?'

After a while Willow steered the conversation to the more mundane—they talked about each other's work, their shared surprise that Laura was still shacked up with the cowboy in Montana and the appalling state of world politics. Harper didn't really care about any of it in that moment but she appreciated her sister's efforts to help pass the time. Small talk comforted her in a way that silence wouldn't have.

Finally, they arrived at the hospital in Newcastle.

'Do you want me to drop you off, park and come and find you or shall we go in together?'

Harper blinked, suddenly realising she had no idea where to find Jasper. For an intelligent woman, she really hadn't thought any of this through.

Her sister, reading her mind as she'd always been able to do, said, 'I'd go to the neonatal ward and, if you can't see him, ask someone.'

Harper nodded. 'Yes. Good plan. Let's park and then go in together.'

Willow took control as they entered the hospital—she read the necessary signs directing them where to go—but when they got to their destination, they came to another obstacle. The neonatal ward had the security of a palace; no one was getting in or out without permission from a stern-looking woman at the desk. Ignoring the people in the adjacent waiting room, Harper approached and cleared her throat.

The woman looked up as if Harper's arrival was a huge imposition. 'Yes?'

'Hi … My name is Harper Drummond, and … I'm hoping to see Jasper Lombard. I …' How on earth could she explain this situation? She shouldn't have come.

'Are you the media?' snapped the woman.

'Yes.' Harper blinked. 'I mean no. Well, I am *in* the media but I'm here because … I heard that a baby was born this afternoon after Claire Lombard was brought in in a car accident and I'm the donor. The *egg* donor.'

The woman raised an eyebrow, clearly thinking Harper had come up with an elaborate story to engineer her way into the situation. 'Even if you *are* a friend of the family, it's parents and grandparents only in to see our babies.'

'But technically she *is* the mother,' Willow interrupted.

'Under Australian law, unless she was the surrogate—' the woman glanced down at Harper's perfectly flat abdomen, '—then she has no legal right to the baby and, as I said, only parents are allowed to see the baby. I'm sorry but suggest you give the family space at this difficult time.'

'It's okay.' Harper put her hand out to stop her sister from saying anything more; the nurse or security guard or whatever she was had a point. She should *not* have come. 'We'll go. Thank you for your time. Come on, Willow.'

Yet as they turned around, they were faced with another woman. A woman in her early sixties with a round face that had numerous smile lines, except she wasn't smiling now. It took Harper a moment to place her.

'You're Jasper's mum,' she said.

At the same moment, the woman spoke. 'I'm Wendy Lombard. You're the wonderful woman that gave Claire her eggs.' Then she closed the small gap between them and threw her arms around Harper.

Harper hadn't known she was capable of so many tears but more poured down her face as she clung to this woman she'd only met once. 'I'm so sorry,' she whispered into the older woman's hair. 'This is so unfair.'

After a few long moments, Wendy finally pulled back, although she slid her hands down Harper's arms and held her hands. Jasper's father stood right behind her.

'It was kind of you to come,' he said, the smile he'd been wearing when they'd met at the balloon base absent now.

'I wasn't sure if I should but when I heard the news, I felt compelled. I can't believe this.'

Wendy nodded. 'We're all in shock. It doesn't seem real.' Then she let go, stepped back and indicated another middle-aged couple a few feet away. 'Harper, this is Joanne and Mike Wallace, Claire's parents.'

Harper didn't know what to say to these clearly broken strangers. The man's arms were wrapped around his wife's shoulders and she was clutching a sodden hanky the way a child might cling to a teddy bear.

There *was* nothing to say.

'This is the generous woman who gave Claire and Jasper her eggs,' Wendy told them.

'Thank you,' whispered Joanne. 'You made our daughter the happiest she's ever been. She was so looking forward to being a mum.'

And then her face crumbled, and she leant into Mike's chest as she let out a gut-wrenching sob. With a look at Harper that conveyed so much emotion, Mike led Joanne over to a row of plastic chairs and sat her down.

'How's Jasper?' Harper asked, her voice low.

Wendy and Paul sighed in unison, then Wendy spoke. 'We haven't seen him or the baby yet. We only just got here ourselves, Claire's folks too. Her brother's on his way, so ...' Her voice trailed off. It was clear she was trying to be strong—for her son and Claire's parents—but struggling to hold herself together.

'The local police called us,' Paul continued, putting his arm around Wendy, 'but they've only given us the bare details. Apparently the baby is a girl.'

Harper nodded, the insider info from Miriam meant she likely knew as much, perhaps even more than they did, but they didn't ask how she'd known to come so quickly. She was about to say something about hospitals being able to do amazing things with premature babies these days, but the door to the ward opened and they all swung round in anticipation.

Jasper stood there, staring at them. Almost staring *through* them.

And if she'd thought Claire's parents broken, he looked a mere shadow of his former self.

The birth of his baby should have been the happiest day of his life.

Instead it was the worst.

Chapter Twenty-two

Jasper hadn't wanted to leave Claire all alone in that god-awful place, but he'd been ushered out and led to another part of the hospital. Once there, Nick and Constable Morrissey led him to a tall woman with long brown hair tied back off her face. Her uniform and the little upside down watch thing clipped to her shirt told him she was a nurse. She introduced herself with a warm sympathetic smile and her hand brushed gently over his arm as she did so, but her name went in one ear and out the other.

All he heard was, 'I'm so sorry to hear about your wife.'

'Claire. Her *name* is Claire,' he said.

'Yes, Claire.' Her expression of pity still etched onto her face, she dropped her hand and turned to a woman behind a reception desk. They exchanged a few words and then she opened a door with some kind of security card and indicated for them to go through ahead of her.

Morrissey stayed behind in the waiting room but Nick accompanied them a little further. It suddenly became clear to

Jasper where they were—the ward for sick and premature babies. He couldn't remember the proper term but on either side of a long corridor were rooms with glass windows and inside those rooms were lots of tiny little box things with babies inside.

He stopped walking and struggled to catch his breath. They were taking him to see the baby.

'You'll have to stay out here I'm afraid.'

Jasper heard the nurse speaking and hope lifted his heart—he didn't want to see the baby, he just wanted to go back to Claire—but then he realised she was speaking to Nick.

'It's only immediate family and medical staff allowed in with the newborns,' she said, then looked to Jasper. 'I'll show you your little girl in a moment, but first I need you to wash up.'

She steered him over to a sink just outside one of the glass rooms. 'Wash your hands right up to your elbows with the soap and then rub this sanitiser on. We want to limit all risk of infection.'

He found himself doing as he was told, telling himself that deep down he owed it to Claire to go and see the baby. It was what everyone would expect him to do.

Moments later, the nurse opened the door and ushered him into a room filled with little baby boxes, the whir and beep of machinery, a couple of medical staff and a few people he guessed were new parents.

'Here she is,' the nurse announced, holding Jasper's arm as she positioned him in front of one of the little boxes.

He gazed down at the tiny red-faced human, naked except for a miniature nappy and the tubes coming out of its nose.

He vaguely registered the nurse speaking. 'Isn't she a doll? Your little miracle. She weighed one point five kilograms but she's doing well considering she's only thirty weeks. I'd say this one's a fighter. This is a heated incubator because she's unable to regulate her temperature yet. We can't let you hold her just yet, but you can put your hand in through the hole and touch her.'

When he didn't say anything, she put her hand onto his arm again. 'Anyway. This is a lot to take in. I'll give you a few moments with her, I'm just over at the desk if you need me.'

Jasper stared down at the baby, taking stock. Although small, this infant looked well-formed—he counted ten fingers and ten toes. Its limbs were a little blue but its chest was rising slowly up and down. He didn't know if it needed help breathing—perhaps one of the tubes was respiratory assistance. A scant scattering of dark hair covered its head. It was scrawny, quite long in body and legs, with no fat to flesh it out. The only indication it was a girl were the pink coloured hospital identity bands—one around its thin wrist and the other its ankle.

He leant closer and read the words—*Baby of Jasper Lombard*—and the date.

This is your and Claire's child, he silently told himself, but he couldn't make the connection between this baby and the one that had been in Claire's belly when she'd left that morning. It simply didn't compute. He felt absolutely nothing for this miniature little stranger.

He'd rather have Claire than this baby. It wasn't even a part of her—it wouldn't grow up to look like her or sound like her. It was no consolation.

Why couldn't they have saved his wife instead of this tiny little girl who hadn't been in the world long enough to miss it?

Why couldn't *he* have died instead? Claire would have been okay without him—she would have devoted all her love and energy to this baby—but he *wasn't* okay. And without Claire, he didn't even know if he could love this child.

His heart heavy, his head sore, he looked up and around, taking in the people staring into the other incubators. They were mostly couples, all smug in love and new parenthood—even if their babies still needed medical assistance, they were all alive and together.

He'd thought he was numb, but that wasn't the case. He did feel something. A burning rage deep within him, an anger stronger than anything he'd ever felt before.

He hated everyone in this room and felt an intense urge to run around and tear the place apart. How dare these couples look so content! How dare the nurse talk to him about miracles and this baby being a fighter!

He had to get out of there. Without a word to the nurse, he barged out of the room, not caring about the noise he made as the door slammed shut behind him. Nick, who looked as if he'd been leaning against a wall taking a little snooze, snapped his head up, but Jasper ignored him as he made a beeline for the exit.

Frustration filled him as he yanked at the door but it refused to open. Nick came up behind him and without a word, touched his hand to a button on the wall. The door clicked and this time when Jasper pulled, it opened.

He didn't know how his parents and Claire's parents had found out—perhaps he'd called them or maybe the police had, it was all a blur—but he emerged into a waiting room full of family, Constable Morrissey and ... Harper.

Harper? How on earth had she found out?

'Jasper,' the small crowd breathed his name in unison, like some kind of pity choir. Their faces wore identical expressions of sympathy and he didn't want any of it, but it was Harper he zoned in on.

'What the hell are *you* doing here?' he asked, stepping right up into her personal space.

She blinked and stepped back a little. 'I'm … I'm sorry. I heard … I just—'

'Jasper,' his dad said sharply. 'Harper came because she cares.'

Jasper screwed his face up, barely able to look at her as he thrust his finger in accusation. 'It's *her* fault we're all here. If she hadn't given us her damn eggs, then Claire wouldn't have been pregnant and she wouldn't have been in Newcastle at all today. If it wasn't for her, my wife would still be alive.'

'Jasper!' exclaimed his parents in unison.

'It's okay.' Harper shook her head at them and clutched the strap of her shoulder bag. 'I'm so sorry for your loss, Jasper. I didn't mean to intrude.'

She turned and fled from the waiting room. Another woman he'd not even noticed before glared at him and then hurried past, following her.

'Oh Jasper,' his mum said as she wrapped her arms around him. When he was little he'd loved nothing more than being in his mother's arms. If he scraped his knee, her kiss could fix it; if someone had been unkind at school or he'd missed out being picked for a team, she could fix it.

But she couldn't fix this.

And if one more person looked at him in the way they were right now or said his name that way again, he was going to scream. He shrugged out of her embrace, because he didn't want their pity or sympathy—that might make this real. Instead, he walked over to the wall and slammed his fist into it, welcoming the pain that exploded from his knuckles.

His dad approached and clamped his hand down on his shoulder. 'Don't do that, son. Talk to us. Let us be here for you.'

But he shrugged him off as well. What did he think they could say or do that could possibly make this better? 'I don't want to *fucking* talk,' he screamed.

He wanted to turn back time, he wanted to *do* something.

'I know you're hurting,' Nick said, approaching with wariness, 'but I'm going to need you to calm down. This is a hospital.'

The sight of Nick's uniform jogged something in Jasper's mind. They'd said Claire had been hit by a vehicle travelling on the wrong side of the road.

'What happened to the driver of the other car?' he asked, dropping his hands to his sides. 'Why were they travelling on the wrong side of the Expressway? How is it even *possible* to travel on the wrong side of the Expressway?'

Nick and Morrissey glanced at each other and this time Morrissey spoke—he'd been beginning to wonder if she was mute.

'The other driver sustained serious injuries and is currently in surgery.' She rubbed her lips together, then continued. 'He was involved in a police chase and entered the Expressway the wrong way while attempting to get away. We believe he was under the influence of drugs.'

Jasper's head spun—her few sentences were so full of wrongness. The fact that the other man, *a drug addict*, had lived to tell the tale; the fact that this could have been avoided if the police had abandoned their chase. How many times had he heard of something like this happening on the news? Anger at the cops warred inside him with anger at the bastard who had killed his wife.

The bastard who was here. Somewhere in *this* hospital.

'I want to see him,' Jasper said, his fists clenching again. He wanted to punch his hand into the man's face as he had into the wall, although this time he wouldn't stop at one hit.

'That won't be possible,' Nick said, firmly. 'I think you should just focus on your little girl now. Let us do our job where the driver's concerned.'

'Because you're so fucking good at that, aren't you?' Jasper shouted again.

'Jasper, *please*. Stop!'

He turned at the sound of Claire's mum's voice to see her sitting crumpled on a seat a few steps away. Her face was blotched red, her eyelashes wet and her eternal smile gone.

'Nothing you can do is going to bring Claire back.'

At the sight of her, something broke inside him and some of his anger drained away. He'd lost his wife but Joanne and Mike had lost their daughter. If anyone could understand a fraction of how he felt, it was them. He took a few steps and dropped into the seat beside her. She opened her arms and he fell into them, resting his head on her shoulder.

The hug he couldn't stand from his own mother, he took from Claire's and he gave one back, clinging to her tightly, never wanting to let go. Joanne and Claire were as close as a mother and daughter could get because of all they'd gone through when Claire was ill as a child. But what was the point of her daughter being saved back then, only to die now? What was the point in letting them fall in love, giving them the promise of such joy, and then ripping it all away?

If Jasper had held any belief in the possibility of a God before now, it had died alongside his wife.

After what seemed like a very long while, Joanne sniffed and looked up at him. He realised his shirt was soaked with her tears and in some ways he envied her them. He wanted to cry, felt like he should, but his eyes were as dry as a piece of burnt toast.

'Tell me about the baby,' she whispered.

For a second he had no clue what she was talking about, and then he remembered. Claire was gone but in her place was a tiny person he was supposed to feel something for. He looked up to see both his parents and hers looking at him in expectation.

He swallowed. 'It's a girl.' He wasn't sure what the police had told them. 'And she's doing okay I guess. She's tiny. And has to be in an incubator for a while.'

He felt stupid but he couldn't tell them anything else because he'd barely listened to the nurse and hadn't cared enough to ask any questions.

'Have you chosen a name yet?' his mum asked.

'Claire wanted to call her Anaya.'

'It's beautiful,' she replied with a sad smile.

'Anaya?' His dad tried it on for size. 'What does it mean?'

He remembered it meant 'God answered', but he shrugged as if he didn't know. Name meanings were a crock of shit anyway and he was only going to call her that because it was Claire's wish, and because it meant he wouldn't have to think of something else.

'Have you got a photo?' asked Mike.

At the same time, Joanne said, 'Can we see her?'

He blinked. How could they be wondering about the baby when their own daughter was lying cold and lifeless on another floor?

'I'm sorry. I … I haven't got one. And, I'm not sure about who can see her.' Had the nurse said something about who could visit?

'Hospital policy,' said a lady he hadn't noticed before from behind a reception desk, 'is parents and grandparents only, but one parent must be present and no more than two people per baby at a time.'

His parents and in-laws looked from the woman back to Jasper.

'You probably want to be getting back to her anyway,' said his mother. 'And we can take turns. Joanne, would you like to go in first?'

'Oh.' Joanne sniffed and pressed a hand to her chest. 'Would you mind?'

The others all shook their heads, so Jasper found himself leading his mother-in-law over to the door. The woman behind the desk pressed a button and it clicked open.

'We have to wash and sanitise our hands before we go into the room,' he told Joanne, following the exact steps the nurse had led him through earlier.

'Of course.' She nodded and scrubbed up as well.

The nurse who'd dealt with him before met them at the door.

'Hello,' she said softly. 'You brought a visitor?'

He nodded. 'This is Claire's mum, Joanne.'

'Hello Joanne.' She offered a sympathetic smile. 'Let's take you over to meet your granddaughter.'

The nurse led Joanne to the baby and Jasper followed limply behind, thankful she'd taken control because he wasn't sure he'd even remember which baby was his.

'Oh!' Joanne gasped, her hand rushing up to cover her mouth as she looked down at the tiny baby.

Jasper peered over her shoulder, wondering if she'd noticed something wrong with the child that he hadn't seen before, but aside from the tubes, its size and the fact that it was in a box, it looked okay. Perhaps even a little less blue at the hands and feet than half an hour ago.

Then Joanne clutched his arm and looked up into his face. 'She's absolutely beautiful.' She sniffed and tears fell down her cheeks again, yet this time they were that weird cocktail of happy and sad. 'Claire would have adored her.'

He nodded and tried to smile, but all he felt towards the little person in front of them was resentment.

Chapter Twenty-three

'Slow down! You'll trip and break a leg in this bad weather.'

Harper didn't reply, stop *or* slow down at her sister's words; she barely even looked out for traffic as she hurried through the car park in her desperation to get to the car.

By the time Willow caught up with her, her hand was on the passenger door waiting for the car to be unlocked. Tears were coursing down her cheeks, their ferocity competing with that of the rain.

'Do you want to go get a drink somewhere?' Willow asked as they slumped into their seats.

'No.' Harper clicked her seatbelt in place. Although part of her craved a stiff drink, she couldn't stand the thought of being in a public place where people could see her falling apart. 'I just want to go home.'

'Fair enough.' Willow started the car.

'Samuel was right. We shouldn't have come. What was I thinking?' She wished she could just crawl into bed and forget this day ever happened.

'You were thinking with your heart. You were hurting and wanted to show you cared. Jasper's family understood that. I think they appreciated you being there—and in time he will too.'

Harper shook her head. 'I don't think so. He's right. If I hadn't interfered in their lives, Claire would probably still be alive.'

'I'm sorry but that's bullshit. How could you possibly have known this was going to happen to Claire? It's not because she was pregnant, it's not because you gave her eggs, it's because she was in the wrong place at the wrong time. Jasper's hurting and in shock. He's showing normal signs of grief—he needs someone to blame right now—but he'll come round.'

'I'm not sure he will.' Harper sighed and swiped at her eyes, unsure if she was crying because of his reaction, because of her devastation and shock at Claire's death or at the prospect of him never letting her see the baby.

The thought of never seeing the little girl upset her more than she'd imagined it would. When she'd first decided to be an egg donor, she hadn't even wanted contact with the child, but as she'd come to know Claire and Jasper better, she'd started to look forward to being a small part of the baby's life.

'Maybe this is my punishment.'

She didn't realise she'd said these words out loud until Willow said, 'What on earth would you need punishing for? I think you're in shock like Jasper.'

'I had an abortion when I was nineteen.'

'Holy shit.' Willow took her eyes off the road and turned to look at Harper as if it were the first time she'd ever seen her.

'Watch the road,' Harper screamed as a car in front of them slammed on its brakes.

Willow snapped her head back to what was happening in front, reacted in time and then pulled off the road and stopped on the gravel shoulder.

'Did I just hear you right?' she asked, her eyes wide.

Harper nodded, knowing her sister wouldn't be judgemental, but rather shocked and possibly hurt that she was only hearing about this sixteen years after it happened. 'I'm sorry I never told you.'

Willow reached over and took hold of Harper's hand. 'Never mind about that. I'm not the important one in all of this. I just ...' She shook her head. 'How did you manage to keep this from me? *Why* did you?'

Harper swallowed, not sure where to start. 'I got pregnant in my second year of university.'

'Was it a one-night stand? I didn't even know you had a boyfriend then.'

'He wasn't really a boyfriend, more a cute guy I liked sleeping with. He was the same age as I was and neither of us wanted a committed relationship. We were both focused on our studies and ...'

Willow nodded. 'So you guys decided you weren't ready for parenthood and chose not to have it.'

'*I* decided,' Harper said. 'I was terrified that he might tell me he wanted us to get married and raise the baby together or something ridiculous like that. His family were devout Christians, but I just knew I couldn't be a mother. Look at the example we had. I didn't want to stuff up a child in the way Laura stuffed us up. I couldn't believe I'd been so stupid, so irresponsible, to get pregnant in the first place, and the relief I felt afterwards only confirmed my feeling that I'd made the right decision. I wasn't sad at all. I was just so grateful that this option was available to me so easily. What kind of person does that make me?'

'You were practically a child. It makes you a human being who was terrified of something she shouldn't have had to face alone.'

'But I never even told him.'

'You shouldn't feel guilty—it was your body, your choice—but I wish you'd told *me*. I could have been there for you.'

'I was the one who stuffed up,' Harper said. 'You'd just left for your big adventure in Antarctica and I knew if I confided in you, you'd be on the next plane back to look after me. You did enough of that when we were growing up. I was finally an adult and it was finally your chance to do your thing without worrying about me.'

But even as she said this, tears streamed down her cheeks. After all these years it felt cathartic to get it off her chest.

'Oh, baby.' Willow leant across the seat and dragged Harper into her arms. She stroked her hair in the comforting way she'd done as a child when Harper was sick, in the way their mother should have but never did.

'You're wrong, you know,' she said after a few moments. 'Our mother may have been a crap parent, but that doesn't mean you would have been. I'm not saying you should have continued the pregnancy—you were so young and had so much potential ahead of you that I believe you made the right decision—but I think you would have made a great mother. You're nothing like Laura, neither of us are, thank God. I know you were only a baby when Dad died so you can't possibly remember him, but I do, and he was an awesome parent. Who's to say you wouldn't be like him?'

'I couldn't take the risk,' Harper whispered, still clinging to her big sister. 'I didn't *want* to take the risk.'

'Man, she really stuffed us up, didn't she? She's lucky she's not in the country right now or I'd go round there and ...' Willow sighed angrily. 'Does Samuel know?'

Harper shook her head. 'No one does. You're the first person I've ever told.'

'What? Not even your doctor, or the counsellor you had to see recently?'

'Nope. I didn't see how it was any of their business.'

'Oh my God, Harper.' Willow pulled back and looked sadly into her sister's face. 'That's a huge thing to bury inside you all these years.'

'I just put the experience in a box and never opened it again,' she said. 'It's not the kind of thing people talk about at dinner parties. Only once in a blue moon do I wonder how my life might have been today if I'd made a different decision.'

'And when you wonder that, do you regret not having it?'

Harper shrugged. 'I don't know. I don't *think* so. Deep down I'm sure I made the right decision—at nineteen I had no money, no stable home, no job. I couldn't have given the child a good life even if I'd had a better example of how to be a parent. But I guess I do feel a little guilty every now and then. What right did I have to make that decision? Maybe my boyfriend would have wanted the baby? Maybe that baby would have been the person to discover the cure for cancer?'

'It wasn't a baby,' Willow said forcefully. 'You aborted a collection of cells. The what-if game is never a smart one.'

Harper didn't reply—of course she was pro-choice but when she saw people like Jasper and Claire talk about how desperately they wanted a baby to love, she couldn't help wondering if she could have made a different decision. Like adoption.

At the thought of Jasper and Claire, the tears that had been starting to ease flooded out again.

Willow squeezed her hand. 'What happened to the guy?'

'I don't know,' Harper said. 'I stopped seeing him after that, and until Samuel I avoided any serious relationships.'

'I see.' Willow nodded. 'Do you think your abortion had anything to do with you deciding to donate your eggs? Perhaps subconsciously you did what you did as some kind of absolution? Not that I think you needed any such thing, but ...' Her voice drifted off.

'I don't know. Until today I hadn't really let myself analyse my motivations, but ... maybe.' She sighed, suddenly too exhausted for this conversation. Whatever her reasons, everything was a big fat hot mess right now. 'Look, do you mind if we don't talk about this anymore? I just want to go home and sleep.'

'Okay.' Willow removed her hand from Harper's and settled back into the driver's seat. 'But I'm here for you, you know that, right? Any time—even in the middle of the night—if you want to talk, you only need to call me and I'm there.'

'I know. Thank you.'

They passed the remainder of the journey to Sydney in relative silence. At some stage Willow put the radio on low, but Harper didn't listen to the music. Her mind was back in Newcastle with Jasper. Her whole body ached whenever she thought of the pain he must be in. She had never known a couple so obviously in love as they were; Jasper must feel as if he'd lost half of himself. Thank God he had a loving family. Thank God the baby did—her heart broke when she thought of Claire gone, but it was a tiny consolation to know that the child she'd so desperately wanted would be surrounded by so much love.

'Are you sure you don't want me to come in for a bit?' Willow asked when she parked her car in front of Harper and Samuel's house.

Harper looked up at the dark house. She guessed Samuel was still out with the partners. She swallowed the prick of guilt that she hadn't gone with him—she couldn't deal with any more regret right now.

'No. I'll be fine. Honestly. Thanks for being there for me today,' she said. 'It means a lot.'

'I'm always here for you, Harps.' As Harper put her hand on the door, Willow leant over and kissed her on the cheek. 'You don't have to go through everything alone.'

'I know. But right now I'd like a little me time. I'll talk to you tomorrow.' Without another word she stepped out of the car. The rain had eased and now only a light drizzle fell as she hurried to the front door.

Inside, she flicked on the lamp and then peeled off her slightly damp coat. Not even the prospect of *Friends* or a whole box of Coco Pops would make her feel better right now, so although she hadn't eaten anything since the Violet Crumble, she bypassed the kitchen and climbed the stairs.

The bedside lamp switched on the moment she opened the bedroom door and she stubbed her toe on the wall as she jumped back in surprise. She swore and rubbed at her foot.

'You okay?' Samuel asked.

'I thought you'd still be at dinner.' She bit down on the impulse to apologise for not being there. If he'd been more supportive earlier, perhaps she would have, but after today's events she wasn't feeling particularly charitable. She braced herself for a confrontation.

But it didn't come. 'I didn't go,' he said, pushing himself up to lean against the headboard. 'I called Stanley and Rodger and gave them our apologies. I told them you'd had a family emergency and they understood. They said we can reschedule when you're feeling better.'

'Oh. Okay.' She crossed the room to her dresser, starting to undress as she went.

'I'm sorry,' he said, his tone genuine. 'I wasn't fair on the phone this afternoon. In fact, I was a complete and utter prick. I've just been really stressed about work lately and I know there's no excuse for my behaviour, but ... Anyway, I'm really sorry to hear about Claire.'

Harper looked into her dresser mirror and then squeezed her eyes shut again. She'd managed to stop crying somewhere between Newcastle and home but one kind word from her husband and the tears had come right back up to the surface.

'Geez, babe, I'm so sorry.' Samuel climbed out of bed and padded across the room to her. He put his hands on her shoulders, spun her round to look at him and then drew her into his arms. 'I should have been there for you. I just didn't realise these people meant that much.'

'No, *I'm* sorry,' she sobbed into his chest. 'I should have been there for you. This was supposed to be your big night. You were right anyway. I shouldn't have gone. It was so awful. Jasper didn't want to see me. I'm not family, it's just ... this situation is so complicated.'

'It is,' he agreed, patting her gently on the back. And she was so grateful he didn't say *I told you so*. He might not have been able to predict this exact disaster but he'd warned her when she'd first raised the idea of egg donation that there could be complications.

She certainly hadn't bargained on making a new friend and then losing her just as quickly.

'It's just so unfair. Claire was such a wonderful person. She and Jasper went through so much to get their baby and they didn't deserve this. I can't believe she's gone.'

'No one deserves to die young, but sometimes shit happens. You did what you could for them, but you can't fix this. You need to look after yourself now.' He pulled back a little and looked down into her face—she couldn't remember him ever seeing her cry like this before.

'Have you had any dinner?' he asked. 'I can go downstairs and fix you something. Maybe pour you a glass of wine? Or would you like me to run you a bath?'

'No. Thank you, but I just want to go to sleep.' She felt so utterly exhausted and craved the oblivion sleep would bring.

'Okay.' He kissed her forehead and then let her go. 'Come to bed then.'

She nodded, took off the rest of her day clothes, pulled on her PJs and then went into the ensuite to wash her face and brush her teeth. It felt wrong to be getting on with such mundane stuff when Claire could no longer do any of them, but she forced herself through her bedtime ritual and then climbed in beside Samuel.

He switched off the lamp again and then pulled her into his arms for a cuddle. Snuggling was so rare for them—in their busy lives they didn't have time for such things—and she knew he was trying his best to comfort her, but even with his forgiveness and support, she couldn't sleep.

Not two minutes after she closed her eyes, Samuel started snoring. Harper wriggled out of his embrace and lay on her back staring into the darkness. She thought of Claire and Jasper, of the motherless baby and of the conversation she'd finally had with Willow tonight. Although she knew her sister wouldn't tell a soul—not even Miriam, unless she gave her permission—she wondered if it was finally time to tell her husband. Should she wake him up and come clean?

It seemed silly now she thought about it that they'd never had that conversation. It wasn't like she'd thought he'd be angry or judgemental—although Samuel came from a strong Catholic family, he himself was an atheist and extremely progressive—but by the time they'd met, the abortion had been so deeply buried in her past that it had simply never come up.

But by not telling anyone, had she made it more significant than it was? Now that she'd finally spoken about it, emotions she didn't know she'd even had were bubbling to the surface. Emotions she couldn't quite decipher.

She rolled over and glanced at her sleeping husband—the outline of his body just visible in the moonlight through the curtains. Why *hadn't* she ever told him? Weren't husbands and wives supposed to tell each other everything? She bet Claire and Jasper hadn't had such secrets.

Chapter Twenty-four

In the early hours of the morning, Jasper found himself sitting in the back of his parents' four-wheel drive, listening to them talking about renting an apartment in Newcastle so he could be near the baby while it remained in hospital.

'I'll get onto it first thing in the morning. I'll ask Sandie and Tom Roberts where they stayed when their baby was born prematurely,' his mum said, talking about a local couple who'd had a son not too long ago.

Claire had mentioned seeing Sandie and the baby in the post office last week and had spent ten minutes telling Jasper how cute the kid was. 'We're already planning play dates,' she'd told him with an excited laugh.

'Perhaps we can get Caroline and Noah to come home for a few months and help out.' His dad's suggestion jolted Jasper back to the present. Claire would not be arranging any play dates now.

'Good idea,' his mum replied. 'Jasper will need to be in Newcastle for the foreseeable future and I think Joanne and I will probably take turns staying with him until Anaya is healthy enough to come home.'

They spoke as if they'd forgotten he was there, or as if he were a child that needed to be organised. How could they just sit there nattering on about logistics and the future when Claire would never have one? In fact, he realised, they hadn't even mentioned Claire—it was all Anaya this and Anaya that, as if her existence made everything okay.

Part of him wanted to tell them to go to hell, to stop making all these plans for him when his life had just ended, but he didn't have the energy to object. His head flopped against the cold glass of the back window and he closed his eyes, wanting to shut out their voices, wanting to simply disappear.

Instead he found himself reliving the nightmare all over again.

Waving goodbye to Claire that morning. The police coming to his house. Seeing her beautiful body all cold and lifeless. Being introduced to the baby and then having to take each of their parents in one at a time to ooh and ahh over it.

They'd all fallen instantly in love. His mum, his dad, Claire's parents—all asking questions of the head nurse and the paediatrician who'd been there while the baby had been delivered by caesarean section. Jasper had tried to listen as they'd been fed information about the baby's state of health, how long it would likely need to stay in the hospital and what its care plan involved, but he couldn't remember any of it. He'd been glad when visiting hours were over and the nurse had ushered them out of the neonatal ward with an apology that they couldn't stay any longer.

Everyone expected him to want to stay with the baby, but he'd just wanted to escape. To be alone—away from his mum and dad, Claire's parents and her brother and his wife who'd also arrived at some stage in the evening. At least he knew Tim would look after Claire's folks so he didn't need to worry about them.

'We're home, darling,' said his mum, turning around from the front seat to look at him. 'Let's get you inside.'

Jasper glanced out the window to see that they'd arrived at his parents' place. 'This isn't my home. It's yours.'

'Your mum thought you might be best staying with us tonight,' said his dad. 'We can take you over to your place in the morning for a change of clothes before we head back to the hospital.'

He shook his head, trying to digest his dad's words. 'We? But what about tomorrow's balloon flight?'

'We've cancelled all flights for at least the rest of the week, out of respect to Claire.'

In all their years of business, Jasper couldn't remember his father ever cancelling a flight for any reason other than the weather or if there'd been a fatal balloon accident somewhere. The latter had happened only a few times in his lifetime and not to anyone he'd known. The reality of what had happened suddenly hit him.

Claire's really gone. She isn't coming home.

But right now he wanted to be as close to her as he could get. And that meant going home to the haven they'd created together. They loved their house and their garden and when they weren't hot air ballooning, they liked nothing more than to simply hang out there together.

'I'm not staying here. I want to go home.'

He saw his parents exchange a look, then his mum said, 'Okay. But I'm going to stay with you tonight. You shouldn't be alone after a day like that.'

'I'm not going to anything stupid,' he snapped, although right now the idea of flying up in a hot air balloon and never coming back down didn't seem stupid at all.

'Oh Jasper, I really don't think—'

'Let him be, Wendy,' his dad interrupted. 'He's right, he's a grown man and I don't blame him wanting some time alone right now.'

She relented with a heavy sigh. 'Okay.'

His dad turned the four-wheel drive around and drove the short distance to his place. When Jasper climbed out of the vehicle, he slammed the door shut behind him but his parents followed.

'Do you want us to come in for a little bit?' asked his mum. 'I could make you a hot drink or something to eat. I really don't like the idea of leaving you all alone.'

He looked down at her standing before him and shook his head. 'No, thanks. I think I'm just going to go to bed.'

With any luck he'd wake up and discover today had been some kind of twisted nightmare.

'If you're sure.' His mum threw her arms around him and held him tight while he stood there like a wooden soldier. He knew she only wanted to comfort him, but he couldn't bring himself to hug her back.

When she let him go, his dad clapped him on the shoulder. 'I love you, son. Call us any time during the night if you change your mind about being alone and we'll be over here pronto.'

He nodded. 'Thanks.'

'We'll be back first thing in the morning,' Wendy said. 'And you'll need to start giving some thought to what kind of funeral you'd like. Do you know if Claire wanted a burial or to be cremated?'

Jasper ran a hand through his hair angrily. 'For fuck's sake, Mum, she only died this afternoon.'

Wendy flinched. 'I'm sorry, I wasn't thinking. I just ...' She sniffed and then wiped her eyes as Paul wrapped his arm around her shoulder and drew her close. 'I'm so sorry, sweetheart.'

'We're all in shock,' Paul said. 'We don't know how to navigate something like this, but somehow we'll get through it together.'

Jasper nodded. Although he didn't want to *get through it*, he felt like a jerk for swearing at his mum. 'I'm sorry, Mum.'

'Don't you apologise, my darling. Go inside. Try and get some rest and we'll see you in the morning.'

He forced himself to give them both a quick hug and then he retreated into the house, closing the door without waiting for them to get back into the car and drive off.

Claire's two cats greeted him at the front door, winding themselves in and out of his legs and meowing loudly for their dinner. *Oh boys.* He dropped to the floor and pulled them into his arms, burying his head in their soft fur. Although Gerry and Sunny had grown to love him pretty fast, Claire would always be their first love. How were you supposed to explain to an animal that their owner was never coming back?

After a short while, the cats squirmed to be let go and started down the hallway. He followed them on autopilot, randomly switching on lights as he went. Despite the cats, the house was eerily quiet. He reckoned he could count on his hands the number of times he'd been here without Claire. As they worked *and* played together, they rarely did anything separately. If they attended a local event, they went together. They both played tennis for the local club and the friends they had in the area were other couples, so if they hung out socially they both went. If they went to Sydney to visit Polly and Scotty and the kids, they went together.

Polly and Scotty! Had anyone told them?

His hand went to his mobile phone in his back pocket and he drew it out. Looking down at the screen he saw he had over twenty missed calls and even more unread messages. Some were from Scotty, some from Polly, others from his sisters and close friends. He guessed bad news travelled fast. Although it was after midnight, he figured that no one would hold it against him if he called them back now, but what the hell would he say? What would *they* say?

No words could make things better so he didn't want to hear any at all.

He dumped his phone on the kitchen table and went over to the spot by the back door where they fed the cats. After shaking dried biscuits into their bowls, he left them to it and grabbed a beer from the fridge. The click-clack of his boots echoed on the floorboards as he walked through the house and his favourite beer tasted bitter on his tongue.

Claire was everywhere he looked.

She was in the sunny bright yellow paint on the walls—her choice, her favourite colour. She was in the floral themed artworks and inspirational quotes in funky frames that hung on said walls. She was in their furniture, a mix of modern and vintage-chic. She was smiling back at him from their wedding photos scattered all over the house.

But nowhere was more Claire than the room they'd spent the last few months doing up as a nursery. He flicked on the light and hesitated in the doorway. In here she'd gone for a pale mint green rather than her usual yellow and they'd painted big white clouds around the perimeter. The furniture was all whitewashed wood. There was the cot and matching change table that had taken hours to put together—flat packs weren't his forte—and the two mobiles, one balloon-themed and made by his mother, the other a floral one Claire had picked up at the local markets.

A low white bookshelf took pride of place beneath the window, already filling up with books and cute cuddly teddy bears from the future grandparents. There was also a whiz-bang pram with a capsule they could switch from the car to the house without waking the baby. Polly and his sisters had sworn by the brand so that's what they'd bought.

But Claire's favourite thing was the big comfy rocking chair. 'Feeding chair', she'd called it. She'd spent days on the internet researching about the best one, telling him she'd be spending hours in it breastfeeding so she wanted it to be perfect. Folded neatly on the seat was a soft white mink throw rug and a feeding cushion in the shape of an animal. Polly had told Claire she couldn't live without one of them as well, that having the right lift could really help in the early days of breastfeeding.

A lump formed in his throat and he put the beer down on the change table. Fancy cushions and comfortable chairs meant nothing now. Claire would never sit in here and nurse their baby.

One day in the not-too-distant future he'd have to bring that baby back here without her. That thought filled him with nothing but dread. How the hell was he supposed to look after a child all by himself? He might be good with his nieces and nephews, good at building Lego models and playing Nerf gun wars, but he didn't know the first thing about infants.

How could he do this alone? He wasn't *supposed* to be doing this alone. That wasn't the plan, dammit.

Why the hell had he let Claire drive to Newcastle by herself? He'd been with her for every other blasted appointment and if only he'd gone with her to this one, they probably wouldn't have been on the Expressway at that fatal moment. And if they had been, he'd have been driving and perhaps he'd have been able to react quicker than she had and avoid the other car altogether.

Damn CASA and their stupid checks. Had Big Basket Ballooning ever failed them before?

He stormed out of the nursery—slamming the door shut behind him—and then went into their room and glared at their marital bed. The doona was a large sunflower print that Claire had chosen. He'd always loved it because it reminded him of the dress she'd been wearing the night they met. On the bedside table sat the book she was halfway through reading, splayed open in a way that always made him cringe. He liked his books kept in good condition, Claire liked hers to look well-loved—it was one of the few things they ever disagreed on.

It suddenly hit him that she'd never finish reading it and at this thought he doubled over in pain. Clutching his stomach, he fell onto their bed. Part of him never wanted to lie on it again, but a stronger, more needy part of him grabbed hold of her pillow and hugged it close. He closed his eyes and inhaled her scent, which still lingered on the pillowcase.

She always smelt of flowers due to the amount of time she spent out in the garden and also the floral shampoo she used on her hair. And as Jasper breathed in that familiar aroma now, he couldn't believe that he'd never be able to smell, see or touch her again. This had to be some kind of cruel mistake. There had to be something he could do to make things normal again. He would do anything to turn back time.

Anything.

He'd give up ballooning tomorrow if it meant he could wake up and have Claire sleeping beside him again.

He'd move to Antarctica.

Hell, he'd become a monk. Even if it meant he couldn't be married to her anymore, at least she'd still be alive.

Yet even as he clutched at these desperate ideas, he knew they were all futile. The house was chillingly quiet—Claire's absence already a gaping hole.

Grief rocked him in waves as he held her pillow close and closed his eyes, craving the sleep that would perhaps bring some reprieve. But two hours later when he was still lying there wide awake—his body physically fine but aching all over—he wondered if he'd ever be able to sleep again.

Chapter Twenty-five

Sometime in the early hours of the morning, Harper must have fallen asleep because when she woke up on Tuesday, Samuel had already left. She hadn't heard him at all. She rolled over to stare at the empty space beside her and the memories of the day before came flooding back.

Claire is dead.

At this thought, she felt shocked all over again and prayed that yesterday was simply a nightmare. But when she crawled out of bed and caught sight of herself in the mirror on her dressing table, she knew this was an empty hope. Her eyes, her cheeks—*she* looked like the nightmare. All red and puffy but at the same time washed out. She was going to need a hell of a lot of make-up to make herself presentable for work. And caffeine. Lots of caffeine.

An hour later when she walked into the studio carrying two takeaway coffees, Lilia took one look at her and she knew she'd failed in her cover-up attempts.

'Are you sure you should be here today?' Lilia asked. 'You look like you've been out on an all-night bender.'

'Luckily this is radio, not TV then, hey?' She thrust one takeaway cup at her producer. 'What's on the agenda today?'

'Well, first up is you telling me what happened last night in Newcastle. Did you see Jasper? Did you see the baby?'

Harper just wanted to blank the last twenty-four hours from her mind but Lilia had held her hand and poured wine down her throat yesterday afternoon while she'd waited for Willow's call, so she deserved some sort of explanation. She flopped into her seat, sighed and then took a long sip of her coffee before giving Lil a brief rundown.

'As for the baby,' she concluded, 'I wasn't allowed in to see her. So I really don't have any idea how she's doing. But plenty of babies have been born earlier than thirty weeks and lived, so I'm hopeful she'll be okay.'

'No wonder you look shattered, that sounds horrid. And that poor man. That poor baby.' Lilia's eyes glittered as if she might break into tears at any moment. 'Poor you. That's a lot to go through. Why don't you take the day off? Go have a nap. I can reschedule today's guest and play one of our pre-records. And we can get Leo to work a little longer and cover the first part of your show. He won't mind.'

'No.' Harper shook her head. Leo was on air every day before her and wouldn't mind helping out, but she didn't want to go home and have nothing for company but her own depressing thoughts. At least at work there was the possibility that she'd be able to think about something else. 'I'll be fine.'

Lilia raised one eyebrow but knew better than to argue. 'Okay. If you're sure.'

'I am, but thanks.' She turned towards her computer screen; this conversation was over. Her first task every day was checking over the latest news and seeing if there were any current affair hot topics that she could discuss on air.

But today the news at the top of her screen was of yesterday's 'fatal accident'—the last thing she wanted to talk about with her listeners. The media had grabbed hold of the story, giving it more attention than a regular car accident because of all the drama involved. The high-speed chase of a drug addict in a stolen car. The tragic death of a young mother to be. The miraculous delivery of a premature baby. Thank God they hadn't got hint of her involvement.

She felt sick as she gazed at the photo of Claire and Jasper on her screen. It was clearly a shot from their wedding day. She guessed the journos had sourced it from Claire or Jasper's Facebook pages, but it seemed in such bad taste to splash their personal life and previous happiness all over the newspapers and internet. How would Jasper feel if he saw all this? And what about Claire's parents? She could only hope that they were too busy with the baby to think about checking the news, and that the media would be respectful enough to give them time to grieve in peace.

As if, said a little voice inside her. At the same time she heard a ping, signalling she had a new email.

Harper clicked the mail icon at the bottom of her screen, happy for the diversion. Although part of her was curious to read if there was any new information about the car accident and the baby, it felt wrong—almost as if she were stalking Jasper—to try and glean such info from news sites.

She frowned, her fingers hovering over her mouse as a name she'd never seen in her inbox before sat right at the top. Wendy Lombard? Her heart skipped a beat as realisation dawned—Jasper's mother.

With shaky fingers, she clicked open the email and held her breath as she read.

Dear Harper

I hope this email reaches you—I went online to the radio station to try and find a way to contact you. I almost called but after last night I wasn't sure whether you'd want to speak to any of us, and I'd probably sob through any phone conversation right now anyway.

Paul and I just want to thank you from the bottom of our hearts for everything you've done—for giving Claire and Jasper the gift of a baby and for caring enough to come last night and pay your respects. Jasper, as I'm sure you'll understand, is devastated and still in shock over Claire's sudden death, but I know that once he has had time to digest all this, he will be appalled at the way he treated you yesterday. He didn't mean what he said. Grief does crazy things to a person.

But in case he takes a little while to come around, I wanted to give you a brief update on Anaya—that is the name of their beautiful baby girl. Claire chose it and we think it fits her perfectly. She weighs a tiny 1.5 kg or 3 pounds in the old way. At the moment she's inside a heated incubator and will probably stay there for a few weeks. The paediatrician told us that once she reaches 1.8 kg she'll be able to regulate her own temperature and go into a normal open air cot.

Right now, we can only hold her little hand through a hole in the side of the incubator but the nurse told us that this afternoon they'll initiate some skin-to-skin contact with Jasper. Anaya's being fed through a feeding tube with expressed breast milk. I didn't know people donated such a thing but they do and it's so good that she can get a little of that goodness, even if just for a short while.

She's also on respiratory support for now but the medical staff are calling her birth a miracle and we are just so thankful that on such a tragic day for our family, there was also this amazing joy.

So thank you from all of us for what you did. Attached are a couple of photos of Anaya and my contact details are below. Please call or email if you want to know anything else. I'm sure in time you'll hear from Jasper as well.

With love,
Wendy.

Harper's gaze dropped to the two photos at the bottom of the screen and she gasped.

'You okay?' Lilia asked from across at her desk.

She barely heard and didn't answer as she gazed at the image of the tiny baby on the screen. It was sleeping, its little hands fisted, tubes sticking out of its button nose. Something in her heart squeezed.

This was what her egg had created. Because of her, this little person was alive. Despite her devastation and sadness over Claire, she couldn't help but smile at the image on the screen.

This baby truly did seem like a miracle.

'Is that the baby?' Lilia whispered from right behind Harper. She hadn't even heard her get up and approach.

'Yes,' she whispered back. 'Her name is Anaya. Isn't she tiny?'

'I think tiny might be an understatement. Wow.' Lilia leaned closer to the screen. 'Her hair's the same colour as yours—not that she has much—and I think she's got your eyes.'

Harper hadn't noticed those details but now that Lil had pointed them out, she couldn't deny it. This baby did bear an uncanny resemblance to her own baby photos. Or the few she had from before her father died and her mum stopped taking them.

'How does it feel knowing that little girl is a part of you?' Lilia asked.

'I'll admit it's a little surreal. And so not the way I was hoping for her to come into the world.'

She thought back to that night at her place when she'd enlisted the help of her friends and family to choose the recipients. At the time they'd ruled out the ads from single women because they'd wanted the baby to have the best family situation possible. They'd wanted to ensure that any child born of her eggs would have the love and support of a father as well as a mother, but if the last twenty-four hours had taught Harper anything it was that life wasn't something you could predict.

'It's terribly sad,' Lilia agreed. 'What a thing to share your birthday with the anniversary of your mother's death.'

'Oh.' Harper swallowed, trying to ignore the flood of emotion that caused a lump to grow in her throat and her eyes to tingle. Last night in the course of a few hours she'd cried more than she'd done before in her whole life and she'd felt certain her tear ducts were empty, but at this awful thought, tears threatened again. Her heart went out to this innocent little baby and also to Jasper, who for the rest of his life would be conflicted about that day.

'Will you go to the funeral?'

She rubbed her lips together a few moments as she contemplated Lilia's question. 'I kind of want to. Although I only knew Claire a short time, I really liked her and I'm heartbroken. But I don't want to upset Jasper again, so maybe I should just send flowers and a card.'

'Sheesh, sympathy cards,' Lilia said as if Harper had suggested sending decomposed road kill in the mail.

'You don't think I *should* send a card?'

'I didn't say that. I just don't envy you the task of choosing one. I had to buy one for a friend who lost her mum to cancer last year and all the poems and stuff inside just seemed so naff. But then again, what can you say to make something like this better?'

'Nothing,' Harper agreed, feeling absolutely helpless. 'This just sucks so bad. I should be sending Claire and Jasper a congratulations card and a gift for the baby.'

Lilia put her hand on Harper's shoulder. 'Are you sure you don't want to take some time off? Maybe you *should* go shopping and buy something for the baby. Maybe that will make you feel better.'

'No. I'm fine.' Harper shook her head and closed the email. Work was what would make her feel better. It had always been her lifeline, the thing that made her happy and one of the few things she *could* control.

With a reluctant nod, Lilia retreated to her desk and together they worked alongside each other in unusual silence. Or at least Harper pretended to work, but she found herself reading Wendy's letter over and over again and staring at the photos of the tiny baby. She wrote a reply, thanking Wendy for taking the time to email and telling her to reach out if there was anything she could do. Then, when Lilia left the office to go grab some lunch, Harper printed off the photos and popped them in her handbag so she could look at them later.

Chapter Twenty-six

The days following Claire's death were surreal. Sometimes Jasper felt as if he were living someone else's life; at other times that he was an actor in some movie he didn't want to watch. He spent the daylight hours in the hospital, sitting by the incubator of a little girl who felt as much a stranger to him as the people who sat alongside the other premature babies. Some of the time he even forgot that he was now alone—he'd fantasise Claire was off getting them coffee or something. And when his phone buzzed with a call or a text message, his heart would leap as his first thought was always her.

Yet every time he lifted his mobile and saw someone else's name on the screen, reality hit and his body turned to ice all over again. Friends tried to call him but he sent short messages in reply telling them he was busy with the baby and that he'd call them later. His mum and Claire's mum took turns keeping him company in the neonatal intensive care unit, but he preferred it when they left him alone. He passed the time just staring down at the baby and waiting for the unconditional love to kick in, but mostly he was just grateful that being with her gave him a reprieve from everyone else's fussing.

At night he retreated to a cheap apartment in Newcastle where he showered and changed his clothes and forced down some dinner—not because he felt inclined to do any of these things but because his mum made him. Most evenings he escaped to the bedroom citing tiredness, but tonight when he arrived at the apartment, he was greeted by half his and Claire's family.

'Hey mate. I'm so sorry,' Scotty said, clapping him on the shoulder and then drawing him into a hug.

'Hi,' Jasper managed. As only he and the grandparents were allowed to visit the baby in the hospital, he'd avoided seeing most of them until now. 'What are you all doing here?'

'We asked Scotty and Polly to come up and discuss the funeral arrangements with us,' Mike replied from a few feet away.

Jasper's stomach turned at his father-in-law's words. He'd been glad when he and Joanne had volunteered to liaise with the funeral director. He didn't know the first thing about organising funerals and he didn't want to learn. Probably that made him a coward—Claire would have been so much stronger if the situation was reversed—but sitting down and talking about flowers and music and whatever else you had to talk about when planning a funeral would just make it real.

As Scotty stepped away, Polly wrapped her arms around Jasper. Within seconds he felt her tears soaking his shirt, reminding him he wasn't the only one suffering here.

'Thank you for coming,' he whispered into her hair.

She pulled back and looked up into his face. He noted the bags under her eyes. 'I just can't believe this,' she said with a sniff.

'You and me both.'

'Your mum sent us photos of Anaya,' she said. 'She's gorgeous and I'm so glad she's doing well. My kids can't wait until she's big enough to come play.'

He nodded. 'Thanks.' Then went through the motions of greeting his sisters and Claire's brother, Tim.

'Do you want to freshen up before we get started?' Joanne asked.

'Nah. I'm fine.' He was far from fine but wanted to get this over and done with—wanted everyone to go and leave him alone to wallow again.

Polly took hold of his hand and led him over to a small table, not big enough for everyone to fit around. Boxes of takeaway pizza and bottles of soft drink sat on top as if this was some kind of party. The thought left a bad taste in his mouth and he knew he wouldn't be able to eat one slice.

He took a seat and his family crowded around—his parents and Claire's sitting on the remaining seats, everyone else standing.

Mike spoke first, taking hold of his wife's hand as he did so. 'This is the last thing I ever wanted to do. You're not supposed to have to arrange your child's funeral but that makes this one of the most important things we've ever done. If Jasper agrees, Joanne and I would like to make this service a celebration of the wonderful, unique person Claire was.'

Around him heads nodded and there were murmurs of agreement. Jasper didn't say a word.

'As Claire fell in love with the Hunter Valley at the same time as she fell in love with Jasper, we think she'd have liked the service to be held there, so we've booked the Catholic church.' He looked to Jasper. 'Most people in our family have been cremated; are you okay with that or would you prefer a burial?'

It wasn't something he and Claire had ever discussed. They'd made plenty of plans for the future—baby plans, travel plans, they'd even joked about retirement plans—but death hadn't been something they'd bargained on happening so soon.

'Cremation's fine,' he said.

'You could scatter her ashes in your garden,' his sister Corrine suggested. 'The place she loved being most.'

But Jasper shook his head. Suddenly he knew what he wanted to do in that regard.

'What's next on your list?' he asked, nodding towards the papers in front of his father-in-law.

The rest of the evening was as much of a blur as the past few days had been. He vaguely registered discussions about flowers, music, pallbearers and the need to choose photos to show on a big screen at the end of the ceremony. He agreed to Claire's parents going to his house and going through the photos on their computer.

And then came the question he didn't even know he'd been dreading until Mike asked it. 'Would you like to say a few words?'

Jasper blinked. For a second he thought his father-in-law was asking him to talk now and then he realised he meant at the actual service. His chest tightened at the thought of getting up in front of a crowd of people and trying to say the right things. What the hell was he supposed to say at the funeral for the love of his life? He wished they were planning his funeral instead.

'You don't have to,' Mike rushed. 'Tim's going to speak on behalf of our family and Polly wants to say a few words as well.'

'I think you should try and say something,' said his dad. 'You don't want to regret not doing so later.'

Jasper nodded. 'I'll say something.' He didn't know what but he owed it to Claire to try.

Joanne twisted a paper napkin between her fingers and sniffed. 'It's such a pity Anaya can't be there.'

'I've been thinking about that,' said his mum. 'Maybe I should see if I can get permission to stay with Anaya without you?'

'You don't want to go to Claire's funeral?' Jasper couldn't help his accusatory tone.

'Of course I want to be there, but the funeral and the wake will take up most of the day and I don't like the thought of Anaya being all alone in the hospital.'

Jasper lifted an eyebrow. 'Alone? That place is buzzing with people. She'll have all the doctors and nurses.'

His mum gave him an apologetic shrug. 'I just don't like the thought of her not having someone who loves her beside her.'

Guilt swamped Jasper at her words—he couldn't honestly say he loved the baby; right now she felt more like an obligation than the blessing everyone else kept going on about. Every time the nurses made him hold her against his bare chest—something they called Kangaroo Care—he prayed he'd feel something. But he never did.

'There is one other alternative,' she began. 'We could see if we could get special permission for Harper to come and sit with her?'

Harper.

Jasper hadn't spoken to her or even really thought about her since his outburst in the hospital the night Claire died. Now that he remembered the less than kind words he'd spat at her, self-loathing washed over him.

He hadn't been fair on her. How would *he* have felt if some guy had spoken to Claire the way he had to Harper? And now he'd had a few days to think about nothing but his wife's death, he realised how unreasonable he'd been blaming Harper for the accident. There was only one person at fault here—that deadbeat drug addict who he hoped would rot in prison for what he'd done.

But Harper? He owed her an apology.

'That's a good idea,' he said. 'Do you think the hospital would allow it?'

'Well,' began his dad, rubbing his beard, 'policy is parents and grandparents only, and Harper technically does fit that description—biologically. There's still a few days until the funeral, so we've got time to make a request to the nurse manager.'

He nodded. 'I'll speak to her tomorrow. Although I guess we'd better ask Harper if she's okay with the idea first.'

'Would you like me to talk to her?' asked his mum.

'No, I can do it. I'll call her when we're done here.'

That settled, Mike closed the notebook in front of him. 'I think we've been through everything. Are you sure you're happy with the arrangements?'

Jasper cringed at his father-in-law's choice of words. *Happy?* How on earth could he be happy about any of this? But he knew Mike meant no harm—they were all suffering and dealing with it in different ways.

'Yes. Thank you for organising everything,' he said.

Joanne sniffed and reached across to take Jasper's hand. 'You've got enough to worry about with Anaya, but if there's anything you think of that we've missed or any other songs that you decide you want played, you just let us know.'

'I will. Thanks.' He slipped his hand out from his mother-in-law's and pushed back his seat to stand. 'I'm going to go call Harper now.'

Polly stood as well. 'Really sorry, Jasper, but we have to be getting back to Sydney to relieve the sitter.' She came around the table and hugged him. 'But don't forget, we're here for you anytime, day or night.'

He squeezed her back and then let go. 'Thanks. I know.'

After Polly and Scotty made a move, his dad and Claire's parents followed. Only his mum, who was staying at the apartment with him, remained and for that Jasper was hugely grateful. Sitting all day by the baby's side was weirdly exhausting and discussing the funeral had taken it out of him as well. Bed beckoned and although he knew he probably wouldn't sleep, he just wanted to lie horizontal for a bit.

'I'll clean up,' Wendy said, patting him on the back as they closed the front door behind everyone. 'You go talk to Harper and then come tell me how you went, and perhaps try and have a bite to eat.'

'Thanks, Mum.' He turned and drew her into him. She'd been taking such good care of him and he hadn't once told her how much he appreciated it.

'You don't have to thank me, sweetheart. And by the way, I hope you won't be angry, but I've been corresponding with Harper via email.'

He pulled back, not sure how he felt. 'What do you mean?'

'I totally understand your reaction to seeing her the other night, but she did something amazing for you and Claire and I didn't want her to be left hanging, wondering or worrying about the baby. I've sent her a couple of photos and emailed her an update every day on how Anaya is faring.'

'Oh, all right.' He let out a deep breath, finding some of his guilt ease at her confession. 'Thanks for that. I guess I'll go call her now.'

'Good boy. I think she'll be glad to hear from you.'

Chapter Twenty-seven

Harper's mobile rang as she loaded dirty plates into the dishwasher. 'Can you see who that is?' she asked Samuel.

He stopped wiping the table and leant across to look down at the screen. 'It's an unknown number. Probably a cold call. Just ignore it.'

And usually she would, but something urged her to answer this one. She wiped her hands on a tea towel and snatched up the phone.

'Hello? Harper Drummond.'

No one spoke for a few long moments. Just as she was about to hang up, she heard a voice she instantly recognised.

'Hi Harper. It's me. Sorry for calling so late.'

The half-loaded dishwasher forgotten, she pressed a hand against her heart. 'Jasper! It's fine. How are you?' She cursed herself the moment the words left her mouth. How the hell did she think he was?

'I'm feeling pretty shit to be honest, but that doesn't excuse the way I treated you the other night. I'm really sorry. I just—'

'Don't you apologise,' she said, sounding a little harsher than she meant. 'I'm the one that should be saying sorry for intruding. I didn't even think about how you might feel about me turning up. I just got in the car and came.'

'And now, looking back, I appreciate that,' Jasper said, his voice a little choked. 'Mum said she's been giving you updates on the baby.'

'Yes. She's beautiful.'

'It's actually because of her I'm calling.'

Harper's knees wobbled and she reached out to steady herself on the bench. 'Is something wrong? I thought she was doing well.'

'She's doing fine,' Jasper rushed. 'The doctors and nurses can't quite believe the progress she's making. She's gaining weight and they reckon another few days and she might not need to be in a heated incubator anymore.'

'Wow. That's wonderful.'

'Yeah. Anyway, I wanted to ask you a favour.'

'Yes?' Her heart stilled.

'Claire's funeral is next Wednesday and my mum was going to miss it to stay with the baby,' he explained, 'but I don't think she should. She loved Claire like another daughter and I think she'll regret not being there later. Could you...?'

Harper swallowed at the terrifying thought of looking after a baby on her own. But it wasn't like she'd have to do anything except be there—the doctors and nurses would be in charge of Anaya's care. And this was a small thing she could do to help. She also had to admit that ever since seeing the photos, she'd been curious about seeing her in person. 'Of course I'll come.'

'Thank you,' Jasper said. 'I really appreciate it, though I still have to run it by the hospital to see if they'll grant us special permission for you to be in the NICU without me.'

'Oh right. Sure.' She suddenly remembered the stern nurse/security guard who'd been at the reception desk that dreadful night. She'd need to be a ninja to sneak by the likes of her without approval.

'I'll talk to the head nurse first thing tomorrow morning and be in contact.' He sighed as if the conversation had been an effort. 'Thank you, Harper, for being so understanding and for being willing to help out. Claire knew from the moment she read your email that you were special. You'll never know how happy you made her.'

Harper's eyes filled with tears. Although she was usually eloquent with words, she had no idea what to say to this poor man.

'Anyway, I'd better be going. But I'll be in touch as soon as I can.'

'Goodnight Jasper.'

Harper disconnected the phone, her heart feeling as if someone had wrapped their hands around it and was trying to drag it down to her stomach. She looked up at Samuel who'd been listening intently.

'You going to the funeral after all?' he asked, tossing the wet cloth in the sink.

She shook her head. 'Jasper has asked if I could go and sit with Anaya while he and his family are in the Hunter Valley for the funeral.'

'Anaya?' Before she could answer, he nodded quickly. 'Right. The baby. Why would you need to do that?'

'To put their minds at ease.'

He raised his eyebrows. 'Aren't they asking a little much? You're only supposed to be the donor. Besides, the baby is so young, it's hardly going to notice a few hours by itself. And as it's still in hospital, the medical staff will be looking after it.'

'*She*, not it,' Harper snapped, her patience wearing thin. Although in theory he'd been supportive this last week—he said the right things and tried to sympathise—it was clear he didn't get her grief about Claire and he'd barely even looked at the photos of Anaya when she'd tried to show him. 'And as you don't *have* a baby, nor a dead wife, I guess you can't put yourself in Jasper's shoes, but this is a small thing he's asked me to do and I want to help.'

Samuel held up his hands in defence. 'You're right, I don't understand. I didn't understand why you felt the need to donate your eggs and I certainly don't understand why they need you to do this, *but* ...' He closed the gap between them and put his hands on her arms. She fought the urge to shake him off. 'As I've told you a number of times, I might not always understand you but I love you and I want to support you. So, would you like me to come with you to Newcastle? When is the funeral? Unless it's Friday, I should be able to shuffle things around at work and make up the time later.'

Like the air slowly being let out of a balloon, some of the irritation she felt at his initial reaction seeped out of her. 'No, I'll be okay. You can't really afford to take the time off—you're already working ridiculous hours—and you won't be able to be inside with me and Anaya anyway. Jasper has to get special permission from the hospital for me to go into the neonatal ward, so it might not even happen.'

But to her surprise, she desperately hoped it would.

'Well, if you're sure. But if you change your mind, I'll be happy to come.' Samuel dropped a quick kiss on her forehead and then let her go. 'I've got to do a bit of reading before coming to bed. Are you going to head up now or keep me company down here?'

'I'm going to call Lilia and give her a heads-up about needing Wednesday off work, but then I think I'll have a soak in the bath. See you when you come up.'

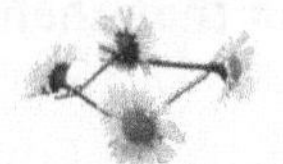

On Wednesday morning Harper got up at the crack of dawn, dressed in skinny jeans, her favourite woollen jumper and knee-high boots, and then tiptoed out of the house while Samuel was still asleep in bed. She usually listened to podcasts on long journeys—mostly overseas shows similar to her own—but today she drove in silence. It didn't seem right to be listening to others talk about their full lives on the day when Claire would be farewelled from the earth, and the boppy music on the commercial stations didn't match her mood.

It had been too early to eat when she'd left, so she'd poured her morning coffee into a travel mug and climbed into the car, planning to stop for a greasy breakfast sandwich at a service station on the way. But her stomach churned the closer she got to Newcastle and she didn't think she'd be able to eat a thing. Her emotions were a weird cocktail of sadness, excitement and apprehension, but they would be nothing compared to how Jasper must be feeling right now.

With this thought, she parked her car and then headed for the hospital entrance. She'd agreed to meet him in the foyer so they could go to the NICU together. Although she was early, Harper saw him and his mum standing off to one side of the reception desk, both of them nursing takeaway coffee cups. They wore Sunday best—Jasper a dark-grey suit that made him look like a model for Armani and Wendy a black skirt and a floral blouse in pinks and purples.

They glanced up as Harper approached and relief swam in Jasper's eyes as he saw her. She couldn't help a sad smile as she noted the bright floral print on his shirt. The few times Harper had met Claire in person, she'd always worn some sort of flower-print clothing or jewellery and it was clear that their attire had been chosen to honour her.

'Harper.' Jasper almost breathed her name as he greeted her with a hug.

'Hi,' she said, squeezing him back.

'Thank you for coming.'

'There's nowhere else I'd rather be.' Harper let him go and turned to Wendy.

'It's lovely to see you again.' Wendy held out a takeaway cup—Harper hadn't even noticed she'd been carrying two. 'This is for you. We weren't sure what your poison was so it's just a simple flat white, but I've got some sugar sachets in my bag if you'd like them. Unfortunately you can't take it in to Anaya—no food, drinks or phones allowed—but it shouldn't be too hot now, so you can drink it quick.'

'Thank you,' Harper said, taking the kind offering. It touched her heart that they'd thought about her on what was probably going to be the worst day of their lives. 'I don't need sugar.'

'You're welcome, love. It's the least we could do.' And then Wendy embraced her as well, taking care not to knock the coffee cup as she did so. It felt weird hugging these people—in some ways they were little more than strangers—yet at the same time it felt natural and right.

'Thank you for all the updates,' Harper said. 'I appreciated them.'

'That's my pleasure.' Wendy pulled out of the hug but kept one arm linked through Harper's. 'And now you get to meet our gorgeous girl in person. Come on.'

Harper's stomach fluttered as they led her through the hospital maze—navigating lifts and corridors to the neonatal ward. She couldn't remember ever feeling this nervous in her life, not even when she'd had the interview with the radio station for her absolute dream job, but she told herself it was silly to be anxious about seeing a baby. Anaya wouldn't know who she was and she couldn't talk, so it wasn't like they'd spend hours attempting conversation to avoid awkward silence.

She absentmindedly sipped her coffee and answered Wendy's polite questions as they walked. Was her drive north hassle free? Who covered her radio show when she wasn't there? Was she planning on travelling back to Sydney tonight?

'You're welcome to stay at the apartment we've been renting if you're too tired to drive,' Wendy offered.

'Thank you,' Harper said, 'but I've only taken today off work, so it'll be easier to head straight home.'

'I'll get back here as soon as I can,' Jasper promised as they finally neared the NICU.

'Oh no, please don't!' She didn't want him to feel he had to rush out on his wife's wake. 'Take as long as you need. I'll be fine here and it's an easy drive back to Sydney.'

Harper took a final sip of her coffee and then tossed it in the bin. She and Jasper left Wendy in the waiting area as they proceeded into the actual ward. As if he'd done so a zillion times before—which he probably had—he went across to a sink, washed his hands, dried them on a paper towel and then took a squirt of sanitiser to rub all over them. She did the same, taking more care over washing her hands than she'd ever done in her life.

He led her down a corridor past a number of rooms, each filled with tiny little clear incubators and lots of high-tech equipment, the kind she'd only ever seen on TV medical dramas. Although she wasn't close enough to see the babies, the hairs on her neck raised a little at the thought of being this close to so many. She'd spent so long avoiding anything to do with them that it felt weird to be suddenly immersing herself in their world.

'She's in here,' Jasper said as he pushed open a door.

Harper surveyed another room full of incubators, wondering which one of them held Anaya.

'Good morning.' The smiley nurse reminded her a little of Mrs Doubtfire, but without the masculinity. 'You must be Harper.'

'Yes, hello.' She wondered if this woman was the nursing unit manager, the one who had fought with the senior hospital administration to get her special access.

'It's lovely that you could come and spend the day with Anaya. I'm her main nurse and I'll be around with the paediatrician to do his morning check-up soon, but I'll also be doing observations throughout the day, so feel free to ask me anything at any time.'

Harper nodded. 'Thank you.'

Mrs Doubtfire's doppelganger looked to Jasper. 'I'll be thinking of you and your family today.' Then she stepped away, leaving him to lead Harper over to Anaya.

Butterflies working up a storm in her stomach, she followed for a few steps until he came to a halt in front of one of the tiny see-through incubators.

'Here she is,' he said simply, peering into the box.

Harper's breath caught in her throat at the sight of the sleeping baby. Anaya was even tinier in person. If not for the little tube going into her nose, she'd look like a porcelain doll.

'She's picture perfect,' she whispered in absolute awe as an unexpected tear formed in the corner of her eye. 'I've never seen anything, I mean any*one*, more beautiful.'

Jasper cleared his throat slightly. 'I hope you brought a book or something. The hours can drag sitting in here.'

A book? The thought had never crossed her mind, but she knew she wouldn't be able to concentrate on anything of the sort. Her eyes went to the circular holes in the side of the incubator. 'Are we allowed to touch her?' she asked.

Jasper nodded. 'You can hold her hand, but you need to put on more sanitiser gel first.' He gestured to a little bottle on the wall behind them.

Without another word, she did as he said and then slipped her hand in the side and stroked a finger over Anaya's tiny hand. Her milky skin was as smooth as it looked, and when she moved a little and curled her hand around Harper's pinkie finger, Harper's heart almost exploded with emotion.

This was the weirdest experience of her life. She'd never expected to have a baby and certainly not with a man she'd only met a handful of times. Yet although technically this was Claire's baby, Harper couldn't ignore the inner voice reminding her of their biological connection. Something squeezed inside her at the thought.

'Well, if you're okay, I'll be heading off now,' Jasper said.

Reluctantly, she removed her hand from the incubator and turned to face him. Although dressed to impress, he looked totally lost and physically drained, as if he hadn't slept in days. She wished there was something she could say to help, but what could you say to a man who was heading off to bury his wife?

She gave him a quick hug. 'Don't worry about Anaya. You take your time to say goodbye to Claire properly. I'll be here in person with your little girl, but with you in spirit. I didn't know Claire for long, but she touched my heart in a way some people I've known my whole life have never managed to do.'

'Thank you,' he said, and then pursed his lips as if struggling to keep it together. She could only imagine the heartbreak he must be feeling and couldn't help wondering if Samuel would be so distraught if she died. Sure they loved each other, but in many ways they lived such separate lives that if one of them was gone, the other's life wouldn't change that much. It was an uncomfortable thought, one she pushed to the back of her mind to deal with later.

Harper watched as Jasper left the room, closed the door and walked along the corridor until he was out of sight. Then she lowered herself into the plastic chair beside Anaya and slipped her hand back into the incubator. Once again, the baby wrapped her tiny fingers around Harper's and then she actually looked up, right into Harper's eyes.

'What are you thinking, little one?' she whispered, feeling a strong and surprising urge to rip open the incubator and lift the baby into her arms. The only babies she'd ever held were those of her best friends, Juliet and Renee, and then she couldn't wait to give them back. But she wanted to comfort and cuddle this one.

Another tear trickled down her cheek, following the one that had formed earlier, and pretty soon she was blubbering a river. She cried for Jasper. She cried for Claire. And she cried for this beautiful little girl. Anaya had plenty of aunties and two loving grandmothers, but she didn't have a mother. As someone who had grown up *with* a mother, but one who was never there in all the ways that mattered, Harper knew what it was like to feel alone, and every organ in her body ached at the thought.

'Here, love, take these.'

Harper blinked at the sound of the head nurse's voice and stared at the tissue box like it was some weird relic from the past.

'We go through a bucketload of those in here,' said the woman, placing a comforting hand on Harper's shoulder. 'And I'm usually pretty tough myself but I must admit this little girl and her daddy have touched my heart. Such a tragedy.'

Harper simply nodded, accepted the tissues and yanked one out.

The nurse drifted away again as Harper wiped her eyes, tasting salt on her lips. Thankfully she'd bypassed mascara when she'd done her make-up that morning otherwise she'd be a frightful sight right now.

As the morning progressed, more people started coming into the ward and filling the seats surrounding the other incubators. She noted a few lingering glances in her direction, but guessed it wasn't because they recognised her—one of the benefits of radio over TV was that you could walk down the street without someone pointing you out. No, these new parents obviously knew the story behind Anaya's birth, but they didn't know about her conception, so were likely curious about who Harper was and why she was there.

But she didn't meet their gazes, talk or even smile at any of them. The only time she let go of Anaya's hand was when the nurse and paediatrician did their rounds. She felt proud and immensely happy when they noted her increased weight and said she mightn't need the respiratory support for much longer.

'We might even be able to try her on a bottle in a week or so,' said the paediatrician, with a big grin that crinkled the lines around his eyes.

Harper made a mental note to tell Jasper when he returned later; hopefully this little bit of good news would cause some light at the end of a dark day.

Chapter Twenty-eight

Jasper had always believed funerals should be a celebration of a person's life, and he'd initially agreed with his in-laws when they'd said they wanted Claire's to be that way. But now, as he entered the church, he changed his mind. The sight of all these people dressed in the bright floral clothes they'd been requested to wear made his chest cramp. They looked more like they were here for a wedding or a party, and that just felt so incredibly wrong.

Claire may have had a happy life, mostly, but she hadn't had a long life. There were so many things she'd still been looking forward to experiencing—so many adventures she'd been robbed of—that coming here today and celebrating her thirty years felt like a kick to the gut. He wanted to rip off his bright flowery shirt and tell everyone else to go home and get changed, but then he saw his in-laws a few steps away.

'Jasper!' Claire's mum threw her arms around him and they hugged long and hard before she pulled back. 'How's Anaya this morning?'

'She's fine.' He nodded, trying to stamp down the irritation that rose within him. Today wasn't supposed to be about the baby.

'Hello, son.' Although he and Mike didn't usually hug, they did so now.

The next few minutes were a blur as Jasper—with his parents and Claire's folks flanking him—headed to the front of the church, pausing every few steps to accept words of sympathy from friends and family. He knew it was a testament to how well-loved Claire was that so many people from their local community and beyond had turned out to say goodbye, but every time someone said how sorry they were, it felt like a knife twisting further and further into his heart. He shook hands with Nick Gilbert and his colleague. Although she'd been with him to deliver the news of Claire's death, Jasper couldn't for the life of him remember her name.

He'd never been so relieved as when he got to the front of the church and could collapse into the first pew, his parents and Claire's taking their seats beside him. Behind them were Claire's three remaining grandparents—one had died after a stroke only a year ago—and Jasper's sisters, who held their kids close. Across the aisle a sombre-faced Polly sat with her five children who were quieter than he'd ever known them to be.

The priest came over and said a few words to him and Claire's parents and although Jasper nodded and said something back, he wouldn't be able to repeat any of the words exchanged. Then the priest touched Jasper's shoulder and retreated to the pulpit as Claire's favourite singer's voice filled the air.

Spend all your time waiting ...

Jasper stood with the rest of the church. He turned towards the back and watched the pallbearers—Scotty, Claire's brother Tim and his own sisters' husbands—start down the aisle carrying the coffin. As Sarah McLachlan sang about an angel and tears streamed down the faces of those around him, Jasper still couldn't believe that it was Claire's body inside that white box.

Less than two weeks ago they'd been lying in bed together plotting their future, and now he'd never hold her again.

After placing the coffin on the stand at the front, the pallbearers all bowed their heads in respect before retreating to sit with their families. The music faded and silence echoed in the church for a few long moments. All eyes were on the coffin with the sunflower wreath on top of it, a wreath that matched Claire's favourite dress. A dress he knew she was wearing today.

Although the weather wild and woolly outside, Jasper felt hot and was finding it hard to breathe in the church. Joanne took hold of his hand and held it tightly as the priest began the service.

'We gather here today to celebrate the life of Claire Joanne Lombard, to pay our last respects and also to try and bring some comfort to Claire's husband, daughter, parents, family and friends who have been deeply hurt by her tragic death. Although we have all come from different places, we have one thing in common. Claire has touched our lives, as she did anyone who ever met her. I personally knew Claire through the tennis club and although she always told me she wasn't a particularly religious person, we had a few deep and meaningful conversations during our friendship, in which I came to understand she was a woman with a great sense of spirituality.'

He went on for a few more minutes, speaking about death and how all life has a beginning and an end. He quoted from the bible and then even read a few verses of Shakespeare before urging Jasper, Claire's parents and all who loved her to hold onto their memories and continue always to remember Claire in their own special way.

Next Tim was invited to the front to speak on behalf of Claire's family.

'Well, this sucks,' he said as he glanced towards the coffin. 'My sister was many things to me—she was bossy and over-protective despite being younger than me, she was my best friend growing up and is still one of the first people I turn to for advice. We grew close as children when I spent a lot of time in the hospital with Mum and Dad sitting with Claire during her long stays there. So close she thought she had the right to tell me who I could and couldn't date.'

He glanced over to his wife and their two year old son, Theo. 'Hannah was the only girl Claire ever approved of and the day I introduced them, she told me if I didn't marry her, she'd never forgive me.'

Laughter echoed throughout the building. Tim paused a moment, wiped his eyes and inhaled deeply before continuing.

'My sister was a fighter and an inspiration in everything she did. From an early age, if she wanted something, she went after it with everything she had until she got it. When she was diagnosed with leukaemia, she decided she wanted to live and that's what she did. No one was prouder than me when she kicked cancer in the arse, and I stupidly thought that meant she'd live forever.'

Tim spoke for a few more minutes, sharing more memories and talking about Claire's love for her unborn child, another thing she'd pursued with her stubborn dedication. Jasper thought Tim may have had more to say, but emotion finally got the better of him and with tears silently pouring down his face, he touched his hand to the coffin and then went back to sit with Hannah and Theo.

Polly took the mic next. Today she wore a bright pink dress that could have been one of Claire's, where usually her choice of clothing was totally different.

'This is the hardest thing I've ever had to do,' she began. 'I've never been good at public speaking, but I'm going to try and hold it together long enough to tell you what my best friend means to me.

Claire is like no other friend I've ever had. She's courageous and fun and always up for adventure, yet at the same time she's the most thoughtful and sensible person I know. She always looks out for me and never lets me go off to do anything crazy alone.'

Again the audience laughed as Polly shared some of those crazy things she'd dragged Claire into over the course of their friendship and Jasper found himself laughing as well, even though he'd heard the stories many, many times before.

'When I had children,' Polly continued, her voice turning serious again, 'even though Claire couldn't easily have them herself, she was genuinely happy for me and no one could have been happier than I was when she announced she was going to be a mother as well. I honestly can't comprehend facing the rest of my life without Claire at the end of a phone line, but my heart breaks even more to think that she'll never get to experience the one thing she wanted more than anything. I'm not the best with words, but I'd like to finish by reading a piece by my favourite Aussie poet—Penelope Bruce—that has helped me navigate my grief these past few days. I hope it might help you all as well.'

It feels like winter is here to stay
I wonder if it's because you've gone away
And so the cold and rain remains because my heart is sad

Maybe the beginning of spring is fickle
Because every day tears course and trickle
Down the sides of my face and brush the sun aside

Maybe the sun is reluctant to shine
Around a heart as heavy as mine
And so in empathy hides behind the clouds

Don't be shy spring, it's your turn now
The seasons must go on somehow
So hang your warmth up in the sky and shine

Because although my heart is sad
Your life and sunshine makes me glad
And reminds me of the goodness and light still here

So come dear spring and let's be friends
And while we know that all life ends
Today we remember to live our life and shine

Polly lifted her head again and looked directly at Jasper. 'I will always love Claire,' she said, 'and I promise I'll always be there for you and Anaya, to talk about Claire whenever you want to, to laugh and cry and to help your daughter know her mother.'

Then she turned to the coffin and blew a kiss. 'Farewell, my friend. I'll miss you.' Taking a tissue from her cleavage, Polly buried her face in it as the tears she'd managed not to cry while speaking broke free.

Jasper watched her return to her family and fall into Scotty's arms as their children looked on in bewilderment, and he understood exactly how they felt. This *still* didn't feel real.

'Sweetheart.' His mum leant close and whispered into his ear. 'It's your turn. Do you want us to come up with you?'

'No.' Wendy let go of his hand and he forced himself to stand.

The few steps to the pulpit felt like the longest walk of his life. And as his hands gripped the wooden edges and he stared out into the full-to-capacity church, he prayed that the words would come.

'Claire and I didn't have time to ready ourselves for her death,' he said eventually. 'And although I've had over a week to prepare myself to stand up here and talk about my beloved wife, every time I tried to make some notes my mind went blank, so forgive me for just blurting out whatever comes now.'

Jasper swallowed and somehow continued. 'I fell in love with Claire the first night we met. You may not believe in love at first sight but there's no other explanation where she and I are concerned.'

Almost forgetting about the teary-eyed faces watching him, he went on to describe that first night and then the five years they'd lived, laughed and loved together. At some point he felt a tear snake down his cheek and another followed fast, but he didn't wipe them away. He kept on talking about Claire, wanting, needing to get everything he'd locked up inside off his chest.

Finally he tore his eyes from the gathered crowd and looked over to the coffin with the sunflower wreath and two photo frames on top. One contained a photo of him and Claire on their wedding day, the other a shot of her lying on their bed with Gerry and Sunny draping themselves over her. 'I wish it was me in that box instead of her,' he admitted, 'yet at the same time I would never want Claire to experience the pain I'm feeling right now.'

Tears pouring down his face, he stepped up to the coffin and looked down. Imagining her lying inside looking up at him, he spoke in a low whisper. 'Goodbye, my darling girl. You might now be gone, but my love for you will never die.'

Then he slowly made his way back to the pew, unsure how he managed to walk when everything inside him was broken.

After that the priest invited anyone else who so desired to come up and say a few words. It touched Jasper's heart that so many people chose to get up and do so. When the last person stepped down from the front, the priest thanked everyone for coming, invited them to head to the club afterwards for refreshments and then stepped back as the slide show Claire's family had put together began.

'Dancing Queen', another of Claire's favourites, exploded from the speakers as a cute baby with honey-blonde hair and big brown eyes appeared on the screen. Her childhood flashed before them—even in the photos of her bald in hospital, Claire's smile filled her face. Jasper reckoned there wasn't a dry eye in the building. His mum shoved a hanky in his hand but he didn't want to use it.

The tears were good, the tears felt cathartic.

As her early years transitioned into adolescence, her love of flowers became obvious. Until she was about twenty-five, the photos were of Claire with her family, her friends and her beloved cats, but as 'Dancing Queen' gave way to Taylor Swift's 'Fearless', the images were much more recent, mostly of him and Claire, and each photo brought with it a memory that would forever live in his heart. There were pictures of their wedding, of them in hot air balloons, on holidays, in their garden, shots from Christmases and birthdays.

But it was the most recent photo that undid him.

A photo he'd taken himself barely two weeks ago. Wearing her favourite maternity jeans and a pink floral top that showed off her pregnant state, Claire smiled proudly at the camera as she cradled her twenty-nine-week bump. The baby might not have been genetically hers but from the moment the doctor had implanted the embryo into her uterus, Claire had loved their unborn child with everything she had. It was hers in all the ways that mattered and those feelings shone from this photo.

Guilt filled his heart that he hadn't given Anaya the love Claire would have expected. He'd stupidly blamed their baby for her death and although he'd sat by the incubator every day since, he'd mainly done so because it was expected of him. But now as he looked up into Claire's eyes, he silently apologised and made a vow to do better.

The photo of Claire pregnant seemed to linger on the screen longer than the others, but as the song drew to an end, one final image appeared. There was Anaya, sleeping (as usual), her hands curled into tiny fists and tubes sticking out of her dainty little nose. Jasper finally saw what his family and even Harper had seen from the beginning.

A beautiful little miracle—all his to love and protect.

His heart, which had held only pain since Claire's death, suddenly beat faster as he stared up adoringly at his little girl. He couldn't wait to get back to her, to cradle her close, to hold her tiny hand, stroke her soft head and tell her how much he loved her.

As Jasper thought these thoughts, Taylor's voice faded and James Blunt's 'Goodbye My Lover' replaced it. The pallbearers approached the coffin, bowed their heads and lifted it from its resting place. His parents and Claire's stood on either side of him and he let their mums link arms with his as they followed the coffin out of the church to the waiting hearse. The last time Jasper had walked down the aisle of a church it had been as a newly minted husband and he couldn't have been prouder with Claire by his side.

Today, although unbearably sad, he was still proud. Proud of Claire and proud of what they'd achieved together. Proud of their little girl.

Goodbye my lover, goodbye my friend, he silently told her as James Blunt's voice echoed through the church. He did feel hollow, exactly as the song said, but he also knew now that he could and would go on. This knowledge made it so much easier to stand alongside Claire's parents and accept the hugs and utterings of sympathy as the guests filed out of the church.

When the final person had paid their respects, Jasper climbed into his car with his mum and dad and drove to the club for the wake. Claire's parents and the rest of their family followed in a procession. The funeral directors were taking Claire to be cremated and Jasper couldn't help feeling relieved that he wouldn't have to watch as she was lowered down into a vault.

Trying to feel grateful that all these people had come to remember Claire's life, he parked his car among the many others and went to mingle. He'd barely stepped inside the hall when someone offered to get him some food. He remembered Mike mentioning that the locals had generously offered to take care of the catering, and he accepted a plate piled high with homemade pastries and cakes even though he wasn't hungry.

Making small talk with everyone—even close friends and family—was exhausting. Everyone wanted to tell him how much they'd loved Claire and share a special memory of her with him, and although he appreciated the sentiment, he just wanted to get back to the hospital. He now accepted that nothing was going to bring Claire back, but believed that he would feel closest to her when he was with Anaya.

After what felt like forever, he surreptitiously dragged his mobile out of his pocket to check the time. His heart sank when he saw that barely an hour had passed. How long was a respectable time to stay at your wife's wake? He knew where Claire would want him to be right now.

Joanne caught him looking and came up to sit on a plastic chair beside him. 'You know, I don't think anyone would mind if you snuck away now,' she said. 'This has been a draining day for all of us, but you must want to get back to Anaya.'

For the first time he could nod his head and admit this was exactly how he felt. 'I really do.'

She put her hand on his knee and patted it. 'We haven't had much time alone, but I just wanted to let you know that you will always be family to me and Mike. If there's ever anything you and Anaya ever need, *anything*, I want you to come to us.' She sniffed. 'As you know we almost lost Claire once before, and sometimes over the last week and a bit, I've asked myself why fate spared her then only to take her now.'

Jasper placed his hand over the top of his mother-in-law's and squeezed it. 'I've asked the same thing,' he admitted. He'd wondered if she'd always been living on borrowed time and if her time to go had really been twenty-one years ago when she'd got cancer as a kid.

'But whatever the answer,' Joanne continued, 'I'll never regret those extra years we had. I'm glad that because of you my daughter knew how it felt to love and be truly loved back, and that she also got to experience being pregnant, something she thought she never would. Now all of us need to love and look after her beautiful baby for her.'

He stiffened a little at Joanne's words—did she somehow know about the ambivalent feelings he'd had towards Anaya? But then he nodded and wrapped his mother-in-law in a tight hug. 'Yes, we do,' he said, 'and I promise that will be my number one mission in life from now on.'

After that, Jasper made his goodbyes and then headed out to his car. His mother had driven him up in it from Newcastle that morning and when he'd said he was leaving, she'd offered to come with him again, but he'd told her to stay in the Hunter with his dad. She'd objected of course, but he'd insisted.

'I'm looking forward to the drive to think in peace. No offence, Mum,' he said, 'but I need to work out how to go forward without you holding my hand at every step. Dad needs you back at home, helping with the business while I'm not able to, and now the funeral is over, you can't keep your lives on hold.'

She'd sobbed, hugged him and then let him go, but not without making him promise to call her when he got there.

It started to rain halfway to Newcastle and although he was impatient to get there, he forced himself to slow down and drive like a granddad. Getting into a vehicle now felt like a dangerous occupation and he found himself so much more aware of other cars on the road.

When he finally parked at the hospital, he let out a sigh of relief and hurried inside, dusting the rain off his jacket. He nodded at the woman behind the NICU desk and then scrubbed his arms up to his elbows. This had become a habit over the last nine days, but for the first time he did so not due to hospital rules and regulation, but because he couldn't bear the thought of taking any germs in to Anaya. He couldn't bear the thought of losing her as he had her mother.

His pulse sped as he strode down the corridor. He couldn't get to his little girl fast enough. It seemed like days, not hours since he'd seen that little face.

He found Harper sitting in the same position she had been when he'd left—her head bent over the incubator, her hand poked through the hole—and wondered if she'd moved at all throughout the day. He silently cursed himself for not thinking to bring her a plate of food from the wake.

'Oh, hi, Jasper,' she said, glancing up as his shadow fell over the incubator.

She sounded surprised to see him but she didn't remove her hand.

'Hey.' Going to the other side of the incubator, he pumped some of the sanitiser gel from the bottle on the wall, rubbed it over his hands and then slipped one in through the hole. Although he desperately wanted to hold Anaya properly, he'd make do with this until the nurse came over. He stroked his finger—which looked ginormous next to hers—over her little hand and actually whimpered.

'You must have missed her,' Harper said.

Trying to swallow the lump of emotion in his throat, he glanced up from the tiny face and met Harper's eyes. 'This is the first time I've ever willingly touched her,' he admitted, and then immediately regretted it. What kind of monster would she think him if he admitted he'd wished Anaya dead instead of Claire?

'Oh,' was all she said.

For a few long moments, they stayed there looking for all the world like two normal parents holding their baby's hands, but this wasn't a normal situation and suddenly he felt compelled to share with this practical stranger.

'You know how I blamed you for Claire's death at first?' he said.

Harper's brow furrowed slightly as she nodded.

'Well, I guess I also blamed Anaya. I couldn't feel anything for her. I felt numb, and although the nurses made me hold her—something called Kangaroo Care, which supposedly helps her thrive—I did it begrudgingly. I could hardly bear to touch her.'

'That's understandable.'

'Is it?' He shook his head. 'Claire would never have forgiven me the feelings I had for our baby, but I couldn't see past my grief.'

When he went quiet for a few moments, Harper prompted. 'But something changed today?'

He nodded. 'I saw a photo of Claire pregnant and I remembered how much she loved and wanted Anaya and something shifted inside of me. I couldn't wait to get back here—to see her, to touch her.'

'The paediatrician said she's doing really well. He thinks she might be able to be transferred to a non-temperature-regulated incubator within days and then we—' she shook her head quickly, '—I mean *you*, will be able to hold her more easily. He even said she might be ready to try a bottle before too long.'

'Wow.' Jasper fought tears again as he gazed down at his little miracle and then decided not to waste his energy. He let them come, realising they were tears of joy.

'I know. She's amazing,' Harper said, sounding as choked as he felt.

'Thank you for being with her today.'

'No, thank you for letting me. How was the funeral?'

He chuckled slightly and she shook her head.

'Sorry. Stupid question.'

It was his turn to smile and his facial muscles ached a little as if they were out of practice. 'It's okay,' he said. 'I know what you meant, and the funeral *was* a good one as far as funerals can be. Heaps of people came, we shared memories and played Claire's favourite music. She'd have liked it I think.'

Harper smiled. 'It sounds lovely. As far as funerals can be.'

'You can go now,' he said, and then realised how blunt he sounded. He didn't mean to be impolite but the truth was he wanted a little alone time with his daughter. 'I mean, you've got a long drive and you must be tired. Sitting in here is more exhausting than I ever imagined it would be.'

She rubbed her lips together and didn't make a move to stand. 'So, is your mum going to stay with you in Newcastle until you can take Anaya home?'

He shook his head. 'We'll be here another month at least and Mum and Dad can't afford to close the business, so she needs to be back in Lovedale helping.'

'And what about Claire's parents? Or other family?'

'Joanne and Mike have their business to run as well—they'll visit when they can. But it's okay. We'll be fine, won't we, sweetheart?' he said, looking back into the incubator at his sleeping angel. From now on it was he and Anaya against the world.

'Okay, well I guess I'll be going then.' Harper slipped her hand out of the incubator but didn't tear her eyes from Anaya as she stood. 'I'll see you later, Jasper. Please don't hesitate to call me again if you need anything.'

'I won't.' When she finally looked at him, he smiled his thanks. 'And I promise *I'll* send you updates now, instead of Mum.'

She nodded, whispered 'thank you' and then, with one final glance at Anaya, headed out of the ward.

Chapter Twenty-nine

As Harper drove back towards Sydney, pain lodged itself in the back of her throat and a feeling of wrongness washed over her—a feeling akin to leaving the house and being unable to remember if she'd turned off an electrical appliance. Only this time it wasn't the iron or oven she felt like she'd forgotten, but her heart.

Although rain fell from the sky, she pressed the button to wind down the window, desperate for air, and fought the urge to turn around and head back to Newcastle. To the hospital. To Anaya.

Jasper's confession went round and round in her head. It was one thing to blame the drunk driver, himself or even *her* for Claire's death, but how could he possibly look down at that gorgeous little porcelain face and feel anything but love and adoration? Even though he now professed to be as besotted as she herself felt—and he did genuinely look that way—she couldn't help but liken his situation to that of her mother.

According to Willow, their mother had been a reasonable parent until grief over the death of their father had changed her. On her own, she hadn't been half the mother she should have been. What if Jasper simply didn't have it in himself to give Anaya all the love she needed?

Harper's phone started ringing through the car speaker, jolting her from her thoughts, and she looked at the screen to see her sister's name. She quickly pressed answer, desperate for the comfort of Willow's voice. 'Hey, big sis,' she said.

'Hey, little sis. How was your day? Are you still in Newcastle?'

Harper sighed—unsure where to start.

'Wow,' Willow said. 'That's a big sigh for a little sister.'

Usually Harper would have laughed at such a comment, but she didn't have it in her. 'It's been a big day,' she said instead.

'You want to talk about it?'

'I'm driving home now. Back to Sydney,' she added as if she needed to clarify that. Suddenly her beautiful house in Paddington didn't promise the comfort it usually gave her. 'Jasper is with Anaya again and ...' The rest of her sentence evaporated as the ball of emotion that had lodged itself in her throat threatened to unravel.

'You sound weird,' Willow said after a few long moments of silence.

Harper let out a snort. 'I just spent the day with a baby who is biologically mine but who legally belongs to another couple, one part of which is dead. How do you expect me to sound?'

'I'm sorry, I just meant ... you sound *different*.'

'I think I am different,' she admitted.

'Oh boy. This sounds like the kind of conversation we need to have over wine, not over the telephone.'

Harper agreed. 'Wine sounds like a very good idea. I'll be back in about an hour.'

'Your place or mine?' Willow asked.

'Can we meet somewhere else? No offence to Miriam or Samuel, but I don't think I'm ready to talk about this with anyone else yet.' Willow would help her sort through her feelings, whereas Samuel would likely get angry and tell her she was being ridiculous.

'Okay. Sure. How about The Drunk Monk?' Willow named a bar in Surry Hills about halfway between both their houses. The place was usually crowded on the weekends but not too bad during the week. 'When can you be there?'

Harper glanced at the time on her dashboard. 'If the traffic doesn't get any worse ... about 6 pm.'

The traffic played nice, and after parking her car down a side street, Harper approached the entrance of The Drunk Monk almost on the dot of six. Willow had already grabbed a booth and she stood when Harper approached. They hugged longer than they usually did and Harper thought about the fact that over the last couple of weeks she'd become both a crier and a hugger. She almost didn't know herself.

When they broke apart, Willow took one look at Harper and said, 'I'm thinking this might call for something stronger than wine. I'm getting you a whiskey.'

Did she look that bad? Harper screwed up her nose. She'd never been a drinker of strong liquor, so one whiskey was likely to knock her on her arse. 'No. I drove here and I need to drive home. A sav blanc will be fine.'

'I caught a taxi so I could drive *you* home. You're having a whiskey.'

Before Harper could object again, Willow turned in her bright red Doc Martens and stalked over to the bar. With a sigh, Harper slumped into the booth seat in the back corner of the dimly lit bar. As she slid her hands over the table in front of her—made out of old whiskey barrels—she remembered that The Drunk Monk specialised in whiskey and pizza.

Her stomach rumbled and she realised that she hadn't eaten all day. She wasn't sure she'd be able to stomach much, but pizza was almost up there with Coco Pops in the realms of comfort food, so perhaps she should give it a shot. As Willow was facing the bar, her back to the table, and Harper didn't want to leave the booth and risk losing it, she dug her mobile phone out of her bag and texted her an order.

She watched as Willow glanced down at the mobile in her hand and then a second later turned around and gave her a thumbs up.

While she waited for Willow's return, Harper texted Samuel to say she was catching up with her sister and wouldn't be home for a couple of hours. Almost instantly he replied:

That's okay. I'm working late. I'll just call some takeaway into the office. x

Harper frowned as she read his message. Where was his question about her day? Was he so self-absorbed that he'd forgotten about her trip to Newcastle? Or did he not rate it as significant?

'Here you are my love.' Willow arrived back at the table carrying two drinks. The first, a martini glass with some kind of red liquid inside, she placed in front of Harper. The second, which looked to be a glass of Coke, she sipped the moment she sat down.

'What is this?' Harper asked, twirling the stem of the glass between her fingers. 'I thought you were getting me whiskey.'

'That—' Willow nodded towards the glass, '—is a Manhattan. Its main ingredient is whiskey but the others might make it more palatable for you. Drink up.'

Harper did as she was told, relishing the slight burn at the back of her throat as she swallowed. Maybe she would let Willow drive her home. 'It's not bad.'

Willow grinned. 'And the pizza shouldn't be long either.'

'Probably a good thing if I'm drinking these,' Harper said, lifting her glass a little. 'I haven't eaten anything all day.'

'What? Not at all?'

She shook her head. 'I was too nervous to eat this morning and then when I was in the hospital with Anaya the last thing on my mind was food. Do you want to see some photos?'

'Sure,' Willow said, but even before the word had left her mouth, Harper was digging into her handbag for her digital camera.

'Phones aren't allowed in the NICU,' she explained as she brought up the first of the hundreds of photos she'd snapped that day onto the screen. She handed the camera to her sister and watched as Willow scrolled through. 'Isn't she just adorable?'

'She's a doll. And she looks like you as a baby.'

'I know.' Ever since Lilia had pointed out the resemblance, Harper couldn't look at the photos without seeing it—and she'd been looking at them a lot—but seeing Anaya in person today had made it even more obvious. 'I've fallen for her,' she confessed.

Willow's head snapped up and she stared at Harper as if she were a stranger. Her eyes widened. 'What exactly do you mean?'

Harper took another sip of her Manhattan, a little bit of liquid courage to tell her sister the weird thoughts and feelings that had been whirling round her head the last few hours. 'I thought I might get bored sitting in the hospital with a baby all day,' she said, 'but I've fallen in love with her. I know she's not legally my child and that I haven't felt her in my womb or given birth to her, but I feel this intense love towards her that I never expected. It's like nothing I've ever felt before. When I look at Anaya, I think my heart might burst. And walking away from her this afternoon was the hardest thing I've ever had to do.'

'Oh boy.' Willow sighed, then reached across and took a gulp of Harper's Manhattan. 'Perhaps we both need whiskey tonight.'

'No.' Harper shook her head and snatched her drink back. 'You need to keep a clear head because as my big sister it's your duty to tell me what to do.'

'What do you mean? What do you *want* to do?' Willow asked.

At that moment, a smiley-faced waiter appeared with a pizza. 'Good evening ladies,' he said as he laid it on the table between them. 'One margherita. Enjoy.' Then he gestured to Harper's glass. 'Can I get you another one of those?'

She was horrified to see she'd almost finished it, but not horrified enough to reject the offer. Desperate times call for desperate measures and all. 'Yes, that would be lovely, thank you,' she said, and with a nod he retreated again.

'So,' Willow said with a confused shake of her head, 'let me get this straight. You've fallen for the baby?'

Harper nodded—much to her surprise she'd fallen hook, line and sinker.

'Does that mean you want to be more involved in her life than originally planned?'

'I think so. Is that insane?' She picked up a slice of pizza and forced herself to take a bite.

'I'm ... uh ... I don't know.' Willow looked uncharacteristically speechless. 'How involved do you want to be? Have you told Jasper?'

'No. Not yet. I didn't get the chance. He practically threw me out of the NICU this afternoon after admitting that until today he hadn't felt anything for Anaya.' Irritation bubbled inside her again. She wished the waiter would return with her damn drink.

'What?' Willow shook her head again as if struggling to keep up.

Harper took a deep breath and relayed the conversation she'd had with Jasper at Anaya's side. 'And after all that, he had the audacity to dismiss me like some kind of stranger. I'm worried, Willow. I'm scared his grief over Claire might be similar to Laura's and that he might neglect Anaya because of it.'

'Hold on a moment.' Willow held up a hand and gave Harper her stern big sister expression. 'You can't jump to that conclusion. Plenty of parents have lost partners and not lost the plot like our mother did. Jasper just buried his wife—he gained a daughter the day he lost the love of his life. He's in shock. Of course he'd be numb. Give the poor guy a chance to step up.'

'One Manhattan,' announced the waiter, delivering the drink to the table with the flourish of a magician.

'Thanks,' Harper managed, sliding the glass towards her. She gulped half of it down and then looked her sister in the eye. 'Perhaps you're right, but I think I had some kind of panic attack in the car on the way back. I couldn't breathe at the thought of being apart from her. It's not just that I'm worried about Jasper's feelings towards her but also because I can't ignore my own.'

Willow raised an eyebrow and let out a deep sigh. 'Do you think you'd be feeling such a strong reaction to the baby if Claire was still alive?'

'I don't know.' Harper shrugged. 'But she's not, so that's irrelevant.'

'I thought you didn't want kids?' Willow didn't have to say she was recalling the conversation they'd had only days ago about Harper's abortion—it was scrawled across her face.

'I didn't. At least, I didn't *think* I did. But I look at Anaya and all I can think about is the fact that she doesn't have a mother. And then I find myself wanting to take on that role. Wanting it more than I've ever wanted anything in my life. It makes me wonder if I've simply been in denial—if I was suppressing that part of myself because I was afraid of repeating Laura's mistakes.'

'Having kids is a big responsibility.'

'I know that,' Harper snapped.

'Hey, chill. I'm on your side here. I'm just wondering, how much custody do you want? Remember you live in Sydney and Jasper lives in the Hunter Valley—how will that work for Anaya?'

'I don't know.' Harper felt tears threatening again. Why did life have to get so complicated? All she'd wanted was to do something meaningful and instead what should have been a simple act of kindness had thrown her whole world upside down. 'I haven't thought that far yet.'

'And what will Samuel think of this?'

Harper actually shuddered. That was not a conversation she was looking forward to having, but then she couldn't bury her feelings for his sake.

As if sensing Harper was close to a mental meltdown, Willow reached across the table and took hold of her hands. 'I think you should finish eating this pizza and then you should go home. Sleep on it. See how you feel in the morning—or even after a few days. Today's obviously been an emotionally exhausting day but as gorgeous as this baby is, you're under no obligation to her. Legally Anaya is Jasper's responsibility and even though Claire has died, that hasn't changed. He might not want you any more involved than you guys originally planned.'

Oh God. Harper's stomach turned and she yanked her hands out of her sister's and pushed the pizza away. There was no way she could eat another bite. She hadn't even thought about that possibility. Would she have a legal leg to stand on now that the situation had changed? Samuel would know. There might be someone at his firm who could help her. But that would mean getting him onside.

'I'm sorry,' Willow said. 'I'm supposed to be here supporting you and I'm not sure I'm doing a very good job. This was just a bit of a shock. I do want you to think very carefully about what you want and what is best for Anaya going forward, but then, whatever you decide, I'll be here for you *and* her a hundred percent.'

'Maybe you're right,' Harper said, feeling defeated. 'I didn't want to have kids because I don't want to stuff them up like our mother did. Just because the situation with Anaya has changed, doesn't mean my example of motherhood has. Why do I suddenly think I'd know how to be a good mother?'

'I didn't say you wouldn't be a good mother,' Willow exclaimed, sounding outraged. 'Laura might not have been a shining example of motherhood, but that only means you have a good example of what *not* to be. I stand by what I said last week—I think you'd make a wonderful mum. If that's what you *want* to be.'

'I think I do,' she whispered, pressing her hand against her heart. Then, 'No, I *know* I do.'

'In that case, kiddo,' Willow said, 'I think there's two very important men you need to talk to. Do you want another drink or shall I take you home so you can get started?'

Harper looked at the near-empty glass and thought another drink a far more tempting prospect than talking to Samuel, but if she indulged in a third Manhattan she'd be in no state to talk to anyone. 'I think I've had enough.' She dug her keys out of her handbag and handed them to her sister. 'Let's go.'

They weaved through the tables to the door. It had been so warm and toasty inside that Harper gasped as the icy winter wind sliced into her cheeks.

'You okay?' Willow asked, sounding anxious.

'Fine.' Well, as fine as she could be. 'Just cold.'

They hurried to her car where Willow turned the heating up high.

'So, tell me about your day.' Harper said, in an effort to give her head a few moments reprieve.

Willow chuckled. 'I spent the whole day sitting behind my desk applying for research grants. Riveting stuff.'

They passed the short journey in relative silence. Willow concentrated on the roads—people drove like maniacs in stormy weather—and Harper found her head falling against the passenger window and her eyelids drooping. She must have actually drifted off for a few moments because the next thing she knew, Willow was gently shaking her shoulder.

'Wake up, Harps. You're home. Do you want me to come in and talk to Samuel with you?'

Willow's words jolted Harper right back to her current woes, and as tempting as it was to have her big sister hold her hand while she had this difficult conversation with her husband, she didn't want to be a coward. 'No. It's okay. Thanks for listening tonight though. I don't know what I'd do without you.'

Willow hugged her hard. 'Feeling's mutual. I love you, little sis.'

'I love you too.'

Then Harper pushed open the passenger door, climbed out of the car and walked on slightly unsteady feet to the front door. She let herself into the dark house, immediately remembered Samuel's text about being home late and exhaled deeply. She wasn't sure whether she was relieved or disappointed that she couldn't have the conversation immediately. After considering calling him and asking him to come home because they needed to talk, she changed her mind and decided to take a bath and wait. He wouldn't be in a good mood if she tore him from his work and she didn't want to start this discussion on the wrong foot.

Two hours later she was washed, dressed in her PJs and fighting sleep. Samuel still wasn't home. Giving in to the urge to climb into bed, she snuggled under the covers and decided she'd talk to him in the morning, when hopefully her head would be clearer than it felt right now.

Who knew? Maybe Willow was right. Maybe she'd wake up and find she'd changed her mind.

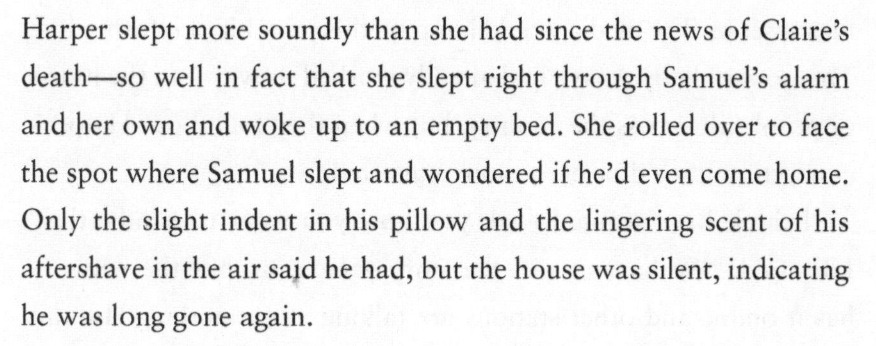

Harper slept more soundly than she had since the news of Claire's death—so well in fact that she slept right through Samuel's alarm and her own and woke up to an empty bed. She rolled over to face the spot where Samuel slept and wondered if he'd even come home. Only the slight indent in his pillow and the lingering scent of his aftershave in the air said he had, but the house was silent, indicating he was long gone again.

Sighing in frustration, she picked up her mobile phone and glanced at the screen.

'Oh, shit.' She leapt out of bed, unable to believe how late she'd slept. She'd be late to work for the first time in her life. As she scrambled to get ready, she texted Lilia:

Sorry I'm late. On way now. Will explain everything when I get there.

Lilia's reply came almost instantaneously.

No worries. See you soon.

She hated the feeling of starting the day behind. Not having time to peruse the news online would usually irritate the hell out of her, but today her head had little room for anything but Anaya anyway. She smiled as she walked into the studio, thinking of her little girl's dimpled cheeks and tiny, tiny hands.

'Morning,' she said to Lilia. 'Sorry I'm late.'

Harper was expecting her to ask about her time at the hospital yesterday, but instead she said, 'You haven't seen the news, have you?'

Her thoughts went immediately to Anaya. Surely if something bad had happened Jasper would have called. 'What is it?' she asked.

'Bryn wants to speak to you in her office in a moment,' Lilia said, referring to the station's senior manager. 'But I thought I'd warn you. News broke overnight that you are the egg donor of the miracle baby born in the car accident.'

'Oh God.' Harper's relief was short-lived as the reality of what this meant set in. The media would jump on this juicy bit of information. The story of baby Anaya had already worked its way into the hearts of people all across the country, but when they found out Harper's connection, they'd be even more interested.

'I think Bryn wants to ask you how you want to handle this,' Lilia said. 'We haven't run the story yet on air, but the network has it online and other stations are talking about nothing else this morning.'

'I wonder how they found out?' she asked. 'Did someone here leak the news? Lucy or the intern?'

Lilia shook her head. 'They wouldn't dare.'

'Maybe someone recognised me at the hospital yesterday and put two and two together.' Even as she spoke, she realised it didn't matter. The fact was that their story was out there and she needed to talk to Jasper ASAP.

In some ways, the media identifying her as the egg donor felt like some kind of sign. An omen. On the day she wanted to declare herself as Anaya's mum, they'd done it for her.

The truth coming out now also gave her a valid reason to return to Newcastle today and speak to Jasper, not just about how to handle the media but about her own hopes going forward.

'Is it possible to reschedule things so I can take today and tomorrow off?' Harper asked. 'After I've spoken to Bryn of course.'

Lilia nodded. 'I think that's a good idea.'

'Thanks.' Harper took a deep breath, then turned and headed down the corridor to face her big boss.

Not one for small talk, Bryn got to the point the moment Harper stepped into her office. 'It would have been good to hear about this from you, rather than from another radio station on my way to work this morning,' she said, peering at Harper over the top of the takeaway coffee in her hand.

'I'm sorry, but when I decided to donate my eggs, it had nothing to do with my work.'

'I understand that, but it does now. The phones have been going crazy all morning with people wanting to get your side of the story. I don't think we can bury this. Our only hope would be a double dissolution or a bomb going off somewhere, but it's been a pretty slow news week so far.'

'It's no one else's business,' Harper snapped. But when Bryn frowned, she sighed and added, 'What do you want me to do?' She knew how the media worked—*everything* was *everyone's* business.

'I've got a friend who works for *The Morning Edition*. She'd like to interview you—and the father of the baby if he's willing. They'll offer you a good fee for speaking to them.'

Harper didn't give a damn about the money and Jasper didn't seem the type to love the limelight, but she could use the interview as an excuse for time off to talk to him.

'I have no idea if that's something he'd want to do, but I can ask him,' she said. 'If you're agreeable, I'm going to take the next couple of days off and go up to Newcastle to talk to him about how to handle this.'

'Okay. You do that. Until then, we won't mention a word about this on air—and I don't need to tell you that it'll be better if you and Jasper don't speak to any other media either.'

'Of course. I'll tell him. And I'll call you as soon as I have an answer.'

When she returned to her office, her phone was going off in her handbag. 'Good news spreads fast, hey,' she muttered to Lilia as she retrieved it. The screen listed quite a lot of unknown numbers and a couple of missed calls from Samuel.

She waited until she was safely in her car and called him on speaker phone. He answered almost immediately.

'Are you okay?' he asked as she navigated out of the car park. 'The news about you being an egg donor is all over the internet. Everyone here is talking about it; of course they knew you were doing it but I've neither confirmed nor denied your link to this case.'

'I'm fine,' she said, heartened that he was concerned about her while at the same time irritated by the way he spoke about the situation as if she were one of his clients.

'You were asleep when I got home yesterday and I didn't want to wake you to ask how the day was, but let's go out for dinner tonight and you can tell me all about it. On second thought,' he said before she could reply, 'I'll bring home takeaway as we might not get any peace out and about at the moment.'

'Actually, Samuel, I'm just leaving work now. I spoke to Bryn, my boss,' she clarified just in case he'd forgotten, 'and she wants me to speak to Jasper about how to handle all this media interest, so I'm heading up to Newcastle again. Not sure I'll be back by dinner. In fact, I think I might pack an overnight bag and grab a hotel room. I'm exhausted from all that's going on.'

She felt guilty not telling him the whole truth—but that conversation wasn't one to be had over a phone, and perhaps it would be best to find out how Jasper felt about her being more involved so that when she went to Samuel she had all the facts.

'Can't you just call him?'

It was on the tip of her tongue to admit that she wanted to see Anaya, but that would open a can of worms she wasn't ready for. 'Some things are easier in person.'

'Okay then. But don't wear yourself out. I'm worried about the stress this is putting you under.'

She thanked him for his concern, promised she'd be fine and said she'd call him when she got there.

Chapter Thirty

Jasper pulled his mobile phone from his pocket as he headed into the rest room. It had been vibrating all morning but as phones weren't allowed in the NICU, he'd ignored it. If there was any emergency with his family, they'd contact the ward directly, so he'd assumed the calls were from people trying to sell him shit or charities wanting money. The number of missed calls from unknown numbers indicated he'd been correct, but in among them was a text from Harper.

He paused to read it:

Hey Jasper—hope Anaya and you are doing well this morning. I assume you've seen the news reports online by now and maybe been contacted by a journalist or two. I'm guessing someone saw me at the hospital yesterday and due to my semi-public status they've jumped on the story. I'm driving up to see you right now to discuss how we address the situation, but it would probably be best if you don't talk to anyone until we've worked out how we want to handle it. See you soon, Harper.

Jasper blinked as he read the message, which had been sent almost an hour ago. The media? Were all those missed calls from journalists? He'd been living in a bubble this last week and hadn't seen or heard what had been said about Claire's accident, but he'd thought it would have been old news by now. The police were keeping him up to date with the driver who'd ploughed into Claire—he'd recovered and had been charged with a number of offences including driving under the influence and dangerous driving resulting in death. They were certain he'd go to prison, although only time would tell for how long. It was easier not to think about that or he found uncontrollable anger welling up inside him again.

Since the funeral, his thoughts had been solely on Anaya and her progress. He hadn't gone back to the apartment last night, choosing instead to stay by her incubator. This wasn't encouraged—parents were advised to try to get some proper rest if they could—but due to his situation, no one had tried to make him go home, so he hadn't heard a news report today or read anything online.

He opened his news app and flinched at the top story: RADIO PERSONALITY MIRACLE BABY EGG DONOR.

What the hell?! The information was scant but obviously someone who'd seen her at the hospital yesterday—maybe even one of the medical staff—must have leaked the news. His fingers tightened around his phone in irritation—this was nobody's business but his and he planned on telling Harper exactly that when she arrived. It seemed a bit of overkill to drive all the way up here to talk about the media, especially when she'd made the trip only the day before, but then again, Harper knew the industry better than he did. And if they were going to be hounded by the press, he would make his position clear and then take his lead from her. He couldn't see her wanting all this attention either.

Ok. Drive safely. I'll see you soon.

After sending his reply, he shoved his phone back in his pocket and continued on to the rest room. He splashed his face with water, shook his head at the sight of yesterday's suit and then went to grab a coffee from the NICU family room. There was a toaster and bread available there, so he forced himself to scoff a couple of slices and washed it down with the coffee before hurrying back to Anaya.

The nurse was standing over her when he returned.

'Hey there, baby girl,' he said, smiling down as he stopped alongside the incubator. He looked to the nurse. 'Harper will be here soon because we have a few things to discuss. Will it be okay if she comes in again?'

The nurse smiled and nodded. 'Of course. She got permission for yesterday and your situation is irregular so I see no need to renege on it. I'll send a message to the desk to make sure they let her through.'

'Thank you.'

'Anaya's doing really well,' she said. 'I've just done her obs and the paediatrician will be here shortly. I think we might have some good news for you, but in the meantime, would you like to hold her?'

He nodded eagerly. Yesterday afternoon he'd done skin-to-skin again and for the first time he hadn't wanted to give her back. Only the knowledge that she couldn't be out of the incubator for too long allowed him to do so.

Jasper sanitised his hands, then sat in the chair and opened his shirt for his baby girl. Once she was settled against his bare chest with a baby blanket tucked over her, the nurse patted him on the arm and moved on.

He glanced down and marvelled at Anaya's tiny perfection. He stroked his finger gently over her head and smiled at her little hand resting against his chest. He felt like a giant in comparison to her. His pinkie finger was almost twice the size of her hand.

'Hey, my sweetheart,' he said. 'Daddy loves you.'

At the sound of his voice, her little eyes peeled open and she blinked up at him. Their gazes met, his heartstrings tugging and a tear slipping from his eye. How he longed for Claire to be able to see Anaya, to feel what he now felt for their little girl. Barely registering the goings on of the NICU around him, Jasper sat there cradling Anaya and telling her about Claire—about how they met, the home they'd built together, the garden she'd one day play in, the cats that would probably take a while to warm to her. 'You are not to pull their tails,' he said with faux sternness. 'Be gentle with them, and they'll learn to love you.'

The more he talked, the easier he found it; chatting to this little person who couldn't yet talk back felt like the most natural thing in the world. He couldn't wait for the day she'd be able to respond.

'I wonder what your first word will be?' he whispered. 'Maybe balloon. Bal-loon.' He repeated and lengthened the word for her like she were a budgie he was trying to teach to speak. Then he chuckled. It would be a while before Anaya would even smile, never mind speak, and longer still till he'd be able to take her up in the air with him, but he couldn't wait. Although his world had dimmed without Claire in it, he suddenly found himself once again able to look forward to things. He felt as if he could breathe again.

When a shadow fell over them half an hour later, he looked up and was surprised to see Harper standing there. He'd almost forgotten about her visit.

'Hi, Jasper,' she said, but her eyes went straight to Anaya. She lathered up her hands with the sanitiser and then stroked her finger down the baby's face, brushing her fingertip against his chest as she did so.

It irked him a little that she didn't ask—this was his and Claire's baby, not hers—but he swallowed the irritation. 'How was the drive?' he said instead.

'It was fine. How's Anaya this morning?'

'She's been quite wakeful. We've been having a little chat, but I think I exhausted her.'

'Little darling,' Harper whispered, again stroking her finger over Anaya's tiny head. Then she finally met his gaze. 'Have you been here all night?'

He nodded. 'Couldn't bear to leave her.'

'You must be exhausted.'

He shrugged. 'I dozed a little.' That was a lie; he'd barely slept a wink but strangely he felt less fatigued than he had in almost two weeks.

'Do you want to go get some lunch and I'll sit with her?' Harper asked.

'I had some toast in the family room here. And a coffee,' he said. 'So, the media? Do you want to fill me in? I hadn't seen anything until I got your message.'

'Oh.' She blinked as if she too had almost forgotten the whole debacle.

'What's going on, Harper? Quite frankly I don't see why Anaya—and how she was conceived—is anyone's business but mine.' He hesitated. 'Ours.'

Harper glanced around them and then looked back at him. 'I agree, but we probably shouldn't discuss it here. As much as I don't want to leave Anaya, there'll be people listening to whatever we say now, so we should probably go somewhere private to talk. Maybe a quiet corner of a café down the road or something?'

'There's a meeting room here that families can use if they need some privacy,' he suggested. 'We can ask the nurse if we can have that for a few minutes.'

'Okay. Good idea, I'll go talk to her.' She turned and walked over to the nurses' desk.

He watched the exchange between Harper and the nurse manager and when she returned, she said, 'The social worker is talking to a couple in there right now, but we can have it when they're done.'

He nodded. 'Okay.'

Before he could say anything else, their nurse arrived. 'Time to put this little munchkin back in her bed,' she said and then gently lifted Anaya from his arms.

As the nurse settled his baby back in the incubator, he quickly did his buttons up again and stood.

'Do you want to sit down?' he asked Harper, gesturing to the chair he'd just vacated. There was only room for one seat next to each incubator, and his mum hadn't raised him to leave a woman standing.

'No thanks. I'm fine. Been sitting for two hours in the car.'

'Okay.' He waited until the nurse retreated before sanitising his hands again—it was almost becoming second nature. Then he lowered himself back into the seat, slipped his hand through the hole and took hold of Anaya's again.

He didn't realise until Harper spoke that she'd done the same thing. 'Isn't her skin so soft?' she said, a smile twisting her lips upwards.

He agreed. 'I've never felt anything softer.'

'She looks good,' Harper commented. 'Maybe I'm just being optimistic but she looks bigger even than yesterday.'

'The nurse said she's really thriving,' he said.

It felt weird talking about the care and wellbeing of his baby with Harper. It should be Claire here holding Anaya's hand and discussing the future with him. However stupid he knew it to be, he couldn't help resenting Harper a little that she wasn't Claire. The injustice of it all had his breathing growing unsteady again.

The nurse came over and cleared her throat slightly, causing both of them to look up at her. 'The meeting room is free for you now. And once you're done, the paediatrician and I want to talk to you about Anaya's progress.'

'Is everything okay?' Jasper and Harper asked at the same time. He heard the terror in her voice that he felt in his heart.

'Yes.' The nurse nodded quickly. 'She's doing better than expected, but we just want to keep you informed.'

'Okay.' He nodded and both he and Harper slowly let go of Anaya's hands.

'Back soon little angel,' Harper said and then straightened.

He led her to the meeting room and then switched the little sign on the door to occupied. The room held a small couch, a couple of plastic chairs, a small table and tea and coffee making facilities. 'You want a drink?'

Harper shook her head. 'I'm okay. I had a takeaway in the car, but you have one if you want.'

'Nah. I'm fine.' He sat in one of the uncomfortable plastic seats.

'Okay.' Harper lowered herself into the other chair and took a visible deep breath. She seemed nervous, which was odd considering the fact that she dealt with the media on a day-to-day basis. She *was* the media for crying out loud.

'So I read one of the stories online after I got your message. Isn't there a way you can make the journalists go away?' he asked. 'It's no one's business how Anaya was conceived and I really don't want to waste time talking to strangers about it when I should be with her.'

'I understand. Totally,' she rushed, leaning forward slightly. 'I only want the best for Anaya as well, but I also know that once a story like this leaks, there are journalists out there who will stop at nothing to be the one to break all the juicy details.'

'Vultures,' he spat. 'What happened to leaving grieving families in peace?'

She didn't answer that exact question, but instead said, 'The station where I work has been fielding calls this morning from journalists wanting to know if it's true that I am Anaya's egg donor. I'm guessing you've had similar phone calls?'

He nodded. 'My phone was on silent but I've had a ton of missed calls from unknown numbers.'

'They'll probably get onto your family as well, so we need to decide how much we want to tell them.'

Jasper ran a frustrated hand through his hair. 'What do you mean how much? Why do we have to talk to them at all? I'd rather tell them to bugger the hell off and leave us all alone!'

She nodded. 'I understand that, I truly do, but I also know that these journalists won't just retreat quietly. They've seen the opportunity for a hot story and they all want their hands on it. So we need to think of Anaya. We could both refuse to comment, but the risk there is that we might have friends—or people we *thought* were friends—willing to talk for cash. It's better if the information comes directly from us.'

'What? You mean someone might get paid to tell our story? I don't know what kind of friends *you* have, but none of *my* friends or family would say a word.'

'And I'm pretty sure mine wouldn't either, but someone saw me here yesterday—the hospital knows who I am. It's out there.'

'So what? You want to deny it?'

'No! Of course not.' She shook her head vehemently. 'But we should consider the money we could get for talking exclusively to one source.'

His eyes widened. He couldn't believe his ears. 'You want to make money out of this?!'

She held up her hand. 'Please, I'm not expressing myself well, because there's something else I want to talk to you about, but ... my boss has a friend who works for *The Morning Edition* and she wants to interview us both.'

He shuddered. 'I'd rather swim with sharks than go on one of those trashy breakfast shows.'

'Look, I know this is a lot to think about but there are journalists wanting to talk to us and they *will* find a way to get a story. *The Morning Edition* is offering a generous fee. It's money you could put in a bank account to go towards Anaya's schooling or something. And if we speak to them ourselves, we can at least somewhat control what they put out there.'

'I admit I don't have a huge amount of experience with the press, but the few times they've written articles about our business, they got half their facts wrong. I'd prefer to say nothing. If we don't say anything, they can't put words in our mouths.'

'Not necessarily,' she countered, 'but it's a lot harder to make stuff up on camera because we'll be the ones doing the talking.'

He raised an eyebrow, still not at all convinced.

Her shoulders sagged and she let out a long breath. 'In the end the decision is yours and I'll respect it. Why don't you have a think about it, discuss it with your parents and Claire's parents and get back to me?'

'I'll think about it, but don't hold your breath. I do *not* want to exploit Anaya.'

'And neither do I. I promise you that.' Harper offered him a tentative smile.

Jasper stood. 'All right then, I'll be in touch.'

'There's one more thing,' Harper rushed. 'It's ... it's something I wanted to ask you before ... before all this media stuff came up.'

His eyes had been on the door, but he looked to Harper's face when he registered the weird tone in her voice. She looked as if she might be about to throw up.

'Are you okay? Do you need some water or something?'

She held up a hand and then took a few breaths. 'Just give me a moment.'

Harper had always appeared such a together person, but the stress of the situation had obviously taken its toll on her as well. She was hunched over, looking like she might crumple in on herself at any moment. But the seconds ticked by and Jasper's concern warred with irritation that she wouldn't just spit out whatever it was she wanted to say. He needed to get back to Anaya.

As if sensing his growing impatience, she finally took a deep breath and met his gaze straight on. 'I don't know how to say this right so I'm just going to say it. I never imagined I would feel anything more than a distant affection for Anaya.' She paused to suck in another breath. 'But Jasper I do. I love her more than I could have predicted and I want to be part of her life. I want to take some of the pressure off, so you don't always have to be the one here with Anaya.'

He blinked as the muscles in his neck and shoulders tensed. Perhaps he misunderstood what she was propositioning. 'It's not a chore to sit with Anaya. There's nowhere else I'd rather be.'

She nodded. 'Trust me, I understand. I feel the same. But you've got to take care of yourself. You can't help her if you're not eating or sleeping properly. If you get sick, they won't even let you in to visit.'

His chest tightened at that thought, but still, what exactly did Harper want? 'What are you trying to say?'

'I want to take on some of that load. I want to be the other parent in her life.'

The way she made Anaya sound like a job irked him. 'We're not a charity, Harper! You don't have to sign up to help us out of some sort of obligation. I will cope, you know.'

'I'm sure you'll do better than cope, and I'm not asking because I think it's something that I *should* do. I'm here, willing and begging you to let me be a part of her life because I want to. I want to be there for her and for you, for the highs and the lows, for everything going forward. *Please* Jasper, I know none of this is what we've planned, but don't push me away. Think of what's best for Anaya.'

His first instinct was a flat-out 'no'—how dare *she* tell him to think of Anaya, she'd signed her rights away the day she'd given them her eggs—but he forced himself to take a breath. When he finally spoke he couldn't help but grimace. 'I didn't think you wanted children. That's what you said in your first email to us. That's what you've said all along. You and Samuel are a career couple and you told us you never wanted to be a mother.'

Harper twisted her wedding ring on her finger. 'I know I said that. And I thought I meant it at the time.' She inhaled deeply. 'You've heard a little bit about my mother, but I've never explained how bad she made our childhood or how little we felt like we meant to her. My dad died when I was a baby and my mum fell apart. She couldn't cope. Willow was only four years old at the time, but she was more of a parent to me than Laura ever was. She wasn't even going to bother sending me to kindergarten, but Willow knew I was old enough to go and she wouldn't let up. My mother hasn't had a job for most of my life. Sometimes she spent her welfare money on make-up and cigarettes rather than on food for her children. I didn't taste fresh vegetables until I slept over at a friend's house when I was ten.

'Of course our friends were never allowed to sleep over, but Mum had "gentleman friends" stay the night. Not that you could call most of them gentlemen. When Willow was sixteen one got drunk and climbed into her bed instead of Mum's. She was angrier at Willow for trying to steal her boyfriend than she was at him for groping her daughter. Mum never bothered to come to assembly or help at school, choosing daytime TV over spending time with us every chance she got.'

Jasper sat speechless as Harper spilled more stories. The things she told him made his skin crawl and his fingernails dig into his hands. Was she suggesting that *he'd* be that kind of parent? That without someone by his side he'd collapse in a heap like Harper's mother had?

Tears spilled down her cheeks as she recounted the horrors of her childhood. It was a miracle she and her sister had emerged as such successful people.

'Why were child services never called?'

She sniffed and shrugged. 'This was over twenty years ago and there were plenty of kids worse off than us I guess. Mum didn't abuse us, she just didn't bother with us much. Willow made sure the three of us didn't starve and she took over mum's budget when she was about thirteen, so I guess things never looked too bad from the outside.'

'Oh God.' Jasper shook his head sadly, emotion clogging the back of his throat. His childhood was like a Disney movie compared to hers.

'Anyway.' Harper sat up straighter and wiped her eyes. 'I'm not telling you all this to make you feel sorry for me. What I'm trying to explain is why I came to the decision that it was better for me not to procreate. I did get pregnant once. I was only nineteen and I was so damn scared that I might be as bad a mother as my own that I got rid of the baby.'

Jasper swallowed, unsure what to say to that. Although Harper's story touched his heart, he didn't want his sympathy for her shitty childhood to cloud his judgement. His priority had to be Anaya. His job was to protect her and do the best for her. His head ached with the responsibility. 'So is wanting to help me with Anaya some sort of atonement for guilt you feel over your abortion?'

'No.' She shook her head adamantly. 'I've thought about that. I've analysed my feelings from every angle. I've talked it over with my sister. I don't feel guilty for choosing to end that pregnancy—it was the right thing for me at that time—but until my eyes fell upon Anaya, I had let fear lead my life. The moment I saw her, I knew in my heart that I would do everything in my power to make her life as good as it could possibly be. When Anaya looked into my eyes, I knew I didn't want to be scared anymore and that I could and would be a good mother.'

His blood went cold and he jolted back against the seat. 'Anaya already has a mother. *Claire*,' he said icily.

'I know.' Harper conceded this point with one slow nod of her head. 'And she always will have. But I'm her *other* mother. I know what it's like to grow up without a female guiding presence and it breaks my heart to think of Anaya not having that either. She might have loving grandmas and fabulous aunties, but ... there's no substitute for a mum.'

And something about the way she said those words, the heartfelt genuineness behind them, dulled his rage and reminded him to think not of himself, not even of Claire, but of Anaya.

His shoulders loosening again, Jasper said, 'If I was to agree with what you're propositioning—and I mean *if*—how exactly would you expect it to work out? We live and work over two hours away from each other. I don't want Anaya to be ferried between the two of us like some child stuck in the middle of a bitter divorce.'

'I don't want that either,' she gushed. 'And I've got to be honest, I haven't had a long time to think this through, but I do know I want to make it work and I'll do whatever it takes to make that happen. We could just take things slowly at first—I could take some time off work or I could come up at weekends and spend time with her then. Obviously you'll be her primary carer—I promise I'm not trying to take her away from you—and I'm prepared to visit frequently once you and Anaya are back home. I don't expect you to bring her to Sydney, I'll ...'

He held both his hands up, indicating for her to stop her desperate rush of words. 'Please. I need time to think this through.' He went to stand, then said, 'What does Samuel think of all this?'

'Samuel will support me in whatever I want, whatever's best for Anaya,' she said, a curt edge to her voice.

'And what role would he play in Anaya's life? She's already got a dad. She doesn't need another one.'

'Of course not. And that wouldn't be an issue because Samuel doesn't want to be a dad. But he's a great uncle to our nieces and nephews, so I guess that's what he could be to Anaya as well.'

With no idea how he felt about any of this, Jasper finally stood. 'Okay then. If you'll give me some time, I'll get back to you.'

She stood as well and looked a little shaky on her feet. 'How much time?'

His jaw tightened, annoyance flaring within again. 'I don't know, okay. Don't rush me on this. I'll get back to you when I'm ready.'

Harper opened her mouth as if to say more, but then quickly shut it again.

He went over to the door and opened it, holding it for her to go through. She walked past him and turned as if to head back to Anaya's room. He cleared his throat and she looked back at him.

'Thanks for driving up today,' he said. 'I'll call you when I have an answer. About the interview and about … this.'

'I was hoping to see Anaya again before I go.'

Jasper folded his arms across his chest and shook his head. 'No. Until we've come to an agreement, I think it's best you leave.'

Her whole face fell, her eyes glistening and her lower lip wobbling, but even though he felt like a jerk, he needed to be alone again with his girl. Harper was asking him something huge—something that would change the arrangements he and Claire had already made with her—and the whole conversation had left him hugely off-kilter.

He wasn't ready to share Anaya just yet. He didn't know if he would ever be.

'Okay, fine,' she said after a long silence. 'But I'm going to take a hotel room in Newcastle so I'll be here all weekend. If you come to a decision or you change your mind and want someone to be with Anaya while you go and freshen up, call me.'

Then, without so much as a goodbye, she turned and hurried towards the door that led out of the NICU.

His fingers shot to his temples and he rubbed them hard, a tension headache exploding behind his eyes as he watched her go. How he wished Claire were here to consult on this. Of course if that were the case, they wouldn't be in this predicament. The contract they'd signed regarding the egg donation clearly stated that he and Claire were Anaya's parents—it would be their names going on the birth certificate. Jasper was pretty certain Harper still had no legal parental rights despite the tragic change in situation, but did that mean she didn't deserve them?

That question on spin-cycle inside his head, he watched the door of the NICU thud shut behind Harper and then headed back to Anaya. She was asleep again, but he sanitised his hands and snuck one into the side of the incubator, some of his tension immediately easing when he touched her smooth skin. He'd do anything for her, but how the hell was he supposed to know what was best? Whatever Harper said, he couldn't see any way for this to work except if they shared the duties—Anaya spending some time with him and some with Harper and Samuel. But he didn't want that kind of life for his daughter. He'd imagined raising her in a loving two-parent family with the cats, maybe a dog and hopefully siblings down the track as well.

'Jasper Lombard?' The voice of the paediatrician snatched him from his thoughts and he stood to greet Anaya's medical team.

'Hi there.'

Dr Roach—a man in his mid-forties who looked like he'd been built for the rugby pitch but was so gentle with the newborn babies in his care—smiled broadly at him. 'Your little daughter is a star,' he said. He glanced down at his notes before looking up again. 'Our monitoring shows that Anaya is now able to breathe on her own, so we're going to remove the CPAP tomorrow morning.'

Jasper must have looked a little blank for the nurse translated. 'Dr Roach is referring to the oxygen we've been giving Anaya through the nasal prongs.'

The doctor nodded. 'And I think she's pretty close to regulating her own body temperature as well, so my prediction is that in the next day or two we'll also be able to transfer her into a normal cot.'

Joy rushed through Jasper's veins as if he'd been injected with happy pills, and his woes about Harper faded into insignificance. 'Wow. That's awesome.'

They both nodded.

'And, not to bombard you with too much good news at once,' Dr Roach continued, 'but if all that goes well, then the next step is attempting to feed her via mouth.'

Jasper swallowed, tingles running up and down his spine. 'You mean ... giving her a bottle?'

'Yes.' Dr Roach scribbled a note onto Anaya's file and then popped the pen back into his shirt pocket. 'We'll need to start slow of course. Learning to suckle will exhaust her and we don't want to overdo it. It'll be one bottle a day at first, but if her progress so far is anything to go by, she'll be taking all her nutrients via mouth before we know it.'

'Thank you,' was all Jasper found himself able to say as he stared down proudly at his sleeping daughter.

As the doctor and nurse moved onto the next baby, Jasper's hand went to his mobile in his pocket. His first instinct was to call Claire and tell her the news. But as his fingers closed around his phone, he remembered two facts: the no phone rule and the reason why Claire wasn't here with him. How long would it take for his head to get around this fact? How long would it be before his every thought when something happened wasn't to text or call her? His heart burnt and his vision blurred a little. He blinked back the tears, not wanting to cry when he should be happy about Anaya's progress.

He needed to focus on the positive. He needed to share this with someone. Harper immediately popped into his mind, but he shook his head. He wasn't making any rash calls. Phoning her now would be cruel—like dangling a piece of fish in front of Gerry or Sunny but not letting them eat it—because he hadn't decided what to make of her request. And his head didn't feel clear enough to make such monumental decisions on his own.

With this thought, he slid his hand back inside the incubator and stroked his finger over Anaya's cheek. 'I'll be back later tonight,' he told her, even though she was still slumbering away.

Then, with a wave to the nurse, he left the ward.

As he stepped out into the waiting area he got a whiff of body odour and grimaced. The bad smell emanating from his person confirmed his decision to go back to the apartment and take a shower, change his clothes. How the nurses had let him hold his baby this morning he had no idea. Claire would be disgusted.

In the car, he called his mum on speaker phone. 'I've got a few things I need to discuss with you and Dad,' he said. 'I know it's short notice but do you guys think you could come to Newie tonight? I'm going to call Claire's parents and Tim and ask if they can come as well.'

'Is something wrong with Anaya?' his mum asked, her voice shrill with anxiety.

'No,' he rushed to reassure her. 'She's doing well. But something else has come up and I need your thoughts on it.'

'Of course we'll come,' said his mum. 'Do you want me to bring dinner?'

'No. That's okay.' He didn't want her tiring herself out when the drive to and from the Hunter would be draining enough. 'I'll order in some takeaway.' He was about to disconnect when he remembered. 'Oh, and have you seen the news?' In the wake of Harper's request, he'd almost forgotten the media issue.

'About Harper being the egg donor you mean? Yes,' she added before he could answer. 'Some journalist called us this morning. Your father told her to take a hike.'

'Good. Thank you. Keep up that silence and I'll fill you in on everything when you get here.'

Chapter Thirty-one

Harper drove to the first hotel she saw, not caring what star rating or facilities it had—simply wanting to be as close to the hospital as possible. After handing over her credit card to the annoyingly talkative woman behind reception and listening to her spiel about the restaurant and breakfast, she couldn't get to her room fast enough. Her heart had been thumping like a brass band since she'd left the NICU; anger, frustration and anxiety playing the part of conductor.

She wasn't sure who she was more upset with—Jasper for not letting her see Anaya again or herself for not choosing her moment better. Asking him to be part of their baby's life when he was clearly worked up about the media had possibly not been the smartest move on her part. She'd stupidly—naively—imagined he'd be overjoyed by her request, but of course it was much more complicated than her feelings.

Usually when Harper stayed in a hotel, the first thing she did was pull open all the drawers and cupboards, and check the minibar and all the little bottles and goodies in the bathroom. But quite aside from the fact that this motel wasn't up to the standard of the places she and Samuel usually stayed and might not even *have* a minibar, she didn't care about any of that right now.

Instead, she dumped her overnight bag on the floor of the sparsely furnished room and made a beeline for the bed. As she stared at the ceiling, which was in desperate need of a new coat of paint, she thought of Jasper's reaction to her confession and her request. He'd listened as she'd told him about her childhood, he'd even appeared sympathetic. For a few seconds she'd felt as if they were on the same page, both of them wanting only the best for their little girl. But then, for the third time since Anaya's birth, he'd basically dismissed her from the hospital, and she had to wonder if his vow to think about what she'd asked was merely a means to get her out of there.

When she'd first arrived and seen Anaya snuggled up against his bare chest, she'd sighed at the sweetness of their obvious bond, but her heart had also contracted with jealousy. The closest she'd been to her baby was holding her hand through that little hole in the side of the incubator and she craved the ability to hold Anaya skin to skin, mother to child.

So when Jasper had sent her packing, she'd wanted to fight him—to tell him he had no right to stop her seeing her daughter, but somehow, thankfully, she'd restrained herself. Her sensible, rational side knew he did have a right. He had every right—and that terrified her like nothing ever had before.

The law was on Jasper's side, and even if she could take him to court and win some kind of custodial rights, that would only make him and his family hate her. And what would it achieve? The bitterness would filter through to Anaya and their daughter would have a childhood as shitty as her own—albeit in a different way. That possibility broke her heart almost as much as the idea of not being involved.

No, as hard as it was to be patient, her best bet was to hope and pray that in time—not *too* much time—Jasper would find it in his heart to let her into Anaya's life. As she closed her eyes, her phone started ringing in her handbag.

She leapt off the bed, almost tripping over her own feet in her effort to get to it. While part of her knew it was too soon, she couldn't help hoping it was Jasper with good news. Deciding it had to be Willow or Samuel checking in on her, she frowned when she glanced down at the screen and saw an international number.

Laura! She hadn't known her mother even knew how to call a mobile from overseas—the few times they'd spoken since she'd been in Montana, it had always been on Skype—but she'd been one surprise after another this last year.

Talk about crap timing.

She considered ignoring the call, but then again, maybe some mindless chatter with her mother would help take her mind off Jasper. Hoping she wouldn't regret it, she pressed accept.

'Hello?'

'What the hell took you so long to answer?' Laura sounded as if she were screaming from the next room. Harper almost dropped the phone, feeling like a little girl being scolded for something that wasn't even naughty.

'I'm ... a little bit busy.' She took a deep breath, already wishing she'd let the call go to voicemail. She didn't have the mental energy to deal with her mother. She went back over to the bed and lay down again, trying to remember who she was supposed to be interviewing at work today so she could tell Laura about that.

'I *know*,' Laura said, her tone accusatory. 'When were you going to tell me I'm a grandmother?'

'What?' Harper sat bolt upright again. 'How did you hear?'

'How did I hear?!' That shrill voice again, worse than nails down a blackboard. 'On the internet. That's how. I know you think I'm a dummy compared to you and Willow but I keep up to date with Australian news. Someone shared a link on Facebook.'

Despite the seriousness of her situation, Harper almost laughed out loud at that. Damn social media—of course it would be there. She hadn't checked her accounts for over twenty-four hours. Taking another deep breath, she told herself to be calm. 'You're *not* a grandmother,' she said, because no matter what decision Jasper made, Harper would never let her mother take on such a role.

'So Facebook is lying?' Laura sounded only moderately placated. 'You didn't give your eggs away to strangers and now one of them is dead and the baby alive?'

'I did donate eggs,' Harper admitted, 'and sadly the recipient is dead and the baby was delivered alive.' Although the bit about 'giving away' and 'strangers' made her fingers tighten around her mobile.

'And you didn't think to tell your own mother what you were doing?'

'No, I didn't.' Harper refused to feel guilty. 'This was a private thing. If Claire hadn't passed away, the media would never have been privy to any of this information and I don't see how it's any concern of yours either.'

'No concern of mine?' The piercing shriek was back, louder and more deranged than ever. Harper seriously considered ending the call without another word. 'I'm your mother. After all I've done, all I've sacrificed for you and your sister, I shouldn't have to hear stuff like this on the internet. You don't think I care that I'm a grandma to a little girl?'

'You're *not* a grandma! The baby already has two sets of devoted grandparents.' Harper was careful not to call Anaya by name.

And no way was she telling Laura anything about her hopes to be more involved in her life. For one, she didn't trust her own mother not to blab to the media—Laura would do anything for a quick bob. And two, just hearing her voice had doubt creeping into Harper's mind.

Seeing Jasper with Anaya today had proven his initial hesitation towards her had blossomed into full-blown love. No one looking at Anaya cradled against him could question that love—it was clear that he'd do everything within his power to make her happy and safe. Maybe Anaya *would* be fine with him. More than fine. Maybe Harper *was* being selfish—like her own mother—in her desire to play a bigger role in the baby's life. Her gut tightened and turned with the uncertainty.

'Are you still there? Are you listening to me?' Laura demanded. 'Why didn't you tell me about giving away your eggs? It's embarrassing, not to mention insulting to find out something like this third hand. Mack wonders what kind of daughters I have that they don't tell their own mother something this huge.'

'Oh my God, you're truly delusional.' Something inside Harper snapped—it was time for a few home truths. 'No, I don't think you have any right to know what I do with my own body. You gave up those rights over and over again during my childhood. You didn't sacrifice anything for Willow and me, but we sacrificed a lot because we had a mother like you. A selfish mother who always put herself ahead of her children.'

Harper barely paused to take a breath. 'Willow and I have been beyond kind to you since we've been adults. We've made excuses, we've dragged you out of scrapes time and time again when it should have been the other way round. But you *never* chose us. The day you didn't turn up when I had the star role at my grade two assembly I finally understood that you weren't what a mother should be.'

'You're not going to bring that up again, are you?' Laura interjected.

Ignoring the question, Harper continued, 'Willow said you wouldn't come, but I believed in you and you let me down. Just as you let Willow down when you called her a whore when your deadbeat boyfriend mistakenly climbed into her bed. If it even *was* a mistake. What would you have done if he'd raped her? No, don't answer that because we both know the truth. We both know who you'd have believed. You let us down over and over again. And because of you, I decided never to be a mother. Because Lord help the child if I turned out like you! *That's* why I "gave my eggs away" as you put it, because I was too scared to use them myself!'

There was dead silence on the other end of the phone, but Harper could tell Laura hadn't hung up. She could keep talking—keep throwing examples at her—but what would be the point? It wouldn't change the past and she didn't want to waste her breath. 'Unless you've got anything else to say, I think this conversation is over. I have more important things to focus on right now.'

And before Laura *could* say another word, Harper disconnected and threw the phone across the bed. Her heart was racing and her blood boiling. She'd never felt such rage, yet at the same moment a massive grin exploded onto her face. She'd finally told her mother what she should have told her years ago. Whether Laura would take any of it in or not didn't matter, because the simple act of getting it off her chest made her feel like the noose that had been hanging around her neck all these years had finally been cut loose.

She now knew with absolute certainty that she was not like her mother and never would be. Whether that was because of her father's genes, Willow's guiding influence as she was growing up or some wonderful freak of nature, who knew? It didn't matter. All that mattered was that she wanted to be Anaya's mother and that somehow she and Jasper would work it out so that Anaya got two loving parents instead of one.

Now that she'd held her baby girl's hand, now that she'd stared down into her tiny but vibrant eyes, Harper couldn't comprehend a life without her in it.

She'd given up on a baby once before, and whatever it took, she wasn't going to do it again.

Chapter Thirty-two

Wendy, Paul, Joanne and Mike arrived at the apartment within minutes of each other, followed soon after by Scotty and Polly. Unfortunately Tim was on a mine site overnight for work and couldn't make it, so Jasper had decided to invite his cousin and Claire's best friend instead. He figured it might be good to have another opinion in case his parents and Claire's were divided.

He hugged them all and led them straight into the kitchen where the food he'd bought from the local Thai restaurant was already laid out on the table.

'That smells delicious,' Mike said, but the smile that went along with his words looked forced. Both his and Claire's parents looked as if they'd aged a decade in the last two weeks.

They were all making an effort to keep going without Claire but nothing had ever felt like such hard work. Although there wasn't really room for anyone else around the table, her absence was as obvious as if there'd been a dragon sitting among them.

Taking a deep breath to try and ease the pressure on his chest, Jasper gestured to the plates and the plastic containers filled with an assortment of rice and spicy food. 'Help yourselves.'

Everyone did so without speaking—the only sounds in the small room the scraping of cutlery against plates. Since Claire's death small talk seemed overrated and Jasper appreciated that none of his family attempted it. When all their plates were full, he put some food on his as well, not that he had much of an appetite. He'd noticed when he'd pulled clean jeans on earlier that they were looser than they had been in years, but food seemed a low priority right now.

He cleared his throat and all eyes in the kitchen focused on him. 'Thanks for coming at such short notice.'

They nodded, smiled and uttered things like 'not a problem' and 'we'd move heaven and earth to be here for you, Jasper.'

'Well, anyway …' His gut tightened as he spoke and he decided to deal with the easiest issue first. 'You might have noticed that the media has found out about Harper donating her eggs to Claire and me.'

'Bloody media,' Paul grumbled. 'Journalists should learn to mind their own business.'

'If it wasn't our story, we'd probably be fascinated by it,' Joanne pointed out with a sad shrug of her shoulders. 'The papers only print stuff because people want to read it.'

'*Anyway*,' Jasper continued, not wanting to get into a debate about the ethics of media, 'Harper drove up to speak to me about it today—apparently *The Morning Edition* wants to interview us. They've offered us money for an exclusive interview.'

'*The Morning Edition*?' Paul's derisive tone told Jasper exactly what his father thought of this.

'By *us*,' Joanne asked, 'do you mean you and Harper or all of us?'

Mike slammed his fist down on the table. 'Does it matter? Paul's right. This has nothing to do with anyone but the family and if they think they can buy us ... well, they've got another think coming!'

Jasper swallowed—while his initial gut reaction had been very similar to his dad's and Mike's, he'd had a few hours to ponder the proposal a little more. What if Harper was right and the media monster continued to run with the story whether they gave their consent or not?

'It would only be me and Harper, I think,' he said. 'I guess they're interested in the whole egg donation angle and the fact that Harper's a bit of a celebrity, but I'd have to clarify that.'

'How do you feel about it, sweetheart?' asked his mum.

Jasper fidgeted with his wedding ring as he spoke. 'It's not something I really want to do, but maybe Harper has a point—she thinks if we agree to the interview, then we'll be able to give our side of the story and hopefully move on.'

Wendy nodded. 'If anyone would know how it works, she would.'

'But it's none of their business,' Mike said again. 'Do you really want them prying into our family?'

'How much money will they pay you?' Scotty asked.

Polly hit him with a look of disgust.

Scotty shrugged. 'I'm just curious. Jasper won't be able to work as much now he's a sole parent, so a little money to put aside for a rainy day mightn't be a bad thing.'

Jasper swallowed. He'd only just begun to come to terms with the fact that he was a widower—he hadn't yet considered how he'd negotiate single fatherhood once Anaya came home from hospital.

'Of course we'll look after Jasper *and* Anaya,' said Wendy, sounding a little offended.

'I don't know the exact amount,' Jasper said. He'd been so affronted that afternoon he hadn't thought to ask any sensible questions. 'I'm torn—I don't *want* to do it, but part of me thinks Claire might want me to. To get the money for Anaya but also to be a voice for other couples like us who might need fertility assistance.'

'Do you really think that's what they'll be interested in, son?' asked his father. 'My limited experience of the media tells me they'll be wanting to know how you plan to cope as a single dad and whether Harper will have any involvement.'

Jasper's stomach twisted as he thought of Harper's request—what would the media make of that?

'Claire was a very private person,' added Polly. 'If the tables were turned, do you think *she'd* want to give an interview?'

Oh how he wished the tables *were* turned. Or better yet, Claire was alive and he didn't have to deal with the media or Harper on his own. But, he knew such wishes were futile. His life had changed and it would never be the same again.

He looked to Joanne. Aside from himself, no one knew Claire better than her mother. 'What do you think? If you're adamantly against it, then I'll tell them no.'

Joanne rubbed her lips together a few moments. 'I think you're right about Claire. She wanted that baby more than anything—she would have done anything for her—so I think if you can put aside the money for her education, then you should do it. But only if you feel up to it. Right, Mike?'

Claire's father still looked doubtful, but gave a reluctant nod.

'It might not be so bad,' said his mum. 'Since Claire died there's been an outpouring of support from our local community, from our friends and family but also from strangers who have heard our story and left messages on the business Facebook page. People really care—they want to know how you and Anaya are doing.'

Jasper let out a long sigh. Nothing could be worse than actually losing Claire. After *that* he could face almost anything else. 'All right then. If no one is adamantly opposed, then I'll tell Harper yes. Hopefully we can get it over with soon.'

'We'll all support you in whatever you think best,' Scotty said and the others nodded and murmured their agreement.

'Thank you. I'll let you know when it's all confirmed.'

His mum nodded as if that was all settled and she was ready to move on. He was too. 'And how is our darling girl today?' she asked.

Jasper smiled. He'd much rather be talking about his girl than the media. 'She's wonderful, thriving.' He filled them in on the paediatrician's report. Wendy and Joanne cried tears of happiness and he had to run into the bathroom for a roll of toilet paper because he'd already exhausted all the tissues in the apartment himself.

'But there's actually a bigger reason I asked you all here tonight,' he said, when everyone had calmed down again. 'Something very important I need your thoughts on.'

Again, the cutlery stopped scraping against plates and his family looked to him, frowns and curiosity etched into their faces.

'Bigger than the media?' Mike asked, raising his bushy eyebrows.

Jasper took a sip of his water, wishing it were beer, but he planned to head back to the hospital soon and wouldn't risk driving even on one drink. Not anymore.

'Harper also ...' He paused, searching for the right words. 'She wanted to ask me ... She *told* me she's feeling very strong feelings for Anaya. Harper ... she wants to be more involved in her life than she would have been if Claire was still alive.'

This news was met with silence. Some of the frowns deepened. Polly was the first to speak.

'What exactly do you mean by *more involved*?' she asked.

He inhaled deeply. 'The finer details would have to be worked out. And I made it clear that *if* I agree to her request, I still want Anaya to grow up knowing Claire as her mother. But Harper wants to be her "other mother" as she put it. She wants to be there to give Anaya a mother's love, but also I guess to do the things women do with their daughters, have the conversations that might be awkward for a girl to have with her dad.'

'I kind of thought I'd be a surrogate mum.' Polly sounded affronted. Scotty laid his hand on top of hers.

'Surely Joanne and I will be around to have those conversations,' Wendy said. 'And Polly, like she said, and Hannah and your sisters. It's not as if Anaya is short on family or love.'

'Polly already has five children of her own,' Joanne pointed out. 'And grandmothers and aunties aren't the same as mothers. Besides, your three daughters don't live close enough to be very hands on.'

His mum opened her mouth to reply, but Jasper got in first. 'Are you saying you think I should say yes to Harper?' He'd thought Claire's parents might be the most opposed to the idea.

'I didn't say that,' Joanne said more forcefully than he'd ever heard her speak before. 'I'm just pointing out the facts. I don't know what to think about anything right now.' Her face crumpled and she leant into Mike.

'Would Anaya go between your place and Sydney, then?' Scotty asked.

'As I said, we haven't discussed how it would work, but Harper did say she'd be willing to make sacrifices.'

'She can't be very involved from two-and-a-half hours away,' Polly said. Jasper didn't mention that by that logic, the same went for her.

'Maybe it'd give you more time for ballooning again, if Anaya spent a little quality time with Harper.' Paul rubbed his beard the way he did whenever something required deep thought.

Ballooning. Jasper got a rush to his head just thinking about it. He'd been so numb since Claire died that flying had been the last thing on his mind—he didn't think he'd ever gone this long without going up. His fingers tingled a little at the thought of rolling out the envelope in readiness for flight. His dad did look exhausted from the extra load he'd taken on due to Jasper's absence. But that on its own wasn't enough of a reason to allow Harper this much access to their lives.

'I'd like to know why she wants to do this,' Mike piped up. 'I know Claire had nothing but praise for Harper, but correct me if I'm wrong, didn't she donate her eggs because she *didn't* want children of her own?'

Joanne nodded. 'That's true. Do you think she genuinely loves Anaya and wants to be involved? Or is she offering this because she thinks it's the right thing to do? Because she feels obligated.'

Although it wasn't his place to tell them everything Harper had told him about her tumultuous relationship with her own mother and the abortion she'd had fifteen years ago, he thought she'd understand if he gave them a little insight. So without going into too much detail, he tried to explain it the way Harper had earlier.

When he'd finished, Joanne spoke first. 'Although it pains me to think of anyone being a mother to that baby apart from my sweet girl, I have to admit it sounds to me like Harper is genuine. Claire spoke to me about her a lot—she liked and respected her—and I think I know my daughter enough to predict that if she could have a say in this somehow, she'd want to give Harper the chance.'

'Yes,' interjected Mike, 'but what if down the track she decides she wants full custody? What if she tries to take Anaya away from Jasper, away from *us*?'

Jasper's heart clenched at the thought. 'I won't let that happen,' he promised. 'We've got official contracts and documentation naming Claire and me as Anaya's parents. She'd need a pretty good lawyer to argue that.'

'And doesn't she just happen to be married to one?' asked Polly.

Fuck! How could Jasper have forgotten Samuel? His hands fisted on the table and his head throbbed with the stress of everything—the way he saw it, whatever he decided there was risk. But if he denied Harper the chance to be a bigger part of Anaya's life, how far would she push it? *Would* she take a custody battle to court? The possibility filled him with dread.

'Look,' Joanne began again, 'this is obviously not the ideal situation, and some sort of official custody arrangements would have to be agreed on, which I hope would take into account Mike and me being part of her life as well. But the notion of a "normal" family is pretty much extinct these days. There are all kinds of families—same sex families, single parent families, blended families. Anaya wouldn't be the only child at school that has two parents living apart. And her parents wouldn't have gone through a messy separation, so she won't have to deal with that kind of animosity.'

Wendy sighed. 'Perhaps you're right, but what role will Harper's husband play? And what happens if Jasper meets someone else? She might not feel comfortable with the arrangement he has with Harper.'

The question about Samuel barely registered as anger welled within him at his mother's mention of him finding someone else. Jasper didn't give a damn how some imaginary woman might feel.

No one would ever replace Claire and he told her this in no uncertain terms.

'Calm down, Jasper,' Paul said, holding a hand up as he inched closer to his wife. 'Your mother didn't mean any offence. You gathered us all here to ask our opinion and we're trying, like you, to work out what that is.'

Jasper unclenched his hands, closed his eyes briefly and then nodded. 'I'm sorry, you're right. But the only person that really matters here is Anaya. Not me, not Harper, and certainly not strangers who may or may not enter our lives in the future. I want to know what you all think is best for my girl.'

Although his family didn't always see eye to eye, they all agreed on one thing—the most important ingredient a child needed to thrive was love.

And thus, by the time Jasper waved them goodbye, he had made his decision.

Chapter Thirty-three

Harper woke to a ringing sound and found herself in a dark hotel room—the only light coming from her iPhone screen. She blinked, taking a few moments to remember where she was and why. Oh Lord, the conversation with her mother came flooding back. How the hell had she fallen asleep with the adrenalin that had been racing through her body after that? Obviously the last couple of weeks had finally caught up with her.

The phone went silent.

'Shit,' she said, sitting up and stretching across to grab it from where she'd left it who knows how many hours before. What if she'd missed Jasper's call? What if he'd rung before and she'd slept through it?

But her heart sank when she glanced at the screen and saw that the missed call had been from Samuel. She remembered the things she'd told Jasper that she'd never had the guts to share with her husband. Sure he'd known living with Laura hadn't been a walk in the park, but he didn't know about Willow's near rape and he still didn't know about her own abortion.

As she was deliberating about whether or not to call back straight away, the phone started ringing again. Her heart leapt—once again hoping it was Jasper and once again feeling let down when she saw that it was not. This time she answered it, forcing a chirpiness she didn't feel into her voice.

'Hi, sweetheart. Sorry I missed your call a moment ago. I was in the bathroom.'

'No worries. How are you? How was the conversation with Jasper?'

It irked her that he didn't ask after the baby. 'I'm fine. Anaya's doing really well and Jasper is thinking about the television interview.'

'If he agrees to go ahead, when do you think you'll do it?'

'I'm not sure yet. Does it matter?' He totally ignored her reference to Anaya.

'It won't be this weekend though, will it?'

She frowned. 'I don't know. I doubt it. Why?'

'Stanley and Rodger have asked if we can reschedule the dinner to Saturday night. You haven't got anything on, have you?'

His tone told her she had better not, and although the last thing she felt like doing at the moment was wining, dining and making conversation with Samuel's colleagues, she couldn't say no to him again. 'Saturday night sounds fabulous.'

It was just over two hours to Sydney. If Jasper had agreed to her proposal by then, she could drive back on Saturday afternoon and return to Newcastle first thing Sunday morning.

'Excellent,' Samuel said. 'Will you be on your way back soon? Do you want me to organise dinner for when you get home or will you grab something on the way?'

She swallowed, glancing at the digital alarm clock on the bedside table. Almost eight o'clock. Why hadn't Jasper called her? Surely he wouldn't leave her in agony overnight.

'Actually,' she said, 'I'm staying here for a couple of nights. To spend a little more time with Anaya ...' *If possible*. 'And of course to school Jasper a little in being interviewed. He's never done anything like this before.'

'Can't you talk him through all that on the phone?'

This was the second time she'd mentioned Anaya by name, but again it was like he didn't even register her. Feeling heat rising within her, she opened her mouth to give him what for when a sound came through, telling her that someone else was trying to call. She pulled the phone away from her ear and glanced down at the screen to see the name she'd been waiting for all afternoon. It was all she could do not to shriek.

'Gotta go, Samuel. I think Bryn's trying to call me.'

Then, without giving him the chance to say goodbye, she ended his call and answered Jasper's. 'Hello,' she gasped, utterly failing to sound cool, calm and collected.

'Hi Harper. How you doing?'

He sounded uncertain, and quite frankly, how the hell did he think she was? But she swallowed this retort. 'I'm fine. How are you? How's Anaya?'

Have you made a decision about me and her?

'I'm good. I've spent the last couple of hours talking with my family and we've come to a decision.'

Her belly went rock solid as she waited for him to deliver it.

'Can you come to the hospital?' he asked.

'What? Now?' Harper blurted before realising how that sounded. She shot to her feet. 'Yes, of course. I'm on my way. I can be there in ten minutes.'

He wouldn't ask her to come to the NICU at this time of night only to tell her no. Would he?

'There's no rush. Drive safely. I'll be here with Anaya whenever you can get here.' And he disconnected before she had a chance to say goodbye.

Harper crossed to the bathroom, switched on the light and checked herself in the mirror to see how much fixing up would be required. She smoothed her hands over the wrinkles in her shirt, then brushed her hair and blotted the shine off her face with tissues. No time to reapply make-up and her hands were shaking anyway, so she could only imagine the kind of damage she'd do with lipstick or mascara.

Two minutes later, she was in her car on the way to the hospital, replaying Jasper's brief phone call over and over in her head. Maybe he'd only asked her there to say goodbye. Did the fact that he was so brusque mean he was about to shut her out? If he had good news, wouldn't he have been more cordial? But surely if it was bad news, he'd deliver it over the phone. These uncertainties gave her heartburn and by the time she arrived at the hospital, she felt in need of a good antacid. She locked her car and hurried into the building.

She took a deep breath and started towards the NICU. As it was now well past visiting hours, the hospital floors were all but deserted and she felt like a trespasser, but she held her shoulders back and continued to her destination, trying to look more confident than she felt.

The nurse/guard at the entrance of the NICU gave Harper a cordial nod as if expecting her, then pressed the button that opened the door to the ward and told her to go on through. Her shoes click-clacking along the corridor sounded so loud but another nurse met her eye and smiled, making her feel slightly less anxious. There were only a couple of other parents on the ward, sitting quietly beside incubators, and they barely looked up as she passed.

At the entrance to Anaya's room, she paused to scrub her arms clean and saw Jasper gazing down at their little girl. The room was dim and quiet due to the late hour.

He looked up when she entered.

'Hi there,' she somehow managed. She tried to read his expression for an answer.

'Hey,' he said, standing, his face unreadable.

Although she desperately wanted him to put her out of her misery, her gaze went to the baby, her heart turning over at the sight of Anaya sleeping peacefully. She didn't know how she'd cope if Jasper told her she couldn't see her again.

'You've made a decision?' she asked, looking up into his eyes.

He nodded. 'Thanks for coming in so late.'

'I want to be here,' she said, and then lowered her voice when she realised how loudly she'd spoken.

Again, he nodded. 'I understand. I spoke to my parents and Claire's tonight, and we all agree that—if it's what you want and you're not going to change your mind down the track—you should be involved in Anaya's life.'

Had she heard right? 'You mean you'll let me be a mother to her?' She blushed as she said this word—it felt awkward on her tongue. It was something she'd never expected to be, something she'd never expected to *want* to be.

'Yes. Anaya has already lost one mother; I don't want to have to tell her one day that I robbed her of another.'

She saw his Adam's apple move slowly up and down as he swallowed, reminding her how difficult this must be for him.

'Obviously,' he went on, 'we'll need to discuss exactly how this is going to work—and I meant what I said about her knowing Claire as her mother as well—but I'm willing for you to be the primary female influence in our little girl's life.'

'Oh my goodness!' Tears spurted from Harper's eyes as she registered he really meant this. She could have kissed him. 'I'm not going to change my mind,' she promised, and it was the easiest promise she'd ever made in her life. There was nothing she wouldn't do for Anaya.

They stood there for a few moments, both staring at the little miracle between them, then Jasper looked up and spoke. 'And about the other thing. You know, the TV interview?'

She nodded—of course she knew—but whatever his decision on that was, she'd respect it. At least she could tell Bryn she'd tried.

'What kind of stuff do you think they'll want to know?'

'I guess they'll ask about you and Claire, how you met, why you needed to do egg donation. They'll probably want to know how I came into the equation, how Anaya is doing now and about your, I mean *our*, plans for the future.'

'Okay. If you really think it'll get everyone off our backs once and for all, then I'll do it.'

'If you're absolutely sure, I'll talk to my boss and let her and my producer handle everything with *The Morning Edition*.'

He nodded. 'I am.'

Harper smiled. There was something else on her mind that she wanted to do right now, and she didn't want to wait another moment longer. 'Do you think I could hold Anaya?' she asked.

'What?' Jasper blinked, unable to hide his alarm. For a second she wondered if maybe she'd misunderstood his agreement to let her be Anaya's mother, but he quickly tried to save face. 'Um ... I guess. If the nurse thinks it's okay this late at night.'

'If the nurse thinks what's okay?' One of the night nurses came up beside them and winked. Her name badge read Leslie. 'Sorry,

I wasn't eavesdropping—the acoustics make it so hard to have a private conversation in here.'

Harper smiled at her. 'That's okay.' She glanced back at Anaya. Should she ask to hold her or should she give Jasper a little longer to get used to the idea?

Jasper cleared his throat. 'Harper would like to hold Anaya, but I told her it might be too late.'

'Oh no, that would be fine. Of course she can.' The nurse's face lit up. 'Just let me finish one little thing and I'll be right back to get her out for you.'

At the thought of what was about to happen, Harper's knees almost gave way beneath her and she reached out to steady herself on the incubator.

'Here.' Jasper gestured to the seat beside the crib. 'Sit down. You'll have to when you hold Anaya anyway.'

As she lowered herself into the seat, she noticed that her legs weren't the only part of her shaking. Her hands were also trembling and she took a few deep breaths, willing the shakes to stop.

'Thank you for letting me do this,' she said. 'I can't imagine how difficult this must be for you.'

He pursed his lips and nodded. As she too was too nervous to speak, they waited in silence for the nurse to return.

'All ready?' Leslie said when she returned. 'You sanitise your hands while I get the little lady out,' she instructed.

Harper did as she was told, rubbing the gel right up to her elbows as Leslie changed Anaya's nappy, talking gently to her the whole time.

When she was finished, the nurse turned back to Harper. 'Right, you'll have to take your bra and shirt off.' She retrieved a hospital gown from a drawer and held it out. 'You can put this on instead.'

Jasper's cheeks coloured and he made to step away. 'I'll go get a coffee or something,' he said, shoving his hands in his pockets.

'No, don't go,' Harper blurted. As much as she wanted to hold Anaya, she didn't want to make him feel uncomfortable. 'I'll go to the bathroom and be back in a moment.'

Then before he could object, she hurried in the direction of the rest room and replaced her upper garments with the hospital gown in record time.

When Harper returned, Leslie smiled at her. 'You ready?' she said, as she gestured to the chair for her to sit. The nurse held the baby with such expertise. And although Harper desperately wanted to hold Anaya, her heart thumped. What if she dropped her? What if Anaya cried and Harper couldn't settle her? She suddenly wished that she hadn't been so quick to refuse all those offers to hold babies in the past. Her breath stilled as she sat and Leslie moved the hospital gown aside and gently laid the baby on her chest.

As Harper felt Anaya's bare, soft skin against her own naked breasts, her heart filled with love, leaving no room at all for anxiety and nerves. In that moment everything felt so absolutely right that she forgot about Jasper's feelings and didn't even care if he got a glimpse of more skin than Samuel had seen in the last few weeks. She barely registered Leslie laying a thick blanket atop them both and tucking it in behind her—she was mesmerised, totally bewitched by the sight, smell and feel of the miracle in her arms.

This instant in time would be forever imprinted in her mind.

After a few moments, Anaya let out a tiny sound—almost like a kitten mewling—and Harper looked up to see Jasper and Leslie smiling down at her.

'I think she loves you,' Jasper said, a mixture of happiness and desperate sadness etched into his face.

She thought about how hard this must be for him. That this was a moment he'd been supposed to share with Claire. She wished there was something she could say to help him.

Instead, she simply said, 'Thank you. I love her too.'

'I'll leave you guys be for a little bit,' Leslie said. 'But I'm just at the desk if you need me.'

As she retreated, Jasper shuffled on his feet. 'Do you want me to go as well? Give you a little alone time with ... with your daughter?'

'*Our* daughter,' she said as she shook her head. 'Stay. We have a lot to discuss.'

Chapter Thirty-four

Harper cringed as her phone started ringing through the speakers in her car; she didn't have to be a genius to know that it would be Samuel, wondering where she was. She'd promised him she'd be home over an hour ago, but after two full days at Anaya's side, it had been incredibly hard to tear herself away.

'Hey honey,' she said as she answered. 'I'm just around the corner. Do you want to pick out a dress for me to wear tonight?'

'Did you get stuck in traffic? We need to leave in less than half an hour.'

'Um ... I'll tell you all about it in a moment. And don't worry, I need a quick shower but I'll dress in record time. Promise.' Then, before he could say anything else, she disconnected.

Her stomach was in knots as she parked the car because it was time to come clean with Samuel. She'd had to make ridiculous excuses about why she'd stayed in Newcastle so long, but she knew she wouldn't be able to return tomorrow morning without telling him everything. And although time was scarce until they had to leave for the partners' dinner, she didn't want to wait until afterwards because this wasn't a conversation she wanted to have if either of them had alcohol in their systems.

The door opened before she reached it and Samuel stood there looking sexy and dapper in his best black suit, his hair slicked back like Pierce Brosnan as James Bond. But he had a dark scowl on his face.

'What's going on, Harper?' he said as he held the door open for her. 'Are you having an affair with Jasper? Is that it?'

'What?' The ridiculousness of his question stunned her. 'No. Are you insane? For God's sake, the man only buried his wife on Wednesday.'

He shrugged, holding his hands out in surrender as the door slammed shut behind them. 'What am I supposed to think? I'm not stupid—I know you don't need three days to school someone for a television interview.'

She winced at his loud voice—Samuel never yelled—but at the same time she understood she'd been unfair to him. 'I'm sorry. You're right—I haven't only been in Newcastle because of the interview.' She paused, opened her handbag and dug out the digital camera. 'I've been there because of her,' she said as she turned it on and shoved the screen in front of his face.

He still looked utterly confused. 'It's a baby,' he said coldly.

'Not just any baby,' she said. 'This is Anaya. *My* baby.'

It took a moment but then his brows folded inwards and he looked her dead in the eyes. '*Your* baby? Last I heard you were the egg donor.'

She swallowed. There was no good way to begin this conversation—there was so much she had to tell him. 'Her birth mother is dead. I can't just desert her.'

'What are you talking about? You signed a legal contract, giving Jasper and Claire all parental rights and responsibilities.'

'Well, things have changed,' she said, clutching the camera to her chest.

'What exactly are you trying to tell me?' he asked, his voice so calm it chilled her.

Standing in their hallway with the clock ticking till they needed to go out didn't seem the best place to tell him, but there'd probably never be a good time or place. 'Something changed in me when I met Anaya. I felt a love and a desire like nothing I've ever felt before. And I've decided I want to be her mother—not just biologically, but in all the ways that matter. I can't walk away from her, Samuel. I don't want to.'

He jerked his head back as if she'd slapped him—in all the years they'd been together, she'd never seen anything shock him like this obviously did. She opened her mouth, not really sure what to say next, but he got in first.

'I thought you didn't want children. I was honest with you from the beginning.' His expression turned from shock to sadness. 'And you always told me you felt the same. Was that all a lie? Did you think I'd change my mind?' He shook his head. 'I knew nothing good would come of this egg donation business. I should never have given you my support.'

Support? What a joke! But she chose to let that go and focus on the now. 'I didn't *lie*. Well, not to you,' she said. 'Until a few days ago, I honestly believed I didn't want to have children, but in hindsight, I conditioned myself not to want them. If anything I lied to *myself*. I made myself believe I wanted other things instead of a family, but all along I think it was a barrier I put up to protect myself. I was scared of failure. Scared of being the kind of mother mine was. So scared I had an abortion.'

'What?' She thought he flinched because her confession disgusted him, but it was sadness she saw in his eyes. And his voice cracked a little when he asked, 'Why didn't you ever tell me? It wasn't my baby, was it?'

'No,' she rushed to reassure him. 'I promise if we'd ever fallen pregnant I would have told you. This was long before we met. I was only nineteen. It had nothing to do with us.'

He ran a hand through his hair, ruffling the perfect style he'd greeted her with. 'I've told you everything about me, Harps. I don't have any secrets from you and I thought you were the same. I thought we wanted the same things in life. What else haven't you told me? What else don't I know about my wife?'

'Nothing. I promise. I'm sorry—I don't want to hurt you, Samuel. I love you, but I also love Anaya.'

'So you've said.' He shoved his hands in his pockets as if trying to control his anger. They weren't big fighters—they'd never thrown things at each other in the heat of an argument, choosing instead to talk disagreements out like the adults they were—but they'd never argued about anything as huge as this before. 'How exactly do you plan on this working then? You say you want to be a mother ... How are you going to do that with the little girl living in the Hunter Valley? Or do you plan to go for full custody? Do you want to *adopt* her? Where will all this leave me? Us?'

'Anaya will live with Jasper to begin with, but I will visit at weekends. And you can come with me. When she's older, she'll be able to come to Sydney and ... stay with ... us.'

He raised an eyebrow and his hands remained firmly in his pockets. 'Do I get any say in this?'

She nodded, her hands now shaking around the camera and her heart beating so fast she could feel it. 'You do, Samuel. I'm not going to give up my baby and I hope that you'll grow to love her and accept us as a package deal, but I'll understand if you can't do that. If you ...'

Harper couldn't bring herself to finish the sentence but they both knew what she meant. A tear slipped down her cheek. She'd never felt more torn in her life—she didn't want to choose between the man she loved and the baby who had stolen her heart.

He was quiet for what felt like an eternity, then took a breath. 'I assume you've already organised all this with Jasper?'

She bit her lip, then nodded.

'This affects me too, dammit. Isn't it something you should have discussed with me before you went zooming off to Newcastle?'

'What? So you could try and convince me I was being ridiculous? So you could try and change my mind?'

He glanced at the fancy clock hanging on the wall behind them—it had been a wedding present from his firm. 'Look, we can't talk about this right now—we've got to go out. Your dress is laid out on the bed.'

Then, without another word, he turned and stormed into the kitchen, no doubt to pour himself a stiff drink. She could do with one too—either that or some heavy painkillers, her head was splitting—but there wasn't time. Although Harper had never felt less like going out in her life, she owed it to Samuel to do this. Whatever happened between them after the dinner, he'd worked hard towards this promotion for a long time and he'd lose face if they cancelled again.

Swallowing tears, she hurried up the stairs, tearing off her clothes as she went. There wasn't really time for a shower but she had a super quick one anyway, careful not to get her hair wet as there definitely wasn't time to blow dry. Wrapped in a fluffy white towel, she emerged from the ensuite to see that Samuel had laid sexy underwear out on the bed beside a black cocktail dress. Highly unlikely *that* would be getting a workout now.

Still, she put them on and then stepped into the dress, cursing under her breath as she almost strained her arm trying to do up the zipper. Usually she asked Samuel for help with hard-to-reach zips, but she wasn't in a mood to ask him for anything. With five minutes until they needed to leave—if they didn't want to be rudely late—she sat down at her dressing table and applied the mask she would wear all night.

Then she went downstairs to find Samuel waiting by the front door, his shoe tapping loudly on the glossy wooden floorboards. Usually he'd compliment her on how she looked. Tonight he simply barked, 'The taxi's waiting,' and indicated for her to go through the door ahead of him. She snatched her coat off the stand and did as he wanted.

Their driver greeted them with a jovial smile and tried to make small talk as he pulled away from the kerb. 'Going anywhere nice?' he asked.

'Just drive, please,' Samuel said and Harper bit down on the urge to reprimand him for his rudeness. She didn't feel like making conversation with strangers either.

Samuel sat as close to his window and as far away from her as possible. Harper wanted to dig her mobile phone out of her handbag and text Jasper to check in on Anaya but she sat on her hands to stifle the urge, not wanting to make things worse than they already were between her and Samuel. She may have only seen her baby a few hours ago, but already that felt like forever—how she'd get through a week without contact she had no idea.

Neither she nor Samuel said a word until they arrived in front of a harbourside mansion in Mosman, where he thanked the driver and gave him a generous tip. Normally he'd assist her out of the car—his parents had drilled chivalry into him—but today he marched up the path through the impeccably manicured garden ahead of her. He waited until she arrived beside him before he rang the bell, but his expression remained grim until the moment the door peeled back.

Then he smiled at Stanley Carter as the older man greeted him with a handshake.

'Welcome, welcome.' Stanley turned his attention to Harper and kissed her on the cheek. 'So good to see you again, Harper. You're looking lovely as usual. Come on in.'

As Stanley held the door open, Samuel put his hand in the small of Harper's back and ushered her inside. The warmth that usually spread through her body at such a gesture was absent and his pressure almost hurt, but she kept a smile pasted on her face as Stanley took her coat, hung it on a hook on the wall, and then led them to join the others in the living room.

Stanley's wife Elizabeth, the other partner Rodger and his wife Tracey were already there, sipping champagne. Greetings were exchanged and Elizabeth summoned the maid—she was the only person Harper knew with house staff—to bring Harper and Samuel drinks.

The Carters' house was the kind of place you saw on *Grand Designs*. Designed by an acclaimed Sydney architect, it had marble floors, high ceilings and huge glass walls to make the most of their million-dollar views. A real log fire crackled beneath a modern-looking mantelpiece, and two fluffy white dogs lay on a rug in front of it—but there was not a speck of dust or fur in sight. To her credit, Elizabeth had made their house feel like a home with large framed photos of her grandchildren on every available surface.

Harper's gaze lingered on the photo of a newborn baby and her heart clenched as she thought of Anaya. Gourmet nibbles were brought out and Harper ate them and sipped her champagne as she tried to keep track of the small talk going on around her, but her mind kept drifting elsewhere.

Finally, Stanley and Elizabeth asked them all into the dining room to take a seat for dinner. Beautifully presented plates of salmon and julienne vegetables were laid in front of each of them, but before they ate, Rodger raised his glass and tapped a spoon against it. The gesture seemed a little ridiculous since there were so few of them in attendance, but Harper knew that the older partners liked a little fanfare.

'It is with great pleasure that we welcome Samuel and Harper here tonight to celebrate his becoming one of our partners. Samuel, you have proven your dedication to your clients and our company over and over again during your time working for us. We value your knowledge, your expertise and your ambition and we hope our partnership is a long and happy one.'

'Thank you,' Samuel said, beaming from ear to ear. He always loved being the centre of attention.

'To Samuel,' Rodger and Stanley said together, as if they'd been practicing for the moment all afternoon.

Harper forced a smile and lifted her crystal champagne flute to join the toast. She *was* proud of him, but after their heated discussion earlier and everything else going on in her life, she had to summon her inner actress to join in tonight's celebrations.

Nothing seemed to matter anymore except the little baby who felt way too far away right now.

As if she'd spoken these thoughts aloud, Tracey directed a question at Harper. 'I promised Rodger I wouldn't ask, but I can't help myself. We've all read the news about the miracle baby. I wouldn't have believed it had you not told us at the Christmas party that you were in the process of donating your eggs, but I have to ask, is it true?'

'Oh, yes. How is the dear little thing?' Elizabeth leant forward, her champagne flute hanging in midair.

Stanley and Rodger looked equally as interested, even though Rodger had apparently forbidden the topic.

Harper felt a little quiver in her stomach and her grip tightened on her own glass. She didn't look at Samuel but she felt his gaze on her nonetheless and was torn between answering the women's questions or brushing them off. Which response would piss Samuel off the least? This was his night and he wouldn't take kindly to her taking the limelight—but nor would he want her to be rude.

In the end, he took care of it for her. 'Yes, the miracle baby is Harper's and she's doing well. She's still tiny of course, but the doctors are happy with her weight gain and she no longer requires respiratory support.'

Harper's mouth dropped open as her eyes shot to her husband. She couldn't have been more surprised if he'd climbed up onto the table and done a striptease. Perhaps he had actually been listening during those few short phone conversations they'd had while she was away.

'That's lovely to hear,' Tracey said, wiping her eye as if she were close to tears. 'Poor little thing. Motherless at birth. And how is her father going?'

'Jasper is grieving for Claire, but finding joy in Anaya,' Harper replied.

'And,' Samuel said, his tone hard to read, '*Anaya* won't be motherless, because she has Harper.'

Rodger blinked. 'But I thought you were only the egg donor?'

Harper looked to Samuel, unsure what he would say to that, but he shrugged as if the floor was all hers. She took it. 'I was, but I've asked Jasper if I can be more involved. A child needs a mother and I couldn't live with myself if I could have given her one and didn't.'

'That's very noble of you,' Stanley said.

She shook her head. 'Oh, that might have come out wrong. I'm not doing this out of any sort of obligation—I fell in love with my daughter on sight and I want to be her mother more than anything.'

Elizabeth picked up her glass and clicked her fingers for the maid. 'Looks like we need another toast. That's such wonderful news. Congratulations.'

The word 'congratulations' didn't seem right when Claire had died, but Harper smiled politely and thanked her.

'There's truly no greater joy in life than children,' Elizabeth said with a glance at the photos that lined one wall.

Tracey chuckled. 'True, and also no greater pain, but still we wouldn't be without our three, would we, Rodger?'

While Rodger grinned and nodded in agreement, Harper saw Samuel lift his glass to his mouth—she guessed to stifle a scowl.

Perhaps Stanley saw it too for he said, 'And what do you make of this, Samuel? Bit of a shock to the system I'd imagine—for someone who adamantly didn't want children.'

The table fell silent as all eyes looked to him. Harper held her breath, wondering if this was where he'd announce that he was leaving her. But instead he said, 'I love Harper, so I'll support her in everything she does.'

Of course he wouldn't make such a declaration in front of his fellow partners, yet his undertones were clear—at least to her—this was *Harper's* decision, not his.

The questions kept coming after that. The women wanted to know all the details, but Harper explained that she had to be careful what she said until they'd done their interview with *The Morning Edition*.

'And when's that?' Stanley asked.

'They've scheduled it for Monday,' Harper said.

'Can we at least see a photo?' Elizabeth wanted to know, her eyes sparkling at the prospect.

'Oh, of course.' Harper went to dig the camera out of her bag and then realised she hadn't put it back after taking it out to show

Samuel. 'Actually, I don't have any on me. We aren't allowed to take photos with our phone and I didn't bring my camera tonight.'

'That's okay,' Elizabeth said. 'Next time.'

But it wasn't okay. Ridiculous tears welled up beneath Harper's eyelids at the realisation that she couldn't just take a look at Anaya whenever she pleased.

'Excuse me,' she said as she stood, folded her napkin and laid it on the table. 'I just need to pop to the rest room.'

'Of course, dear. You remember where it is, don't you?'

Harper fled, taking her handbag with her. Hopefully by the time she returned the conversation would have moved on to something Samuel was more comfortable with, because if they asked any more questions about Anaya she was likely to burst into tears. The baby had only been a part of her world for a matter of days, but already being away from her felt like losing a vital body part.

She slipped into the bathroom and closed the door behind her, trying to catch her breath and willing the tears back into their ducts. Then she sat down on the closed lid of the toilet and pulled out her mobile phone, suddenly remembering she could access the early photos of Anaya on her email. As she gazed down at the baby—even tinier then than she was now—her breathing slowed again and she smiled at the screen.

A message popped up from Lilia:

Bryn's given me Monday off to come to Newcastle with you. Shall I drive us both? Pick you up at five? It'll be like being on breakfast radio again. x

She stared at the message. Samuel wasn't the only person she needed to tell about her change in situation. Willow had been calling daily to check in but Harper had been too busy with Anaya to call her friends and tell them what was going on. She made a mental note to phone Juliet and Renee as well.

Actually I'm heading back tomorrow morning. Will call you on the way to fill you in on everything. xx

Then she slipped the phone back into her handbag, checked her eyes weren't too puffy, flushed the toilet for effect and went back to join the party. As she'd hoped, the men were now talking business and the women were discussing Tracey's daughter's upcoming wedding.

Dessert—usually her favourite dish of the night—came and went and she barely tasted it, never mind enjoyed it. Everyone else appeared to be having a jolly old time and she feared they could go on all night, but Harper wanted to go home and get the drama that was brewing on Samuel's face over and done with.

Finally Tracey put her out of her misery when she announced she'd turn into a pumpkin if she didn't go home soon. Taxis were called, arms were slipped back into coats and Harper was genuinely grateful when she thanked Stanley and Elizabeth for their wonderful hospitality.

Samuel assisted her into the waiting taxi and once again, neither of them said a word as their driver navigated the streets back to Paddington. As they walked up the short path to the house, Harper's heart beat madly again, but she told herself *what will be will be*—she'd already got the important stuff off her chest. Samuel unlocked the door and held it for her to go through, but he still hadn't met her gaze and she had no idea what to expect.

When she couldn't stand the weird silence a moment longer, she said, 'Well, do you want me to sleep on the couch?'

'No.' He loosened his tie, then yanked it off and tossed it onto the hall table. He looked exhausted, older than his thirty-seven years. 'I want you to come to bed with me.'

'What? For one last fuck?'

He blinked and then grimaced. 'Harper, please, there's no need for that. And what do you mean *last*? Are you leaving me?'

'I thought you might be throwing *me* out.'

'Why would I do that?'

She sighed. 'You weren't exactly pleased by my news earlier.'

'I was shocked,' he said forcefully. 'All the time we've been together, I've thought we were on the same page about having a family. Then you not only tell me you think you actually *want* to be a mother, but that you've already got a baby. With *another man*. How do you expect me to feel?'

'I ...' She shook her head, unable to find the words.

Samuel took a step towards her and put his hands on her arms. 'I'm not going to pretend I'm happy about this; it's going to take some time to get used to the idea, but I meant what I told everyone tonight. You are my wife, I love you and I meant every word of my wedding vows. You might have changed, but I haven't. You're still the only woman I want in my life and I want us to work through this.'

Harper sniffed—unable to believe her ears. She'd been certain it was over between them. The tears she'd been holding back all night broke free and rolled down her cheeks.

'I hope those are happy tears,' he said, sounding slightly uncertain.

She nodded. Sniffed. 'They are. I seem to have become a bit of a crier these last few weeks.'

Samuel wiped her cheeks with his thumbs as he gazed down at her. 'Then I guess we'll have to buy a few more boxes of tissues.'

Harper went to laugh, but the sound got lost as his mouth claimed hers.

And although she was physically, mentally and emotionally wrung out, her body reacted to the passion in his kiss. Relief and love for him washed over her. She slid her hands round his back and held him close as she met each delicious stroke of his tongue with one of her own.

It wasn't long before he was tugging at the zipper of her dress. She stepped out of it as it pooled onto the floor and her nipples hardened when his thumbs traced them through the lace of her bra. Harper shivered as Samuel dropped to his knees, peeling her knickers down her legs as he went. She leant back against the hall table and moaned as his mouth found the apex of her thighs. They hadn't slept together since Claire's death—since Anaya's birth—and thus he brought her quickly to release.

She'd barely caught her breath before Samuel stood and spun her around, placing her hands on the table in front of them. As he thrust into her from behind, she held on hard and enjoyed the ride. The sex was rougher than usual—almost like he couldn't help himself—but she didn't mind. It was good, better than it had been for a while, and part of her was simply grateful that he still wanted her. That he wanted to make things work.

Afterwards, he took her to bed and held her close.

'I can't wait for you to meet Anaya,' she said as she snuggled against him. 'I know you're going to love her. In fact, why don't you come back with me tomorrow morning? I want to spend as much time as I can with Anaya before I have to come back to work for Tuesday, but we could take two cars?'

'I've got a busy schedule next week and I need to work tomorrow.'

She bit her lip, trying to stifle her disappointment. *Baby steps*, she told herself. 'Maybe next weekend then.'

'Yep. Maybe next weekend.'

Then Samuel kissed her on the forehead and they both fell asleep.

Chapter Thirty-five

As the cameraman and journalist finished setting up in the living room, Jasper retreated to the bedroom for a few moments peace. The apartment was full of strangers. In addition to the television crew, there was Harper's producer, Lilia, and a local make-up artist who'd seemed very excited to be given this gig. He crossed over to the dresser, grimaced at his reflection, yanked a tissue from the box his mother had bought over the weekend and dabbed it at his face. He'd never worn make-up in his life and he didn't see why he had to start now, but everyone had said it was something about looking better for the camera.

Quite frankly, he didn't give a damn what he looked like on screen—he was a grieving man and a new dad, not a TV star. With this thought, his gaze drifted to the framed photo of him and Claire which he'd asked his mum to bring from home. He reached out a finger to touch her face and startled at the feel of cold glass, when he'd stupidly been expecting her warm, soft skin.

'You were so beautiful,' he whispered, still not used to speaking about his wife in the past tense. 'And you'd be so proud of our little girl.'

He only wished Anaya was truly theirs—biologically—so that perhaps she'd grow up to look a little like Claire and share some of her mannerisms. But that wish was as useless as the one he had every time he lay down to try and sleep—the wish that he could hold his love just one last time, smell her, taste her, talk to her and truly have her answer back. Countless times he'd spoken to Claire's photo, but no matter how much he'd pleaded for her to give him a sign that she could somehow hear him, her photo remained mute.

Instead he had Harper to talk to. Harper to share Anaya with.

Jasper was trying his best to get used to that idea, but he wasn't sure he ever would. At his suggestion, she'd stayed in the apartment last night, rather than take a hotel room again. After leaving Anaya in the hospital, they'd returned here and shared a takeaway Chinese meal, but the conversation had been awkward. They'd talked about her husband—apparently he might come up the following weekend—and although that suggested Samuel was accepting of Harper's decision, Jasper was struggling enough with her involvement without complicating things further. After the dinner had been eaten and the mess cleaned up, they'd retreated to their separate rooms until the morning.

As he puffed out a long breath of air, a knock sounded on his door. He straightened and ran his hands through his hair, which had some kind of gel in it. 'I'm coming.'

He opened the door to see Harper's producer Lilia standing there. They'd been briefly introduced earlier but hadn't said much to each other.

'Sorry to bother you,' she said, offering him a gentle smile, 'but they're ready for you.'

'Thanks.' He followed her into the living room, idly wondering what her background was. With long, jet black hair, tanned skin, dark eyes and thick black eyelashes, she had an exotic look about her.

The TV crew were settling Harper into one of two chairs and the curtains were drawn so the room was dim except for the artificial lighting that had been set up to shine on them.

'Look, I know I'm here for Harper,' Lilia said, as Jasper waited for Helen Frey, the interviewer, to direct him into his chair, 'but if you need anything, please don't be afraid to ask. Harper's used to this kind of thing but I guess you're not, so if there's some special coffee you like or a snack that will help you relax, then I can go out and get it.'

'Thanks. That's kind of you.'

'No worries.' She winked at him. 'I'm here to help.'

'Where do you come from?' he asked her, unable to ignore his curiosity.

'Liverpool,' she replied, her dark eyes sparkling.

'I meant ... what's your family background?' His cheeks heated, hoping he hadn't offended her with his question.

'It's all right. I was just teasing.' She reached out and squeezed his arm. 'We're Assyrians. My grandparents migrated from Baghdad in the sixties.'

'Right.' He flinched and shook his arm free because the touch of a woman that wasn't Claire felt wrong. He looked away from Lilia and waited for the signal from Helen.

When she summoned him to his chair, he joyfully stepped forward.

'Take a seat, Jasper. Get comfortable.' Despite her words, Helen put her hands on his shoulders and repositioned him the moment his butt hit the chair. 'The microphone pack isn't pressing into you, is it?'

'No. It's fine,' Jasper lied. Earlier the cameraman had fit him and Harper with tiny microphones and at that moment the pack was digging painfully into his back. It would probably leave an imprint, but he didn't want to say anything that would prolong this agony. The sooner the interview was over, the sooner he could wipe this powder off his face and get back to the hospital.

'Great. Awesome.' Helen grinned at him and Harper, but then her face suddenly fell as if she'd remembered the reason they were sitting here. 'I mean, good that you're comfortable. Let's get started.'

She sat in a chair positioned slightly off to the right of them and explained that this would be more like a conversation than an interview. 'I want you to relax and try and forget the camera. Look at me, not Eddie.'

Jasper guessed Eddie was the camera guy's name—they'd been introduced earlier but, like the make-up artist's name, he'd forgotten it almost immediately. While Helen rolled off a few more instructions, the make-up girl rushed over to pat more crap onto their faces and he resisted the urge to swat her hand away. Then Helen gave the signal and the camera started rolling.

'Jasper, I want to offer my sympathies for the loss of your wife. I know I'm not alone in feeling for you and your family; the whole of Australia has been touched by Claire's horrific accident, which ended with your daughter Anaya being delivered by caesarean section.'

He nodded and muttered 'Thanks,' even though she'd already uttered almost exactly the same sentiments when she arrived. This bit was for the camera, which somehow made it feel less genuine. He had to work hard not to clench his hands into fists. It all felt so wrong—sitting here, talking to strangers about Claire's death and their personal business.

'Anaya was born at thirty weeks gestation and required assistance feeding and breathing. How's she doing now, two weeks later?'

Jasper swallowed, a rush of love coming over him as he thought of his baby. 'She's thriving.'

He looked to Harper and she smiled, encouraging him to continue.

'The doctors removed the respiratory support on Friday and now Anaya's breathing well on her own. Yesterday they transferred her from a heated incubator to a normal cot because she doesn't need help regulating her temperature anymore. And today, we're going to try to feed her with a bottle for the first time.'

Jasper willed away the emotion that welled in his eyes at this prospect.

'That's wonderful,' Helen said. 'How long do they expect Anaya to be in hospital?'

'Another month, perhaps a little longer.'

'I can imagine you have mixed feelings about that,' she said.

Jasper frowned. 'What do you mean?' He couldn't wait to move back home with Anaya, to stop living out of a suitcase and to have her with him twenty-four seven.

'Having a baby is undoubtedly one of life's biggest joys, but losing a spouse is at the opposite end of that spectrum. There must be an internal war going on inside your head, grief fighting happiness. And bringing your baby home without your wife is going to be tough.'

'Yes.' His fingers went to the wedding band on his left hand. He knew the interviewer wanted more than one-word answers but he couldn't find the words to explain how he felt.

Helen pulled a tissue from the box beside her and leant forward to offer it to him but he shook his head. He got the feeling she wanted him to shed a few tears—that would make good television—but he wouldn't cry because she wanted him to.

'Tell us about how you and Claire met,' she said after a few seconds silence.

And so he did. It was good to speak about Claire. Remembering things they did together made him feel alive again, and by the time she asked him about Claire's infertility, the answers came easily. He explained how she'd suffered ovarian failure due to treatment for childhood cancer, but that she'd desperately wanted to experience pregnancy and have a child of her own.

'And that's where Harper came in?' Helen asked. Before he could reply, she turned her gaze on Harper.

'Egg donation is a gift in Australia and therefore not as common as it is in some overseas countries. What made you—a married career woman with no children of your own—decide to donate your eggs?'

'Well, I …' Harper hesitated and Jasper's heart went out to her as he watched her search for an answer. Until that moment, he hadn't imagined that this would be as difficult for Harper as it was for him, if not more so. Her reasons for donating were personal, and she wouldn't want to air her dirty laundry on national TV.

Just when he thought she wasn't going to be able to answer, she did.

'My husband and I agreed when we first met that having a family wasn't a priority. Samuel has a large family of nieces and nephews, so we got our kid fix with them and we are both dedicated to our careers. We didn't think we'd have the time to give a child what it needs and didn't want to enter parenthood unless we were a hundred percent certain. But then one day I had some guests on my show who were having a baby with an egg donor and I thought perhaps it was something I could do to help a similar couple.'

'What did your husband, your family and friends think of your decision?'

'They were supportive,' Harper said. 'In the end, it was my body and they understood that.'

'And the plan was that Claire would have the baby, she and Jasper would raise it as their own, and that you wouldn't be involved?'

Harper nodded. 'That's right, to an extent. We agreed that I would keep in contact and would see them once or twice a year. We all wanted to be honest with the child—he or she would know I was the donor, and Claire their mother.'

'But now all that's changed, hasn't it?' Helen paused only momentarily, before continuing. 'Sadly, Claire isn't able to be a mum and you have decided to take on that role. What happened to not wanting children?'

Jasper noticed tiny beads of perspiration on Harper's forehead and he almost told Helen to stop the questions right there. Why did anybody else need to know any of this? But Harper simply said, 'Anaya happened. From the moment I saw her, I felt the connection and everything inside me changed.'

Helen snatched up another tissue and this time she was rewarded when a tear slipped down Harper's cheek. But Jasper knew her emotion wasn't for the cameras. It was real—her love for Anaya shone in her voice and in her face and he suddenly knew he'd made the right decision to allow her into their lives. She wasn't Claire and she wouldn't mother their baby in the same way Claire would have, but he believed she would give Anaya what she needed all the same.

Helen asked them about how they planned to navigate shared parenthood and Jasper did his best to take the heat off Harper. Finally she seemed to have exhausted her curiosity and the interview was over.

The cameraman began to pack up his equipment and the make-up girl said her goodbyes and then slipped out the front door.

Helen congratulated them on a job well done. 'I know this wasn't easy for either of you and I thank you for taking the time to talk to me. Before we go, do you have any photos of Anaya you could send us? We don't need many but the viewers would love to see her—she's the star of this story.'

Jasper and Harper exchanged a look—a couple of photos wouldn't hurt—and then both nodded. 'I've got some on my camera,' Harper said. 'Lilia, did you bring your laptop? If so I can send them through in a moment.'

Lilia had been so quiet that he'd almost forgotten she was there.

'Yes,' she said, 'but give me your camera and let me take care of that. I know you guys are desperate to get back to the hospital.'

'Oh thank you,' Harper said, and Jasper forced a smile in Lilia's direction.

'You're welcome. And—' she dragged some sandwiches in plastic containers out of her oversized handbag, '—I made you both some lunch. I figured you're probably sick of greasy takeaway food by now.'

'You are an angel.' Harper kissed her friend on the cheek as she accepted the offerings.

Lilia's cheeks flushed crimson. 'Don't be silly. Now, is there anything else either of you need me to do?'

'I don't think so.' Harper looked to Jasper and he shook his head.

'Thank you so much for lunch,' he said, his stomach rumbling even though two seconds earlier he'd been planning on bypassing food to head straight to the NICU.

'It's my pleasure. Now you two get going. I'll see Helen and Eddie out, send through the photos, then lock the door and pull it shut behind me.' Lilia looked at Harper. 'I'll see you back in Sydney tomorrow.' It came out more like a question than a statement and Harper took a few moments to reply.

'Yes. Bright and early.' But she didn't sound enthusiastic about this prospect at all. Jasper didn't blame her—it'd break him to go almost a week without seeing their baby—but Harper had chosen to keep working now so she could take extended leave when Anaya finally came home.

Since Harper had to drive back to Sydney later, they drove in separate cars to the hospital but parked nearby and went inside together.

'You did well in the interview today,' she said as they walked the corridors that he now knew better than the lines on the palm of his hand. 'It can't have been easy having to talk about Claire like that.'

'It wasn't as bad as I imagined,' he admitted. 'But I'm glad it's over. Not sure I want to watch it on TV either. You did well too.'

She snorted. 'No need to be kind, Jasper. I almost fell apart.'

He chuckled—something he couldn't remember doing since the morning Claire had walked out of his life. 'But you didn't. You pulled it together and I think we offered a united front.'

'Yes, I think we did.'

They proceeded in comfortable silence to the NICU, then washed and sanitised their hands before heading inside. This had become such second nature that Jasper had started washing his hands the moment he got back to the apartment as well, before he did anything else. He mentioned this to Harper and she laughed.

'Probably not a bad habit,' she said.

'I guess not,' he agreed as they came to a stop beside Anaya's crib.

They both gazed down at her.

'Is there anything more beautiful than a sleeping baby?' Harper asked.

'If there is, I can't think of it,' he said. 'When I look down at her, I immediately start to relax. They should bottle the feeling.'

Moments later, nurse Leslie came over to join them. 'How was the interview?' she asked.

Jasper shrugged. 'It went all right, I think.'

And Harper nodded her agreement. 'It's out of the way now anyway.'

'Excellent. And your little angel is doing well this morning, so are you ready to attempt to give her that first bottle?'

Again Harper nodded and Jasper replied, 'Are we ever?' He couldn't remember ever being as excited about anything in his life.

Feeding a baby—especially a premature one—turned out to be way more work than he'd imagined. Leslie took them to the 'bottle room' in the NICU and talked them through the process as she readied the milk.

'Is there some sort of manual we can read to remember all that?'

The nurse smiled at Jasper's question. 'I thought men didn't follow instructions.'

'This one does. Especially when it's something as important as this.'

'I'd like to read a manual like that too,' Harper said, looking as terrified as he felt.

'Don't worry,' Leslie said, and gestured for them to follow her back to Anaya. 'There'll always be someone to help you while you're in here with us, and we'll make sure you're experts before we send you home.'

Jasper hoped she was right but vowed, when he went home on the weekend, to pick up those baby books Claire had been devouring before she died. He'd teased her that she was studying them as if she were preparing for an exam, but now he wished he'd done the same.

Leslie put the bottle down on the shelf behind Anaya's crib and then looked back and forth between them. 'Who wants to go first?'

Of course *he* did. But he glanced up at Harper and remembered the way she'd spoken about Anaya during the interview. 'Do you want to?' he asked.

'What?' Harper blinked as if she'd heard him wrong. 'Are you sure?'

He was tempted to retract the offer, but reminded himself he had all week to take a turn whereas Harper had to be back at work tomorrow. 'Yes. You do it.'

'Thank you,' she whispered, her hand pressed against her heart.

'That's settled then. You sit down and I'll grab our star.' As Harper lowered herself into the chair, Leslie changed Anaya. 'We want her to be as comfortable as possible before trying to feed,' she explained.

Anaya woke during the process and whimpered a little, but stopped fussing the moment Leslie placed her in Harper's arms.

'Hey there, little lady,' Harper cooed, offering her pinkie finger for Anaya to grab onto.

'Can you pass the bottle?' Leslie asked Jasper.

He retrieved it and handed it to her.

Leslie crouched down on the floor beside Harper and Anaya. 'Now be aware, this might be a slow process. Her suckling reflexes are still developing and if she does manage to drink, she'll tire quickly so it won't be long, but we'll try again tomorrow.'

She lifted the bottle to Anaya's tiny mouth and gently teased her lips with the rubber teat. Harper stared down intently and Jasper did the same, waiting to see how she'd react.

Like the envelope of a hot air balloon slowly opening for the air, those tiny lips peeled back and Anaya's mouth closed around the teat. This time the whimper came from Harper and a smile grew on Leslie's face. Jasper began to breathe again.

'That's the way,' said the nurse softly. 'Good girl. She's a natural.'

Pride in his baby girl made him stand tall. After Claire, he hadn't thought he'd ever feel such love towards another person, but he was suddenly close to bursting with it.

Leslie gestured for Harper to take the bottle and then she stepped back and stood beside him. 'You want to take a photo? As I said, she probably won't last long this first time.'

'Of course. Good idea.' As Lilia still had Harper's camera, he took his out of his backpack and snapped a few shots.

Harper smiled for him and then looked down to Anaya. 'I think she's asleep,' she said.

He leant in to take a look. Sure enough, Anaya's little lids had closed again and her mouth hung loosely around the bottle. She looked adorable and had satisfaction scrawled across her face, but Jasper couldn't help the pang of jealousy. For a moment he wished he'd been the one to feed Anaya first, but then he told himself to stop being stupid.

It didn't matter who fed her. The important thing was that she was making progress.

Chapter Thirty-six

'Was that the spunky Jasper?' Lilia wiggled her eyebrows suggestively as Harper put her mobile down on her desk.

'Lilia! He's a new widower! And anyway, I thought you were happy with ...' The name of Lilia's new beau eluded her; there'd been so many before him she'd lost track. 'What's-his-name.'

'Jasper's wife might be dead—God rest her soul—but I'm not. The man is a thing of beauty and you know how much I like beautiful things.' She reached down to stroke her latest handbag, which sat on the floor by her feet.

'Yes, it was him.' Harper laughed despite herself, and it felt good because she hadn't done so for days. It was only Thursday—three days since she'd last seen Anaya—but it felt more like a year. 'He was just telling me that Anaya drank almost double today what she did yesterday and that they might try her on two feeds tomorrow.'

'Oh, that's wonderful news,' Lilia exclaimed.

'Yes, it is.' Harper sighed deeply.

'So, why the glum face then?'

'Because ...' She stared at the little photo of Anaya she'd printed out and stuck on the bottom corner of her computer screen. 'It's hard hearing about all these little achievements she's making and not being there to experience them. I feel like I'm missing out on so much. I feel like I should be with her instead of here.'

'And so the mother guilt begins.' Lilia laughed.

'And then I feel guilty because I *want* to be with her rather than here.'

Lilia's expression turned serious. 'I can't imagine what you're going through, but for what it's worth, I think you're right to take holidays when Anaya leaves hospital, rather than now. She's being properly looked after by the doctors and nurses but when she goes home, that's when Jasper will need all the help he can get.'

'I know.' And in theory, Harper did, but being away from Anaya was proving harder than she'd imagined. No matter what she was doing at work—researching, paperwork, interviewing—her daughter was always front and centre in her mind.

Lilia opened the bottom drawer of her desk and pulled out a large package wrapped in shiny silver paper and garnished with a fancy pink bow. 'I was going to save this till you were heading to Newcastle tomorrow afternoon, but I hope if I give it to you now, it'll cheer you up a little.'

Harper blinked as Lilia stood and dropped the present into her lap. 'What is this?'

Lilia smiled. 'Open it and you'll see. It's not much, but since you didn't have a baby shower but now have a baby, I wanted to get you a little something to mark the occasion. I hope you'll like it.'

Happy for the distraction, Harper yanked at the ribbon and tore off the paper with far less care than she usually took. She gasped as it fell away to reveal the most gorgeous bag she'd ever laid eyes on—from her favourite Aussie designer no less. It was a 'thing of beauty', to use Lilia's phrase, made with a combination of gorgeous velvet and embroidered fabrics in shades of red, black and purple. Harper knew it would have cost Lilia a good portion of her weekly wage and her eyes watered as she looked up at her friend. 'Thank you.'

Lilia shrugged. 'It's a nappy bag in case you were wondering. Even though you've joined the mummy ranks, I couldn't have you going around with one of those ugly ones I see so many people carrying.'

Harper laughed, placed the designer nappy bag on her desk and then stood and wrapped her arms around her friend. Neither of them said anything—they didn't need to—and when Lilia finally pulled back and said it was almost time to greet today's guest, Harper found she did feel better. There were just over twenty-four hours until she could get in her car and drive north again, and tonight—in the name of keeping busy—she'd scheduled dinner with Juliet and Renee.

For the first time, the prospect of baby talk didn't make her want to stick her fingers down her throat. In fact, she was very much looking forward to it.

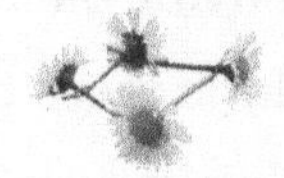

Harper met her two oldest friends at a restaurant in Darlinghurst. They squealed like schoolgirls when they saw her and then wrapped their arms around her as they offered their congratulations.

It still felt awkward when people used this word in relation to her situation. The staff at the station had all signed a big card for her with the word printed in massive pink letters across the front, and Samuel's partners' wives had sent her a big bouquet of cloth nappies designed to look like flowers. And while she appreciated the enthusiasm of her friends and colleagues, guilt hovered over her like a dark rain cloud whenever she dwelt on the fact that she only had this because Claire didn't.

'We saw you on TV the other morning,' Juliet said as they bustled into the restaurant.

'You looked stunning,' added Renee. She opened her mouth to say something more, but an attendant with a name badge that read Keisha greeted them at the entrance and asked if they had a booking.

Harper nodded. 'Under Harper Drummond.'

'Fabulous, come this way.' The attendant picked up three leather menus and led them to a table in the far corner. 'Can I bring you some drinks to start?'

Juliet clapped her hands together. 'We're celebrating. I think this calls for champagne. Bring us a bottle of your finest. This one's on me.'

'Ooh, good idea,' Renee said. 'I'll buy the next. Sam's just stopped breastfeeding so I'm a free agent tonight and I plan to enjoy myself.'

'Right then. The best bubbly we have, coming right up.' Their waitress laughed as she retreated.

Harper opened her menu and glanced down to scan the options—the last two weeks she'd been living on muesli bars and takeaway, so the prospect of something a little more upmarket had her tastebuds watering—but her friends didn't appear in the slightest bit interested in the food.

'So, welcome to motherhood,' Juliet said, grinning. 'Isn't it wonderful?'

Harper sighed and decided to be frank with her friends. She put down the menu. 'To be honest, it's all a bit surreal at the moment—and while I adore Anaya and am so damn thankful she's in my life, it's bittersweet because of Claire.'

Her friends' faces fell. They looked suitably chastised. She hadn't meant them to feel bad but it wouldn't feel right to sit here celebrating her entrance into a club that only a few weeks ago she didn't want to be a part of. 'And it's hard being so far away from the hospital. I can barely concentrate on work.'

'I'm so sorry,' Renee reached across the table and squeezed Harper's hand. 'We're excited but we're being insensitive. How is poor Jasper holding up? When he spoke about his wife on the TV, I couldn't stop bawling. Matthew even had tears in his eyes and the only other time I've ever seen him cry was when the Sydney Swans lost the grand final. Jasper seems like a really good guy.'

Harper nodded. 'That is a perfect way to describe him. I don't think I've ever met someone so in love with their spouse. If it wasn't for Anaya, I don't think he'd be coping at all. She gives him a reason to get up in the morning.'

Renee sniffed and Harper felt a little bad for lowering the mood of the night. 'Anyway,' she said, 'how are Sam and Kiara?'

Her friends blinked in surprise and Harper realised she'd never actually asked them this question before. Shame washed over her. She thought they'd been baby-obsessed since becoming mothers but now she saw things for how they really were. Without being aware of it she'd been living in self-preservation mode, steering clear of all things baby in case—*heaven forbid*—she might start craving things she didn't want to crave.

'Sam's doing really well,' Renee replied after a few moments of shocked silence. 'I think I was more upset about him stopping breastfeeding than he was. He's just started climbing—as if walking wasn't bad enough—so we're having to baby-proof all the high cupboards and doors as well.'

Harper smiled. 'How old is he now?'

'Almost sixteen months,' Renee said.

'I didn't even know you knew their names,' Juliet exclaimed.

'Juliet!' Renee tossed her a warning look.

'What?' Juliet shrugged. 'It's true. She's never shown the slightest bit of interest in our kids.'

Renee glanced down at the table.

'It's okay,' Harper said. 'Juliet's right.' *They* hadn't been bad friends; she had. And she owed them an explanation. 'I'm sorry for not showing the interest I should have in your children. I'm not making excuses. I realise now how wrong it was and although it's no excuse, I do have a reason.'

Juliet leant back in her seat and made a face that said *this will be good*. 'We're all ears.'

Talking about her childhood and the abortion should have been getting easier, but it wasn't. Her stomach churned. Thankfully, just as she opened her mouth to begin, Keisha returned with three glasses and a bottle of Veuve Clicquot. The woman had barely poured her glass before Harper grabbed it and gulped down a mouthful.

'Are you ready to place your orders?'

Renee smiled back apologetically. 'Can you give us a few more moments, please?'

'Sure thing.'

As Keisha retreated and Juliet and Renee each took a sip, Harper began. They had all met in high school so they were already familiar with her less than perfect example of motherhood, but both were shocked when she admitted how much this experience had shaped her. Both women took Harper's hand when she told them about her abortion.

'Oh Harper, I wish you'd told us earlier,' Renee said.

'Me too.' Juliet nodded, her earlier anger banished. 'We could have been there for you.'

Harper nodded and swallowed the lump that rose in her throat. 'I wish I had now, but there's no changing the past. I'm just sorry it meant that I wasn't excited for you two when you got pregnant like a good friend should be.'

'Forget that now.' Renee waved a hand in front of her face. 'We're certainly not always the perfect friends either, but the fact we're still here putting up with each other after all these years shows there's something between us.'

Juliet lifted her glass. 'I'll toast to that.'

'Me too,' Harper said. Toasting friendship and letting go of past demons was something she could definitely do.

Keisha returned to the table as they lowered their glasses. 'Ready yet, ladies?'

They smiled sheepishly at each other.

'What's *your* favourite dish on the menu?' Juliet asked their waitress.

'The char-grilled beef sirloin with parsnip mash and honey-roasted heirloom carrots. Chef does beef better than I've ever tasted anywhere. Even better than my mum.' Keisha leant in close and put a finger to her lips. 'But don't tell her I said that.'

They all laughed.

'That sounds fabulous,' Harper exclaimed, snapping shut her menu. 'You sold me.'

'Me too,' Julie said.

'I'm not supposed to eat roasted food on my diet, but ...' Renee threw her hands up in the air and grinned. 'To hell with it. I'll have what they're having.'

Keisha chuckled. 'That was easy then. Thanks ladies.' She collected their menus and went off to deliver their order to the kitchen.

'About your job,' Juliet began, a pensive expression on her face. 'Can't you just take maternity leave? Surely your contract entitles you to parental leave.'

She nodded. 'Yes, it does but it's not as straightforward as that. Legally Anaya is Claire and Jasper's baby—and he still wants her name on the birth certificate—so we have to work out some sort of guardianship agreement. Until that is in place, I don't have any rights to maternity leave. I've asked Samuel to talk to someone at his firm about the situation for me but he's pretty busy at the moment as well.'

Juliet rolled her eyes. 'Since when is Samuel *not* busy?'

Harper ignored her. 'I've got plenty of holiday leave, so I am going to take a couple of extra days off here and there while Anaya is still in hospital, and when she goes home in a couple of months I'm taking six weeks. If I can get maternity leave, I'll look at taking it on top of that.'

'It sounds exhausting, but if anyone can do it, you can,' Juliet said. 'Me? If I were in your shoes I'd probably just quit my job and embrace full-time motherhood.'

Harper knew her friend didn't mean any offence by this statement—even at school Juliet's life ambition had been to have babies and keep house—but as much as she adored Anaya, she couldn't imagine being one of those stay-at-home types. She wanted Anaya to grow up to understand that women could be as successful as men in the workforce and that doing a job you truly loved brought immense joy and satisfaction.

'How's Samuel handling this whole situation?' Renee asked, giving Juliet another look as she changed the direction of the conversation.

Harper fiddled with the necklace at her throat. 'He's being very understanding and supportive.'

'When will he be able to meet Anaya?'

'Not for a while. It's only parents and grandparents in the actual neonatal ward.'

'That's a pity,' her friends said at the same time.

'There'll be plenty of time for them to get to know each other later. Anyway,' Harper said, smiling at Juliet, 'you haven't told me how Kiara's doing.'

This time Juliet smiled and happily filled them in on the many milestones her almost two year old had recently achieved and Harper listened carefully, making mental notes of what she and Jasper had to look forward to with Anaya.

Keisha delivered their meals and conversation continued as they ate. She hadn't over-exaggerated the chef's talents—the beef was impossibly tender and Harper had never known parsnips could taste so good. Although they were already full to bursting, they couldn't resist the citrus curd, French meringue and nut crumble that Keisha recommended.

Finally, at almost eleven o'clock, Harper looked up and realised they were the only people left in the restaurant. After the initial moments of discord, the evening had flown by and as they stood to leave, she thanked Juliet and Renee for being so supportive and understanding, and also for helping her get through what would otherwise have been a long night on her own.

'Have a safe trip to Newcastle tomorrow,' Renee said as she hugged Harper goodbye.

'Yes.' Juliet nodded as she did the same. 'And be sure to send us more photos of your gorgeous girl. I'm getting clucky again but I've got to convince Jared that it's time for another. He's a sucker for newborns so your photos might just do the trick.'

Harper laughed and promised she would.

Chapter Thirty-seven

Jasper startled awake when his alarm clock rang at three o'clock on Saturday morning. His body clock, which used to wake him at this time of its own accord, had changed over the last few weeks. Now he took hours going to sleep and usually woke without an alarm at about 7.30 am, then got ready and headed into the hospital. But today, for the first time in almost three weeks, he wasn't going to see Anaya.

Today he was at home—although it no longer felt like home—and he was going up in the air instead. He forced himself up off the couch, dragging his hands over his face and fighting the urge to snuggle back under the throw rug. When he'd arrived late last night, he hadn't been able to face the prospect of sleeping in the marital bed without Claire, so he'd opted for the couch with Gerry and Sunny at his feet instead. The cats barely moved when he got up, and a lonely silence echoed through the house.

As he'd driven away from the hospital yesterday, his emotions had once again been at war inside him. Part of him thrummed with excitement at the prospect of flying again, but he also struggled with the guilt of leaving Anaya and the knowledge that he'd be working without Claire. They'd been a team for almost five years and he wasn't sure he knew how to work with anyone else anymore. This morning, as he padded down the hallway to the bathroom and threw himself into the shower, that guilt and grief felt stronger than ever.

By the time he'd dragged on his clothes and headed outside to his car, the only thing stopping him driving straight back to Newcastle was the knowledge that he'd be letting his parents down if he did so—they had two big groups booked in this morning.

His headlights lighting the road ahead, Jasper drove the familiar route to the balloon shed, marvelling at how unfamiliar everything felt. He parked his vehicle next to his father's and then headed into the shed. The last time he'd been here they'd been getting the equipment ready for the Civil Aviation Safety Authority's annual check and he realised he'd never even asked his dad how they'd fared. Had the check even gone ahead? He shook that thought from his head, not wanting to dwell on anything about that day. He had tortured himself enough in the weeks since.

'Hello, son,' said his dad with a wave as Jasper entered the building. He was in the tiny kitchen off to one side of the shed filling two reusable coffee cups with the Big Basket Ballooning logo on the side.

'Hey, Dad.' Jasper headed over to him, his nose twitching as he caught the aroma of bacon and eggs. Sure enough, on the bench beside his father were two packages wrapped in greaseproof paper.

Paul chuckled as he followed Jasper's gaze. 'Your mum told me I was to watch you eat that. She's scared you're wasting away.'

Jasper picked one up and started peeling back the paper. He took a bite and moaned as the flavours exploded on his tongue. 'She worries too much,' he said between bites. 'I'm okay, honestly. Sad, obviously, but I'm eating. It might not be great food, but nutrition is the least of my worries right now.'

Paul held up his hands as if he were the victim in an armed robbery. 'Hey, no need to explain to me. I'm just following orders. And you're allowed to be sad. Are you sure you're up to all this today?'

Jasper swallowed. He wasn't sure at all but he couldn't put it off forever. He wanted to fly, but the thought of facing a bunch of excitable strangers filled him with dread. 'I'll be fine.'

Whether or not his father believed him, he nodded. 'Let's get this show on the road then,' he said as he picked up his coffee and breakfast.

They climbed into the four-wheel drive and drove in silence to the site they'd chosen for today's launch. Jasper was grateful his dad didn't try to make him talk. Even when they stopped the vehicle in a paddock and began their testing, he only spoke about what they were doing and Jasper threw himself into the work, happy for the distraction. If he focused on ballooning today and tried not to dwell on the fact that Claire wasn't with him, maybe he could get through this.

By the time they returned to the shed, Wendy and one of their other employees, Luke, had arrived, and a few eager passengers were starting to emerge from cars. Jasper took a deep breath, trying to ignore the butterflies dancing in his stomach. He'd done this more times than he could count, but for some reason he was nervous. As he looked at the animated smiles on the faces of the people that were arriving, he fought the urge to get back into his car and escape. How was he supposed to be all jovial with these strangers when he was still coming to terms with a life without his wife? What if they'd seen his story on the TV, recognised him and wanted to talk, ask questions?

Paul paused as he headed for the shed and looked back to Jasper, a frown on his face. 'You coming, son?'

'Yes.' He couldn't let these people down and he couldn't let his parents and the business down either. This business was Anaya's nest egg. If anyone said a word about Claire or their baby, he'd politely tell them he preferred not to talk about it.

Thankfully, it soon became apparent that most of today's passengers were tourists from Japan, and none of them appeared to have heard about Jasper and his miracle baby. Either that or they didn't care, which was fine by him.

Despite this, the group were one of the most excited he could remember having for some time. Even before his dad had finished the safety spiel—during which he was interrupted a number of times with questions—their enthusiasm was beginning to grate on Jasper's nerves. When they were split into two groups and he was introduced as one of the pilots, every person in his group wanted to take a selfie with him.

Again he almost walked out, but the tired lines around his dad's eyes kept him from doing so. Instead he summoned a smile he didn't feel and acquiesced to the photos, telling himself that the only way to get through the next few hours was by pretending. He'd imagine he was an actor in a film—a happy actor who wanted to win an Academy Award for his performance—and try not to let the fact that he'd never excelled at drama classes at school bother him.

This decision helped him make small talk as they piled the passengers into the bus to take them to the launch site.

As he lifted his foot to climb in with them, his mum came up beside him. 'Do you want to drive my chaser car today?' The usual routine was for his dad to drive the bus while the two crew members each took a vehicle with a basket trailer and Jasper sat among the passengers answering questions. But today he couldn't have been more grateful to his mum for offering to swap places.

'Thanks,' he said as he kissed her on the cheek and took her keys.

While his parents finished getting everyone onto the bus, he drove ahead on his own, Luke following closely behind with the other trailer. His mind kept drifting—to Claire, to Anaya, to Harper—but he repeated the word 'actor' over and over like a mantra as he tried to slip into his old self.

Once he'd parked in the middle of the paddock they'd chosen to be today's launch site, there was plenty to keep him busy. He and Luke unloaded the baskets, envelopes and other equipment from the trailers and prepared them so that by the time his parents arrived with the passengers they were ready to start filling the balloons. Everyone split into their two groups and as usual they encouraged the passengers to participate in the set-up process. Lots of photos were taken of the balloons coming to life—photos of the action, shots of the sun rising behind them and more selfies than a busload of teenagers could ever take.

One by one the passengers were instructed to climb into the basket and take their assigned places. One woman had a minor panic attack but Jasper spoke softly to her, reassuring her she was in good hands.

'I have an incident free record,' he said, 'and I don't intend to break it this morning. Come on, I promise this will be the best fun you've ever had.'

She let out a long sigh and then nodded. 'Okay. I'll do it.'

From there the flight went smoothly. Jasper couldn't have asked for a better group—they followed the safety instructions to a tee and asked really sensible questions. They oohed and aahed over the scenery and took numerous photos of the vineyards and rolling hills below them. After a while he found he wasn't acting anymore, but genuinely enjoying their company.

The time flew quickly as it always did up in the air and his guests expressed bitter disappointment when he told them it was time to head back down. As the basket returned to earth, bumping three times along the ground before planting itself, Jasper glanced across the faces of his passengers and grinned. The tourists climbed out, their voices buzzing with excitement as they relived the experience to each other. As they helped deflate the envelope and roll it back up to fit inside its plastic casing, some of them were already planning another flight.

And Jasper couldn't blame them. He could hardly wait until tomorrow morning when he was scheduled to take another group up into the air. Until today, he hadn't realised just how much he'd missed flying these last few weeks.

As always, Jasper, Luke and his parents took their clients to a local café for breakfast, and despite the bacon and egg roll he'd scoffed earlier, Jasper ate heartily. Maybe it was the fresh country air or perhaps the company and conversation, but the appetite that had been all but missing lately seemed to have returned.

'It was good to have you back,' Paul said, patting him on the back as they waved goodbye to the last of their guests. 'I hope you enjoyed yourself a little.'

'I did. I really did,' he said, still smiling.

Standing beside them, Wendy also smiled. 'That's wonderful, sweetheart. Have you got any plans for the rest of the day?' She didn't give him time to answer. 'I was thinking we should look at setting up your spare room.'

He stared at her blankly, no idea what she was on about. 'The spare room? What for?'

'For Harper of course. Isn't she coming up here for a while once the baby is out of hospital? We can't expect her to stay in a hotel for such an extended period—and she'll want to spend as much time as she can with Anaya—so I assumed she'd stay with you. And I thought we should at least put a double bed in the spare room so when her husband comes up to visit, they'll be comfortable. You can borrow one from our place.'

His good mood deflated faster than a rubber balloon with a hole in it. While he was up in the air, he'd almost forgotten. He'd been able to enjoy the stupid fantasy that things were how they'd always been and to pretend that the only reason Claire wasn't on the ground chasing for him was because she was with their baby. Although his mum meant well and was only trying to help, her mention of Harper brought reality crashing down.

The glee he'd experienced while flying whooshed out of him and he felt like an empty shell again, someone who was going through the motions out of necessity, not desire.

'Actually, I might head back to the hospital for a few hours,' he said, already digging in his pocket for his car keys.

Paul frowned. 'I thought you weren't heading back till tomorrow. Isn't Harper there with Anaya now?'

'Yes. But *I* want to be there as well.'

Or more to the point, he didn't want to go back to his house where the silence and absence of laughter would only remind him of what he'd lost.

Chapter Thirty-eight

Seven weeks after Claire's death, Jasper took Anaya home from the hospital. As much as it pained Harper not to be there on this monumental day, she chose to stay away. Welcoming the baby into his house without Claire would be hard enough, so she decided to give him a day to settle in before she arrived for her six week stay.

But she'd packed her car, said goodbye to Lilia and the team at work, met Samuel near his office for dinner and then gone to bed early before driving up to the Hunter Valley first thing the next morning.

'It's not even eight,' Jasper said when he opened the door to her. 'You must have been up at the crack of dawn.'

'I couldn't sleep,' she confessed. 'Too excited. So how was your first night?'

In reply, he yawned. 'Let's just say I don't think she's a huge fan of her bassinet, and she may be nocturnal. She's lucky she's so damn cute because I didn't manage to settle her until four o'clock, when we both collapsed on the couch. Then she was up again at six demanding a bottle.'

Harper swallowed the impulse to say something about co-sleeping not being safe, especially with a premature baby. But really, what did she know? Although she'd spent the last few weeks devouring every parenting handbook she could get her hands on, she still didn't have any more personal experience than Jasper did. And she didn't want to start off their already unorthodox arrangement by undermining him. 'Where is the little cherub now?'

'On the couch again. Go on in if you want and I'll make us both a cup of coffee.' He tried to stifle another yawn. 'Lord knows I need one.'

As Jasper headed into the kitchen, Harper dropped her handbag to the floor by the door and turned off the hallway into the living room. Although everything looked much the same as it had when she and Samuel visited all those months ago, she felt Claire's absence strongly and could only imagine how hard being here must be for Jasper. She didn't linger long on this thought because her gaze went to the couch where Anaya was sleeping peacefully in some kind of floral cushion fort.

Jasper had left plenty of space around her and Harper had to admit that—wrapped up tightly like an insect in a cocoon—she looked pretty damn safe. Although she didn't mean to wake her it had been two days since she'd seen her and she couldn't help reaching out and scooping her up. Anaya's eyes blinked open and she made a little murmur as she looked up into Harper's face. She quieted again as soon as Harper sat on the couch and settled her on her chest.

Jasper returned with the coffees a few moments later, but she didn't drink hers until it was cold because she wouldn't risk a hot drink near Anaya and she didn't want to put her down. It felt different snuggling with her here than in the hospital, where there'd always been a nurse not far away if things went wrong. But Harper didn't feel nervous. On the contrary she was excited, as if she were just setting off on the biggest adventure of her life.

'Every time she cries,' Jasper said from his position on the armchair, 'I expect a nurse to turn up to tell me what to do. Then when they don't, I'm terrified I'll stuff up and do something wrong. But I feel quite chuffed when I manage to change and feed her all by myself. Haven't quite got the sleep thing down yet, but it's early days.'

Harper laughed. 'I was just thinking something similar about the nurses. Well done for surviving the first night. Do you want to have a nap or something now I'm here?'

Before he could reply, the front door opened. 'Yoo-hoo,' came Wendy's cheerful voice. Harper had seen Jasper's mum a few more times on her weekend stays in Newcastle and had grown to adore her. Wendy didn't always have a filter when she spoke, but she meant well—and her warm smile was contagious.

'Hi Mum,' Jasper said, barely lifting his head off the chair as she entered the room.

'I'm sorry,' Wendy gushed, rushing over to the couch, 'I know I said I wouldn't come over too early but I'm just so excited to have you home. And I couldn't wait to see the little love.'

'You mean you wanted to check up on me,' Jasper said, his tone good-natured. Harper knew that Wendy had offered to stay with Jasper the first couple of weeks but that he'd politely declined.

'If I let her move in, she'll never leave,' he'd confided one day in the hospital. 'I may as well get used to doing it on my own from the beginning.'

She hated it when he said stuff like this because it reminded her that in the long term he *would* be doing it alone—at least during the weeks—and she wished she could do more. She was also going to miss a lot of important milestones because of her work and home life in Sydney.

'Can I hold her?' Wendy asked, plonking herself down alongside Harper and stretching out her hands.

'Mum, Harper only just got here,' Jasper said. 'Besides, Anaya looks comfy there.'

She met his eye and gave him a grateful smile. Like a little girl not wanting to share her doll, she was reluctant to give her up so soon.

'Sorry.' Wendy looked a little sheepish. 'I just couldn't help myself. But I guess there'll be plenty of time for cuddles now that our girl is home. How about I make you breakfast? You'll both need all your strength to look after this little one.'

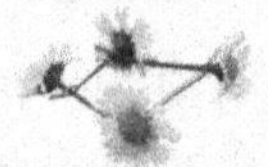

Harper had booked a hotel in town for the duration of her stay, but in the end she only spent two nights there. Both nights she was at Jasper's house until late and then returned early the following morning. He was the one to suggest the spare room was hers if she wanted it and she eagerly accepted his generous offer.

The only person less than enthusiastic about this situation was Samuel.

'What the hell, Harper?' he said when she phoned to update him.

'It just makes sense for me to be on site,' she explained. 'Practically and financially—there's no point paying for a hotel room I'm only using for a couple of hours a day.'

But Samuel didn't care about the money. 'How am I supposed to feel about you living with another man? What will people think?'

'I'm not *living* with another man—and surely I don't need to remind you that he's just buried his wife! I'm only staying with him so I can spend time with my daughter. And you know you're welcome to come up whenever you want. Jasper's happy for you to stay here too and I'd love for you to spend some time getting to know Anaya.'

'All right.' Although he relented, he sounded like a child who hadn't got his own way.

'In fact, why don't you come up this weekend?' Harper asked. 'We could take Anaya out for a bushwalk in the national park—and Jasper's mum is cooking a roast for lunch on Sunday.'

'I'll see what I can do,' he promised, but, almost four weeks later, he'd only managed to make the journey once and hadn't stayed the night, citing his usual excuse of too much work.

Although Harper would have liked to see him more, that one visit hadn't gone as well as she'd hoped. But she was usually so busy with Anaya that she didn't have time to miss him. At first she couldn't believe the amount of time, work and energy a baby needed—Wendy had been spot on—but she loved every minute of it.

Jasper returned to work four mornings a week, helping his folks whenever they had big group bookings. Anaya still tired quickly, and tended to drink small amounts at regular intervals. They usually bathed her in the early evenings, then Jasper would give her a feed before heading to bed so he could get up early. The days he had to get up for work, Harper was on night duty, and when he wasn't, he took that time slot, so that at least one of them got a good night's sleep.

At least that was the theory, but it didn't always work out that way. Harper found she couldn't lie in bed in the middle of the night if she could hear Anaya crying at the other end of the house and Jasper always got up if Harper was taking a while to settle her. It was then, during the early hours of the morning, that friendship began to blossom between them.

During the day, their conversations were mostly functional—revolving around Anaya's feeding, bathing and changing—but at night she saw glimpses of the real Jasper. A man raw with hurt from the loss of his wife, a man struggling to accept his new way of life. She encouraged him to talk about Claire by asking questions about their time together. Some things she already knew but she still enjoyed listening to him talk about the night he and Claire met, about their ballooning adventures and travels, about all the tiny things she did that both infuriated and attracted him. And she hoped it helped him in some way also. Anaya certainly seemed to like it and Harper soon realised that the baby settled most quickly when listening to her father talk about Claire. She guessed it was the soothing tones of his voice rather than his actual words, but thought it poignant that in some mysterious way Claire was still there with them, the three of them working together to do the best for their child.

On the mornings when Jasper was out of the house, Harper got up early to feed Anaya and then took her into bed where they'd usually doze another couple of hours before the next feed. At this point, Harper would get up, feed Anaya and then shower with her in the pram close by. In the city, walking had been something she did to get from point A to point B, but as her morning swims weren't possible here, she took to taking Anaya out instead.

If they were lucky, they got out early enough to see the hot air balloons floating in the sky above them. The beauty of this sight always took her breath away.

'Your daddy's up there,' she'd say to Anaya as the baby gazed skyward from her pram. And Harper would smile at the knowledge that Jasper was doing what he loved. Only when he was interacting with Anaya, sitting out in the garden or when he'd just returned from a balloon ride, did she see a glimpse of the smile he'd been wearing the day she'd first met him and Claire.

Harper got to know the best café close by and she'd walk there to get a proper coffee every morning. Within a matter of days, the owners knew her by name and had her order ready seconds after she stepped through the door. It didn't take long to discover their cakes were as good as their coffee, so it was lucky she was doing all this walking or she'd be the size of a house by the time she had to return to work.

But she didn't like thinking of that day.

Although she missed Lilia's company, and still tuned in every afternoon to listen to her replacement, she didn't actually miss her work as much as she'd thought she would. It was true that looking after a newborn was a full-time job. She kept busy doing things that would previously have bored her senseless—washing nappies (Claire had bought cloth ones) and little clothes, rinsing bottles and making milk, cleaning—but doing them for Anaya made the mundane fulfilling.

She even attempted to cook a few times, but it soon became apparent that it was better to leave that task to Jasper or Wendy. Jasper politely suffered through a few meals, but he wasn't a great actor and she could see he didn't enjoy eating them any more than she'd enjoyed cooking them. At least three times a week, Wendy and Paul stopped by with an esky full of home-cooked meals and baked goodies. And on the weekends, when Claire's parents came up to visit and spend time with Anaya, Wendy went all out cooking a roast with all the trimmings. Harper loved her time alone with Anaya, but she also enjoyed the time spent with Jasper and his family much more than she'd expected. They were such a warm, loving family—the kind of family she'd longed for as a child—and she was glad Anaya was going to grow up to be a part of that.

Everything was all going swimmingly—or so she'd thought—until one day, just as she and Anaya were about to step out for their morning walk, she saw Jasper pull up at the house hours early.

Chapter Thirty-nine

The radio came on, the news jingle sounding, the moment Jasper turned the key in the ignition.

'In news just in,' began the announcer, 'at least eleven people on board a hot air balloon have died when it caught fire and crashed on a ranch in Nebraska. This is one of the deadliest balloon accidents to occur in United States history.'

The news reader moved on to other things quickly, but neither Jasper nor his dad heard anything else. In the middle of the paddock, the four-wheel drive idling in the dark, they looked at each other in shock. Although accidents such as these happened occasionally, Jasper could only recall a handful in the last decade.

'Do you know anyone in Nebraska?' he asked, mentally going through his contacts in his head, making sure none of his friends were working in that state.

Paul shook his head but the sombre expression didn't leave his face. 'I don't think so.' He let out a heavy sigh. 'This will make things interesting this morning.'

Jasper didn't have to ask what his dad meant. Taking a deep breath, he gripped the steering wheel tightly as he drove back to the Big Basket Ballooning premises. Sure enough, when they arrived, his mum and Luke were there to meet them in the car park.

'Have you heard the news?' Wendy asked, her voice high-pitched and her hand pressed against her chest.

'Yep.' Jasper and Paul nodded.

Wendy sniffed. 'It's just awful. Two of this morning's passengers have already phoned in to cancel,' she said as car headlights started down the gravel road towards them.

This wasn't surprising. Not everyone who had booked in for today would have heard the news yet, but once they did, the majority of them would likely have second thoughts.

Paul ran a hand over his beard. 'Let's see who arrives and then decide what we're going to do. I'd feel happier postponing today's flights in a show of respect to those who have lost their lives—it's what we did last time something like this happened.'

'But that time,' Wendy pointed out, 'we found out the night before so we could contact everyone involved.'

Paul sighed. 'Yes, that's true. We don't want to disappoint anyone who has travelled a long way to be here.'

Wendy and Luke agreed, and although Jasper nodded, his stomach twisted into a knot at the thought of flying today. There'd been few serious balloon incidents in Australia and nothing of this magnitude since 1989 when two balloons had collided in the air over Alice Springs, but perhaps it was only a matter of time. He and his dad prided themselves on their safety record but he'd bet the pilot of the Nebraskan balloon did too. Sometimes freak accidents happened.

He'd learnt that lesson the hard way all too recently.

And what would happen to Anaya if he—like Claire—died in such an incident? He wasn't foolish enough to think he could coat himself in bubble wrap and prevent anything ever happening to him, but was going up in a balloon four or five times a week tempting fate? When Claire was alive, they'd made an agreement that only one of them would ever fly at the same time, so if something tragic did happen, their baby wouldn't be left an orphan.

But now Claire was gone and he hadn't given a second's thought to that agreement, or to flying these last few weeks.

He followed his parents and Luke into the shed as their passengers started to arrive. Usually he could feel the nervous excitement of the passengers pre-flight, but there was a different kind of buzz among the group gathering this morning. The ones who hadn't heard the news already were quickly informed by those who had, and feelings were divided.

Some people still wanted to go up. 'What are the chances of another accident happening so close to this one? Statistics would tell us we're probably safer ballooning today than on any other day.'

Others weren't so certain. 'I thought ballooning *was* safe?'

And while his father tried to reassure the passengers that yes, ballooning was one of the safest forms of travel in the world but very rarely accidents did occur, Jasper stood by without saying a word. A cold sweat spread across his skin at the thought of climbing into the basket. Fear had never been part of his vocabulary, but suddenly it lodged itself in his throat, making him unsure if he could go up in the air even if that's what they decided.

'Will we get our money back if we don't want to fly today?' a lady with orange frizzy hair wanted to know.

'Of course,' Wendy rushed to placate her. 'We'll either give you a full refund or you can choose to reschedule for another time.'

'No, I want my money back,' demanded the woman. 'No way I'm going up in a hot air balloon after this.' She gestured to the chubby man standing beside her. 'It was all Eric's stupid idea anyway.'

'If you'll come with me to the office now, I can arrange the refund,' Wendy said, indicating the lady should follow her.

Others who'd also been turned off hot air ballooning for life hurried after her, leaving about ten people standing around looking uncertain. After more discussions among themselves and with Paul, the remaining group agreed that it didn't feel right to fly today anyway. It was decided they'd go home and phone in a few days to either re-book or request a refund, depending on how they were feeling by then.

Although ballooning accidents *anywhere* were bad for business, Jasper breathed a sigh of relief as the shed emptied of people. Without a word to either of his parents, he snuck out the door and hurried to his car. The thought of all those people dying brought the memories of that awful day only nine weeks ago rushing back. A fresh wave of grief washed over him as he imagined American cops approaching the families of the deceased to give them the bad news. Then he thought of Anaya being on the receiving end of such a message and he decided he would do everything in his power not to let that ever happen.

Less than ten minutes later, he parked haphazardly on his driveway and rushed inside, desperate to see her, to hold her close. He opened the front door to find Harper putting Anaya into her pram.

'Hi,' she said looking up. Her smile quickly transformed into a frown. 'What are you doing home so early? Is everything okay?'

'You haven't heard the news?'

She shook her head. 'I haven't had the TV on this morning and Anaya and I have been too busy to check my phone, haven't we, sweet pea? Why? What's happened?'

'There was a hot air balloon accident in Nebraska. At least eleven people are dead.'

'Oh, God.' Her hand rushed to cover her mouth. 'That's awful. I'm so sorry. Did you know anyone involved?'

'No. We don't think so.' He crossed to the pram, unclicked the strap Harper had just done up and lifted Anaya to his chest. He cradled her close, breathing in her fresh baby scent, never wanting to let her go again.

'Oh, well I guess that's something,' Harper said. 'But still, what a tragic accident.'

He looked her in the eye. 'I've decided I'm giving up ballooning.'

'What?' She screwed up her face. 'No, you can't! Is that why you're home early?'

'We decided to postpone today's flight out of respect for those who'd lost their lives. As you might guess, the passengers who were supposed to go up today were a little uncertain after they heard the news. And it made me realise I've been an irresponsible parent to put myself in such danger every day.'

'But you and Claire ... You told me that hot air ballooning was one of the safest ways to travel. Sure, accidents happen—but they can happen anywhere, anytime. Hot air ballooning is what you love. It's your life.' She shook her head. 'You can't give it up. What will you do if you don't fly?'

He shrugged. 'No idea, but I'll work something out. Anaya's my life now and she's more important than anything else. I need to do what's best for her and she can't afford to lose another parent. Who would look after her if I died too?'

Harper's head snapped back as if he'd slapped her. '*Me* of course. *I'm her mother.*'

Jasper flinched at her words. No matter how good and present she'd been with Anaya these last few weeks, he would never get used to the fact he had a baby with a woman other than Claire.

'You're having fun now, but this isn't your real life. If Claire hadn't died, you wouldn't even be here.' He saw the hurt in her eyes as he spoke, but he couldn't hold his tongue. 'What happens when the shine of new baby wears off and you remember that you don't even *want* children? And I know how much you miss your work—you listen to the show every afternoon. Don't tell me you'd be prepared to give all that up?'

Harper narrowed her eyes and spoke in a tone he'd never heard from her before. 'I'm not playing a game, Jasper, so don't presume you know what I think or feel. Whatever *you* think, I love Anaya just as much as you do and I want everything for her as well. There are plenty of career mums out there who manage to hold down a job and a family. But if I ever had to choose between work and Anaya, she'd always come first. So far I haven't pushed you to make our parental agreement formal because I know you've got enough on your plate right now. But maybe it's time we spoke to lawyers because I promise, if the unthinkable happens and you can no longer be there for Anaya, I *will* be. End of story.'

'Really?' he scoffed. She sounded genuine and maybe she truly believed this to be the case, but she was forgetting one key player in their situation. 'Does that go for Samuel as well? Would he move heaven and earth for Anaya if the need arose? Because quite frankly, I don't think he even likes her.'

Harper blinked then opened her mouth, but before she could say a word, he continued.

'I think you're fooling yourself that Samuel's okay with this situation. If he really cared about Anaya—*hell*, if he really cared about *you*—don't you think he'd make more of an effort? He's visited only once in almost a month and didn't even hold her while he was here. He barely even looked at her.'

When Anaya started to cry, he realised how loudly he'd been speaking. Silently cursing himself for scaring her, he rocked her closely against him.

'Please, Jasper,' Harper pleaded, taking a step towards them. 'You're upsetting her. Let's sit down and talk this through sensibly. Claire wouldn't want you to do this.'

'*Claire*,' he said through gritted teeth, 'would have wanted me to do what is best for our baby. There's nothing to talk about.'

Then, without another word he turned and hurried out into the garden.

Chapter Forty

Harper jumped as the front door slammed shut behind Jasper and Anaya. She was too shocked to cry. Not only her morning, but suddenly her whole life, had been turned upside down. Again. Jasper's words of a few moments earlier echoed loud and clear in her head: *If he really cared about you, don't you think he'd make more of an effort?*

She'd been so preoccupied the last few weeks—so lost in the wonderfulness of her newborn daughter—that she'd pushed aside her niggling thoughts about Samuel and his relationship with Anaya. This baby thing had been thrown on him out of nowhere and she'd expected him to take a little time to get used to the idea. Yet although his apparent acceptance of the situation had surprised her, she'd taken him at his word that he wanted to make it work.

Was that foolish? Was his declaration of support too good to be true?

Actions speak louder than words—Laura had taught her that—and Jasper was right; Samuel hadn't done anything to show he wanted to nurture a relationship with Anaya. During their phone calls, he changed the subject or ended the call whenever she tried to talk to him about Anaya. Since that first, almost disastrous, Sunday visit, he'd found excuses not to return.

She shuddered now as she finally allowed herself to remember that day.

She'd been so excited about introducing him to Anaya, but from the moment he'd climbed out of his car Samuel had made it clear he wasn't there to see anyone but her. Claire's parents had also been up for the weekend, and along with Jasper's parents, they'd bent over backwards to include Samuel in conversation and make him feel welcome, but his responses had verged on rudeness.

And when she'd asked him if he wanted to hold Anaya, he'd said something about having a bit of a cold and not wanting to pass on his germs.

Hah! What a load of codswallop! She'd stupidly been grateful for his thoughtfulness, but in all their years together she couldn't recall Samuel ever once getting ill. He was the only person she knew who had never taken a sick day in his whole working life.

The back of her throat grew tight as she recalled his words from the day she'd told him she wanted to be Anaya's mother: *You might have changed, but I haven't. You're still the only woman I want in my life and I want us to work through this.*

The only woman.

Did that also preclude Anaya? By *work through* it, had he actually meant he'd stand by her while she came to her senses? Perhaps Samuel—like Jasper—believed that in time she'd tire of motherhood and then they could forget this whole thing ever happened and go back to how things were.

'Oh my God.' Her words echoed in the empty house and she reached out to steady herself on the pram as realisation hit hard.

He'd told her outright he hadn't changed and that he only wanted *her* in his life but she'd heard what she wanted to hear, believed what she wanted to believe. Now she could see that Samuel had no more interest in Anaya or being a stepdad than her own mother had in parenting herself and Willow. They'd grown up feeling like they weren't good enough, like they were a burden, and Harper would rather die than subject her child to that kind of life.

Jasper might be right about Samuel, but he couldn't be more wrong about her. Her love for Anaya might have come as a surprise—to no one more than herself—but now nothing mattered more than her daughter and she would prove it to him.

Not bothering to change out of her walking clothes, she snatched her car keys from the hook by the front door and headed outside. Jasper and Anaya were nowhere to be seen, but she couldn't put this task off a moment longer.

As she drove towards Sydney, she rehearsed in her head exactly what she'd say to Samuel. He might be good at convincing judges and juries of his way of thinking, but she wouldn't let him pull the wool over her eyes again. She'd ask him to prove his commitment to her and Anaya by coming back with her tonight and making a damn effort and if he didn't ...

Well, would that really be the end of the world?

She thought about what she'd be missing if she and Samuel parted ways and came up with an embarrassingly small list—sex and the fresh croissants he sometimes brought her in bed of a weekend morning. The shocking truth was she'd barely missed him these last few weeks. Phone calls had been exchanged because *she'd* made the effort, but they were usually over quickly. They weren't like Jasper and Claire who had lived *and* worked together. They weren't like Jasper's parents who sometimes sat for hours in the garden just talking to each other. Or Joanne and Mike who spent all day every day working together in their bookshop and loved it. They weren't like Willow and Miriam, or Renee and Juliet with their husbands. All those couples spent time together—doing both mundane things like watching TV or grocery shopping and also exciting things like going on holidays or seeing concerts—because they *wanted* to.

Harper tried to remember the last time she and Samuel had gone out anywhere together that wasn't something to do with his work. There was the hot air ballooning and Christmas at his parents' place. Only two occasions in almost a year, and yet neither of them had thought that weird. The only thing Samuel ever seemed to want to do with her was have sex and when she thought about it, that was pretty much the only thing she wanted to do with him.

Had she seen something in Samuel all those years ago that told her he'd be a safe bet? Had he given off a vibe even from their very first meeting that he didn't want children? And had she stayed with him all these years because it made keeping *her* resolve not to have a family easy? What did it say that she'd taken so long to tell him about her abortion? Surely if they were that close, she'd have opened up earlier?

These were the questions that played in her head the rest of the drive to Sydney.

It was just ten o'clock when she hit the city, and the traffic wasn't too bad. She parked her car in a fifteen minute space right out the front of Samuel's office building and hurried inside, making a beeline for the elevators that would take her to his firm's level.

Samuel's office was close to the elevators, but as she emerged and started in that direction, one of the receptionists called out to her. 'Excuse me. Can I help you?'

Harper paused a moment, infuriated that the receptionist didn't recognise her, although she shouldn't be too offended as she couldn't recall the woman's name either. 'I'm Samuel's wife,' was all the explanation she gave as she continued on her way.

'Oh, right.' The receptionist shot to her feet and hurried round the desk after her. As her heels click-clacked on the polished concrete floors, she said, 'You shouldn't go in there, he's in an important meeting.'

'Well, this is important too,' Harper said, not glancing back at the receptionist as she came to his office door and flung it open.

It took less than a second for the sight before her to register in her head.

Important meeting, her arse. Or perhaps that should be Annika's arse?

Of course, there were no tan lines on the CrossFit junkie's perfectly taut, brown butt, yet, as Samuel glanced up and registered Harper standing there, he dropped his arms, leaving two white imprints where his hands had just been gripping her tightly.

'Harper!' he exclaimed, shoving Annika away and rushing to pull up his trousers from where they lay bunched around his ankles.

Annika yanked down her tiny skirt, her cheeks reddening as she fled from the room, not daring to meet Harper's gaze. Harper shut the door behind her and calmly stepped closer to his desk. She couldn't help but notice the red, lace g-string that Annika had abandoned in her haste lying atop a pile of files, a torn condom wrapper just beside it.

'How clichéd,' she said as she looked from it right into Samuel's eyes. 'How sad. But at least you were playing it safe.'

The compromising position in which she found him with Annika only cemented Harper's decision.

'I'm leaving you, Samuel. Our marriage, for what it was worth, is over.'

'No!' He shook his head, fumbling to do up his belt buckle as he spoke. '*That* was *not* what it looked like.'

She raised an eyebrow, wondering if it was uncomfortable standing there with a condom wrapped around his unsatisfied dick. 'What kind of fool do you take me for?'

'It only happened once. It *hadn't* even happened yet. You interrupted before it could happen. But what do you expect? You've been so damn preoccupied with the baby. We haven't shared a bed in almost a month. And when I came to the Hunter Valley to see you, you wouldn't let me touch you.'

Argh—there was so much in those few sentences that made Harper want to scream, but instead, she held up her finger and spoke calmly. 'For one, my baby has a name. She's called Anaya. For two—' another finger, '—you've inconvenienced yourself only once in almost four weeks to come visit me and even then you only stayed for a few hours. You were supposed to be coming to see me *and* Anaya, but your only concern was getting me alone for five minutes to have your wicked way. I wasn't about to sneak off and have sex with you in the middle of Sunday lunch with Jasper and Claire's family.'

He opened his mouth as if he had something to say about this but she shot up a third finger and rode right over the top of him.

'And three, whatever sordid scene I walked into right now, doesn't matter anyway. I'm not leaving you because you're a lying, cheating prick, although this certainly makes my decision easier. I was coming today to ask you to be honest with me about Anaya. Did you ever really mean it when you said you'd accepted my decision to be her mother? That you were happy to have her in our lives?'

She watched his Adam's apple move slowly up and down as he deliberated how to reply. 'I don't think I ever said I was *happy* about it,' he confessed.

'So what were you hoping? That the shine would wear off after a while, that I'd just abandon my little girl and come back to you?'

He didn't have to say anything; his expression said it all. That's exactly what he'd believed would happen.

Fury burnt within her at the two men in her life who didn't believe in her love and dedication to her daughter. Well, she'd show them!

'Right then.' She let out a heavy sigh. 'I guess that's it.'

'I'm sorry, Harper,' he said, his mouth downturned, a pained expression tainting his normally handsome face. 'But I never wanted a baby. All I ever wanted was you.'

'Really?' He sounded so sincere that she might almost have believed him if his actions matched his words, but the knickers on his desk made him a liar. 'Are you sure? Or did you just want someone who didn't demand too much and who you could *fuck* whenever you felt the need?'

It was a rhetorical question, she didn't expect an answer. She already knew it.

'Honestly Samuel,' she continued, 'I see it now, what we had wasn't magic. It wasn't even anything special. If you truly loved me, you'd have supported me these last nine weeks instead of turning to someone else for a little bit of action. I deserve more than that—and if I've learnt anything from Claire, it's that life's too short to settle for something that's just okay. I know I'm not completely blameless—I did change the goal posts on you and perhaps I never gave you my true self, but, as we've both made our positions clear, as neither of us are willing to compromise, I think the best thing for both of us is to move on.'

He leant back against his desk and crossed his feet at his ankles. 'If that's what you want, then I'm not going to waste my breath trying to change your mind.'

'I wouldn't expect you to.'

'But, this is your decision, not mine, so don't think you're going to milk me for all I've got. You'll get exactly what you're owed legally and that's it.'

The fact he thought she would proved he didn't know her at all. She clenched her keys tightly in her hand. 'That's fine, Samuel. I'll pop round to the house one day soon when you're at work and I'll take what's mine and not a tea towel more. Now, shall I send Annika back in?'

Then before he could say another word, Harper turned and walked out on her marriage.

She held her head high, her shoulders back, and smiled politely at a couple of Samuel's colleagues as she made her way out of the building. She should be more upset, and perhaps she was simply still in shock, but she found herself nothing but angry. Angry at Samuel yes, but also angry at herself that she'd taken so long to see her marriage for what it truly was.

As she stepped outside into the sunny spring morning, she went to reach into her bag for her phone, desperate to speak to her big sister. Only then did she realise she'd left Jasper's house without either her bag or her mobile.

Dammit.

Harper stamped her foot upon the footpath as she pondered her next move. All she had with her were her car and its keys, so she'd call into Willow's office on her way back to the Hunter Valley. But first, her office—she needed to talk to Bryn.

Chapter Forty-one

Jasper didn't know where he was going. He only knew he had to get away before he totally blew his top at Harper. Part of him wanted to sit among Claire's flowers and feel her calming presence, but he didn't want to risk Harper coming out and seeing him like this. Or worse, trying to talk some sense into him. How dare she tell him what Claire would have wanted. They'd barely even known each other.

His breathing ragged, he didn't stop walking until he got to the bushland of the nearby national park, another place he and Claire had loved spending time together. The wildflowers were out in full bloom—their soft pinks and purples and the bright yellow and red ones all swaying in the breeze. Today, the sight of them felt like a punch in the gut. Wildflower season, Claire's favourite time of the year, and just one more thing she wasn't here to experience.

And in that moment, he hated her! She'd always been a bit of a distracted driver—often turning the radio up full blast and dancing like she was at a nightclub instead of sitting in a car. Surely she must have seen the other vehicle approaching. Surely she could have done *something* to save herself. He didn't want to do this alone, dammit! He didn't want to do it with a stranger and he didn't want to give up ballooning.

But what bloody choice had she left him?

His parents were going to be devastated, but he hoped in time they'd come to understand. And what *would* he do if he didn't fly? Hot air balloons were the only job he'd ever had and he wasn't qualified to do anything else. He'd always imagined that when his dad eventually retired he'd take over at the helm of Big Basket Ballooning, but now, unless one of his sisters and brother-in-laws wanted to come home, he guessed they'd have to sell or shut down.

Hot tears dripped down onto his daughter at this prospect, but she slept soundly, not even flinching when he brushed them away with his thumb. She was the definition of perfection. He couldn't get enough of her, could spend hours simply watching her like this; yet at the same time it broke his heart looking at her and knowing that Claire wouldn't be here, sharing parenthood with him as they'd planned.

Jasper's anger shrivelled up as the sadness once again consumed him, making his chest hurt and his throat tight.

What right did he have to feel resentful about giving up ballooning?

At least he was here to make the decision, and no matter what Harper said, he knew if the positions were reversed and Claire were here instead of him, she would have done the same. Therefore, no matter how hard the next years, decades, however long he had left were, he needed to accept his new reality. He needed to think of their daughter first and himself second, and not let his grief for Claire consume him because he didn't want Anaya to grow up in a bubble of sorrow.

He sat there in silence—his thoughts a jumbled mess of hot air balloons, Nebraskan strangers, his parents, Claire and Harper—until finally Anaya stirred in his arms. At first she only whimpered a little, her head moving from side to side as her mouth searched for a mid-morning snack, but when she didn't find one, she began to howl.

'Hush, now sweetheart. It's okay,' he said over and over as he hurried back to his house. 'Daddy's sorry. We'll be home soon.'

Less than an hour ago he'd been accusing Harper of not being fully committed to Anaya, and yet he was the one who'd taken her away without a thought of her basic needs, such as milk and sun protection. He thanked God she'd woken hungry before the sun had reached its full dangerous potential and he swore he'd pick up his game from now on. No more leaving the house without the full shebang of baby paraphernalia.

He also owed Harper an apology. No matter his grief, the accusations he'd made about her marriage were uncalled for. Out of the two of them, she'd been the one to make the most sacrifices for Anaya.

But when he returned to the house, he found it empty and her car gone.

'Shit,' he said, before remembering the little ears in his arms. Looked like he hadn't been the only one who needed some time out. He'd give Anaya her bottle and then call Harper and ask her to come back so they could talk. She was right. If this peculiar situation was going to work, they needed to make it official. Jasper owed that to her *and* Anaya.

He popped the baby in the pram while he fixed her milk, and as she wailed, the cats got up from their spot by the kitchen window and fled down the hallway, no doubt to go and hide under the bed. Mere seconds after he lifted Anaya into his arms again and teased the rubber teat against her lips, she clamped her mouth around it and started suckling. She'd grown in weight, length and strength since they'd brought her home but the effort of feeding still exhausted her. Before the bottle emptied, she was asleep again.

Jasper changed her nappy—marvelling at how she could sleep right through the exercise—and then grabbed his phone and carried her to the couch, where he laid her down and then sat guard beside her. Almost one month at home and she still hated her bassinet with a passion, but neither he nor Harper could bear leaving her to cry herself to sleep. Not just yet anyway.

At the thought of Harper, he took a deep breath and found her number on his phone. Where not long ago Claire was always at the top of his recent call list, now Harper took pride of place. Ignoring the way his heart cramped at that thought, he pressed call and lifted the phone to his ear. Almost immediately he heard ringing coming from the hallway and sure enough, after a few moments, Harper's voicemail clicked in.

He silently cursed but didn't leave a message as instructed. Instead, he checked that Anaya was safe and then went into the hallway and found Harper's bag and mobile in the bottom of the pram. The fact she'd left the house without them showed him how upset she'd been, making him feel even more like a prize jerk.

When she still hadn't returned an hour later, he lifted Anaya from her slumber and bundled her into her car seat. He wasn't sure where to look but Harper couldn't have gone far without her things and he figured driving around trying to find her would be better than sitting at home wishing he could take back the things he'd said.

Jasper checked the main street with its café, post office and general store and then he drove by his parents' place on the off-chance she'd gone to speak to them. When he couldn't find her anywhere he reluctantly returned to the house and fed Anaya her next bottle of the day. As more hours passed, anxiety began to grow within him. What if something bad had happened to her? What if she'd driven down some back road and had a car accident? His pulse raced at the thought and his skin grew clammy. If something happened to her he didn't know if he could handle the guilt.

And what would he one day tell Anaya?

Samuel. Maybe she'd called him. Or her sister. Deciding to phone one of them, he went to the pram to retrieve Harper's mobile and cursed with frustration when he couldn't unlock the screen. He dumped the phone back in the pram and ran his hands through his hair.

Perhaps he should call the police. Or was that overreacting?

Telling himself this was exactly what he was doing, he decided if she wasn't back in another hour, he'd ring Nick down at the police station. With that decision made, he settled with Anaya on the couch and tried to watch a couple of episodes of *Homeland*.

Sixty minutes later, just as he was picking up his own phone to dial, the doorbell rang. He sprang off the couch, which woke Anaya, so he picked her up and carried her to the door. Harper had a key but after the way they'd left things, he wouldn't be surprised if she'd chosen not to use it. At least he hoped, because if it wasn't her, he was seriously going to start to worry.

'Thank fuck,' he said, as he opened it. 'Where the hell have you been?' In his anxious state he forgot she had no obligation to keep him informed of her whereabouts. 'I'm sorry. None of my business, but I couldn't help worrying when I came back and found your phone and bag here, but you gone.'

She nodded. 'I'm sorry about that. I didn't even realise that I'd left them behind until I got to Sydney.'

'You went all the way to Sydney and back?'

'Yep. I had things to do, people to see.'

He exhaled deeply. 'Well, I'm glad you're back. I wanted to talk to you. You coming in?'

'Yes.' She stepped inside and closed the door behind her. 'But I've got things to say too, and I'd like to go first if that's okay with you.'

His parents had raised him that ladies always went first, so he conceded. 'Okay. But you've had a long drive, so how about I make us some coffee? Want to hold Anaya while I do so?'

Harper held out her arms, 'Yes, please,' as he passed their daughter over.

'I'll be right back,' he said, turning and heading into the kitchen.

Five minutes later he joined Harper and Anaya in the living room. They were sitting on the couch, so he put her mug and a plate of Anzac biscuits his mum had made down on the coffee table and then took the armchair for himself.

As he lifted his drink to his mouth and took a sip, Harper repositioned Anaya against her chest and then looked him straight in the eye.

'I went to Sydney to see Samuel,' she began. 'You said he's not invested in Anaya and—'

'I'm sorry,' he interrupted, lowering his mug to his lap. 'That was out of line and unfair. I shouldn't have said it. The balloon accident in Nebraska rocked me, it was too close after Claire and I—'

She shook her head. 'No, you were absolutely right. Samuel is not and never will be invested in Anaya. I think I knew this deep down already, but I confronted him today and he admitted that, like you, he was just waiting for me to lose interest in her.' Her brow furrowed and she scowled. 'But that's not going to happen,' she added forcefully, 'and so Samuel and I are separating. We're getting a divorce.'

'What? Geez, Harper, I'm sorry.' He felt as if the break-up of her marriage was somehow his fault. 'When I lost it this morning, this is the last thing I wanted. Are you sure you can't work it out?'

Harper rubbed her lips together a moment as if gathering strength. Then, 'No. This isn't all because of Anaya. Her arrival merely helped show up all the cracks that were already in our marriage. I'm not going to bore you with the sordid details, but this is the right decision. For all of us.' She took a breath and continued. 'After I ended things with Samuel, I went to work and spoke to my boss. I've put in a request for some unpaid leave so that I can be here with you and Anaya for up to a year before I have to go back to work.'

'Harper.' The guilt twisted like a knife in his gut. 'You don't have to do any of this to prove your love. I can see how much Anaya means to you.'

'I don't *have* to,' she conceded, 'but I *want* to. It's not forever. I love my job and I want to be a working mother. But I can't bear the thought of being so far away from Anaya, so I've asked my boss to look into a possible transfer for me to the Newcastle station.'

'Wow,' Jasper breathed. This was a lot to take in. He hoped Harper wouldn't regret any of these life-changing decisions.

'There's one more thing. I'm going to look into buying a small place of my own, so that you can have your own space again.'

He opened his mouth to say that wasn't necessary but she held up her hand to shut him up.

'This is your and Claire's home, and you need time to properly grieve and work out how to *be* without her. You don't need me breathing down your neck.'

'Thank you,' he said, the lump that had appeared in his throat making the phrase not much more than a whisper.

She smiled. 'I know this isn't what either of us planned or wanted for Anaya, but I believe that together—with the help of our families and loved ones—we can give her a good life.'

Jasper nodded and smiled back. 'So do I.'

Harper glanced down at their daughter. 'I think she might be stirring again, but there's just one final thing I want to say.'

'What is it?' She'd left her marriage, quit her job and moved towns within a matter of hours. He didn't know what else was left.

'I want you to promise to give a little more thought to your decision to give up ballooning. It's what you've lived and breathed your whole life. It's a passion you shared with Claire and something that's been in your family for generations. I want that for our daughter. I want her to see that her parents—including Claire—lived life to the fullest and didn't let fear stop them from doing what they loved.' Harper cocked her head to one side. 'What do you say, Jasper?'

And what could he say? This amazing woman had turned her whole world upside down to prove her love for their daughter.

'Okay, Harper,' he said. 'I promise.' And then he closed the distance between them and gave her and Anaya a great big hug.

Epilogue

Claire couldn't believe it had been almost half a decade since she'd left the earth. It still felt like only yesterday, but over the years she'd come to accept her destiny. She hadn't been happy to go at first—no, she'd kicked and screamed, yelling at the powers that be that they'd made a terrible mistake.

It wasn't her time to go. She had a husband who loved her, who needed her. And didn't they see her bulging bump?

But then she'd looked down and realised the bump was gone. Her baby was gone. Never had she been as distraught as she was in that moment, but she calmed a little when she discovered the baby had lived. By some miracle, her daughter had been born in the wreckage of that car accident. It broke her heart that she wouldn't be there to raise her, but she took some comfort from the knowledge that her body had borne the brunt of the crash and saved the child.

And while she might not have been beside Anaya in person—not in the hospital when she'd had her first feed or when Jasper had brought her home to the nursery they'd created together, not when she'd said her first word or the day she'd started kindergarten—she'd been there in spirit. Guarding her and the people around her as she grew from a tiny infant into a little girl full of life and enthusiasm.

Jasper had been broken at first, but as he'd cradled their little girl in his arms, she'd known it would only be a matter of time before he fell in love. She'd had faith in him. He was wrong; she wasn't angry at him for taking a little longer than she did to feel that connection. He was grieving for her as she was for him, and grief had a tendency to warp the mind a little.

But as wonderful as Jasper was, a girl needed a mother and Claire had wept that she wasn't able to fulfil that role. In her mind she'd auditioned her closest friends and family and although they'd all been willing, she hadn't been able to truly let go until she'd seen the look on Harper's face the day she'd first met Anaya.

And then she'd known. The only woman who would ever come close to loving her daughter as much as she had was her biological mother. So she'd set to work on Harper, sowing the seeds of what she wanted to occur. And Harper must have been halfway there already for it hadn't taken long at all for her to come around to the idea.

Claire had felt a little bad that this had meant the end of Harper's relationship with Samuel, but that feeling had been short-lived. Sometimes one door closes because there's something better behind another one.

That had certainly been the case for Harper.

Claire gazed down now on the scene unfolding on the ground below. Harper was standing there watching as the envelope of the balloon filled with air. She leant into the tall, dark, handsome man beside her—clichéd perhaps, but there are reasons for clichés—and placed her two hands protectively on her growing bump. Her face shone with a happiness that rivalled the glow of the rising sun behind her.

Harper had met Regan the first day she'd started a new job in Newcastle. He was a technician at the radio station and she couldn't believe it when he told her that he too lived in the Hunter Valley, not far from the little unit she'd just purchased to be closer to Anaya and Jasper. After that they carpooled whenever they could, and during those journeys to and from work, a wonderful friendship had blossomed. It had taken almost two years for Regan to work up the courage to ask Harper on an actual date, by which time her divorce had come through from Samuel. In the meantime she'd been contemplating trying online dating.

Lilia still hadn't had much luck in that department, but she persisted—saying it was fun kissing toads in pursuit of Prince Charming—and Harper had to admit, her body was craving a little action.

And damn the action had been good—Claire had overheard Harper telling her sister and had twinged a little with jealousy. Aside from motherhood there were a few things she really missed from earth—companionship, her cats, her garden, hot air ballooning and sex.

Anyway, back to Harper.

She and Regan had both been burnt by love before and took their time easing into a relationship. By the time they realised they'd finally found the one, Harper was almost thirty-nine. Regan wanted kids and although he doted on Anaya as if she were his own, Harper found she *wanted* to have a baby with him. So they'd had a lot of fun trying, but to no avail. Six months and then a year passed, and when they consulted Dr Ballantine for assistance, he'd done his tests and then suggested she could perhaps use an egg donor of her own.

The irony of this hadn't been lost on her but a few months later Regan's sperm had fertilised the eggs of a yoga teacher from Byron Bay. Due to Harper's age, they'd transferred two embryos to her uterus and both had taken hold. The twins were due on Christmas Day, but whether or not they were born on that date, they'd be a gift to everyone in their extended family.

'Is it ready yet?' Anaya's angelic voice tore Claire's gaze away from Harper and Regan. Her little girl was jumping up and down beside the almost fully-filled balloon while Jasper poured air into the envelope.

Like her daddy, Anaya had grown up in a world where hot air ballooning was as natural as breathing, yet this would be the first time she was allowed to go up herself and her excitement was uncontainable. Jasper had tried to make her have an early night but she'd barely slept a wink and had leapt out of bed the second he'd crept into her bedroom to wake her up.

'Very close. Are you ready?' Jasper asked as he shot another burst of hot air into the balloon. Orange flames glowed within it.

'I was born ready!' Anaya exclaimed and Jasper chuckled.

Then Paul, Mike and Regan helped him lift the basket off its side and the bright multi-coloured balloon rose off the ground. Anaya held her breath, her big brown eyes wide as she looked on. Claire had never forgotten her first flight and she knew Anaya was about to have the best fun of her life. She only wished she could be properly present to experience it with her.

The moment was also bittersweet for Jasper. As he climbed into the basket, he held his hand out for Anaya and she scrambled up over the side to join him, while Claire's mum stood by with a box ready to hand to him.

A box with Claire's ashes inside. Staring at *that* was a weird feeling indeed.

Jasper had waited five years—until Anaya was old enough to join him in the air—to finally let Claire go.

'Thanks, Joanne.' He took the box, placed it carefully by his feet, and then gave his parents the nod to unlatch the ropes that tied the basket to the ground.

'Stay still,' he told Anaya. 'You don't want to fall out before we lift off the ground.'

'I don't want to fall out once we're in the air, *either*,' she replied.

Jasper smiled. And Claire knew he was thinking that although they weren't biologically related, Anaya had some of her traits. A feisty nature and stubbornness being two of them. 'That you don't,' he said. 'Now, hold on tight because we're about to lift off.'

As they floated up, their family and friends growing smaller beneath them, Anaya was silent for almost the first time since she'd learnt to talk. Jasper did his stuff, watching his daughter as she soaked up the experience; he'd explain the ins and outs to her next time.

When they were about as high as they could go under today's weather conditions, he spoke. 'You know who is in this box, don't you?'

She nodded. 'My other mum, Claire.'

'Yes, your other mum.' Jasper's voice was choked and Claire could tell he was fighting back tears. She hoped he *would* cry in front of their daughter—it did little girls good to know that big, grown men also hurt from time to time. 'She loved you very much you know.'

'I know,' Anaya said solemnly. 'Even though she never met me, even though I came from Harper's egg, Claire loved me before I existed.'

'She did. Ballooning is something your mum and I loved to do together, so I decided to scatter her ashes up here. That way, whenever I fly, I'll feel like she's with me.'

Oh!

If Claire could still cry right now she would, but that was one thing they didn't think necessary in the afterlife.

'And because we were a little family of three,' he continued, 'I wanted to wait until you could come up with me and do this. Are you ready?'

'Yes. Do you want me to pick up the box, Daddy?'

'That would be great, sugar.'

Anaya did so—handing it to him as if it were the most precious thing she'd ever carried. Jasper checked the direction of the wind again, and then, with Anaya's little hand holding his, they lifted the lid on the box and tossed its contents over the side of the basket.

Silent tears streamed down Jasper's cheeks as what looked like tiny particles of sand were carried away on the breeze.

Goodbye, my love.

'Daddy? Are you all right?' Anaya asked. She was gazing up at him with a worried expression on her face.

'Yes.' He sniffed, put the lid back on the box, placed it on the floor and then wiped his eyes on his sleeve. 'Yes, I am, because I've got you.'

As he pulled her into his arms and kissed her head, Anaya said, 'You know how Harper has Regan, and Aunty Polly has Uncle Scotty, and Uncle Tim has Aunty Hannah ...' She went right down the list of all Jasper's sisters and all the other couples she knew. 'Do you think you'd be even happier if you had someone grown up to talk to as well?'

Jasper spluttered as if this was the last thing he'd expected her to say. 'Do you ... do you have someone particular in mind?'

'I was thinking Mum's friend Lilia was nice. And she told me last time I saw her that she'd really like to go up in a balloon as well.'

'Did she now?' A slow smile spread across his face at Anaya's innocent-sounding suggestion, when in actual fact Claire had been the one to put the idea into her little girl's head.

It was time for Jasper to move on—he was still young and there was no reason for him to miss out on intimacy and companionship simply because she could no longer share it with him. Lilia was a genuinely kind-hearted person and had had such terrible luck with men so far that she deserved a little fairy-dust as well.

And she was gorgeous but totally different in looks and personality to Claire, which made it easier to bear the thought of her and Jasper together.

Anaya nodded.

'Thanks for looking out for me, precious,' Jasper said. 'I promise I'll give it some thought.'

Acknowledgements

Thanks as always must go to the wonderful team at Harlequin and HarperCollins Australia, with a special mention to Sue Brockhoff, Annabel Blay, Adam van Rooijen and Natika Palka who have worked super hard to bring *Gift* to readers!

In addition to the in-house team, I want to thank my editor, Lachlan Jobbins, for putting up with my stubbornness when it came to certain aspects of the plot and also my agent, Helen Breitwieser, for always being in my corner.

One of the main issues in this book is egg donation and I want to thank Mel Holman for inspiring this aspect of the story and also for being so incredibly generous with her time and information about her experience.

Egg donation is the serious issue in this book and hot air ballooning is the fun one! My first hot air balloon ride was in Northam, Western Australia, with the fabulous crew at Windward Balloon Adventures. Thanks guys for that first taste—I'm now totally hooked. Also special thanks to Martine Scattini who came with me to 'research' this aspect of the story.

A shout out to my dear friends Kristen Francis and Leila Noble who helped me with the neonatal care research and answered my other baby and hospital questions. And also to Louisa West who answered my stupid questions about the legal profession.

Thanks always to my writing support team—especially my 'writers camp' gals (you know who you are) who help me get the words down with our sprinting sessions. And also to my writing pals who help me procrastinate with Voxer; what did we do before we discovered this fab app?

My writing career would not be possible without my wonderful readers—so I thank everyone who has bought one of my books in the past and has chosen also to buy this one. I wish you the happiest reading experience and don't forget to let me know what you thought of the book. I'm always happy to hear from readers via Facebook, Instagram or my website: www.rachaeljohns.com.

Thanks also to the bloggers and journalists who review and help spread the word, and to the wonderful folks who champion the books in those magical places called 'libraries'. Cheers to the booksellers across Australia and New Zealand—you guys rock!

And last but never least, my cheer squad at home—to my husband, Craig, my mum, Barbara, my mother-in-law, Ronice, and my three sons for helping out and putting up with all the craziness that comes with living with a writer.

THE PATTERSON GIRLS

by Rachael Johns

Winner of the ABIA General Fiction Book of the Year

How can four sisters build the futures they so desperately want, when the past is reaching out to claim them?

When the Patterson daughters return home to Meadow Brook to be with their father after their mother's death, they bring with them a world of complication and trouble. The eldest sister, obstetrician Madeleine, would rather be anywhere but her hometown, violinist Abigail has fled from her stellar career, while teacher Lucinda is struggling to have the children she and her husband so desperately want. The black sheep of the family, Charlie, feels her life as a barista and exercise instructor doesn't measure up to that of her gifted and successful sisters.

Dealing with their bereft father who is determined to sell the family motel, their loves old and new and a series of troublesome decisions doesn't make life any easier, but when they go through their mother's possessions and uncover the shocking secret of an old family curse, they begin to question everything they thought they knew.

A warm and wise novel about secrets revealed, finding your soulmate and the unique bond between sisters.

'Reminds me of Monica McInerney's family-focused narratives ... a great book to curl up with on a lazy Sunday afternoon.'—*Australian Books + Publishing* on *The Patterson Girls*

THE ART OF KEEPING SECRETS

by Rachael Johns

Little secrets grow up to be big lies...

They've been best friends since their sons started high school together, and Felicity, Emma and Neve share everything ... or so they thought.

But Flick's seemingly perfect marriage hides a shocking secret which, with one word, threatens to destroy her and her family's happiness. Emma is in denial about a potential custody battle, her financial constraints, the exhaustion she can't seem to shake off and the inappropriate feelings she has for her boss. And single mum Neve is harbouring a secret of her own; a secret that might forever damage her close-knit relationship with her son. When the tight hold they have each kept on their secrets for years begins to slip, they must face the truth. Even if that truth has the power to hurt the ones they love, and each other.

Perhaps some secrets weren't made to be kept.

'A compelling and poignant story of dark secrets and turbulent relationships ... The characters were funny and flawed and filled with the kind of raw vulnerability that makes your heart ache for them.'—Nicola Moriarty, bestselling author of *The Fifth Letter* on *The Art of Keeping Secrets*

talk about it

Let's talk about books.

Join the conversation:

 on facebook.com/harlequinaustralia

 on Twitter @harlequinaus

www.harlequinbooks.com.au

If you love reading and want to know about our authors and titles, then let's talk about it.